PRAISE FOR

The Education of Mrs. Brimley

"[A] scintillating take on the classic lessons-in-love theme. Her witty dialogue, sexy hero, and delightfully intelligent heroine—who understands the value of a well-rounded education—are sure to garner her a wide readership."
—*Romantic Times*

"Oh, what a joy to read! Truly humorous . . . Wonderful writing." —*The Romance Readers Connection*

"Both original and charming, the book is a sensual indulgence that reveals a promising new talent in the genre."
—*A Romance Review*

"[A] fun and fascinating tale that readers are sure to enjoy . . . Emma and her sensual teacher Nicholas . . . will charm readers with their wit and bring up the temperature with their hot encounters." —*Historical Romance Writers*

"Victorian romance fans will enjoy this fun frolic starring two likable protagonists who fall in love while he trains her in the art of love. The droll double entendres make for an intelligent, amusing historical as the student teaches the teacher as much as he does her." —*Midwest Book Review*

"[A] terrific first novel . . . The witty dialogue, steamy situations, and appealing characters combined to form a delightful book." —*Romance Junkies*

THE

Seduction

OF A

Duke

DONNA MACMEANS

B

BERKLEY SENSATION, NEW YORK

THE BERKLEY PUBLISHING GROUP
Published by the Penguin Group
Penguin Group (USA) Inc.
375 Hudson Street, New York, New York 10014, USA
Penguin Group (Canada), 90 Eglinton Avenue East, Suite 700, Toronto, Ontario M4P 2Y3, Canada
(a division of Pearson Penguin Canada Inc.)
Penguin Books Ltd., 80 Strand, London WC2R 0RL, England
Penguin Group Ireland, 25 St. Stephen's Green, Dublin 2, Ireland (a division of Penguin Books Ltd.)
Penguin Group (Australia), 250 Camberwell Road, Camberwell, Victoria 3124, Australia
(a division of Pearson Australia Group Pty. Ltd.)
Penguin Books India Pvt. Ltd., 11 Community Centre, Panchsheel Park, New Delhi—110 017, India
Penguin Group (NZ), 67 Apollo Drive, Rosedale, North Shore 0632, New Zealand
(a division of Pearson New Zealand Ltd.)
Penguin Books (South Africa) (Pty.) Ltd., 24 Sturdee Avenue, Rosebank, Johannesburg 2196,
South Africa

Penguin Books Ltd., Registered Offices: 80 Strand, London WC2R 0RL, England

This is a work of fiction. Names, characters, places, and incidents either are the product of the author's imagination or are used fictitiously, and any resemblance to actual persons, living or dead, business establishments, events, or locales is entirely coincidental. The publisher does not have any control over and does not assume any responsibility for author or third-party websites or their content.

THE SEDUCTION OF A DUKE

A Berkley Sensation Book / published by arrangement with the author

PRINTING HISTORY
Berkley Sensation mass-market edition / April 2009

Copyright © 2009 by Donna MacMeans.
Excerpt from *Kissing Midnight* by Emma Holly copyright © 2009 by Emma Holly.
Cover art by Leslie Peck.
Cover design by George Long.
Cover hand lettering by Ron Zinn.
Interior text design by Kristin del Rosario.

ISBN: 978-0-425-22806-7

BERKLEY® SENSATION
Berkley Sensation Books are published by The Berkley Publishing Group,
a division of Penguin Group (USA) Inc.,
375 Hudson Street, New York, New York 10014.
BERKLEY® SENSATION and the "B" design are trademarks of Penguin Group (USA) Inc.

PRINTED IN THE UNITED STATES OF AMERICA

10 9 8 7 6 5 4 3 2 1

For my wonderful husband,
I shall love you always.
And thank you to Anna Sugden and
Cassandra Murray for chocolate and laughter.

· Prologue ·

THE ADDRESS WASN'T THE MOST FASHIONABLE IN Paris. Indeed, the row of merchants obviously catered to a less refined clientele than the Winthrops and the Vanderbilts. Furtive figures bundled in drab, well-worn cloaks scurried down the avenue as if winter winds, not fresh spring breezes, chased their backs. A highly polished hackney cab, rarely seen in this neighborhood, slowed in front of an ancient bookseller, the subtle scent of improved fortunes in its wake. A pickpocket lingering near a doorway took interest. A prostitute hesitated, waiting to see if a masculine hand would grasp the doorway prior to exiting. However, when a comely face with a pert nose and two wide, curious eyes peeked out the window, she continued on her way.

Francesca Winthrop, one of the world's richest heiresses, emerged from the cab, exhilarated by her purloined freedom. Her mother would likely lock her away in her room for weeks on end if she discovered Fran had traveled alone to such a shady district. But then her mother, absorbed in shopping to furnish yet another residence, would likely not even realize Fran had left their rented rooms.

Euphoria filled Fran's heart and lungs, making even this dingy street one of the most beautiful in the entire city. The air was sweet, the day positively radiant. Unable to contain the smile fueled by her happiness, she nodded to two women who had stopped to stare at the newcomer.

The cause of her joy had a name that she could share only with the woman within the shop. Her mother may have traveled across the Atlantic to purchase the very latest fashions from the House of Worth, but not Fran. She had come to see Madame Aglionby and seek her counsel.

Fran swept inside the obscure bookstore. Pausing to savor the musty fragrance of aged book leather and well-loved pages, she envied her old tutor's life surrounded by so many stories and fabled adventures.

"Francesca, is that you?" The proprietor's wife, thin and elegant with threads of silver in her dark hair, threw her arms wide. "You've been away too long. Come give your old tutor a hug."

Fran carefully maneuvered her elaborate day dress through the aisles. The new fashionable narrow silhouette allowed her to negotiate the aisles, but the attached bustle and tiebacks could topple several stacks of books with an ill-considered turn. She stepped into Madame Aglionby's friendly embrace, relishing the attention she rarely received at home.

"Let me look at you." Madame Aglionby pushed her to arm's length. "You are positively glowing!" Her lips twisted into a knowing smile. "I think there's a man to blame, *oui*?"

Words could not escape the bubble of excitement that blocked Fran's throat. Finally, she could speak of Randolph and know that her words would go no further. For now, she merely bobbed her head to her friend and former teacher.

"I have set the kettle for tea. Come. Sit and tell me all about your young man." She led the way to the back of the store and brushed aside a small stack of books with various foreign titles, before she frowned at Fran. "But first, tell me this. Does your *maman* approve?"

The question burst Fran's euphoria. Her smile faltered as she propped her lavender parasol against the table and slid into the offered chair. "Randolph has forbid me to speak to Maman about him. He feels it would be better if we appear only to be friends. He's afraid she will not be pleased." She reached across the table and grasped the older woman's hand. "I know you would like Randolph, though. I wish you could meet him. He's so very smart. He works for the law firm that handles Papa's accounts. He's well traveled, and he plays polo." She couldn't list his attributes fast enough, so marvelous was her beau. She sighed heavily, unable to contain her yearning. "I can't wait until he kisses me."

Madame Aglionby drew back, her arched eyebrows lifted in question. "He has never attempted to kiss you? Does he know of your desire?"

"I . . . I'm not sure." A heat rushed to her cheeks at her admission. She fiddled with the fine bone handle of the parasol to avert her gaze. "I'm afraid I don't know how to go about it. Not many men have tried to . . . you know. The ones Maman has chosen for me have been so old." She shuddered. "I never wanted to encourage their affections."

She raised her eyes to her French tutor, knowing that she was the only one who could be trusted with her plea. "I'm afraid I don't know how to go about attracting a man's notice."

After a moment's hesitation, Madame Aglionby laughed, a light, tittering sound of disbelief. Warmth and affection filled her gaze and eased the discomfort of Fran's confession.

"My dear, you have already attracted a young man's notice. You need only be yourself and all your wonderful attributes will shine through."

If only that were true. "I don't think I have wonderful attributes," Fran said. "At least, not the kind that encourage a man in that manner." She hesitated. "I don't know how to flirt with a man." She swallowed. This was the primary reason she had come to visit her old tutor. Looking askance at Madame, she asked the question that had burned deep beneath her stays across the vast Atlantic Ocean. "Can you show me? Maman always said you had a way with men."

Madame leaned back in her seat. Her lips thinned, her expression suddenly cold and distant.

"I'm so sorry," Fran gushed, immediately regretting that she had caused displeasure. That had not been her intent. "I'd forgotten that Maman had made those foolish accusations about you and Papa."

Her former teacher studied her a moment, then the sharp angles of her face softened. "That's all right, my dear. Had it not been for your mother's insistence on my dismissal, I would never have met Monsieur Aglionby and established my life here." She gazed with affection at the shelves of books that reached from floor to ceiling in all directions. "I'm spending my life surrounded by old friends. I'm content. In fact . . ." Her gaze swung quickly back to Fran. "You have, of course, maintained your skills in French?"

"I've been translating children's stories for some time," Fran responded. "They may not be the most difficult of translations, but I enjoy—"

The teacher held up her hand to indicate enough. "I may have something that might help you. My husband procures journals for a gentleman with certain . . . proclivities. Recently, he uncovered the personal diary of a well-known courtesan."

Fran's breath caught. Her eyes widened. A properly reared daughter should not know that such women existed, but, of course, a properly reared daughter probably lived with less discord than she.

"The diary reveals her methods to attract and encourage the men who might purchase her services."

"How do you know this?" Fran asked. Polite society never acknowledged that other world. That a diary should exist . . .

A smile played about the corners of Madame's mouth. "Even though one is married, one still maintains a certain curiosity."

Madame stood, smoothing the wrinkles from her plain skirts. "Antoine cares more about the price fetched for the journal than the one who pays for it."

"The price should not be a problem," Fran said, eager to see the secrets the diary might contain.

"I thought not," Madame said with a slight smile. "The book is in our private quarters. It will take me a few moments to locate it. While you wait . . ." She glanced about the room, her gaze resting on a white box on a counter. "Perhaps you can begin to encourage your young man by sending him a letter."

"I have been writing to him." Fran protested. "I've told him about the places we've visited, and the weather—"

"Not that kind of letter, my dear." The teacher retrieved the stationery box, complete with writing implements. "You need to tell your Randolph how you feel about him." She pulled a sheet of fine vellum from the box. "Tell him how you long to feel his arms around you. Tell him that you await his kiss."

Fran's mouth dried to the consistency of paper. She'd never mentioned those things to Randolph. "Won't he think that such language is . . . improper?"

"The battle for a gentleman's heart is rarely won with proper etiquette. Study the lessons in the diary and you'll have him begging for a glimpse of your lips. Try your hand with the letter and I shall find the book."

Madame started down the aisle toward the staircase that led to the living quarters, but stopped midway. "Francesca, you probably should keep this book well hidden from your *maman*. I doubt she will approve."

"Maman has little interest in my reading material. I doubt she will even notice the addition of a journal."

"Be wary and do not underestimate your *maman*," the tutor cautioned. "There's not much that she misses. Her eyes and ears are sharper than her tongue, and she has honed that instrument to a fine cutting edge." Her eyes narrowed and all humor fled her somber face. "Be very careful."

· One ·

Three months later
Newport Beach, Rhode Island

WITH ALL THE MALICE SHE COULD MUSTER, FRANcesca Winthrop whacked the wooden croquet ball beneath her foot, sending her mother's ball careening across the manicured lawn, over the edge of the Newport cliffs, and possibly into the blue gray waters of the Atlantic Ocean. Pity, it wasn't her mother's head.

"Really, Francesca, that show of spirit was entirely unnecessary." Alva Winthrop signaled one of the dozen servants standing about for just such an occasion to search for her ball at the rocky base of the cliff, before feigning laughter for the benefit of the other society matriarchs watching the match. "Most women would be positively thrilled to learn they were about to marry a duke."

"Most women have at least met the man they are to marry, or had a say in the selection," Fran replied, careful to keep her voice low and her smile in place. *Never show emotion, or else risk the scorn that follows.* She'd been fed those words in infancy along with her pabulum. An only child, raised in a lonely edifice to enormous wealth, she learned her lessons well. A tear, a stutter in public earned her a slap across the face from her mother in private. Thus to the others in the game, Francesca Winthrop maintained a calm façade. Deep inside, however, she screamed her protest.

"I won't do this, Maman." She glanced away, bracing herself for her mother's anticipated reprimand. "I'm . . . I'm in love with someone else."

"Nonsense." Alva smoothed her hands over her white muslin skirts. "Love has little to do with the stewardship of great families. You've known since birth that your destiny was to bring a title to the Winthrops. With your father's money and your new husband's title, you'll be received into the best households on both continents."

"No, Maman, with the influence of your new son-in-law, *you'll* be the one received in those *best* households," Fran said, trying to ignore the stabbing pain caused by her mother's lack of consideration. Yet, it had always been that way. Her opinion in matters of her own future were . . . insignificant. Reality constricted her throat, making words difficult. "I shall be the one tied to a man I don't know and whom I don't love."

"We all make sacrifices, dear. You'll learn to adapt. He'll arrive in two days. We'll announce your engagement at the costume ball this Saturday."

Three days! Her mother had been planning that ball for two months, and Fran had been dreading it for at least as long. Now she would not only have to find the fortitude to face a room full of people but an unfamiliar fiancé as well. Dread, as hard and as solid as one of her painted croquet balls, fisted into a tight knot in her stomach.

An errant honeybee buzzed Alva's hat, perhaps mistaking one of the silk roses for the real thing. Alva waved a gloved hand to chase it away. "I don't know why you insist on maintaining those ridiculous beehives. I certainly won't miss them when you move to London."

London! Fran hadn't quite digested news of her imminent engagement before encountering this second cannon volley. She'd have to move to London and live among total strangers. The comfortable solitude that she'd maintained her entire life would vanish. The knot in her stomach leapt to her rib cage, inhibiting breath. She was dizzy, light-headed.

Alva squinted disapproval toward Fran for a moment, then shifted her gaze, her face brightening. "Look, Simpson has found my ball. I'll just go see to its proper placement."

Fran forced words past her constricted throat. They emerged in a harsh whisper, a testament to the unexpected blow dealt to her future. "Why now, Maman? You must have known of this earlier. Why not wait to tell me in private?"

Alva Winthrop stopped and turned, her glance stern and sharp. "Do try to aim for the wickets, dear. It's the winning that matters, not the course one takes to get there."

Fran stood paralyzed. For a moment, she contemplated hitting her bonus ball directly toward her mother's heel. The resulting injury might give her pause over the injury she was causing her daughter. In her saddened heart, however, she knew that it would be a worthless gesture. Her mother was impervious to another's concern.

Not only had her mother not asked about her love interest, she hadn't even acknowledged the difficulty and reluctance Fran had experienced in sharing that information. Obviously, her only daughter's personal desires were of less import than the advantageous placement of a croquet ball.

Fran gazed beyond the lawn to the familiar tranquil Atlantic. A few sails billowed in their escape from Narragansett Harbor. The Fall River steamer, a tiny spot on the deep blue horizon, chugged along on its daily foray between Newport and Long Island.

"Randolph," she whispered with all the yearning in her heart. "Where are you? Why haven't you written?" If ever she needed his comfort and advice, now was the time. In the brief interval between her return from Paris and his departure for Germany, they had managed to share two hasty kisses and several long precious glances filled with yearning and desire. He had promised to write every day while he traveled on behalf of her father's business. Yet not one envelope had arrived since his departure three months ago. Now she would be pitted against her mother over plans for her future without even the written assurance of his devotion. Did he even know what Maman had concocted? If only she could go to Randolph, speak to him directly.

Facing the vast expanse of the ocean, even her father's gift of height failed to protect her from feeling small, insignificant, and utterly alone. Three days! What if she couldn't abide the Englishman? Her mother might not have cared about such things, but this was not her mother's life. She must take action. She must formulate a plan.

"Francesca, stop dawdling. We're all waiting on you," her mother called from the lawn boundary.

For the sake of her mother and appearances, Fran composed her expression, then turned back toward the game. Leaning over her mallet, she did as she was told and aimed her ball for the wickets, but her thoughts focused far away, on the other side of the ocean.

WILLIAM CHAMBERS, MARQUESS OF ENON AND MOST recently Duke of Bedford, sat beneath a potted palm in the eloquent parlor of the Fall River steamer anticipating imminent death. After all, death would put an end to the turbulent discord in his stomach, fueled by every rise and fall of the steamer's hull. The eight-day trip across the Atlantic Ocean had proved less than comfortable, but to add insult, he was ushered aboard this steamer with no time for recovery. His stomach rolled again, bringing the taste of bile to his throat. Could any woman, even one as rich as Midas, be worth this hell on water?

"Chambers. Chambers, old fellow, is that you?"

William forced one resistant eye open to focus on the opulent form of Henry Twiddlebody. Just when he thought he had sunk to the bottom of the barrel, life provided assurances in the form of Twiddlebodys of the further depths possible. Hesitant to move, for fear it would encourage the vile mixture in his innards to vacate its contained premises, William simply nodded to Henry. Unfortunately, the fool apparently assumed the gesture to be an invitation as he pulled a chair practically to William's knees.

"I say, old fellow, you're looking a bit green about the gills. I take it you've never held a commission in Her majesty's fleet, ey?"

Damnation! Trapped by a Twiddlebody and too ill to make an exit. Life couldn't get worse. William pressed his lips tightly together while the man chuckled at his own wit.

"I'm sorry to hear about the passing of your father, my boy. He was a good man." He looked askance at William, a smile tilting his lips under a full, wily mustache. "I guess I should be calling you 'Your Grace' now that you head up the estate."

William could almost feel what was coming next. Ever since he had discovered how his father had hopelessly squandered the family's estates with gambling debts, the most unsavory characters had found reason to approach him for an audience.

"I hadn't thought to see you this far from London, but it is fortunate indeed." Twiddlebody shifted his corpulent mass in the groaning chair to sidle closer to William's ear. "I hold some of your father's paper, you know. I wouldn't mention it normally, but as the old Duke has gone on to his just rewards, I thought perhaps you could redeem the marker. It's my missus, you see; she's been feeling poorly and—"

"Enough," William interrupted. "My solicitors have assured me all debts will be resolved shortly. I'm sure once you return to London, the matter will be settled."

Twiddlebody drew back, his eyes round with surprise. "You've uncovered some money then. I was led to believe . . ." His eyes narrowed and he leaned in closer, spewing a foul breath in William's face.

"Just what are you doing so far from home, Your Grace? You're not planning on ducking out of your father's responsibilities, are you?"

Anger bubbled up from William's gut, blacker than the poison churning in his innards. Perhaps his face reflected a bit of his fury, as Twiddlebody pulled back, a bit of horror reflected on his face as well.

"I apologize, Your Grace, I didn't mean to imply . . . I mean to say, there isn't a more honorable man in London than yourself, a gentleman in every sense of the word, a member of the Jockey Club, a man known for his charitable support. Even your father admitted as much. If you say the debt will be paid, then I'm as sure as I'm an Englishman that it will be."

If the steamer hadn't taken that moment to pitch suddenly to the left, William would have chanced his uncertain legs to carry him away from the insulting bugger. But if he stood, he was liable to be tossed into Twiddlebody's lap, a more demeaning hell he could not imagine.

"Which brings me back to the issue of why you've ventured out on the high seas," Twiddlebody continued. "You say there'll be sufficient funds to cover your father's . . . er . . . misfortunes." He hid his mouth beneath his hand as if in deep thought, which William believed was highly unlikely. "This steamer is headed to Newport, a known vacation spot for the rich, and away from New York City, the American business capital." Twiddlebody's eyes lit up, and he sat back, a grand smile spreading from ear to ear. "Why, you're going to catch yourself a wealthy bride, aren't you?"

He chuckled to himself while William plummeted into deep mortification. The heat in his face would well be mixing with the aforementioned green to render a shade only his artist brother could fathom.

"Wait till I tell the missus," Twiddlebody prattled. "London's most eligible catch o' the day is hunting for a fat purse in America. Hearts will be breakin' back home, you can bank on that." He issued a hearty laugh as William lamented that his upholstered chair wasn't deep enough to swallow him whole. "You always were the responsible one. I had thought to present my markers to that younger brother of yours, but I'll take them to your solicitors first thing upon return." Twiddlebody stood to take his leave, then shook his head. "Wait till I tell the missus."

William scowled at the thought of their father's debts being presented to Nicholas. Wouldn't he enjoy that? After all the years William had preached about obligation and responsibility to his black sheep brother, it would be more than humiliating to have men of Twiddlebody's ilk chasing after Nicholas in pursuit of payment for debts their father had incurred. Obviously William should have spent those years preaching to his father instead of Nicholas. Now that his brother had found his muse in that schoolteacher, his successes mocked William's competence as the head of the family. William's scowl deepened, just another item on a long list of his own shortcomings.

Not that he wasn't happy for his brother. Wasn't it William's actions that directly led to the discovery of Nicholas as a great artist? Of course his brother did not exactly appreciate his methods, nor did he appreciate his overtures to the schoolteacher. William grimaced. Naturally, he would not have suggested the things he had if he'd known about their relationship.

Still, Nicholas appeared quite content with his new respectable life, while maintaining a similar degree of respectability, in the face of his father's defaults, was costing William a small fortune. Only the threat of insolvency could have forced him to take this drastic measure. He had sworn never to remarry after his previous wife's death. However, thanks to the old Duke's lack of control, severe and even hurtful remedies had been required.

His fingers reached to rub a spot on his shoulder, a reminder of one of those hurtful remedies. If Deerfeld Abbey went on the auction block, proof of his family's ruination would be rampant. Even Nicholas would be drawn into the fray. William's pride as the oldest would not withstand that blow.

Thus he'd marry the woman suggested by his solicitors and keep the beggars from running off to Nicholas. After all, what did Twiddlebody call him? The responsible one? Was he being responsible marrying a stranger for the sake of her money, or was he merely being lazy? Was it honorable to sacrifice one's future happiness for the sake of the family, or was it foolish and lacking in respect? At one time, marriages arranged to enhance the family fortune were commonplace. Why then did this very circumstance make him feel lower than . . . a Twiddlebody?

The steamer mercifully docked before William could slip further into his maudlin thoughts. Although loathe to navigate the slightly swaying deck without benefit of a handrail, the lure of stationary dry land proved too much to ignore. He joined the crowd of men, women, and children funneling down the gangplank.

In the crush, one young lad in short pants with tears rolling down his cheeks pressed his tiny body up against the thin

wooden wall that channeled the departing passengers like
sheep down a chute. William quickly surveyed the open ground
at the base of the ramp and noticed a frantic woman calling
someone's name. Without regard to his rebellious stomach,
William swooped the lost lad up and tucked him under his arm
like a folded copy of the *Times*. The child screamed and kicked,
earning William the glare of many of the departing passengers,
but he carried the boy down the ramp and deposited him at the
feet of the mother. He barely heard the woman's words of
gratitude while he searched the landscape before him. In New
York, a gnarled old attorney had met him at the gangplank of
the *Britannic* and rushed him to the Fall River steamer for the
second leg of his voyage. Now, however, there didn't appear to
be anyone—

"Your Grace?"

William turned sharply, a bit too sharply for his poor
stomach to reconnoiter. He had a brief glimpse of a tall man
in a white linen suit before he felt the blood rush from his
head down to his toes.

"Whoa, steady there." The man grabbed his arm. "Take a
moment to find your land legs."

It wasn't his legs that presented the problem, William
thought glumly. Still, he preferred the stranger believe that
misconception.

"Promise me that you aren't here to take me to another
boat," William gasped.

The man laughed. "I have a rig tied up across the way.
Once we collect your luggage—"

"I have no luggage," William interrupted, starting to feel
human once again. "That is to say, I haven't any luggage here.
There was some difficulty with unloading my trunk off the *Britannic*. My man stayed behind to ensure its safe arrival in
Newport."

The man nodded. Now that William could focus on something other than his own discomfort, he could see the stranger
wasn't much older than a student still at a university. He looked
gangly, but comfortable in his white linen, far more comfortable than William felt in his frock coat and tails.

The stranger presented his hand. "Stephen Young, esquire. I've been sent by Whitby and Essex to welcome you to Newport, Your Grace."

William accepted the eager handshake, but grimaced. "'Your Grace' reminds me of my father." He neglected to add that the address reminded him as well of the unpleasant and dishonorable circumstances his father had left for William to resolve. "Perhaps we can dispatch with that particular address while I'm here? Perhaps we can pretend I'm just another American during my stay."

Stephen's glance suggested it would take more than a dropped title to allow him to pass as American; still the loss of the formalities felt good. As if all his difficulties could be so easily dispensed if he just declined the title. Life didn't work that way, but for a brief period of time he could pretend.

"I saw what you did for that little boy," Stephen said. "That was very considerate of you."

William, feeling stronger by the minute, took a good look at his surroundings. A bustling little seaport this was, though not with the industrial shipping that fouled the Cheapside of the Thames. If anything this port trafficked in people of various classes judging from their attire. The air held a wholesome freshness to it, more attune to the countryside than his familiar London. Indeed the hills and the trees reminded him of his brother's home in Yorkshire. Nicholas would approve of this place.

"The little boy lost his way," William said, still studying the tiny city of Newport. "It can be frightening to suddenly discover that everything you knew is lost." He glanced back at Stephen Young, esquire, who stared at him in a most peculiar fashion. "Shall we go?"

"This way, Your . . . sir."

William followed the young man to a simple one-horse rig and climbed aboard.

"Tell me, young squire," William teased, coaxing a smile to the boy's serious face. "How did you recognize me amongst all the other passengers?"

"Your clothes, sir."

"Ah yes," he frowned down at his trousers, "I suppose I do look a bit worse for wear. My man stayed behind in New York to escort my trunk once unloaded."

Confusion passed over the young man's face for a moment before it cleared. "No, sir, you look fine. A bit too fine, if I may say, for Newport, sir."

"Oh," William murmured, glancing about. Indeed, with the exception of the obvious laborers, the few men that passed by, and his young escort, all wore light linen suits better suited for the July heat than his frock coat and tails. He must stand out like a mule on a racetrack. "Then let's be off. And perhaps you can point out a suitable haberdashery along the way?"

The ride was short. Looking back toward the water, William felt he could have just as easily have walked the short distance, if it had not been all uphill. His guide pulled the rig to the front of a grand hotel with a wide veranda on busy Bellevue Avenue. A sign proclaimed the establishment to be named the Ocean View.

Mr. Young prepared to hop out of the rig when William restrained him with a hand to his arm. "Tell me, squire, before you go, are you familiar with the purpose of my trip to Newport?"

The young man's smile lit up his fair features. "Of course, Whitby and Essex are handling the negotiations."

"I see . . ." William said, contemplating his next question. It really shouldn't matter. He would do his best by the wealthy American, as any honorable man might, and yet . . . He leaned forward, lowering his voice as befitting a discreet conversation.

"And do you know of the young woman to whom I find myself engaged?"

A wide smile blossomed on the younger man's face as he gazed beyond the horse's ears. "Frosty Franny? Everyone knows her and her honey."

The smile collapsed once he glimpsed William's scowl. A deep red darkened his features.

"I'm sorry, sir. That's just how the local papers refer to her.

She's not really . . ." He cleared his throat. "Miss Winthrop, yes, sir, I know of her."

William nodded, his scowl still firmly in place. It was most disconcerting not knowing what his fiancée looked like. Alva Winthrop's letter advising of her daughter's availability had arrived at a most fortuitous moment. There had been no time for the exchange of photographs. Yet, this man's odious reference to her, attached to what he hoped was not some reference to her feminine virtues, made him wonder if he should not have waited a bit before embarking on this venture. The need for money was great, but great enough to be tied forever to a . . . a laughingstock? A woman had made a fool of him before. Once in a lifetime was enough.

"Everyone in Newport knows of Miss Winthrop," the man repeated, his tone sufficiently apologetic. "You are a lucky man to have secured her, sir."

He averted his gaze, thus William couldn't quite judge the honesty of that last proclamation. But as he studied Stephen's profile, the man squinted. "If I'm not mistaken"—he tilted his chin toward the opposite side of the street—"I believe there's your fiancée now."

"Where?" If William hadn't been raised on decorum in the way other young lads were raised on porridge, he would have pushed his escort aside to better view the women strolling beneath the elms that shaded the storefronts across the avenue. He bent forward, much to the protest of his still queasy stomach. "Which one?"

Stephen hopped from the rig, giving William a better view. He proceeded to tie the horse to the hotel's post.

"She's heading up the avenue toward the shops."

A tiny peal of a bell pulled William's glance across the avenue to the fancy gold lettering advertising a series of commercial establishments. A swaying bustle disappeared into the interior of one, while two other ladies approached the grouping.

"Which one?" William asked, wishing the two ladies would turn so he could see more than their profiles. Not receiving an answer, William slid across the seat and lowered himself to the street. Dodging the fashionable carriages, he dashed across the avenue in pursuit of the woman who would soon be his bride. If only he knew which woman that would be.

SILENTLY CURSING THE TINY BELL AND AWKWARD GLANCES that announced her presence, Fran quickly slipped to the side of the tobacconist's front display of gaily painted cigar boxes so she could view the street without being seen. Ever since she had balked at her mother's proposal two days ago, spies in the form of her mother's matronly friends had watched her every move and hovered always within earshot. Fortunately she had anticipated such a turn of events and had taken measures to arrange for transport on the Fall River steamer without her mother's consent. Still, she needed to lose the two bloodhounds on her trail if her plan to reunite with Randolph was to succeed.

Mary, her maid, should have already secreted a bit of luggage with a few travel garments to the steamer's boarding ramp. If Fran could make it to the steamer undetected, she stood a chance of purchasing transatlantic passage to Germany without interference. From there she'd find Randolph. She wasn't sure how, but she felt confident that the love in her heart would lead to his door. They would marry and be forever free of her mother and her purchased Duke.

First, however, Mrs. Kravitz and her annoying daughter needed to continue up the boulevard, so she could exit unnoticed from this aromatic sanctuary. Fran inhaled the rich masculine scent of tobacco, letting a smile tease her lips. They would never think to look for her in this male bastion. If anything, Mrs. Kravitz would search for her in the millinery shop next door. Or better yet, continue down the avenue believing they would spot her around the next corner. Fran risked a glance toward the window.

Mrs. Kravitz hesitated outside the shop, near the painted wooden Indian, glancing up and down the street. Her daughter, Phoebe, cupped her hands on the glass window itself and peered in. Fran quickly pressed her spine to the wall to escape notice, holding her breath that they would continue on their way.

"Miss Winthrop, what a surprise to find you here. Are you purchasing something for your father, perhaps?"

Fran nearly jumped out of her corset. The gravelly voiced proprietor stood close to her elbow. Too close, Fran thought, squelching the panic that such close proximity generated. However, with her own back pressed to the wall, there was no place to retreat. She placed a gloved finger to her lips, silencing the inquisitive man, then slowly shook her head.

He glanced toward the front window, his face relaxed into a smug expression. "I see. Is it Mrs. Kravitz you wish to avoid?" His lips twitched in a suppressed smile. "Or the unusually dressed gentleman?"

Gentleman? Her pulse picked up in surprise, but she maintained her outward calm. What gentleman?

Her glance slipped to the window. True to the proprietor's description, a man dressed in evening attire detained the two bloodhounds. He was handsome enough. Handsome, single, and wealthy, if Mrs. Kravitz's posturing with her daughter was any indication.

Fran turned to her side so as to get a better view. Mrs. Kravitz and her daughter were too preoccupied with the broad-shouldered stranger to pay attention to the happenings inside the shop. If they had just ambled a little bit farther along the walk, their conversation would have been kept them too engrossed to see her leave. But with the women blocking the entrance, even a potential suitor for Phoebe Kravitz couldn't distract sufficiently from Fran's exit.

The stranger had a strong chin that imbued him with a sense of authority, she noted. Unfortunately, that was Randolph's weakness. Randolph's chin seemed to retreat backward toward his neck. A bit of guilt at comparing her true love's attributes to those of this man flashed through her thoughts, but she dismissed it. She was merely being observant, not judging unfairly.

Perhaps Randolph's lack of chin had inspired those scratchy

muttonchops that he favored. Why did men believe that fashion to be attractive? This man certainly didn't require facial hair to create interest. His intriguing smile and strong, firm lips certainly had Phoebe Kravitz moonfaced. Although in truth, just watching the way his lips wrapped around words caused a ripple of excitement beneath Fran's stays as well. She almost envied Phoebe as the target of the stranger's rapt attention.

She raised her gaze to his eyes, dark blue intelligent eyes that missed nothing. Including her, she realized as his gaze shifted slightly, and he raised one dark brow in acknowledgment. Her heart pounding, she slid back against the wall. Oh, why did he have to intervene at this moment?

The whistle from the Fall River steamer rent the air, announcing its anticipated departure for Long Island. She was running out of time! She needed to be on that ship. She needed to find a way to Randolph, to the quiet, uncomplicated life of a barrister's wife.

"Miss Winthrop, are you sure there is nothing I can show you?" the persistent shopkeeper inquired. "I just received a new shipment of Turkish cigarettes? Perhaps your father would like a box of some Havanas?"

"Is there another exit from your store?" Fran asked. She tilted her head toward the window. "I don't wish to disturb the patrons at your front entrance."

"Why, yes," the proprietor replied cautiously. "We would have to go through the back storeroom, though. It's a bit dusty." He frowned down at her skirts. "We're not accustomed to fine ladies, like yourself, visiting our establishment. I'm afraid your beautiful skirts—"

"That is of little concern." Hope leapt to her throat. If she hurried, she still might make it. "Can you show me the way?"

She followed the man through a pair of curtains and wove her way around stacked wooden crates and wood shavings. A light covering of ash and dust mingled with brown flakes littering the floor. Mary would have a fit when she saw the state of her hems resulting from this quick detour, but no matter, that was of little import. Her guide reached the back door, opening it to a less traveled though much steeper Newport street. Fran ushered through. Once free of the establishment, she raced down the hill toward the port.

I'm coming, Randolph. I'm coming. Her hat slipped its moorings about midway down the hill and tumbled off to the side of the road. She lost one of her fine slippers, but continued in her madcap race. Slippers could always be replaced, but an opportunity to change the course of her future, less so. She approached the wharfmaster's building and foot traffic increased. She stopped short, her heartbeat pounding in her ears, her stays making breath difficult. All those people! Panic fueled her self-doubts. Could she do it? Could she plow through that crowd of strangers?

The steam whistle blasted two bursts, the warning signal that it was pulling away from the dock. Fran lifted her skirt so as not to trip and rushed toward the melee. She raced around the building and down to the ramp before she stopped, her chest heaving from the exertion, her hair long and loose from the loss of hairpins, her skin tingling from the assault of the wind, to see the steamer approaching Castle Rock on its departure from the bay.

"You're too late," Mary called amidst several pieces of luggage further down the dock. "I tried to tell them, Miss Winthrop. I really did. But they left anyway. They said they couldn't wait and to try again next time."

Too late. The words stabbed her heart as tears burned her eyes. *Too late.* She could tell Mary that there wouldn't be a "next time." Once her mother heard tales of her reckless run through the heart of town to catch a boat that wouldn't wait, she would be locked in her room again. Her mother held no tolerance for public inappropriateness. She could tell Mary that this was her one shot at freedom and it had disappeared in a blue gray wake and a steam cloud trail. She could say many things if the lump in her throat wasn't squeezing the ability to talk right out of her. *Too late!* Her lip trembled.

"Miss Winthrop?" Mary approached, her eyes wide and her mouth twisted in a concerned moue. Her gaze swept from her untidy hair, past the twisted day dress to a bare toe poking through a rip in her stocking, visible beneath a dusty hem. Her voice dropped to a near whisper. "What happened to you?"

A vision of the overdressed stranger with a raised eyebrow and an intriguing smile slipped into her mind. He happened. He was responsible. And with whatever means she could find at her disposal, he would pay.

· Two ·

WILLIAM THANKED MRS. KRAVITZ FOR HER RECommendations of suitable housing establishments and returned across the avenue. Although he had heard that Americans were a bit forthright, he hadn't appreciated the difference until just now. Back home, a proper lady would never speak to a strange man without introduction. Yet this matron introduced herself and her daughter only a moment before listing her daughter's rather ordinary attributes. He shuddered. Heavens be praised that the daughter was not the woman he sought. A king's ransom would hardly prove sufficient for a sane man to go through eternity with Miss Kravitz and her mother in his pocket.

He should feel relief that this young miss was not his betrothed, yet instead he felt apprehension. What if his Miss Winthrop was as plain and dull as Miss Kravitz? He hadn't considered that his future wife would be dim-witted, but now he supposed he would have to face the possibility. He could deal with his wife being plain, but pleasant features would be appreciated. A wicked smile crept to his lips. Pleasant features like those arranged on the woman in the window. Just what was she doing spying on his conversation? Just when he thought this might be yet another American tradition, the angel disappeared. One could well relish being tied through eternity with someone resembling that young miss. Pity that such refined attributes would be wasted on a servant girl as no self-respecting lady would patronize a tobacco shop.

Still, he must be realistic. At the advanced age of twenty-six, his Miss Winthrop was most likely a dour-faced simpleton.

He truly hoped that the appalling reference to "Frosty Franny" was not an attribute to some deformity of her features, but perhaps it was. Given her considerable financial assets, why else would she still be available? No, better to forget about the beauty in the window and prepare oneself for someone like Miss Kravitz. The future of the Chambers legacy depended on his sacrifice, and sacrifice he must.

William stepped into the Ocean View lobby and discovered Stephen Young in deep conversation with a familiar face.

"Percival? Percival Hunt, you old dog. What are you doing here?"

A wide grin spread across his friend's face. He stood and offered his hand. "Stephen was just telling me you were in town. Look at you!" A sparkle lit Percival's eye. "Were you pulled from the captain's table?"

William waved his hearty chuckle aside. "It's a bit of a long story, and I'm in no mood for the retelling. You, however, did not answer my question. I'm surprised to see a familiar face this far from our old haunts."

"I've been in New York learning a bit about my father's shipping interests when we received an invitation to a rather grand soiree. To decline such an invitation here is akin to denying the Queen."

"Well, you mustn't do that," William said, wondering if the "grand soiree" was the same fancy dress ball Mrs. Winthrop insisted on holding in his honor. If so, his arranged engagement would soon be known to all and sundry tomorrow. Would the sizeable fortunes involved make him the object of envy? Or would he become the butt of laughter and ridicule as suggested by that nickname? Already he felt the target of curious glances and sly smiles.

Percival tilted his head toward the third man in their midst. "Whitby and Essex handle many of our contracts. They usually keep Stephen buried beneath law volumes. I was rather surprised to see him here."

"It seems Whitby and Essex are involved in a great many contracts," William murmured.

"And then to see you." Percival slapped William on the

back. "By God, I would never have expected to see you summering in Newport."

"To be honest, I have been invited to a grand soiree, myself." He lifted a hopeful eyebrow toward Stephen. "Do they do that frequently here?"

Percival laughed. "Newport is like London in season. Each family tries to outdo the other. And if you've come for the ladies, you've come to the right place." He winked. "You're still a widower, are you not?"

"Yes, but . . ."

"You and I shall have a great time. I'm anxious to hear of your family. How's Arianne?"

Stephen took that moment to hand William his room key and exchange handshakes. It seemed the senior partner, Mr. Whitby, would be expecting him back at the law firm. After offering future assistance if required, he left the two men to continue their discussion in the limited privacy of a hotel lobby.

William leaned forward. "Tell me, Percy, have you made the acquaintance of a Miss Francesca Winthrop?"

"Why, that's the very family I alluded to earlier." Percy smiled. "But no. I arrived in New York earlier in the summer after the grand dames of society had left for cooler climes. I was rather hoping I'd be fortunate enough to gain an introduction at the costumed affair."

"I suspect that can be arranged," William murmured, taking some relief in the fact that Percy hadn't mentioned any missing frozen appendages in connection with Miss Winthrop.

"Pardon?" Percy asked.

"Nothing. Nothing. Just idle speculation on my part." William settled back, eager to turn his mind away from Frosty Franny. "I noticed a patron of the racetrack on the boat coming over. Is there any chance of a confluence of horseflesh in the area?"

AS ANTICIPATED AFTER THE MORNING'S FAILED ATTEMPT at escape, Fran had been locked within the sparsely furnished prison of her bedroom. Her options for escaping tomorrow's mandated engagement had narrowed as she was no longer trusted or allowed outside of the house, even to tend her hives.

"Trust me," the mother had said as she turned the key in the lock. "I know what is best."

The time spent isolated allowed her anger to cool into a quiet desperation. She couldn't blame the handsome stranger for her demise. He wasn't responsible for her mother's heavy-handed manipulations. Besides, she most likely would never see him again. She wouldn't see any familiar faces again if she was forced into this marriage and shipped away to London.

The exile to her room did, however, allow her time to work on her translations. She'd finished one volume of German fairy tales that she'd begun a month earlier. However, when she reached for the next volume, she uncovered the French cour-tesan's diary. She'd forgotten that at Madame Aglionby's sug-gestion, she'd hidden the purchase amongst the children's volumes she'd also procured that day. Her face warmed as she thought of the scandalous letter she'd written Randolph at the tutor's suggestion.

Was that why he hadn't returned her correspondence? Was he shamed by her candor? It would be like Randolph to ques-tion her sense of propriety. After all, he was the one who in-sisted they remain proper and respectable. *Until the time is right,* his voice murmured in her head.

"Too late," she gave voice to her thoughts in the empty room. She drew her fingers across the unmarked cover of the diary, experiencing a tingling deep inside. She hadn't read much beyond the few early entries where the woman described how life had forced her hand to sell favors to men for money. The woman's hand was light and artful, her grammar and construc-tion superb, but the situation she described, deplorable.

Another world existed on that furthest end of society. A world whose inhabitants were identified by a quickened step and a furtive glance, whose antics were whispered about in dimly lit corridors. Her father had frequented that world from time to time, it was no secret. He would shout his exploits when the arguments with Maman left the house still and cold.

Had Randolph? Had his silence meant that he had turned away from her, just as her father had turned away from Maman?

She couldn't remember where she had placed the journal when they'd returned from that Paris shopping trip, so she hadn't the chance to employ any of the advice by the woman known only by the letter *B*.

Her hand reached for the forgotten journal when an unanticipated knock on the door altered its course. Instead, she grabbed another book to place on top of the wanton diary to hide it from sight.

"*Entrez*," she called, without any real interest in the intrusion. Since her mother had locked the door several hours earlier, her only visitors were the servants bringing her meals. The sooner the interruption passed, the sooner she could return to the licentious material. A key scraped metal in the lock, and the door slowly opened. Harrelson, the butler, forced his head inside.

"I'm sorry to intrude, Miss Winthrop, but you have a visitor."

"A visitor?" A memory of the handsome stranger that had buggered her escape immediately popped into her mind. But that remote likelihood, coupled with the even more improbable possibility that her mother would permit such a visit, swept the fanciful notion from her brain. "Who is it?"

"Mr. Whitby of Whitby and Essex, miss. He has asked to speak with you."

"My mother's attorney wishes to speak with me?" Her mother had never seen fit to include Fran in any of her frequent consultations with Mr. Whitby. Pawns were rarely allowed legal counsel. That the man waited for her now must mean he had something private to discuss. Something for her ears only. A cautious delight threatened to spill to her lips. Randolph must have sent a letter.

"I put him in the gold room," Harrelson intoned.

Fran nodded and stood to smooth the wrinkles from her extravagant day gown. Worth had created it and many others specifically for her on their last trip to Paris. She checked her hair in the small wall mirror that Alva had selected for Fran's room.

The Winthrops, like the rest of the elite society, only lived in their Newport "cottages" for six to eight weeks in the summer. The rest of the year was spent at their estate in Hyde Park or in their New York town house. Much like her gowns, the Newport cottage had not been designed for comfort. It was meant to impress, or more appropriately, stun a discerning eye with its opulence. The gold room, so named because of carved gilt walls, served as both a reception room and a ballroom. Although other rooms had proportions more conducive to an intimate conversation, the pure opulence of this room took a visitor's breath away. Thus, it was used to flaunt the owner's advantage when serving as a reception area. Alva had always maintained appearances were paramount, and in anticipation of tomorrow's ball, the gleaming surfaces had been polished profusely.

Fran, however, felt none of the confidence the room's designer had intended. Instead, her stomach fluttered as if a dozen hummingbirds had taken residence.

"Mr. Whitby." She nodded with a quick, casual curtsy. The elderly man's full white beard absorbed the room's warm gold reflection as if he had stumbled into a fountain of youth. Or perhaps the anticipation of Randolph's letter had made the world young and fresh and beautiful. She knew he would write. She could rely on Randolph. Just as she had been taught, she kept the smile in her heart and not on her face. "You asked to see me?"

"Yes. Thank you for obliging, Miss Winthrop. I hesitate to disrupt your mother at such a busy time."

A small sense of annoyance registered in Fran's chest, knowing as she did the reason for her mother's activity. "How may I assist you?"

Whitby scowled. "Yes, indeed. I brought some papers that require her signature. Papers that she had insisted be drafted in the most extreme urgency. Now I've been informed that I cannot deliver them due to her costume fitting or some such activity."

"I see." Fran worried her lip with a sense of unease. In all her years, she could not recall a single time that her mother turned away Mr. Whitby, who had served as a close friend and confidant.

"I wonder if you could take these papers to her?" Whitby asked. "I would not trouble her if not for her very insistence on their necessity."

"Yes, yes, of course," Fran replied absently, taking the offered sheath of papers neatly tied with a blue ribbon.

Whitby looked down, as if embarrassed to meet her gaze. As an invited guest to the ball, he knew its purpose and most likely her desperation to avoid it. "There is no hurry to return the papers once they are signed. I'll send someone in a day or so to collect them. Thank you for your assistance, Miss Winthrop."

He collected his hat and turned to leave. His imminent departure pulled Fran from her maudlin thoughts of the upcoming nuptials.

"Mr. Whitby?" she asked, delaying his departure. "Have you received any news from Mr. Stockwell? Has he completed his business affairs in Germany?"

"Oh." He glanced nervously about the room. "I had hoped not to be the one to tell you."

A sense of foreboding dimmed her earlier exuberance, still she maintained her countenance even though events were making it increasingly difficult. *Never show emotion, or risk the scorn that follows,* her mother had always counseled. "Not to tell me what, Mr. Whitby?"

"Randolph has married a German girl. We're hoping he will be instrumental in representing our client's interests in that part of the world. Now that steam has made shipping more reliable, the world is becoming a smaller place." His lips pulled tight in a sad smile.

She stood still, her smile frozen on her face, her mother's axiom pounding in her brain. Never show emotion. Appearances are paramount. Her heart screamed at the loss of her future, the loss of a quiet life as Mrs. Stockwell, the loss of children loved for themselves and not for the position they could bring her in society. All her hopes and dreams dissolved in six short words. *Randolph has married a German girl.* Her last foothold in a sane world crumbled, and she felt as if she had tumbled into a deep, black abyss. Still, she smiled and nodded as if she had known it all along.

"You must pass along our congratulations, Mr. Whitby, when next you see him."

"Good day, Miss Winthrop." The attorney tipped his hat and stepped around her to leave. She stood frozen with her smile, fighting back tears. Her mother would have been proud.

She wasn't sure how long she stood alone in the gold room, a devastating hole boring through her heart. The gilded mirrors surrounding her reflected so much glitter and gold, they managed to disguise the passing of time. Perhaps that's how so many years had slipped away from her, she wondered. It had all been a trick of those mirrors.

Had Randolph's affections been a trick as well? Those mirrors made them all believe they had more time. She was twenty-six years old, abandoned and alone. Her mother planned upstairs, her hard-fought battle to gain admission to New York's Four Hundred—the most elite group of American society— driving her to purchase a title by selling her daughter. It was all so worthless, so pointless.

A tear plopped onto the sheath of papers in her hand, the sound amplified in the vast empty room. She rubbed the moisture from her cheek, unaware she had been crying. It would do no good for her mother to see her this way, and see her she must if only to gain her signature on these documents.

As she left the room and began to slowly climb the winding staircase to reach her mother's bedroom, she noticed a housemaid with a laden tea tray.

"Sally," she asked. "Is that for Maman?"

"Aye," she responded. "I'm taking this tray to her now. Is there something you'd be wanting?"

She placed the sheaf of papers on the tea tray, thus eliminating the need to see her mother and evidence of a family's betrayal.

· Three ·

"CHAMBERS, I DON'T THINK THIS IS A GOOD IDEA." Percy glanced at his reflection in the mirror, twisting from side to side, admiring the fit of the military blue jacket with the gold braid trim of a Prussian prince. "This costume was meant for you. The note said as much."

"Ridiculous." William picked up the brilliant green papier-mâché frog head that would ultimately complete his costume. "I much prefer wearing your costume. This headpiece will allow me the freedom to move throughout the crowd without the demands placed on a performing pig."

"So now I'm a pig, am I?" Percy laughed. "Seriously, why are you doing this?"

The painted face on the frog held a ridiculous grin, the eyes much larger than those on a natural frog. It would certainly hide him completely. William slipped the hollow construction over his head until the neck opening rested on his shoulders.

"Hiding in that mask won't stop my questions," Percy said. "We've gallivanted about Newport all yesterday, and you've still not told me why you're here."

The mask muffled the sound of Percy's voice. William heard the gist of the question. He just wasn't sure he wanted to answer it. He peered out the two holes placed for vision. He could see, but not clearly. The world took a darker turn when wearing the mask: confining, hot, trapped. Yes, definitely the latter. As restrictive and uncomfortable as the headpiece felt on his shoulders, he didn't remove the covering. He picked up the green gloves that had come with the costume.

"You're going to propose to her, aren't you?"

William raised his head but didn't address Percival's question. To speak of what he was about to do would make it too real, too embarrassing.

"Miss Winthrop. She's the reason you're here, isn't she?"

He started to reply, but the sound amplified inside the mask, making the sound of his own voice painful to his ears. Placing hands on either side of the head, he lifted it off his shoulders. If only he could lift the responsibility of the family name as easily. The warm, humid air of Newport brought relief to his overheated face.

"You shouldn't be embarrassed," Percy said after a glance. "Men have married women for their dowries for centuries. It's a part of England's tradition."

William looked away, discomfort souring his stomach. "It's not part of my tradition. I had thought never to marry again after Catherine died. If there were any other way . . ."

"You must have loved Catherine a great deal," Percy said, sympathy evident in his voice.

William frowned. Percy never knew of Catherine's infidelities. Revisiting past injustices would serve no purpose now. He picked up the sword that had accompanied the prince costume and tested the point with his finger. "The engagement is to be announced tonight at the ball."

Percy's eyes widened. "Tell me then, why are we switching costumes?"

"I'd like a chance to view the chit without her knowing that I'm her intended." William handed the sword to Percy, who placed it in its scabbard. "Women act differently once they discover I have a title. It was difficult enough as a marquess, but I've discovered the shorter the title, the more ridiculous the pursuit. They mask their true selves."

He tapped the giant frog head, reflecting on his choice of words. "This is my last ball as an unencumbered man," he continued. "I'd like to experience how it feels to be an unknown."

He didn't feel the need to mention his faint hope to locate the woman in the window. At this late juncture he wasn't sure what could transpire even if he were to locate that particular miss. Once his engagement was made public he would be ethically bound to his new fiancée. However, donning the frog disguise would provide more opportunity to observe both the costumed guests and the servants.

"But the Winthrops are expecting a duke." Percy practiced a stern expression in the mirror.

"Then be a duke," William replied. "Just look disapproving and nod your head ever so slightly when introduced. There's really nothing to it."

"There's everything to it!" Percy insisted. "We're talking about marriage. You said yourself that the Winthrops plan to announce your engagement tonight. I will not stand before the elite of Newport and pretend to be engaged to a woman I don't know. It's not honorable."

William sighed. "I won't let it go that far. When the time comes, I'll announce my presence to the Winthrops. I will not prevail upon you to do something less than honorable." Although by Percy's own words, William was again struck how his whole situation was little less than the public purchase of a mistress. Where was the honor in that?

Percy appeared mollified, but still hesitant. "Are you sure they won't know instantly that I am not you? Have they not seen your photograph?"

"That young attorney assured me the negotiations were finalized much too quickly for the exchange of photographs. As I would arrive about the same time as the mail from London, it was decided that such an exchange would not be necessary. After all, she is marrying for my title, not for my appearance." Just as I'm marrying for her money, he silently added. He could be an old geezer and she a pox-marked hag for all that it mattered.

"Look at you," William said, pointing to Percival's reflection in the mirror. "What woman wouldn't be pleased to find herself shackled to such a handsome figure of a man? I suspect the poor girl will be beyond disappointment when she discovers that I'm to be her true groom."

"Nonsense," Percy remonstrated. "You've always done well

with the ladies. I'm sure once you remove that ridiculous headpiece, she'll be overcome with her good fortune. What woman wouldn't wish to find herself betrothed to a handsome duke?"

William grimaced. He rather expected the chit to be overcome with joy no matter his appearance by virtue of his title alone. That was what his last wife did. Once the vows were spoken, her true nature emerged.

His brother Nicholas had married the most non-appropriate woman he could find and a happier couple William had never seen. The jealous longing that surfaced whenever his thoughts turned to Nicholas pulled at his chest. What would it be like to share a life with a woman who truly loved a man for himself and not his wealth or title? Did such women exist? If they did, he had run out of time to find them. The duty and responsibility that came hand in hand with his title had made that kind of happiness little more than a pipe dream.

He lifted the frog head and settled it on his shoulders once again and peered through the small holes that allowed sight. He squinted at his absurd reflection in the mirror. "What woman indeed?"

"MISS WINTHROP, YOUR MOTHER WON'T LIKE BEING tricked like this."

"My mother is an old hand at trickery," Fran said, remembering her mother's frequent use of guile to manipulate others. She adjusted the peacock mask to conceal most of Mary's face. "As long as the evening ends with my engagement to the Duke, she'll forgive your involvement."

And if she throws a sufficient fit, enough to make the Duke drop his engagement proposal, so much the better, she thought smugly. She stepped back from her regally attired maid, pointing her in the direction of the mirror. "There. You are stunning. Everyone will believe you are a rich American heiress."

Mary frowned at her reflection. "Your parents will know. I'm not nearly as tall as you, Miss Winthrop. I don't know all those fancy words you use, and I've never tried those fancy dances." She pulled on the revealing bodice. "Maybe we shouldn't do this."

"Nonsense," Fran reassured her, readjusting the folds of the elaborate costume. Indeed, poor Mary appeared a bit overwhelmed by all the blue and green feathers. But the low décolleté displaying Mary's ample assets would draw all the attention. No one would notice the heavy garment dragging on the floor from Mary's lack of height. "You will be the princess of the ball. You don't have to dance if you don't want to. Just stroll about the rooms downstairs and pretend you are me."

She doubted the deception would progress that far. Her mother was well acquainted with Fran's abhorrence of crowds and strangers. Once Maman realized that it was not Francesca in the peacock costume, Fran imagined the ball, and more important the engagement, would be cut short. At a minimum, she'd gain more time to effect an escape. At best, the resulting scandal would give the Duke sufficient motive to search for his bride in England and not on these shores.

She glanced at her own reflection standing behind Mary, wondering if her mother would appreciate the irony of her choice of costume. Fran wore the free-flowing folds of fabric that symbolized the French statue given to the United States as a gift, Liberty Enlightening the World. The costume currently was a popular one at fancy dress balls, as fund-raising efforts for the monument's pedestal had been sluggish. Mr. Evarts had approached the Winthrops to lend support and had left several sketches of the statue behind. Once erected, he had said, the statue would serve as symbol of liberty and escape from oppression.

She had purchased the costume several months ago in anticipation of the many costumed balls that ended the summer season not realizing she'd have occasion to use it in her own bid for liberty. How appropriate as tonight she hoped for an escape of her mother's oppression.

"You won't let me be engaged to no duke?" Mary's wide eyes pleaded with her in the mirror.

"No, I won't let that happen," Fran reassured her. However

much she disliked the future her mother had planned for her, she couldn't in good faith send her maid to stand in her stead before an altar. No, she must conspire a way for the Duke to denounce the engagement.

"Now remember the plan. You're to go downstairs just as the Duke enters the foyer, not a moment before. We'll know him by that costume Maman selected. Curtsy, just as we practiced, when you're presented."

Mary nodded and attempted a wobbly curtsy in front of the mirror. Fran remembered the hours her mother used to make her practice the movement as a young girl. She hadn't wobbled like that in twenty years. Surely, a conceited, pretentious old duke would be offended by such an awkward display. A smile crept to her lips. And if her mother caused a scandalous scene, so much the better.

"I couldn't curtsy better myself," Fran lied. "The Duke has never met me so he won't suspect a switch. Just play it by ear."

"Where will you be? What if your mother confronts me?" Mary's eyes grew big and round. "What if I'm discharged as a result?"

"Tell her I made you do it," Fran responded. "Tell them it is all my fault. She'll believe you. Maybe that will make the Duke call off this ridiculous arrangement."

They exchanged places. Fran sat on the chair before the mirror, while Mary vigorously stroked her long hair with a brush. "Are you sure you don't want me to put it up, Miss Winthrop? Your mother would want you to have it high like a proper lady."

Fran retrieved one of the sketches of Bartholdi's statue from the vanity drawer. "It should resemble this lady's hair. Gathered at the nape in a series of folds with finger curls below the ears," Fran said, appraising herself in the mirror.

Mary smiled. "You look like a young girl with your hair down around your shoulders. You have such pretty hair."

Indeed, she did look younger this way. Not at all like the old spinster she was bound to become now that Randolph had abandoned her. Perhaps that was the true motive behind this sham engagement, she thought. Her mother might just want to see her properly married. As quickly as she entertained that thought, she abandoned it. Her mother was interested only in what her pawn could do for her. She had no concern for her daughter's wishes or happiness. Alva's desires were all that mattered. That was the way it had always been.

Fran pressed a copper crown that radiated seven spikes in a sunburst design into her hair. "This headpiece should stand out above the crowd. I should be easy enough to find."

She hesitated. If all transpired according to plan, the commotion at the doorway should prove sufficient to dissuade the Duke. But if not, she had an alternative plan. A cold shiver slipped down her spine.

"If you don't find me in the ballroom," she said, hoping events would not progress that far, "ask someone to check the gardens."

NO ONE KNEW BETTER HOW TO STAGE A DRAMATIC entrance than her mother, Fran thought, which explained the wide, multilevel Siena marble staircase solidly stationed in the middle of the house. From their position on the mezzanine level, Mary and Fran could lean over the ornate iron-and-bronze rail to the gathering below. Alva had spared no expense for the ball from the look of the decorations. A large bronze fountain, filled with floating lotus blooms and water hyacinths, bubbled directly beneath them. Hummingbirds and brightly colored butterflies had been brought in specifically to flutter about the spectacular floral masterpiece. She suspected a few of her honeybees had found their own entrance as well, drawn to the overwhelming floral scent of lilies and roses. A white-wigged footman dressed in Louis XIV fashion stood just beyond the fountain, announcing the names of the guests as they arrived.

Had Fran not already recognized the Duke's costume the moment he strolled through the decorative grille into the entryway, she would have known by her mother's effusive efforts that a person of societal import had arrived.

"Now!" She urged Mary with a slight push. Mary tentatively approached the wide, sweeping turn of the staircase to descend to the main floor, her blue and green silks rippling on the smooth steps behind her.

Fran retreated behind a giant potted fern to observe her plan unfold. Guilt and uncertainty roiled in her stomach. She wouldn't have taken such desperate measures if the stakes, her very future, weren't so critical, she reassured herself.

The fair-headed Duke, dressed in a regimental uniform, had the athletic build and soft charm that many would call handsome. He was not as old as she had imagined, nor as corpulent. Her attention, however, was drawn to the Duke's companion, a man dressed in tails as if for a formal evening, but with the head of a frog, reminding her of a favored storybook character from her childhood. Holding a hand to her mouth to soften the chuckle that rose to her lips, she imagined the princess in *The Frog King* would have had little difficulty befriending such a well-formed amphibian. She cautiously moved forward, risking discovery, to see his direction.

"His Grace, the ninth Duke of Bedford, and Mr. Percival Hunt," the footman announced.

Her mother's face lit with an internal glow. Rising from a curtsy, she stepped forward to receive her special guest. She looked so carefree and happy. When was the last time her mother had looked so joyful?

Doubt surrounding the appropriateness of the switch began to gnaw at Fran's nerves. Her mother beamed approval of the handsome young man. Anticipating her mother's disappointment when she discovered the trick, Fran felt a moment of guilt. Perhaps this plan was not the clever solution she had envisioned.

She quickly descended a few steps. Her mother wouldn't approve of the costume switch, but she'd never forgive the planned deception with Mary. However, Fran had barely touched the fifth step when she realized. Mary had reached the bottom of the stairs. The deception was in play. Fran would be too late to stop it.

"Your Grace," her mother, beautifully attired as a Venetian princess, extended a hand toward the staircase. "Allow me to introduce my daughter, Miss Francesca—"

Her mother stopped in mid-introduction and stared hard at Mary. No one else would probably have noted the difference, but Fran saw the joy drain from her mother's eyes. A cold, passionless steel returned in its stead.

Mary's peacock feathers flitted in constant motion as she bent in a surprisingly graceful curtsy with arm extended. Fran herself could not have executed it better. "Miss Francesca Winthrop, Your Grace," she said, her voice strong and clear.

"Well done, Mary!" Fran whispered before retreating back to the landing. Too involved with the scene below to leave, but too afraid of her mother's reaction to remain in sight, she slipped back behind the fern.

"Miss Winthrop," the Duke smiled and accepted Mary's hand, bestowing a kiss on her fingertips. Her mother tilted her Venetian headdress, searching the staircase without a change in expression, not once correcting the Duke's false assumption.

Fran's heart sank. This was not going according to plan! She had counted on her mother creating the sort of stir that would have kept the old society matrons chattering for weeks— the sort of stir that would cause the Duke to hesitate and not agree to the negotiated engagement. If Fran had more time, she knew she could convince the Duke she'd make an unsuitable wife. Duchesses don't go to extraordinary lengths to avoid strangers. They certainly don't spend their time translating myths and legends from ancient and foreign texts. And they don't have hurtful names given to them by newspapers who don't understand her fear of crowded places.

Yet her mother nodded her approval as the Duke placed Mary's dyed-blue glove on top of his military sleeve and led her toward the gold ballroom. Fran had to admit, they did make an attractive couple. Mary's smile broadcast her delight as they made their way to the crowded ballroom.

She glanced back toward her mother, who flagged down a footman. Alva whispered something in his ear. The man glanced up the staircase. Afraid she'd been spotted, Fran dashed down a hallway toward the servant's stairs. Her hasty flight carried her down to the butler's pantry and then out to the gardens through the delivery courtyard. It was time for her secondary plan, the one she was loathe to take, but under the circumstances, had no choice.

SWEAT STUNG HIS EYES AND TRICKLED DOWN WILLIAM'S temple within the closed confines of his papier-mâché prison. Although the open bottom of the frog head mask extended a good foot beyond his chin, the breeze stirring the ostrich feather of the lady before him never penetrated to soothe his heated cheeks. Even a glass of cool champagne, awkwardly manipulated under the bottom of the mask, couldn't reduce his discomfort.

"Are you quite all right in there?" asked a lady dressed entirely in white feathers who purported to be a swan.

William nodded, finding that method of communication less painful than speaking. His vision, slightly obscured by a sheer mesh cloth covering the huge frog eyes, allowed him to observe Percy's progress with the lady peacock from a distance. The girl possessed no semblance of grace or elegance and her irritating feathers flitted and fretted as much as those bloody bees who kept thinking his bulbous green head was some kind of exotic flower.

Still Percy seemed captivated by the chit, which offered some vague hope that she might eventually prove somewhat suitable as a duchess. He doubted she would measure up to his aunt's rigid standards for the title. Even with her substantial dowry, she was nevertheless American.

He glanced about the room as much as the mask afforded with a bit of awe. The things he could do with the money spent on this room alone. The gold and the glitter, the artistry on the ceilings and in the statues tucked into the corners of the room, and all of it new. According to Percival, this was not the result of centuries of inheritance, one generation building upon the foundations laid by another. This was all newly purchased and placed, and this "cottage" only one of the family's many newly purchased manors. Why, the money spent on this residence alone would save Deerfeld Abbey and all of its tenants.

Another breeze stirred the draperies near the open door to the gardens. The temptation to blend into the cool night and remove the tormenting frog mask proved too great a temptation. Enjoying a bit of his anonymity, William managed to walk around the edges of the ballroom without once encountering an ambitious young lady or a hovering matron. The novelty pleased him, though the thought of removing the head pleased him more.

The crowd inside had spilled out to the terrace, making it difficult to move without stepping on a lady's skirts, or stumbling about in a most undignified manner. He was afraid his murmured apologies never escaped the confines of the mask. The light from the ballroom reached beyond the terrace before fading into the dark night. He thought he spied a path that led away from the crowds and eagerly sought it out. The farther he walked along the path, the sooner the music provided by the ballroom orchestra became replaced with the faint soothing sound of ocean waves meeting stone. Such a clean, refreshing sound. William reached up and removed the mask, letting the late summer breezes rejuvenate him as well. The moon shimmered on the undulating swells, making him feel small and insignificant: a simple man, not a duke with the weight of a dynasty on his shoulders.

"It's beautiful out here, is it not?" A woman's voice interrupted his reverie.

At first, William didn't respond, believing the woman's question must be directed to a gentleman who might have accompanied her. He could well imagine a man's motives on bringing a lady to such a secluded spot. A smile teased his lips. Some things remained the same on both sides of the Atlantic. He stole a glance in the direction of the amorous couple.

However, there was no couple. Just a goddess wrapped in bed linens. His breath caught. Moonlight shimmered on a copper crown on her head, giving the illusion of a halo to the heavenly presence beneath. The drape of the cloth hid her body but the comely shape of her face and shoulders suggested a form of equally pleasing proportions. The ocean breeze tugged at the folds of cloth, and he found himself wishing for a bit of a gale.

She stepped closer accompanied by the fresh scent of the gardenias. He longed to touch her, to feel if she were real or just a figment of his imagination.

"It's so peaceful away from the crowds, away from prying eyes."

This time he knew she spoke to him and to him alone, yet he was afraid he would sound like a bumbling idiot if he chanced to open his mouth. Her eyes skimmed his face and briefly settled on his lips as if she recognized his difficulty. She lowered her gaze to the hideous frog head, and broke into a soft, pleasing laugh.

"I saw you earlier. You arrived about the same time as the Duke, did you not?"

He nodded. Where had she come from? He couldn't recall hearing footsteps behind him, and he certainly didn't see her before she announced her presence. Such an appealing woman shouldn't be alone out here, in the dark.

"I'm sorry," he said. "I hadn't meant to disturb you." He glanced about, looking for a matron or a chaperone hidden in the shadows. "In fact, I didn't realize anyone was here."

"Oh." Her eyes widened. "You've an accent. You're British. I suppose it wasn't just coincidence that you arrived with the Duke. Are you a close friend?"

"Well, yes actually." He silenced the soft chuckle that rose to his lips, but couldn't suppress the resulting smile. Little did she know just how well he knew the Duke.

She stepped nearer. In spite of the ocean breeze and the lack of the stifling frog mask, a bead of sweat ran between his shoulder blades beneath his shirt. There was something familiar about the girl, though he couldn't recall having met such a vision with her long finger curls, and dressed in such a titillating fashion among the many introductions he'd borne of late. The nymph moved so close a mere inch separated his knuckle from the hardened nub pressing through the silk of her costume. His groin tightened and all memories of recent introductions faded.

"What's he like?" she asked, her voice innocent yet seductive.

"The Duke?" He forced the words through his constricted throat, resulting in the strangled utterance of an adolescent boy. Control yourself, he silently commanded. Just because such posturing on her part would be tantamount to a sexual invitation in England doesn't mean society works the same way here. His hand clenched by his side, he drew a deep breath. A mistake as his lungs soon filled with the evocative essence of gardenias and moonlight. "He's a good chap. Strong, reliable, and true." His words rushed. "A good judge of horseflesh, I'm told."

And other flesh, his body reminded him, as the breeze stirred the gathered drapes of cloth covering her chest, bringing his gaze back to that enticing nub. His mouth watered with the urge to coax the titillating swell into something harder, firmer. His body responded with a rise of its own. "Some women find him handsome."

"Do they?" Inexplicably, and with a certain measure of awkwardness, she stroked the lapel of his jacket and tilted her head back as if expecting to be kissed.

Shocked, he had intended to raise his hand to force release of his lapel, but his fingertips reached instead for the dewy skin of her cheek. He traced the soft curve of her jaw and ran his thumb lightly across her full lower lip, wondering if he dare taste what she offered.

Remembering the excessive comforts evident at the cottage, gold and silver, the floral towers and abundant champagne, the thought suddenly registered that perhaps this goddess was meant to be his for the taking. A smile pulled at his lips. These Americans, they think of everything. The frog mask slipped from his grasp and thumped to the ground. He wrapped his arm around her waist and pulled her to him.

"I'm not sure how these things are accomplished here . . ."

he whispered, letting the urgent nature of his needs take over. After witnessing the opulence at the ball, he wouldn't be surprised to discover a bed hidden beneath the cover of trees, a gilt-edged bed at that. He dragged his lips tenderly across her forehead, inhaling her sweet scents and preparing for an outright assault on her tantalizing mouth. "But if you're offering what I believe—"

A sudden clamor of footsteps behind him interrupted. His spine stiffened. Dallying with a light skirt was one thing, but he did draw the line at public performances.

"Francesca Winthrop!" a woman's shrill voice wailed. "Francesca, you foolish girl, what are you doing?"

· Four ·

SHE HADN'T INTENDED TO LOSE CONTROL OF THE flirtation. While she had hoped that a minor indiscretion would lead to discovery and cancellation of the engagement contract, she hadn't expected to enjoy indiscretion quite this much. His British accent played like music to her ears, while the expressive quirk to his eyebrows touched her deep inside. He had a secretive smile, as if he found humor in the most mundane things. His wide shoulders and strong frame seemed oddly familiar. Perhaps they reminded her of the knights in her illustrated copy of Arthur's tales. Yes. That must be it, she reassured herself. Like those knights of old, tonight he was saving her from a future not of her choosing.

However, even with all these vaguely familiar physical attributes, his eyes managed to captivate her more than the rest. The night obscured the color, but she saw an interest in the depths that melted her bones and wobbled her knees. Randolph's glance had never produced that effect and for the first time she felt gratitude at being unencumbered. Once the stranger had wrapped his arms about her and pulled her into his warmth she struggled to keep her wits about her. A clean, masculine scent filled her nostrils. Her eyes closed, her lips parted to receive an eagerly anticipated kiss. She waited . . . she waited . . .

Fluttering her eyes open, she saw his gaze turned to the left. With a subtle pressure on her side, he shifted her behind him as if to protect her from some savage beast. She bent to peek around him and saw he was indeed facing the most cunning and savage of all opponents—her mother.

"Francesca. It will do no good hiding behind this stranger. The damage has been done. Come out now and face the consequences." Her mother harrumphed.

Although her handsome paramour tried to keep her safely behind him, she stepped around his restraining arm and moved to his side. When his lips opened to speak, she placed her fingertips to still his words, and yes, perhaps lingered a bit longer than necessary. She would have liked to have felt the pressure of those lips, just once. Perhaps once this was all over . . .

His eyebrow rose in that endearing fashion, pulling her answering smile before she turned to face her mother's ensemble.

The Duke and Mary stood behind Maman. The family attorney, Mr. Whitby, was aligned to the Duke's left. Her father and Mrs. Kravitz joined the group a moment later along with other curious guests, providing a rather satisfying audience. Normally, such a gathering would intimidate her into nausea, but not tonight.

Tonight, the crowd provided only a mild tinge of discomfort. With their presence, there could be no doubt as to the scandal and thus no better assurance of being released from this pledge. Fran's gaze skipped to the bewildered Duke standing behind Maman, disappointed that he didn't look more annoyed. She had hoped he'd be angry at her indiscretion. Could he truly value her dowry more than his pride?

"Your Grace," Fran said, holding the folds of her costume out to the side as she executed an elegant curtsy.

"Your Grace," her mother intervened, "allow me to introduce my *real* daughter, Miss Francesca Winthrop." She turned back to Fran. "I suppose you had some purpose for this foolish dalliance with this . . . this . . ." Although Alva's head bobbed at least six inches beneath the stranger's, Alva still managed to look down her nose at him. "Ne'er-do-well."

A disgusted look crossed the young Duke's face as he stepped around her mother. Fearing that the Duke might harm the duped stranger in defense of her honor, Fran held her hand up in restraint.

"Please, Your Grace. No one would cast blame if you wished to call off the engagement—"

"Francesca!" her mother gasped.

Fran swallowed the panic induced by the growing audience. She had to see this through to the conclusion—then she could hide from the crowd. She stepped in front of the Duke so she could address him directly.

"Your reputation must remain above scandal. As you can see by my actions, I am not suitable to be your duchess. Nothing has been announced; the taint on my honor would be slight."

No doubt Maman would send her overseas just to be rid of her, Fran thought with an inward smile. She could continue her studies alone and in peace. The more she contemplated that alternative, the more she was convinced that her actions had been just. Finally, the future she longed for, one of simplicity and solitude—no fancy balls, no crowds of endless faces. She was almost grateful to the Duke for providing this opportunity.

"There shall be no need of that." The stranger's voice, so deep and rich and close, sent a quiver through her chest, or perhaps it was his ominous tone. Either way, she didn't need or want the stranger's interference. Her plan had worked perfectly so far.

"This does not involve you," Fran murmured. "I'm afraid you've been a bit of a pawn."

"On the contrary, it most certainly does involve me," he said with that damnable quirked eyebrow that nearly touched his hairline.

"Allow me to make the introductions," the young Duke stepped forward with a wide grin.

"Miss Francesca Winthrop, I wish to present Duke Ne'er-do-well, the ninth Duke of Bedford."

Her mother gasped. Fran turned on her heel and said in a low accusation, "You tricked me."

"It would appear we are well suited." His eyes smoldered with a fire that quickened her pulse and induced the mild panic that hitherto had been the prerogative of a crowd, not an individual. The intonation in his voice reminded her that she had endeavored to trick him as he had her. A jolt of realization chilled her spine. Perhaps in this man, she had met her match.

He raised his voice sufficiently to extend to her mother. "Under the circumstances, I see no reason to call off the engagement." His gaze shifted back to her. His appreciative stare warmed her in places unseen. "Indeed, I see every reason to hasten the wedding."

"But that's impossible," Fran gasped, recognizing that he proposed hurrying the one thing she hoped to avoid. "It will take at least a year to arrange everything. There's the matter of the invitations and my gown—"

"One month should be more than sufficient," her mother said behind her.

"Maman!" Fran turned round on her.

"Did I neglect to mention that I ordered your wedding gown that last visit to Paris? The local modiste can make the final adjustments. We'll have the wedding here. Invitations will be delivered within the week." Alva looked steadily at the Duke. "One month."

He nodded, then reached in his pocket before lifting Fran's left hand. "I will forgo asking for your hand on bended knee. Such an unbecoming formality would serve no purpose with an arranged merger." He slipped a ring onto her finger. "Shall we go and make the formal announcement to your friends? At least, to those that didn't follow the promenade out here."

She stared, still in shock over the outcome of her desperate plan to claim a future of her own choosing. The thin band felt alien and cold and less of a symbol of love than a symbol of how her future had suddenly narrowed. Gone were her dreams of a meaningful academic pursuit of languages and translation. Instead she was to be the wife of a stranger picked out by her parents and mired in the endless ennui of society's expectation. This man, this duke, stood in her way, blocking the path of her planned pursuits. She studied his face, suddenly realizing why he had looked so familiar. She grimaced. "You're the man who blocked the egress from the tobacco shop!"

His smile sent a shiver down her spine. "And you are the goddess in the window."

SO THE LITTLE MINX HAD TRIED TO DERAIL THE EN-gagement. William gripped her hand tighter so she couldn't escape before the official engagement announcement was made. He pulled her toward the crowded ballroom. Not that he supposed even a public announcement would stop her if she was willing to sully her own reputation to avoid a wedding. He'd have to watch her like a hawk until the deed was done.

Perhaps news of his father's disreputable debts had spanned the Atlantic before his arrival, spooking her desire to be linked forever with his name. Perhaps she doubted the integrity of someone who would marry for money. He glanced her way with empathy. He supposed he could forgive her that. Hadn't he entertained similar Thoughts?

He imagined he could forgive her many things with both beauty and a sizeable dowry to match. Many men would. So then why was she still available? He frowned. Something was being hidden from him, he guessed. Something that the mother thought might reverse his decision.

They neared the ballroom and her steps faltered. He glanced at her face and saw a beautiful woman, albeit a terri-fied one. Terrified of what? Of him? She certainly wasn't terrified when she almost seduced him into unpinning that costume of bed linens. If the others hadn't intruded . . . his gaze dropped lower to the breast that had begged for his ministrations earlier. Although the enticing nub no longer pushed its defining shape through the fabric, he could respect her desire not to show others what he now considered his alone. He removed his dinner jacket and slipped it over her delicate shoulders.

She glanced at him, her brows lifted in question.

"I hardly think this . . . costume . . . is befitting a future duchess," he explained, not sure how else to convey his concern with her father and familiars so close at hand.

"You find exception to my attire?" she challenged him. "You would question the way I dress?"

"Really, Francesca," her mother intervened. "The Duke is correct. Your attire is most unsuitable. Lady Liberty indeed."

"She symbolizes escape from oppression," she replied, defeat evident in her voice.

William glanced askance at his future mother-in-law, grateful that she would remain an ocean away once the wedding was completed. That was not at all the reason he objected to the costume, but this was not the time for such confrontations. Instead, he worked the three buttons of the jacket front so Miss Winthrop's pert attributes would be covered. "Trust me in this," he said quietly, for her ears alone. "I know what is best."

She blanched. Even in the moonlight, he saw her eyes widen and the color drain from her face. He thought she might swoon and prepared to catch her should she fall. Bloody hell, if the woman was sick, she shouldn't be out in the night air.

But she turned way from him and stood facing the sea. He thought this might be another ploy to escape, but she made no effort to run. Instead her spine stiffened and her perfect posture became more rigid. She raised her chin and all vestiges of emotion fled her face.

Belatedly he realized that by fastening the jacket he had effectively trapped her arms inside the overlarge covering, rendering her much like a deranged women at Bedlam. But even that did not stop her as she followed her parents into the ballroom, moving with a grace that would define a queen. Her father announced the news of her engagement with great charm. He himself smiled and waved to the well-wishing crowd, but his future bride merely nodded at the appropriate moments. Even in the oversized coat, she appeared detached, cold, and distant, as if she were above them all in status and breeding. He suddenly understood the impetus of that ridiculous nickname. Silly Americans, they simply did not recognize proper carriage and decorum when they saw it.

Satisfaction and a sense of accomplishment rippled through him. Even his father, had he lived to witness this occasion, would be proud. Miss Winthrop's haughty public demeanor, her perfect posture and grace, and most important, her fat purse, meant he had found his perfect duchess.

Still, one niggling thought intruded. This cold and arrogant woman bore little resemblance to the passionate seductress he had lusted for just scant moments ago. Was that just a ploy to escape the arranged marriage? Which woman would show up for the marriage, or more important, the marriage bed?

"Congratulations, Your Grace." Percival appeared by his side. "It appears fortuitous that we exchanged costumes."

"Fortuitous, indeed," he said, considering the ramifications of her ruse. He glanced at Percival. "I would prefer that we keep my intended's attempts to forestall the engagement a private matter between us. Should word leak out, I will insist that it was a planned dalliance between two secret lovers."

"Agreed," Percival said with a wide smile. "Though one wonders why she would be inclined to avoid such an advantageous engagement?"

William wondered the same, though he didn't offer a reply to Percival's query. Perhaps there was another in her heart? Only a woman of some experience would be able to play that sweet seductress as well as she had, and her age would suggest she'd had ample opportunity to test her feminine wiles on others . . . and what of that sudden, unexpected bout of illness? He frowned, working the facts to their logical conclusion. Perhaps there was a reason that the mother was anxious to marry off her only daughter so quickly. Could his intended be ruined goods in need of a quick husband? Not that it would deter him from the wedding—the money involved was too significant to ignore. However, he had a right to know if Miss Winthrop already carried the seed of another inside her belly.

"You promised me an introduction to your intended," Percival said, glancing at the sea of faces. "But she seems to have disappeared."

"What?" William glanced quickly about. "She had been

here just a minute ago." But she was gone. Just as she had disappeared from that window in the blink of an eye, so had she disappeared from the celebratory gathering.

"Another time then." Percival laughed. "With the wedding so close at hand, I'll be in town for that event as well. Although if Miss Winthrop continues to be elusive, I may have to wait until your honeymoon."

William smiled at his friend's jest, but his mind continued its earlier quandary. If indeed Francesca carried another's babe, would she admit the fact if confronted? How would he know months hence if a babe was early or belonged to another?

He thought of Emma, his brother's wife, remembering how her body blossomed when ripe with child. There were clues, long before the final stages of pregnancy. He couldn't remember exactly when those changes manifested, but his artist brother was bound to have recorded such events. If he, in his role of husband, could avoid intimate relations until those signs appeared, or failed to appear, then he would know for certain.

That shouldn't be difficult. Every society provided outlets for a man in need. One just needed to know where to look. After that brief but pleasant interlude with Miss Winthrop, such a diversion would complete what her invitation began.

"Percival, I think we've done all that can be accomplished here. What say we go find entertainment of a more accommodating nature?"

HER FATHER FOUND HER NOT FAR FROM THE HIVES. It was her place of seclusion, the one place she knew her mother wouldn't venture. Without her smoker and mask, Fran knew not to venture beyond this appropriately placed boulder, but her mother wouldn't even come this close for fear of being stung, hence the boulder became a refuge.

Her father recovered the Duke's evening jacket from the grass where she had thrown it. He carried it with him and used the sleeves to dab at the moisture on her cheeks.

"Franny? Are you all right?"

"Oh, Papa," she said, choking back a sob. Her fingers twisted the engagement ring, a band supporting six colored gems, around and around her finger. "I'm doomed. My worst fears realized." She sniffed, hoping to keep fresh tears at bay. "Can't you do something to cancel this farce of an engagement? This Duke is unbearable."

"He didn't seem so unbearable when you were locked in his arms near the garden's edge."

Grateful for the night's coverage, she felt heat rise to her cheeks. "I thought he was someone else."

She'd thought he was kind. She'd thought he was attractive. She hadn't realized he was in league with her mother. *Trust me in this. I know what's best.* How often had she heard Maman say those exact same words while manipulating her to do her bidding?

She swiped at her cheeks. "He'll expect me to be a duchess. He'll expect me to be like Maman." She shifted her position to face her father. "I can't be another's pawn. Not again. Please, Papa. Surely you can do something?"

Although her father generally left the social arena to her mother's administration, she prayed this time he would take up her cause. Surely he'd see that she'd be trading one oppressor for another. As the provider for the family's abundant finances, her father's final word was law.

He laid the Duke's jacket beside her on the rock. "You know your mother and I don't always see eye to eye, Missy. It's one of the reasons I spend so much time away."

Hope ignited in her soul. Her father wouldn't let her down, especially when he referred to her by the pet name he'd given her as a child. They had always shared a special relationship insofar as Maman's demands. Her parents' frequent loud disagreements were not a secret to her or anyone else in the household. She raised her head, meeting his gaze with anticipation. If anyone would stand up to Maman, it would be him.

"This time . . ." He took her hand in his. "I agree with your mother."

Shock glued her to the boulder or she would have fallen

off in disbelief. Her throat constricted to the point that her words emitted in a wispy plea.

"Why, Papa, why?"

"I want grandbabies, damn it." He straightened, his height adding power to his words. "Enterprises like mine do not run on their own. I want to leave a legacy. I want heirs."

"But I don't love him," she pleaded.

"Perhaps in time . . ." He looked away for a moment before returning her gaze, his face twisted in agony. "For God's sake, Franny. We've given you plenty of opportunities to find someone. You're twenty-six, and you're not getting younger."

"I'll be away in England, living with strangers." It was her trump card, her final play to wring her father's guilt into a reprieve. "I may never see you again."

"Well, there might be a way . . ." He looked at his feet while he kicked at the dirt near the base of the rock.

"What?" Her voice strengthened. "There's a way to stay here?" *A way to avoid this marriage?*

"I've informed that duke of yours that any children you may have will be educated here in the United States, and not at some hoity-toity foreign school."

"Children?" Her voice reflected her disbelief. If the plan for her to stay in America involved children, then, she assumed, it involved marriage as well.

"Oh, he wasn't happy about it. I can tell you that. And I had to compromise a bit on the heir. But I'll not pay to have my grandchildren look down their noses at me like some snooty Englishman."

Pay. Even her beloved father didn't hesitate to admit the only way she could secure a husband was to buy one. Her one small flame of hope extinguished in a wisp of smoke. "So I'll still have to marry the Duke?"

It was his turn to look surprised. "Yes, of course, Missy. You'll marry the Duke. That's what this expensive party is about, isn't it?" He waved a finger under her nose. "But if you're as smart as all those fancy tutors said you were, and if you want to come home and live here with your family, then you should get yourself with child." He averted his gaze, taking particular interest in some geranium blossoms by the boulder. "Your mother . . . did she ever explain . . . ?"

"I'm not a fool, Papa, I know how babies are made." There were some subjects she'd prefer not to discuss with her father. Years ago Madame Aglionby had reluctantly explained how such things were accomplished to stem her incessant questions. Of course, she'd been too young then to ask the sort of questions she should have. Then, of course, that awful row between her parents followed soon after, which led to Madame's hasty departure and the end to her source for answers.

"Then you'd best do what's necessary with that fancy duke of yours," her father said while averting his gaze. "And do it as soon as possible."

· Five ·

"YOU SHOULDN'T BE CRYING, MISS WINTHROP. YOUR eyes will be all puffy for the ceremony."

Fran sat in front of her boudoir mirror while Mary twisted her hair in elegant ropes and braids, all to be hidden beneath a veil of fine French lace anchored with orange blossoms. "I don't care. Let my eyes be red and puffy. I should be marrying Randolph." Her admission brought a fresh downpour of tears.

"Why do you say such a thing? Didn't Mr. Stockwell marry some German girl?"

Fran nodded, dabbing her eyes with a white handkerchief elaborately embroidered with her wedding date. Mary pried a hairpin apart with her teeth before securing another section of hair.

"Then you shouldn't be crying over some married man. Besides, that husband of yours looks handsome enough. He's not going to want to see that you've been crying over someone else's husband."

"Maman has had me so involved in dress fittings and the like, I have barely seen Bedford. Papa took him to New York to show him around . . . I'm not sure he even recalls what I look like. Besides this veil will cover my face. Even Maman . . ." Fran stopped her fidgeting and glanced up at Mary in the mirror. A sly smile blossomed.

Mary shook her head. "You can stop that thought right there, Miss Winthrop. Changing places at a wedding is serious business. Besides, your mother almost dismissed me after I wore your costume at the fancy dress ball."

"But she didn't," Fran said. "I convinced her that I forced you to do it."

"Which you did," Mary reminded her. "But I'm not pretending to be you at your wedding." She secured the last orange blossom in her hair and glanced at the mirror. "Besides, I could never fit into that elaborate gown."

Fran wasn't sure she fitted in it herself. The lacing was so tight, she could barely take a full breath, which made her sigh sound like a huff. "There has to be something I can do to escape."

The mantel clock whirled out a tune announcing the time. Each tone resonated, then faded in the big room, leaving emptiness in its wake. The lonely, forlorn sound may as well have been tolling in her heart, Fran thought. Empty, lonely, and . . .

"Where is everyone?" she asked, realizing that no other household noises competed with the clock's chime.

"At the church, I imagine. Your mother left a while ago to make sure everything is as it should be. She intends to make this the wedding all Newport will be talking about for years. Don't you worry, though. Ferris is waiting to drive you to the wedding. You're to arrive in style." Mary beamed into the mirror. "The cabriolet is covered with roses. You've never smelled the like."

"Ferris is driving?"

"Um-hmm," Mary said, surveying her efforts in the mirror. "Your mother bought new livery for all your attendants. Ferris looks especially handsome, and those two matched grays to pull the carriage—"

"Is he waiting outside now?" Francesca asked with a glance to the window. "I imagine we'll need to be leaving shortly."

Mary walked over to glance out the window. "Lord Almighty! Look at all those people waiting at the gate. Why, there must be crowds from here all the way to Trinity."

Francesca's eyes widened and her pulse increased its tempo. Why must there always be crowds? She was so tired of being placed on public display. Had she married Randolph, it would have been different. No one would care about a barrister's wife.

But married to a duke . . . Her stomach roiled. She glanced to Mary. "What about Ferris?"

"Yes, he's there. Mighty handsome, I must say."

"He must be thirsty waiting in that hot sun," Francesca suggested. "Why don't you have him come into the kitchen for some cool lemonade before we leave?"

Mary parked a hand on her hip. "Are you up to something, Miss Winthrop? Because I don't want to be a part of any tom-foolery. Not today, at least."

"No, no," Fran said, hoping the lie didn't show on her face. "I'm just concerned for his welfare. Go ahead and invite him into the kitchen. I'll be down in just a moment."

Mary left as she was bidden. Fran waited near the window until she saw Mary and Ferris leave the carriage unattended. Mary hadn't exaggerated about the crowds. Could she negotiate the carriage by herself without accidentally trampling someone? She'd never driven a large carriage before. Would the crowd let her break through the line to escape to the harbor?

"I hope you are not considering another foolish scheme, Miss Winthrop."

The low masculine voice with a distinct accent sent a shiver down her spine. She spun away from the window. His large frame blocked the door. It seemed he was always blocking her plans for escape. Only this time there was no back exit. She sidled to the far wall, putting as much distance between them as possible.

"You!" she challenged. "You're supposed to be at the church. You're not supposed to see the bride before the wedding. Perhaps you should go."

"And leave you to slip away and avoid the proceedings?" He must have noticed the color draining from her face as a knowing smile tilted his lips. "What were you planning this time?" He pointed that well-defined chin toward the window. "Make off with the driver for some remote love nest? Is that the reason for this rushed wedding? Have you been scandalous with the servants?"

How dare he! How dare he insult her, suggest she was some light skirt, granting her favors like a common trollop. Before she knew what she was about, she had crossed the room with her hand raised to slap the indecent suggestion right off his face. But he caught her hand in mid-flight, then blocked her ineffective efforts to kick at him. He swung her around, pinning her back to his chest, his hands holding her forearms immobile.

The exertion required by her brief rail conflicted with the restraint of the tightly laced wedding corset needed to mold her midriff to the gown. The stays felt as if to cut into her sensitive flesh, the constriction forcing her bosom to rise and fall in rapid succession. Her hand slipped to her stomach as she fought for breath.

His warm breath glided over her shoulder to the bluff that swelled above the top of her corset, defining the path of his gaze. His hands slid down the length of her arms to cover her own where she clenched them at her stomach. He encircled her within his arms much like a safe harbor sheltering a ship.

She was tempted to linger there. Her breath seemed to come easier encased in his arms. She felt protected, similar to the familiar comfort of being surrounded by her beekeeping gear. Still, she struggled to hold on to her anger. She needed to maintain her guard. Opportunities to escape matrimony were becoming increasingly rare.

"You shouldn't exert yourself," he said, his words warming her ear in a most delicious fashion. His hand pressed against the layers of fabric that covered her belly. "Trust me. It can't be safe for you or for—"

"Trust you?" She immediately stiffened her spine. He had almost lulled her into forgetting she was trading one set of iron shackles for another. "You think your judgment will keep me safe? Might I remind you that a forced marriage to a stranger is fraught with risk."

She batted at his fingers to release her. His hand slid to her elbows, before he marched her to a gilded chair near the door. Then he gently pushed on her shoulders till she perched on the edge of the cushioned seat, her bustle and voluminous layers of white satin and lace occupying the remaining space.

"I suppose that is true," he said, with a stern glare. "But an innocent should not suffer for it. Sit here and catch your breath."

If the act of drawing breath had not been so very difficult, she would have asked to which innocent he referred. However, one glance at the authoritative figure in a cutaway black jacket answered her query. Surely her own innocence would suffer as a result of his actions. Tonight, she would lose her claim to innocence entirely. A tantalizing flutter danced within her rib cage, the aftereffect of her exertion, she quickly decided. "Why aren't you with the others?"

"I thought I might accompany you to the church, just in case . . ."

"In case of what?" she asked, though she suspected she knew the answer.

"In case you tried what you were just about to attempt." His brow raised in conjunction with the tilt of his lips. He crouched in front of her and took her hands in his. Through the white lace of her gloves, a warmth traversed up her arms, reminding her of the comfort she had found earlier in those arms. The flutter within her chest expanded, but this time she knew better than to blame her corset. It was him, the man with the slight pout to his lip and the calm assessment in his deep blue eyes. The wrong man to make her heart race and her knees weak. Lord help her, but it was the wrong man! She pulled her hands from his.

A flash of disapproval rippled across his expression, yet he still extended his hand to her. "Shall we go? I suppose your *maman* is frantic at the absence of the bride and the groom."

Fate and her mother had left her no place to hide, no place to run. She closed her eyes and retreated deep inside herself, abandoning all plans of escape. Aware of the people outside the gate, she imagined she was walking on the ocean shore, allowing the waves to wash softly over her feet. With each pass, her panic lessened . . .

As if from a distance, she felt a tug on her arm, leading her out of the room. She heard cheering, or was that the roar of the waves breaking on the reef? The cloying scent of roses wove its way into her consciousness. She must be near the

cliff walk, near the gardens. It would be over soon . . . this
quiet stroll along the shore . . . all be over . . .

WILLIAM WAVED AND SMILED AT THE CROWDS LINING
the street. This aspect of American life was not so very different from what Francesca could expect in England. He glanced
to her side of the cabriolet and noted her fixed forward gaze. It
would have pleased him to see her at least offer a smile to the
many well-wishers. One might think he was leading her to the
gallows.

If there was one thing he had learned through his life experiences, it was that duty and responsibility often called for one
to do the necessary, rather than the preferred. Wouldn't he
have preferred to run off to Yorkshire and dabble with paint as
his brother had done? Or use his knowledge of Thoroughbreds
to maintain the finest stables in England instead of painfully
selling the stock in an attempt to shore the depleted estate coffers?

Duty, responsibility, and sacrifice. His shoulders ached
from the weight of those words. He rubbed the familiar spot
on his shoulder and stole a glance at his bride-to-be. Perhaps
she was just learning the harsh rules she'd be expected to
abide by as his wife. He squeezed her hand, just to remind her
that he would see her through this. But she didn't respond.

She sat straight and proud, removed and distant—resigned,
like a modiste's life-sized fashion doll. She was indeed that—
fashionable. Lily would at least have to hold her tongue on that
note. His mistress hadn't been pleased when he ended their
relationship to come to America for a bride. Duty, responsibility, sacrifice . . .

The wedding proceeded exactly as his mother-in-law had
planned. It was a shame she hadn't planned that her daughter
at least smile during the ceremony. He glanced at her askance.
Most women in England would give their eyeteeth to take
her place by his side, yet she appeared as if she were facing
the magistrate. Didn't the woman realize that he was saving
her from the special kind of social chastisement reserved for

unwed mothers? You'd think she'd be grateful for that charity alone. She certainly hadn't quibbled over his earlier reference to her innocent babe and her hand seemed drawn repeatedly to protect that area of her person. Such actions seemed to confirm his suspicions of her pregnancy.

He stood a bit taller, quite convinced that he was doing the right thing, the responsible thing, by sliding a wedding band onto her finger. One might expect her to take delight in the value of the family heirloom. Yet, if anything, the lace-clad woman to his right diminished slightly with her barely audible vow to love, honor, and obey.

The deed was done. The cleric blessed the union. William looked askance at his new wife. It was fortunate indeed that demonstrations of affection were never exchanged in a society wedding. A stone column held more warmth than his bride. They turned as one to face the guests, then walked down the aisle together, as solemn as if marching behind a casket. At least, with the cold chill emanating from his wife, he should have no difficulty delaying consummation of their vows. No difficulty at all.

THE BRIDAL LUNCHEON PASSED IN A BLUR, observed from a distance. Fran contained her panic in a tight uncomfortable ball that roiled in her stomach. She managed a practiced smile to deal with the endless line of well-wishers. Her mother had indeed outdone herself with the extensive guest list, few of whom Fran was acquainted with. Even her bridesmaids were unknown to her at a personal level. All were daughters of her mother's friends. Of course, her mother had kept her so isolated, she hadn't had the opportunity to collect friends. Hers had been a quiet, lonely existence.

Periodically, she would feel a tingling at the base of her spine. She glanced over her shoulder to discover that *he* was watching her, taking her measure. Then his brow would lift, almost imperceptibly, an acknowledgment perhaps. He'd done the same that day when she hid in the tobacco shop window. His conversation would continue without apparent effort.

She envied his ease. All these people had to be strangers to him, yet he slid into their conversations like champagne into a glass. There was no awkwardness about him, none of the forced courtesies that she was required to exercise. He seemed to genuinely enjoy the company of strangers. They relaxed in his presence, while she managed to frighten them away. The Duke and her mother shared that talent to put others at their ease. Even as the thought entered her mind, her mother took a position by the Duke's side, laughing and chatting as if she had been involved in the conversation from its inception.

Fran turned her attention back to the woman she had been talking to earlier, but the woman had moved on. Fran discovered she was facing an empty corner of the room, and took comfort in the temporary reprieve.

"Are you enjoying your party?"

Currents raced about her rib cage; why did his voice, and his alone, affect her in such a manner? In a sense, his British accent reminded her of the sweet and innocent fairy tales from foreign lands that she sought to translate. Yet when she turned to face him, she recognized there was nothing sweet or innocent about the man before her. The fact that he'd just married a stranger only proved the ruthless means he'd take for money alone. She stiffened her resolve to resist the allure of his voice.

"This is not for my benefit," she reminded him. "It is for Maman. She has finally gotten her wish." They both glanced toward the mother of the bride, dressed as if for a coronation.

"I'm sure she wished for her daughter's happiness," William offered. "What mother wouldn't?"

That was the least of her mother's concerns, Fran knew. Such minor considerations as happiness meant nothing compared to obtaining a duke as a son-in-law. Such a social coup had already launched her into the company of the cream of society, the Four Hundred. She recognized several of the guests as members of that valued group. But Fran said nothing. They were, after all, in a public venue, and her mother's lessons of concealing one's thoughts, even from a husband, had been well learned.

"Are you ready to depart?" he asked. "The amenities have been served. We should be on our way."

Oh, yes! She wanted to cry. *Take me away from here.* But then she remembered the reason why newlyweds were permitted to leave before the rest of the guests and she shook her head. She was in no hurry to face the humiliation that was bound to come when a man claimed his wife.

His gaze skittered across her face, before resting on her lips. "I'm not a monster. I promise, I will not hurt you."

He seemed so sincere, she was tempted to believe him. But she knew better. Who else but a monster would bind her in matrimonial ties, then carry her off to live among strangers?

She knew that tonight would involve pain. Madame Aglionby had warned her that a certain amount was natural on the first coupling. She knew eventually she would have to forebear additional pain in order to produce a child, but surely that long path could wait to commence for an hour or two.

"A little longer, Your Grace?" she asked, pleased that her mother's training kept the desperation from her voice.

She saw a slight flinch, again barely perceivable. The thought that he suppressed his emotions almost as well as she pleased her. At least they had that in common. But then he looked down his rather long, noble nose at her, and all thoughts of commonality vanished.

"No," he said, lifting her gloved hand to his lips. "Procrastination will serve no purpose. We'll leave now." He grasped her elbow, then walked her toward her parents to extend their farewells.

Her throat constricted, making speech difficult. For all her arguments with her mother, she discovered a sudden hesitancy to leave. After all, her mother had been her only companion for years on end. She kissed her father's cheek, feeling tears burn in her eyes. He held her at arm's length for a moment, seeming to have a similar difficulty for words.

"Remember," he managed, then attempted a smile. "I trust you will have news for us when next we meet. As soon as possible, Franny. Don't disappoint me."

She understood his meaning. He expected news that she

was with child. If only she could accomplish that goal without Bedford's assistance.

Her father shook Bedford's hand, then turned away with a glimmer of a tear on his cheek. Bedford quickly guided her toward the carriage waiting to whisk them to the grand suite of the Ocean View.

Once seated in the cabriolet, Fran pulled her skirts away from him, lest he get the impression that she wanted to share more than satin and lace. "That quick departure, sir, was uncalled for."

"Good heavens, woman, you were talking to walls. It was time." He settled into his seat. "As my wife and duchess, you must learn to appropriately carry on your end of the conversation. We'll be in England soon and proprieties must be maintained. I'd be more inclined to lock you in the attic than allow you to be observed talking to the furniture."

"You'd lock me in an attic?" She stared at him, appalled, though the expression was wasted. The Duke watched the passing providence with more interest than he appeared to afford his new wife.

"You'd not *allow* me to talk to furniture?" The latter appalled her more than the suggestion of the attic. Her mother had frequently locked her in her dismal bedroom. Why should an attic be different? Still, it carried an ominous tone.

If he insisted he had authority over the small matter of choosing the object of her conversations, then certainly he would exercise it in other areas as well. The tight ball of discord expanded, building more pressure under her too-tightly laced corset. She had no more freedom than her mother's Pomeranians, all that had effectively changed was the holder of the leash.

"Come now." He turned toward her. "I was merely trying to say that in the future you'll have a responsibility to talk to people. Don't try to tell me that you haven't avoided doing just that. I've been watching you."

"Watching me?" She pretended to be surprised. She'd felt the strange tingling that signaled his gaze too often not to know the truth of his words.

"You're skittish, like a new filly. That might be well and good for this colonial province but the British aristocracy requires maturity, worldliness." He regarded her as one might a child. "Have you memorized the volume of lineage that I supplied?"

She recalled a thick, dusty old tome that listed family after family with all their respective connections. The book had been delivered shortly after their announced engagement. She had barely glanced at it, given the immediacy of the wedding and all that entailed.

"I had thought you meant the book to be used for reference purposes, Your Grace," she said quietly, still reeling from his insult of her maturity. "I used it to properly place the wedding gifts according to which family—"

"Good heavens, woman! Don't you understand the necessity of knowing the society amongst whom you will be expected to circulate?" His pointed words stabbed at her pride. "Why, an English schoolgirl learns this at her mother's knee."

"I'm not British, sir. I'm American," she said with bravado.

"Please. There's no need to remind me." His lips quirked a moment before he sighed. "I suppose we shall have to review some of the more important families tonight."

"Tonight? But tonight is our wedding night. I was not expecting to receive an education on my wedding night."

"An education?" He glanced to her midriff, his eyes narrowed slightly. "No, I suppose you weren't. More's the pity."

She felt insulted, though she wasn't exactly sure why. Certainly, his misguided allusions as to her intelligence or sanity, for that matter, would be insult enough, but there was something else. Something that made her both indignant and overheated at the same moment.

"I assure you, sir, that I'm a most able student. I believe I shall have plenty of time to study the lineages once we board the SS *Republic*." She neglected to mention that she would never be able to concentrate on such a detail-laden memorization exercise tonight. This, after all, was *that* night.

Already her rib cage felt aflutter as if bees had taken residence and were frustrated by their confinement. Every unanticipated bump beneath the carriage wheel, every accidental touch, every uncertain glance seemed magnified in importance, an uncomfortable sensation that she imagined would only increase until the awkward moment of consummation. Her voice squeaked in a higher tone than normal. "Must we study the volume tonight?"

She thought she noticed a hesitation in his manner, as if he was giving her plea serious contemplation. However, she must have been mistaken. His brow lowered in displeasure.

"I see no reason why we should postpone what you should have already accomplished. The sooner you begin, the less the likelihood you will fumble when presented to society upon our return."

She stared at him, confused. What had happened to cause his displeasure? A cold foreboding slipped down her spine intensifying her anxiety about the evening ritual a hundredfold. She shifted to face forward, mirroring his staunch expression. While a part of her sobbed, her mother's voice echoed in her head, never *show your fear*.

The ride to the hotel was mercifully short. They arrived and hastily retreated to their suites. Only the garments they would need for that evening and the morning's departure for New York were available. Everything else had already been shipped overseas, or packed by the servants to accompany their passage.

"Your Grace." Mary curtsied the moment Fran entered the room that tonight would serve as her private quarters. "It was a beautiful wedding and you looked so lovely in your gown. I think you looked just like one of those fairy princesses you've told me about from your stories."

Fran very much doubted that. All those fairy princesses were happy with their prince. She on the other hand had the distinct impression she'd been given in wedlock to the devil himself.

"I'll be happy to shed this dress," Fran replied as Mary began to unfasten the back. "I never realized satin could be so heavy." Or perhaps it was her nervous expectations that weighed heavily on her mind. Certainly her spirits weren't lifted as the multiple layers slipped from her frame.

"I understand a meal is to be delivered, Your Grace, or directly for—"

"Don't call me that," Fran snapped.

"I can't very well call you 'Miss Winthrop' anymore," Mary said, her head lowered in contrition. The sight added guilt to the long list of Fran's overflowing emotions. She suspected the local papers reflected Mary's sentiments that marriage to a duke signified a romance worthy of a fairy tale. Perhaps it did, she thought despondently, recalling a French fairy tale she had translated, although some might not consider the Duke's handsome features those of a beast.

"No, I suppose you can't." Fran softened her tone and glanced at the gold ring on her left hand. "Duchess doesn't suit either. It sounds like the name of one of Maman's Pomeranians."

Mary, working on the petticoat fastenings at the small of Fran's back, tried to hide her smile, but the mirror reflected the pull of her cheeks and Fran knew she had been forgiven her earlier display of annoyance.

"I suppose Mrs. Chambers would be correct here in America," she continued, "but that doesn't feel correct either."

"Perhaps it will after tonight," Mary said, a knowing smile tilting her lips.

Her words brought a shiver to Fran's spine, and fear leapt anew to her throat. She glanced quickly at the closed door that adjoined her suite to that of her new husband. Her mother had described with a shudder the physical sacrifices Fran would be expected to make as a wife. That singular act frightened her more than any of the duties she'd be expected to perform as a duchess.

"Nevertheless, when we're alone, would you continue to call me Miss Winthrop? I'm losing my home, my parents . . ." She raised her eyes in a silent plea to Mary's reflection in the mirror. "I don't want to lose my name as well . . . not yet."

"Yes, miss." Mary's curt response held a sad note. She cast a worried glance toward the mirror, then bent to the silent task of unfastening the numerous hooks and buttons that were the basis for the resplendent gown.

"What is this?" Fran asked, noting a small beribboned box resting on a vanity cluttered with orange blossoms and snippets of lace.

"A late gift I suppose," Mary said. "It arrived during your luncheon."

"I wonder who sent it. Was there a card?" She pushed aside the lace.

"No, ma'am. This is all there was."

Fran quickly dispensed with the ribbon, opened the box, and discovered a gold pin shaped in the form of a honeybee.

Her eyes rounded with wonder. "It's lovely," she said. "I wonder who sent it? It must be from someone who knows of my passion for bees."

"I imagine it's from your new husband, miss."

Fran's mouth tightened. "I don't think so. Any gift from him would be ungainly large and covered with heraldry, just to remind me that his is a glorious line, while mine is just . . . American."

She held the pin closer for inspection. It was indeed excellent craftsmanship, with intricate lines.

"Your mother?" Mary suggested, squinting herself at the pin.

"Maman would never give something so plain as to not have a single gemstone. No, a gift from Maman would be large enough to proclaim wealth, not small and elegant."

"That only leaves your father," Mary said.

"Hmm." Her father might have sent this as a reminder, that like bees in a hive, she must do her duty and bear children. However, she had another person in mind—Randolph. Only someone with the sensibility of a poet, like Randolph, would understand the symbolism and significance of a honeybee. No other wedding gift had arrived from him. Obviously, the law office had kept him abreast of developments concerning her father, their client, and thus her wedding. Perhaps this was Randolph's way of saying he understood that she had to follow her parent's wishes. A deep sadness built within.

"Would you like to wear the pin on your nightgown?" Mary asked. "Or perhaps the wrapper?"

"No," Fran replied, replacing the pin in the box. "I don't think that would do."

As Randolph had never written informing her of his marriage, she had not felt the need to advise him of her engagement. Guilt tinged her sadness. Now that the deed was done, she should acknowledge her changed marital status and thank him for the gift. She slipped the box into her toiletry case. It would only be good manners to write him a note, the sooner the better.

Once Mary had untied all the cumbersome layers of smooth satin and stiff petticoats and had put them away, she slipped a lacy concoction over Fran's head, allowing the sheer fabric to settle over her unbound body.

"What is this?" Her eyes widened, her voice barely more than a whisper.

"It's a gift from your *maman*." Mary smiled. "Isn't it lovely? She said she had it commissioned in Paris when you were there last April. The pattern is so elegant and fragile."

Fran glanced at her reflection in the mirror, then gulped. The peignoir set was more illusion of fabric than the actual item. Every natural curve of her body was clearly visible, unbound and unrestrained. The creamy lace teased the eye with its strategically placed filigree. Certainly the garment was never designed to withstand a solitary night's slumber. She imagined it would tear indiscriminately with the slightest touch. Perhaps that's the purpose, a mischievous voice whispered in her head. A warmth spread across her chest that by no means could be attributed to the open-weaved lace.

"Is there not a wrapper?" Fran asked, a tremble in her voice. "This could hardly be considered decent."

Mary smiled, but kept her opinions to herself. She held a barely opaque robe designed more to tease than to cover. Suddenly the prospect of what was to happen, of what was necessary to happen for her to return back to her home in the shortest period of time, brought a cold shiver.

A knock at the adjoining door caused Fran's breath to catch and her anxieties to peak.

"Mary, whatever happens—don't leave me alone with that man," Fran pleaded. Before Mary could reply, the door opened.

He entered her bedchamber unbidden, dressed in loose trousers and a silk robe. Her gaze was drawn to the enticing intersection of the lapels where a hint of curling black hair teased the eye. She had seen bare-chested workmen before in her travels throughout Europe. Somehow, that a gentleman— that her husband—would be similarly molded seemed primitive, uncivilized, yet enticing in a fundamental forbidden way.

Mary, hairbrush in hand, quickly bobbed into a curtsy, while Fran remained seated in an effort to corral her fears. *Never let another know your true thoughts,* her mother's words counseled. Fran maintained a calm visage as her mother had taught, while internally she gasped and shrank in fear.

"Leave us," the Duke said. Mary returned the hairbrush to the dressing table then crossed the room. After she had passed the Duke, she turned at the door and glanced back at her mistress, an apologetic lift to her brow.

"Good night, Miss Winthrop." She silently closed the door behind her.

Traitor, Fran thought, envious of her maid's freedom. If only she could just leave rather than face the ravaging her mother had assured her would occur on her wedding night.

Bedford glanced over his shoulder and frowned, then turned his attentions toward her. "How is my . . . Lady Liberty . . . this evening?"

He started walking toward her. She stood, choosing to face her challenger on two feet rather than trapped in a chair. Her back ramrod straight, her shoulders back, her head held high in a regal disdain, it was posture to which she had been groomed since her first steps. The effect intimidated most, but seemed to have little effect on him. He hesitated a moment, then continued in his advance. His eyes traveled the length of her before an appreciative smile tilted his lips.

Heavens! In her haste to stand, she'd forgotten about the barely there peignoir. She fought the telltale heat that threatened to blossom on her cheeks. He may ravage her as she understood a new husband was honor bound to do, but he didn't need to know of her embarrassment.

"I thought you might have a certain natural reluctance about tonight," he said, his deep voice setting her skin to tingle. He stepped behind her. She stiffened, wishing he would stay where she could see him. The bristles of a hairbrush touched the crown of her head. She flinched.

"But I'm pleased to see I'm mistaken."

Belatedly, she thought to pull the flimsy wrapper tighter across her body. From his close proximity, he probably could tell her heart fearfully hammered in her chest. One minute she wished he'd just do the deed and be done with her, the next she hoped to earn a small reprieve.

"I don't love you," she said, as the brush gently glided through her hair.

"I don't suppose you do. You hardly know enough about me to like, much less love." His hand soothed the curtain of hair away from her face, his knuckles brushed her cheek in an oddly intimate gesture. Mary had brushed her hair a thousand times, but never had the act held such an intimate effect.

"I assure you," he said. "Love has little to do with marriage. I should know, I've been in one loveless marriage already."

"You're married?" She twisted her head to the side, but still could not see him. "How can that be?"

"My wife died years ago. Didn't your mother tell you I was a widower? Perhaps not. It hardly matters when one is in need of a title"—he hesitated—"and a husband."

"I have no interest in your title, sir," The only title she'd ever longed for was that of barrister's wife. That fantasy was now an impossibility. "That was my mother's dream for me, never my own."

"Is that why you planned that little diversion the night of our engagement? To thwart your mother's plans?"

That had been the second time he had referred to their initial meeting. What did it matter now? Her plan had failed. "You hid your identity as well as I recall. Why did you do that?"

"I was pursued as a simple marquess, but once I ascended to the title of Duke of Bedford, I find I am a highly sought trophy among marriage-minded females. I thought to escape the competition just once before the knot was tied. Might I remind you, my dear, that you won the prize sought by many."

"Hmph. A prize I did not want."

"We all must make sacrifices to secure our dreams." She heard the smile in his voice. "I promise to provide the life of privilege and luxury most women dream about in exchange for the funds to make it so."

"A life of luxury holds no interest for me," Fran replied. "My dream was to marry another, then live a quiet life in a small house in New York. Can my father's funds make that wish yet come true?"

"Another?"

The soothing motion of the hairbrush hesitated before the silver handle clattered on the vanity tray. He stepped around to face her, a smug expression teasing his lips. "I suspected as much. But you do understand that now that you are my wife, there will be no others. You will leave that possibility behind as surely as you have left your parents' home."

He placed his hand on her shoulder and slowly drifted down her arm. His fingertips surprised her with their hard strength. Randolph's touch hadn't that tautness, that sense of purpose. The contrast caused a tremor near her spine. She briefly closed her eyes to prevent him from seeing the impact of his touch, but he was watching her so closely even that simple reaction was noted.

"And you, Your Grace?" She marshaled a challenge. "Am I to understand that similar restrictions apply to your . . . activities?"

"Would you care?" He smiled. "You've already indicated you house no affection for me."

Strangely, she did care. She thought of the hurt we'd witnessed on her mother's face when rumors flourished about her father's relationship with her tutor. She thought of the hurt that would be imposed on her children, if Bedford harbored affection for another.

He lifted his hand from the inside of her elbow and raised it to the side of her face, stroking the curve of her cheek. He stood so close, she could sense more than feel the scrape of her breasts against his bare chest. To her embarrassment, her breasts sought that very contact as her nipples pushed through the tiny openings in the lace. She prayed he wouldn't notice.

But he did. He glanced down. The fingers that stoked the line of her chin paused. The tiny lines at the corners of his eyes deepened.

"I won't deny that I've had a dalliance or two in my past. I am a man with a decided appetite. However, if my eyes don't deceive me, I believe you may have appetites of your own."

He placed his full palm on her breast, as if to measure her fullness like a farmer testing the ripeness of fruit. She tried to stifle her gasp to no avail. Her knees threatened to buckle, but she locked them tight.

"But from this day forth, I shall be the only one to satisfy your hunger. I will know every curve, every taste, every nuance of your flesh. I will possess every inch of you. I will bury myself deep within your luscious womb till you cry out for release. You will welcome me whenever I wish as is your wifely duty, and I shall endeavor to make it a welcome experience. Is that understood? You have bought a title, a husband, and a father for your . . . for our children, but I will never be cuckolded. From this night forth, there will be no other. Resign yourself to it."

His gaze bored into her. Whatever he saw in her eyes seemed to dilute the desire she had read in his face. He stepped back, his glance slid down her body to rest near her midsection. "Is there anything you'd like to tell me before we formally begin our lives as husband and wife? Any . . . developments of which I should be aware?"

"No, Your Grace." She shifted uncomfortably, tempted to

tell him how her insides melted like beeswax beneath his gaze. His words had unleashed a delicious quivering near her womb. She studied his mouth—firm lips, expressive lips, demanding lips. How would they feel pressed against her neck, her shoulders, and below? She tried unsuccessfully to repress a shudder of anticipation.

He noticed that as well.

"I suppose in many ways we are still strangers, and perhaps your woman's sensibilities aren't prepared to give yourself to someone so unknown to you." The hand that had so recently tested her breast slipped behind his back, giving him the air of a dictator, one without the benefit of a uniform.

"I shall give you this night. Make of it what you may. Tomorrow, we shall begin our journey as husband and wife and return to our new home."

She thought he might kiss her. His gaze appeared fixed on her lips and his upper arm twitched as if it was difficult to keep his hand hidden. She wanted that kiss, yearned for that bit of tenderness after the hard words he had spoken.

He leaned toward her and she offered him her lips. He pressed his lips to her forehead.

"Good night, wife."

Then he turned and left.

Fran sank back on the chair, trembling like a flower petal beneath a honeybee's dance. Conflicting emotions of relief and disappointment warred within. If his words were to be believed, he wouldn't be demanding her physical offering this evening as had been expected. While this loosened the tight grip of anxiety in her stomach, another worry quickly replaced it. Why? Why wasn't he demanding that which she understood was to be expected?

Not that she particularly wanted to be ravaged, but the act was necessary if she were to produce an heir and thus return to her home soil. Common knowledge suggested a woman only had to be alone in a room with a man for him to take advantage. Wasn't that why her mother insisted those old biddy chaperones be present whenever a man paid her attention?

Well, there were no biddies in the room and she was still

very much virginal. Was something wrong with her? Did those gossips that called her Frosty Franny behind her back know something that she was not privy to? They'd whispered that speaking with her was akin to feeling a cold nor'easter shiver their bones. She'd always discredited such nonsense in the past, but what if she did somehow exude a chill wind? A jolt of realization stabbed at her heart. What if that was the reason Randolph had not made advances?

The problem had never been with Randolph; it had been her all along. She apparently lacked that essential quality that other woman had in abundance. That inviting quality that attracted strangers to take notice, that warm glow that made them comfortable, that gentle encouragement that made the women open to ravishment—those are the qualities she needed if she ever hoped to become pregnant.

Unfortunately, those were the sort of qualities that her father's money couldn't buy. One couldn't go into Madame Dubonnets's establishment and request a veil of enticement to be added to a bonnet, or a sprig of invitation to bait one's bustle. Indeed, if it was a matter of attire, this lacy peignoir would surely have done the trick. No, it had to be an inherent quality, something one was born with, or learned from one's peers.

If that was only possible. If nothing else, she had always been an apt student. Hadn't Madame Aglionby always complimented her on her ability to assimilate languages? Madame Aglionby . . .

Lost in thought, Fran barely heard the knock on her door. She glanced at the connecting door to her husband's quarters, but the knock repeated at the main entrance to the room. She called out permission to enter. Mary appeared with a heavy volume.

"I was instructed that you required this volume this evening."

Exasperated, she sighed. This was no doubt the Duke's doing, as were Mary's sad eyes. Spending one's wedding night alone with a book hardly fit her vision of a fairy tale princess. Especially this boring old tome. Another book came to mind.

"Mary, do you recall the set of books I set aside for the transatlantic passing?"

"Yes, ma'am. I've kept them separate so they wouldn't be placed in the ship's hull as you requested."

"I'm interested in the one I picked up in Paris, do you recall? Small, black, without a title?"

"The one tied with a ribbon and hidden in your bureau?"

Mary reddened slightly under Fran's prolonged glance. "Yes, that's the one. Is it close by? Could you retrieve it yet this evening?"

"Yes, Your . . . ma'am." Mary started to turn toward the door, then stopped. A frown worked at the corners of her eyes. "I hadn't thought you'd be needing me this evening, this being your wedding night and all. My mother had planned a farewell gathering as she won't be seeing me again for a while . . . I was wondering . . ."

Fran sighed, trying to avoid the look of pity on Mary's face. She glanced about the room. "After you've found the book for me you're free to enjoy the rest of the evening on your own. Just be sure you don't miss the ferry. I can't imagine surviving the trip without you."

Mary rewarded her with a big smile. "I'll be right back, Miss Winthrop."

· Six ·

My Dearest Randolph . . .

She penned the words on softly scented stationery while waiting for Mary's return with the journal. The next lines were most difficult. Though she longed to tell him how much she wished he were the man exchanging vows with her at Trinity Church, she could not properly form the words. Would such a declaration change anything?

In truth, she had begun to suspect that it wasn't love for Randolph as much as fear of marriage to Bedford that caused her such angst. When Randolph hadn't replied to her letters, she'd noted her ardor had significantly cooled. Still, he had been her best chance for freedom at the time, and a far more familiar suitor than Bedford. She would have been content with Randolph, but he had chosen another. What was done, was done.

Opting for a more formal reply than the salutation indicated, she expressed good wishes for Randolph and his new wife, as she was sure they would have extended the same to her had they been present today. She hesitated over thanking him for the pin. A new wife might not approve of such an intimate gift to a former acquaintance. She kept the references vague and uncertain in case he might share the letter with his wife.

Mary knocked on the door, then entered. Fran placed the freshly penned letter aside to dry before accepting the leather-bound journal from Mary. So much had changed since she discussed the prospect of marriage with Madame Aglionby. In the space of a few months, she felt she had aged several years. How naïve she'd been to think she could choose her own husband. Sadness pulled at her throat.

She ran her fingers over the aged cover of the courtesan's journal. Would it have made a difference? Perhaps if she'd read it earlier and gleaned its nuggets of wisdom and if Randolf hadn't left so suddenly for Germany, she'd be Mrs. Randolph Stockwell and not the Duchess of Bedford.

However, reflection on what could have been would offer no assistance on her current dilemma. Best to set the past aside and move forward with the future.

She placed the book in the center of the writing desk, secured the top on her ink bottle, then placed her writing implements aside for Mary to pack in the morning. After she adjusted the oil lamp to assist reading, she tenderly opened the cover and bent her head to study the courtesan's secrets of seduction.

My dearest confidante, I am in desperate straits. I haven't eaten for three days. Rain and sewage fill the dark alleys that I have been forced to call home . . .

SHE READ FOR AT LEAST AN HOUR, ENTHRALLED WITH the trials of Bridget, the name she assigned to the lone initial. Bridget appeared to be an educated woman abused by a deceitful lover, then abandoned by an uncaring society. Without family or friends to give her shelter, she was cast to the streets of Paris to survive, until the highly paid and exotic courtesan Fatima brought her to Folly's Desire, a house of ill repute.

Fran's eyelids grew heavy as she turned page after page, reading the details of life in that other world, the one never discussed. Some of the events candidly discussed in the pages shocked her to say the least. She wished she had someone with whom to confirm the accuracy.

Of course she had been told from her earliest memories that there were two types of people: those with the means and refinement to move amongst high society, and those without sufficient funds and culture to do so. From reading the journal, it appeared that division among ladies of pleasure existed with similar lines of distinction. There were those that were groomed to be companions of the elite and those that satisfied the more common man.

Bridget obviously could read and write. That, more so than beauty, seemed to satisfy a certain criteria established for women placed in the former division.

Perhaps that explained the kinship Fran began to feel with the journal's author. Society pretended that women like Bridget chose that path of survival due to some basic evil or spiritual failing at heart, but Fran wondered if that were true. Had she been placed in a similar plight without means or family to provide the basic necessities, would she have eventually turned to a house of pleasure? And once there, wouldn't she be placed in a capacity to associate with well-bred men of society based on her own education and knowledge?

She thought about her father and the whispered rumors she'd pretended not to hear about his passionate pursuits outside of the home. Would her father frequent such a place as the one Bridget described in the journal?

The question made the reading more personal, more immediate, and she found herself forgetting her purpose for studying the journal in the first place. Time passed and her eyes burned from a combination of fatigue and the smoke of the lamp. She had decided to read one more page, and there she found sudden insight. She reread the passage to be sure.

Fatima has ordered that all the necklines of my gowns must be lowered to an indecent level. She declared I must display my bosoms to their best advantage. Old men will drool, she said, to see the plump pigeons powdered and perfumed, then thrust forward like a fancy sugary behind glass. Something so sweet and close, men will believe they can almost taste the treat, yet will be denied the opportunity until they pay sufficient coin for the privilege.

The more tempting and frequent they are displayed, the higher the purse. Such display, which has been vehemently discouraged throughout my youth, shall be diffi-

cult for me to manage without shame. However, Fatima assures me I will adjust with practice and the financial rewards shall be well worth the discomfort.

A sudden enlightenment jarred Fran. It all made sense. A woman's breasts were a defining characteristic of the feminine gender. Emphasis therefore on the presentation of a woman's chest only served to remind men that one was a woman, and thus a suitable object of lust. Did not her bees do something similar? When the male bees were presented with a sight of the queen's enlarged abdomen, they began a mating ritual that ensured the continuation of the hive. The insight pushed her back in the chair. Why hadn't she thought about this presentation aspect before?

Although her objective differed slightly from that of Bridget, the process should be similar. She would need to prominently display her own sugary and thus entice the Duke to do all that was necessary to produce a child. Otherwise she'd be doomed to spend the rest of her days in a world not of her choosing.

She stood, the small of her back welcoming the change of position, then moved before the full-length mirror. Dressmakers and salesclerks had often lavished praise upon her girlish figure and graceful beauty, but she had always suspected that was a ploy to encourage additional spending for items she just didn't need. She couldn't recall ever having objectively examined her own form before. There had never been a need.

In the soft yellowish light of the gas jets, she tried to see her body as another might view it. She had smallish breasts, she decided. The mounds were sufficient enough to distinguish her from a boy, but she doubted anyone would express more than a passing interest in them. They certainly were not the buxom proportions of Phoebe Kravitz. A smile crept to her lips. She recalled earlier observing crumbs of white wedding cake on the rose silk covering Phoebe's ample bosom.

However, as she studied her own reflection in the mirror, she realized that any crumb she might have dropped would undoubtedly fall straight to the floor. Was this the reason the Duke had abandoned her on her wedding night? Were her bosoms insufficient to entice men? They certainly were in comparison to Phoebe Kravitz.

Fran turned from side to side, her sudden enlightenment causing her to reassess any cruel notions previously thought about her mother's friend's daughter.

Perhaps Phoebe was trying to implore her own form of a sugary temptation within the confinements of society fashion. Perhaps she was inviting men to feast at her bosom. Would the Duke like that? She giggled, envisioning her stalwart, resolute Duke bent in half in an attempt to reach the appetizers offered by the far shorter Phoebe Kravitz.

What began as a silly conjecture quickly turned into something else entirely. She imagined the Duke nuzzling her own chest. His lips feasting on her skin, laving at her nipples—an action mentioned in the courtesan's journal. A delicious tremor, emanating from that very spot, shivered through her. Dear heavens, did men truly do that?

She couldn't reconcile Randolph to such an image, but the Duke—she shuddered—she wouldn't put anything so base, so common, so . . . physical . . . past him. The lazy shuttering of his eyelids and the subtle twitch to his lips made her think that he might even enjoy such an activity. A sudden heat washed through her. Would she? She picked up the white lacy fan designed to accompany her wedding dress and fluttered up a current that pushed her hair away from her face.

"Don't be silly," she scolded herself. The man is so arrogant he probably included instructions in the marriage contract that his bride's head must never be higher than his own. Should such a man deign to eat crumbs, it would only be with a silver spoon. Hah! Again, she was being silly. His grace would never settle for crumbs. He'd insist her chest support an entire meal.

She laughed at the mental image, then glanced at the mirror. The laughter died in her throat. Her paltry denizens would never do.

If the journal was correct in its suggestion that men are drawn to women with obvious feminine attributes, she would have to be a bit more confrontational to attract the Duke's attention to that area of her anatomy. She returned to the desk to scan the journal's pages, hoping to find suggestions on how to best accomplish that.

HE WAS AN IDIOT. HE WAS A FOOL. WILLIAM TOSSED amid the sheets in a large and painfully lonely bed. He had every right to claim her, and he very nearly had done precisely that. Any doubt that she was virginal disappeared the moment he saw her in that lacy bit of nothing. She was the very advertisement of carnal pleasure. Oh, what his brother could do with that temptress as a model. The thought made him punch his pillow into submission.

Then she pulled that wispy garment so tight across her curves in feigned modesty, though he suspected it was to emphasize her feminine form, and thus fan his desire to consummate the marriage.

These Americans were a strange lot. Why couldn't she just tell him she was with child? She had to know that her secret could not remain so for long.

A disturbing thought intervened. Had his father's reputation for a short temper traveled all the way to America? Did she fear that once he ascertained that she was not a virgin he would seek revenge in some manner?

If she would just admit to any babies already breeding in her womb, then he'd happily share with her the more pleasurable aspects of marriage. If only he could trust her to answer him honestly if he were to pose the question.

No. Abstinence was better. The issue of paternity was too important to live with uncertainty. He had just assumed not consummating the marriage would be easier than it was proving to be. He had thought they could spend the evening getting to know one another, sharing confidences, small pleasures. But from the moment he had entered her room, her proud arrogance, wrapped in that enticing lascivious concoction, pulled at him like a champion yearling. She had a defiance that challenged, and a body that begged to be touched. His cock had sprung to attention the moment she flaunted herself for his viewing. She was his for the handling, lawfully, albeit unwillingly, wed.

Damnation. He should have been the first. Her mother was right. The girl had been groomed for royalty. The Queen herself could not have been more stiff-necked. With a body made for a man's pleasure—his groin tightened—he should have been the first.

She hadn't even flinched at his mention of her child and need for safety. It was conclusive proof, to be sure. Why else would such a tantalizing piece still be on the market? He shook his head. These Americans . . . where was their sense of morality?

He glanced toward her room, noticing the soft glow of a gas lamp beneath the door. At least she seemed to be taking his suggestion to study the family lineages. The book contained well over two hundred families she would be expected to know. The poor chit. Her father's money would never buy her acceptance into the higher circles of society. But if she studied hard and showed proper deference, he imagined the ton would tolerate her. That should be enough. After all, she would be in England and permitted entrance to the grandest soirees. What more could a woman want?

He would wait. That was the plan. Time was his friend in this. She could only conceal her condition for a limited period. He would wait.

Yet her lamp burned on, teasing him with that little sliver of light. She was awake, studying his prestigious lineage. She might have a question. She might welcome an interruption. The more he thought it, the more he determined she wanted—no, needed—an interruption. He slipped a robe over his shoulders, then slowly opened the connecting door without a warning knock.

She glanced up, startled. Inexplicably, a flush tinged her cheeks as she closed a slim black volume and slid it near a small stack of books to her right. He noticed the lineage volume sat on a table more than an arm's reach away.

"I'm sorry, did I disturb your slumber, Your Grace?" she

asked, fidgeting with the flimsy cover that did nothing to hide the lace that accentuated her curves.

He cautiously moved forward, his eyes drawn to the hinted valley between her breasts. "I saw your light and I wondered . . ."

Damnation! As if he wasn't already having difficulty lifting his gaze, the chit slowly rolled her shoulders allowing those comely denizens to thrust out over the desktop much like a figurehead on the bow of a whaling ship. Moisture fled his throat. His fingers ached, anxious to prove that her womanly assets were not carved from wood, but were rather soft, firm, warm . . .

"Your Grace?" She intervened, interrupting his thoughts. "You wondered . . . ?"

His fisted hands stabbed at the pockets of his silk robe, his gaze still fixed to her comely chest. "I wondered if I could be of assistance in your studies?"

The question startled her, or perhaps it was his continuing stare. Her flush deepened, then spread across the exposed skin of her chest. He dragged his gaze upward, but she glanced away, inexplicably concerned with straightening the small pile of books.

"I had supposed that you were following my suggestion in preparation for your introduction into British society, but I see that I was mistaken."

She rose from behind the desk, allowing the sheer covering of her peignoir to slip off her shoulder and puddle on the floor. His cock thickened and brushed his thigh in its ascent. My God, she was beautiful and brash in the way of Americans. Though she stood as stiff as his eager cock, there was little doubt of her intent. She was offering herself to him. Suddenly, it didn't matter that they were strangers. She was desirable, willing, and his. Against his better judgment, he stepped forward.

"I was merely writing thank-you notes for the wedding gifts, Your Grace. Maman prepared a journal listing, you see. But if the light bothers you . . ."

It was a lie. A pen with a dry nib lay on the desk blotter,

the cap to the tiny jar of ink securely fastened. She may have been writing earlier. Indeed, some correspondence lay stacked on another corner of the desk, but she was not writing when he entered the room.

Her gaze was direct, it was just not focused on him. She stood rooted to the spot, as if tied to a tree; a sacrifice offered to appease a demanding dragon.

He winced a bit at his role in that scenario, but he paused to wonder. Was she using his lust to distract him? What had she been doing in the middle of the night, if not studying lineage? Why had she felt the need to lie about it? His gaze slipped to the correspondence, his eyes quickly scanned the top note.

My Dearest Randolph . . .

He couldn't fashion the rest from this distance, but it didn't matter. Seeing the other man's name cooled his desires as if he'd been doused in the Atlantic. She'd been writing her lover, the father of her unborn child.

The seductive shadows that flickered across the lace no longer interested him. She bent to douse the lamp. It was just as well. The man's name served as a reminder to stick to his original plan.

"Good night, Your Grace." Her voice drifted to him in a sultry tone that he'd not associated with her before. He could hear a smile in her voice almost as if the four words were an invitation rather than a salutation. Of course, she wanted him in her bed, he reminded himself. She needed a good shake in the sheets to cover proof of her condition. He congratulated himself on being wise to her trick. He had almost succumbed to her charms.

"Good night," he replied, backing to his room. Was this to be the way of it? She would tempt him to cover proof of her past indiscretion and he would resist? He must resist.

He cursed beneath his breath. Who would have imagined a simple arranged marriage could prove so complicated?

Sooner or later she would no longer be able to hide the truth of her condition and on that day she would truly learn the price paid for this game. He swore it.

· Seven ·

BRIDGET'S JOURNAL WAS A GODSEND. OTHERWISE, Fran would never have anticipated that the thrusting forward of one's chest could rob a man, such as the Duke, even briefly of speech. She'd noted the direction of his gaze. With the journal's assistance, she'd be breeding in no time. With that goal in mind, she greeted Mary with an unusual request.

"You wish me to lower all of them?" Mary's voice plaintively indicated what she thought of modifying the necklines on Francesca's wardrobe.

"You can sew, can't you?" In her haste to follow the wondrous advice of the journal, she'd forgotten to consider Mary's skills. She couldn't recall ever asking that Mary alter a garment before. Normally, she would just purchase a new one.

"Of course, I can sew, miss, but . . . how low did you wish me to make them?"

Fran drew an imaginary line across her chest.

Mary blanched, "Down to the berries?"

Fran's expression must have relayed her ignorance, as Mary lowered her voice and explained.

"They call them that because of how they look. All pink and pebbled, just like berries—you see."

"Oh." Fran smiled, finding it interesting that both Fatima and Mary used sweet, edible references to describe that particular female anatomy. Perhaps it was more than coincidence. Perhaps . . . a flash of heat jolted through her chest.

"Are you sure you want them that low, miss?"

Fran tried out her best modern, knowing woman smile. "I'm hoping to attract the Duke's interest." His interest certainly piqued when she rolled her shoulders back last night. He couldn't seem to take his gaze off her "berries," even though she hadn't had occasion to perfume and powder them. Yes, a little more of that sort of attention and she'd be with child in no time.

Mary glanced toward the bed, a smile blooming on her lips. "I'm glad he came to his senses, then. I'm sure you'll continue to hold his interest no matter how you dress." She stood in the middle of the room, her hands on her hips. "All your evening gowns show off your bosoms. I can't alter your walking suits and day dresses to that extreme." For a brief moment, Fran imagined her mother's censure in Mary's expression. "You know full well, Miss Winthrop, that exposing that much skin during the day in public just wouldn't be proper."

Mary was right, though Fran was loathe to admit it. After Bedford left her room last night, she had visions of looking so "succulent" in the mornings that she needn't worry about meeting the public. In fact, she would prefer to be confined to her stateroom so as to avoid meeting them, no matter how appropriate her attire.

"Besides," Mary continued. "Sometimes you can create that kind of interest in a man even if your neckline brushes your chin. It's a matter of letting him know what's under the dress, if you know what I mean."

"Under the dress? Why would a man be interested in bustles and crinolines?"

Mary sighed, apparently losing patience with Fran's lack of understanding. She dragged a hand down the front of her apron. "Under the dress. Sometimes if a man knows how you look in your smalls, he imagines you attired just so, no matter what you wear over top."

"I see," Fran said, and indeed she did. Mary's counsel sounded remarkably like Fatima's advice on the value of attire for advertising. She glanced at Mary with new appreciation. Did everyone know these rules of seduction, except her?

Mary rummaged through the few unpacked garments for appropriate attire. The Duke had requested that they take a train to New York City, rather than the shorter journey across the water. Though she had no say in the decision, the result pleased her. Travel by her father's railcar was far more private than public display on the Fall River ferry.

Mary removed a dark blue traveling suit for the day's departure. "Now my sister, Pauline, she has a red corset that's as bright as a sunset. My mother says it's a sign that she's going straight to the devil, but it's something a man isn't likely to forget, that's the truth."

Not likely to forget . . . Fran mulled over that possibility. All her corsets had been purchased in New York, all her plain white and ivory corsets—trimmed with satiny ribbons and fancy lace. None of them were the color of a bright sunset and certainly none of them were unforgettable.

"Oh, no, Miss Winthrop," Mary gasped. "You have that scheming look in your eye again. You're a legal married woman now. It'll do no good for you to start planning an escape."

"An escape?" Fran smiled. "I assure you, Mary, I wasn't planning an escape." Perhaps a capture, she thought, but not an escape. "I was just thinking about what you said. An unforgettable corset might be just the thing I need."

She glanced about the room for a piece of paper, her gaze briefly touching on her letter to Randolph. She opened her jar of ink, dipped the nib of a pen, and scratched out an envelope addressed to Randolph Stockwell in care of the law firm, before starting a second message on another piece of paper. "Stewarts Retail Emporium maintains my measurements on file. Could you send this telegram before we leave for the train?"

"Yes, miss."

"I'm asking them to send an unforgettable corset"—she paused and smiled at Mary before continuing to scratch out her instructions—"to the SS *Republic* in my name." She straightened. "Then we'll see if the Duke has a concern for what's under the dress."

With Mary's assistance, Fran began to dress in the dark blue traveling suit. Given the privacy provided by her father's private railcar, no one would see her beyond Bedford and the traveling servants. In light of her recent experimentation, she chose not to wear the modest handkerchief linen fichu with fancy cutwork that she'd normally button around her neck and tuck inside the lapels of the jacket. Instead she covered her chest with perfume and powder before buttoning the jacket down the front of her.

Fran could feel Mary's disapproval as she pinned her hair in place.

"Only the Duke will see me in father's private railcar," Fran explained. "My evening dress exposes more than this jacket."

Mary still scowled. "Evening is evening and day is day, miss."

"There's a purpose in my actions, Mary. I know what I'm doing."

She seemed unconvinced.

Fran sighed. She didn't owe Mary an explanation, but they'd been together for so long, she would have liked her approval. "Tomorrow, I promise to wear every item that you lay out, but for today let me be as I am."

Mary replied with a curt nod, then lifted the handwritten note to take to the front desk to be telegraphed.

"Mary, could you post the letter on the desk, as well?" Fran asked. "I don't wish it to be forgotten in the packing."

Fran couldn't exactly hear all of Mary's mumblings as she headed for the door, but she could have sworn she heard the words "straight to the devil."

WILLIAM GRIMACED IN FRONT OF THE MIRROR AS Hodgins, his valet, fitted and brushed the back of his day jacket. Morning had arrived much too quickly.

"Is all as it should be, Your Grace?" Hodgins asked. "Would you prefer the worsted?"

"No. This is fine," William quickly replied, not anxious to disclose the true reason for his anxiety. Although the brandy he'd consumed after that second confrontation with Francesca was partly to blame, his uncertainty was another. What awaited him on the other side of the door, the sensuous temptress of last evening, or the cold fashion plate from the wedding? He had the unique sense that he had married two distinctly different women, and he wasn't completely sure which he preferred. They both had a certain appeal, but they both could prove equally disastrous.

"I was just thinking about the trip home," he improvised with a quick glance to gray skies framed by the window. "I had some . . . difficulty on the trip over."

Hodgins followed his gaze before offering a sympathetic glance in the mirror. "It was a wise decision to take the train to New York even if it does lengthen the trip to the city. I should not like to be tossed upon an angry sea in that small steamer."

Hah! William groused to himself. The day could be as clear as glass and he suspected it wouldn't matter. He was a man who needed solid footing beneath him and he suspected the woman who waited for him in the next room could make even terra firma less so.

"I'm sorry I wasn't available to assist you on the ferry, but do not fear," Hodgins offered. "I won't leave your side this time."

William turned and scowled.

"Unless, of course, you require it of me," Hodgins quickly added.

"I'm not a child, Hodgins," William muttered, heading for the door. He was too old for such nonsense as hangovers and mal de mer. Damn it, he would simply force his stomach into compliance. That was all there was to it.

At least, until he opened the door and saw coddled eggs and greasy sausage. His stomach turned. "I think just the fruit and toast this morning."

"Excellent choice, Your Grace."

Before he could be seated, the door to his wife's room opened. He straightened, then turned toward the door. "Good morning, Your Grace," he managed, before he fully assimilated the vision before him.

Her face radiated such elegance and beauty, he thought the confounded morning light was playing tricks. A bit of pride of possession shimmered through him. A man could do worse than greet that face every morning.

She nodded in response. The hint of a mischievous grin barely noticeable on her lips reminded him of her comparable youth that blasted through his morning haze to mock him. Lord, she had been up as late as he writing that blasted letter to her lover. Why didn't she look as tired as he felt? That thought managed to intensify the pounding at his temples.

His gaze traveled downward from her pert chin and froze on her chest.

"Did your maid not return in time to assist you with your attire?"

Her coquettish smile disappeared the moment her glance caught Hodgins. Strange. Hodgins would shrivel away and die if his actions ever upset a lady. Why would she react in such a manner? He hadn't much opportunity to contemplate that as she accepted the offered seat immediately across from him.

"Mary arrived early this morning," she said. "She has such a delightful family. They are bound to miss her while she's in England." Her lashes fluttered with forced innocence. "Why do you ask?"

"Because it appears you've forgotten part of your wardrobe."

He waited as his wife refused the cup of coffee offered by Hodgins. She spoke in such a formal tone, one would think she was addressing the Queen. Frosty Franny, she was to be then. That was a relief. It was easier to keep one's distance from a rose when the thorns exceeded the length of the petals. "We have sufficient time before departure to remedy the situation."

She glanced down as if to examine herself. "Really?" Her gaze returned to his. "What part?"

He sputtered; surely she couldn't be serious? "The part that covers your"—he placed his hand on his chest—"virtues." Confound it! Surely the girl knew the proper way to dress. "As my duchess, there are certain standards of dress—"

She leaned forward slightly, as if to give him a better view.

"My virtues, as you call them, will be even more prominently displayed when I dress for dinner. Why does the sight of them now disturb you so?"

"They don't disturb me," he protested, but it was a lie. They disturbed him so that his throat held all the moisture of dry toast. They disturbed him in that they flaunted what he longed to have but was denied. They disturbed him in the thought that other men could appreciate what should be his alone. He took a sip of coffee and felt it burn a path down his gullet. "Perhaps in this country, it is acceptable to flaunt one's . . . virtues . . . in public. However, in England the standards are higher."

"We're not in public, Your Grace." She took a delicate bite from a piece of toast slathered with butter. The oil cast a sheen on her lips that offered a new temptation—a temptation he felt all the way to his groin.

"This is true, but we soon shall be. We need to travel to the railcar and there's every possibility that the roads will be lined with well-wishers much as they were yesterday. Trust me, you will want to adjust your attire." *If only so I can keep my gaze off the attractive cleft between your breasts*, he wanted to add, but didn't.

She grew quiet, pensive, and pushed her eggs about the plate. The silence added tension to the room rather than detracted. He supposed it was a bit much to expect her to thank him for his advice, but she really did need to understand about the rules of the society she was about to enter. Thank heavens his aunt would be waiting at the abbey to help mold her into an acceptable English lady. He'd have to keep his suspicions of the duchess's pregnancy to himself, of course. He doubted his aunt would be as generous as he in accepting the bastard child.

The sudden thunderous sound of rain striking the roof overhead pulled both their gazes upward. The storm that had been threatening all morning had arrived.

Francesca's brows raised, a victorious glint shone in her

eyes. "Even if well-wishers wait in the rain, they'll see a closed carriage roll by."

His eyes narrowed. Confound the woman, the rain, and all of this unrefined country. Why did everything have to be a battle? It wasn't that he was asking for some grand sacrifice, just a little show of decency on her part.

"I say this for your own good." His voice sounded stern to his own ears, but she needed to understand—the sooner, the better. "It is unacceptable for a duchess to be inappropriately attired. If your maid does not know this, I shall secure one for you that is more attuned to the mores of society."

She gasped. "You'd remove Mary?"

Thunder roared overhead, and he found it necessary to raise his voice to be heard. "If she cannot dress you in a decent and mature fashion, and address you properly as your position deserves, then yes, we'll leave her behind with her delightful family who won't have to miss her leaving them after all."

His head still throbbed from last night's excesses, and the blasted thunder did nothing to alleviate the pain, nor did this confrontation first thing in the morning. He sipped his coffee, then attempted to modulate his voice in something less than a shout.

"There are many young women, educated in the dictates of the polite world, who would be more than willing to serve in Mary's stead. A good many indeed. We would have no difficulty in finding a replacement."

She stilled, and in that moment he could actually see her spirit wither. The mischievous glint in her eyes withdrew. The radiant spark that so impressed him with its freshness and youthful intensity faded.

A three-stone weight dropped in his gut. He'd been too harsh. He wished he could take back the words, modify their impact. He didn't mean to browbeat the girl, just prepare her for the road ahead, provide her with the necessary resources.

"I'm afraid I've lost my appetite," she said, patting her lips with her napkin.

William gained his feet while Hodgins rushed to assist the

Duchess. The servant was trained to repress his opinions of his employer, but William felt his unspoken censure just the same. Once the Duchess was on her feet, William signaled Hodgins with a swift glance to the door and the servant wisely took his leave. Francesca turned away.

"No, wait," he said, quickly rounding the small table to reach her before she found the sanctuary of her room. He grasped her arm so she couldn't escape. Not that he'd blame her if she tried. "I'm sorry. It was not my intent to hurt you. I'm . . . I'm just concerned that you're not prepared for the road that lies ahead."

He wanted to pull her into his arms and comfort her, but he wasn't sure he'd earned the right.

"Mary wanted me to wear a fichu." He had to strain to hear her thin voice over the rain. She wouldn't look at him, she probably couldn't bear to look at such a monster. He felt lower than the muck at the bottom of the Thames.

"She said to present myself without it was improper. She's my closest . . . my only . . . I should have listened to her." She raised her glance up to him, and he promptly decided even the muck was too lofty for him. Unshed tears glimmered in her beautiful eyes, clumping her lush fringe of sooty lashes into spikes that stabbed at his heart. "It was my fault. Please don't send her away."

He couldn't help it. He drew her tight to his chest and wrapped his arms around her. She was like a crumpled bird, one that had fallen from its mother's nest. Was that what he had done? Robbed the nest before this fledgling was ready? He hoped not. Pressing his lips to the delicate shell of her ear, he inhaled the sweet essence of her, the freshness of sun, and wind, and—a smile slipped to his lips—rain. He nuzzled a bit closer and murmured, "Of course, Mary can stay."

She pushed back, her hands on his forearms. Her gaze urgently searched his face. "She can stay? You won't change your mind?"

His smile broadened to see the glint return to her eyes. "Yes, she can stay."

By God, he'd bring her whole bloody family along if it

would keep that glow in her cheeks. In fact, he was about to suggest that very thing, when his downward glance got lost in the beckoning valley between her breasts. He cleared his throat and slipped his hands to span her trim waist fortressed by satin and stays. There was safety in knowing so many layers protected him from succumbing to the welcoming flesh beneath. However, the rise and fall of her chest so readily exposed by her lack of covering teased a similar stirring from another part of his anatomy. He cleared his throat, hoping the action would clear his thoughts as well. "Why didn't you listen to her?" .

She tilted her head, nibbling on her lower lip in consideration. "Is there nothing you find attractive about my person?"

He almost laughed, but she looked so serious. Silly girl! He found far too many attractive diversions about her person. That was the crux of his difficulty.

"I find your eyes most attractive," he said, pleased to see she responded with a timid smile. "And the elegant shape of your cheekbones will be the envy of all who see you."

She lifted her gaze, the fire returning to her eyes. "Is that all?"

"I like the pert tip of your nose," he said with a quick kiss to mark the spot. Which in hindsight might not have been wise, for now she was close, intimately close. He nuzzled his nose down the length of hers, drowning in her sweet, honeyed scent. "And there's this."

She must have felt the magnetic attraction that brought him close as she parted her moist lips in anticipation of his kiss. He was tentative, at first, not wishing to frighten her with demands as he had earlier. However, she shifted against him, pressing the length of her close. She met the pressure of his kiss with her own, timid, almost innocent in nature—which he knew without doubt she was not.

A name reared in his head. *My Dearest Randolph.* She was kissing him and thinking of another man. With a groan, he took what was rightfully his. He tightened his hold about her and plundered her mouth with his tongue, seeking to eradicate the taste of another man from her memory. He kissed her again and again, not aware of her response, just the need to rub out any thoughts of another and mark this territory as his own.

He suckled on her lower lip when she pushed hard against his chest, breaking his hold, then stepped back. Her eyes were wide, rounded. She held the back of her hand in front of her lips.

"Wait," he said, still drugged from the taste of her. He wanted more, needed more. He reached for her, but she stepped back.

"I . . . I must change," she said, slipping quietly into her room.

The door closed. She was gone.

What the bloody hell did he just do? He banged his fist on the door frame in abject frustration, knocking loose several paint chips. The sound brought Hodgins to the opposite door, but he waved him away.

He knew better. Didn't he spend hours last night reminding himself of the logic of his plan? Didn't he determine to stay away from the chit until the proof of his suspicions presented himself? Yet an inexplicable frenzy grabbed control of his mind once he tasted her lips—complete loss of his senses. How could such a thing happen? It certainly had never occurred with Lily, his current mistress, or with any of the other women with whom he'd enjoyed the occasional dalliance.

Randolph. The name burned a path through his brain like one of those acids they'd experimented with at Eton. He was the only explanation for this sudden need of absolute possession. William rubbed his fist and gazed out the window at the slowing rain.

Certainly, it was no secret he was competitive. He had to be. His father had driven him hard to be the best. To be second was to fail. He had accepted that Randolph had left his mark on Francesca before him—unfortunate, but true. Francesca didn't strike him as overly impetuous but she was, after all, American. He would have been content to treat her as his wife with gentle kindness. But that was before he saw that cursed letter. He could tolerate what had occurred before him, but now that Francesca had joined her name to his, he would not tolerate divided loyalties. He would eradicate Randolph from her thoughts, from her dreams, from her very consciousness, but first he had to gain her trust.

He rested his forehead against the cool glass pane. He'd done a bloody good job of mucking that up as well. He'd terrified the girl with his need to possess. Her rounded panic-filled eyes would haunt his dreams. He'd be lucky if she deigned to speak to him again.

He took a deep breath, letting it calm his racing pulse. Control. It was the only recourse. He was the experienced one. He would guide them safely through this passage. He'd need to rein in his jealousy, of course. Give the girl some distance. Let cooler heads prevail. Let her learn to trust him, especially once the babe in her belly made its presence known.

Patience, control, and especially distance—that would be the plan.

· Eight ·

FRAN PRESSED HER BUSTLE INTO THE DOOR, EF- fectively barricading it with her body should he forcibly try to enter. The door shuddered briefly at her back, reminding her that similar shudders ran through her body. What had just happened? She pressed her fingers to her lips, feeling the swell of them.

Certainly, she'd been kissed before. Randolph kissed her twice before he left for Germany. One could not have been in love without that gentle exchange of trust and devotion. But there was nothing gentle about Bedford's kiss. This was a kiss of passion the likes she could not have foreseen. It was demanding, consuming, powerful.

What did it mean when one felt the titillating vibrations of a kiss past the portals of decency and all the way to her core? She could feel the sensation still, humming with an intensity that made her feel incomplete, as if her body required something more.

The wood stilled at her back, allowing a calm to replace the rush of sensation she'd fled from earlier. A gentle, yet heady, refrain began to bubble inside her, until it bloomed on her lips.

It worked!

The guidance provided by the journal worked! Be it the powder, the perfume, or the advertisement afforded by her lack of covering, it worked!

Bless you, Madame Aglionby—she sent a silent prayer skyward—for providing a means to direct my destiny. With the journal's help, she should be with child in no time. A gentleman would never resist his wife's desire to have her baby in her home country. Her father had already negotiated the issues of schools. She'd have to spend some time in England, but now at least she had the means to minimize her stay.

Of course, she'd have to be more careful about applying these valuable principles of seduction in a public venue. Just the suggestion had almost cost her the services of Mary. The prospect of living among strangers was daunting enough. She needed Mary's support and friendship if she was to keep her head above the fray.

She crossed the room to retrieve the abandoned fichu and proceeded to attach the linen piece and anchor it inside her jacket. She was just checking her appearance in the mirror when Mary returned from her errands.

Mary glanced at her then smiled. "Pleased to see you've come to your senses, miss."

"About that, Mary. I think it would be wise for all concerned if you addressed me as 'Your Grace' or 'madam' henceforth. I suppose I need to adjust to the sound of it and bid 'Miss Winthrop' adieu."

Mary's smile broadened and a bit of relief registered in her eyes. "If it pleases you, Your Grace."

AS EXPECTED, THE RAIN HAD DISCOURAGED THE PRE-dicted crowds and the newly married couple was able to begin their journey without ceremony. In order to catch the train that would take them to the Grand Central Depot in New York City, they had to first take a short ferry ride to Wickford, Rhode Island. A carriage would then convey them to the docks where the SS *Republic* waited. Even though the trip to New York would have been shorter on the Fall River steamer, Fran supported Bedford's preference of the train, believing as she did in procrastination as it related to their eventual destination.

Fran clutched a satchel that contained her writing implements, two small volumes she hoped to translate on the transatlantic crossing, the tome of lineage that Bedford decreed she learn, and the courtesan's journal. The trip on the ferry proved a bit difficult. The deck chairs were too wet to use, due to the recent rain. Fran found a chair in the first-class stateroom and tried to busy herself with her translations so as to discourage conversation from any other passengers. Bedford, however, stationed himself along the rail and stared at the horizon.

She thought he looked a tad pale when they departed the vessel, but didn't comment. Although she had limited experience with the male gender, she had noted that such observations regarding the unseating by a horse, a missed swing of a polo mallet, or insufficient sea legs were rarely appreciated.

Bedford had brought stacks of congratulatory telegrams from family, tenants, political organizations, employees, and friends. Once they had boarded the private parlor car, he used those to quiz her on her knowledge of family. It was tedious and tiring, especially when combined with the rhythmic sway of the railcar.

"What ho!" he exclaimed, after opening an envelope. "This one is from Queen Victoria herself." He glanced at her, pride radiating from his face. "We are truly honored."

"That's lovely." Fran smiled, without attempting to match the Duke's enthusiasm. She noted his reaction to the Queen's telegram certainly exceeded his response to the formal congratulatory note sent by President Rutherford B. Hayes. The British seemed to place much greater importance on these trivial formalities.

His face paled when he read the next telegram. "It's from Bertie." He glanced at her. "Prince Albert Edward. He wishes to meet you."

Fran thought she might have been introduced to him once, though those introductions quickly became blurred in her memory. "That's nice of him."

"Too soon, too soon," Bedford muttered shaking his head. He picked up some sheets of paper and searched for a pen. "We won't be ready."

He lapsed into his list making without conferring further

with Fran. She pleaded a headache and retired to the private sleeping car.

It was an excuse to escape, of course. The lineage assignment held no real interest or challenge. Bedford certainly encouraged her to rest, so she took advantage—and brought her courtesan's journal with her.

UNDER THE TUTELAGE OF FATIMA, THE DEMAND FOR Bridget's company increased and her entries became less frequent. She grew fatigued by the physical demands made of her person and, in order to keep those requests minimal, began to engage her patrons in conversations.

At first, she bantered lightly about the arts, but she found that frustrating as few of her patrons cared a fig about anything more than the art of pleasuring them. She began asking them questions, at first about what pleased them, and then about other topics—their family, their occupation, even their politics. She kept track of her questions and some of their responses in the journal, which gave Fran a chuckle.

The important discovery to Bridget was that her patrons not only purchased her time to advance these discussions but, in many instances, regarded her as a complete person and not just a convenient vessel. Some of the men even asked her what would give her pleasure. Unfortunately, Bridget didn't provide details to that issue, much to Fran's chagrin. She would have liked to know that answer herself.

Bridget's popularity increased and Fatima noticed. She announced the time had come for Bridget to find a patron who would want her services exclusively. To draw such a gentleman's attention, she advised Bridget to determine her most attractive attribute and mark the spot with a beauty mark. Without fail, the eye would be drawn to the desired location reminding the gentleman of her charms, while her mode of dress would advise of her availability. Bridget's conversation skills and education, combined with this reminder of her beauty, should make her highly desirable.

Highly desirable . . . Fran closed the journal, wondering

what that would feel like. She knew she was highly desirable because of her father's offered dowry, but what would it be like to be highly desirable because of one's self? She wondered what charm Bridget would choose to accentuate with a beauty mark. If Bridget had Fran's face and form, what charm would she choose, if any?

Fran picked up an ornate hand mirror and critically scrutinized her face. Bedford had said he liked her eyes and nose, but he seemed to spend extra attention to her lips. She knew that he appreciated her chest when it was thrust before him. That memory brought a smile.

It's a shame that her chest wasn't closer to her eyes and nose; then all her charms could be concentrated in one place. She tilted the hand mirror sweeping from chest to face and back. Perhaps if her neck wasn't so unusually long, she'd be considerably more attractive.

The sound of movement on the vestibule between cars alerted her to imminent arrival of another. Probably Mary coming to help her dress for dinner. Good. She could help her with this issue of charms.

"Do you think my neck is overly long?" she asked when the door opened to the sleeping car.

"Is that possible?" a deep male voice answered, sending tingling vibrations down her spine. She adjusted the position of the hand mirror to see Bedford behind her. "A neck is after all a neck, is it not?"

She swirled around to face him. Embarrassment at being discovered in such a narcissistic endeavor sent heat to her face.

"But I would say that yours is a particularly elegant neck, much like that of a swan."

He reached out and drew a finger down the length of her neck. Her lids lowered almost in imitation of his. She imagined he could feel her quickened pulse through the tips of his fingers. However, almost immediately he withdrew his fingers and stepped back, shifting uncomfortably before her.

"I thought you were resting, but I see you've been reading." He started to reach for the journal on the bed, but she grabbed the book and pressed it to her chest before he could examine it. One quizzical brow raised, but she didn't offer an explanation. "I've come to see if you felt up to the public dining car."

She could well imagine all those strange faces gazing at them in the public car. Just the thought raised gooseflesh on her arms. "A private meal, if you please."

"Private it shall be then." He narrowed his eyes and glanced down the length of her. "Are you feeling well? Queasy, perhaps? I'm told that happens. I can request a light fare, if that would help."

Obviously he had mistaken her sudden flush upon his arrival to the onset of illness. She smiled, preferring his interpretation to the truth. "I feel fine, though I appreciate your query."

She waited for him to leave, but he hesitated a moment before pointing toward her chest. "What are you reading that has so captured your interest?"

This was difficult. She couldn't very well disclose that she was studying a woman of the sporting nature because she obviously hadn't the basic knowledge of seduction that most seemed to have been born with. In the recesses of her mind, she could still hear the taunt of "Frosty Franny." Even the press had recognized her deficiencies. Embarrassment burned a path up her neck, causing her to be grateful that she was wearing the fichu. It hid the resulting flush from his eye.

"It's a German childrens' tale," she lied. "I translate them into English," she added, hoping the part truth would mitigate the lie.

Interest sparked his eyes. "Amazing. I had not suspected that of you." He gestured that she should sit on the bed. "Tell me about the story."

She complied, though that was not her wish. She'd prefer he was in the other railcar, not seated on the opposite end of the bed. Granted it was her plan to lure him here eventually, but she wasn't prepared. Not yet. She hadn't dressed appropriately nor had she determined her best features.

"It's the story of a little girl whose most prized toy is a ball of pure gold." She improvised with the story most fresh in her memory. He nodded his head encouraging her to continue. "Her father has warned her to be careful, but she loses the ball in the bottom of a deep pond."

"Are there illustrations?" he asked, gesturing to the book.

"Oh . . . no, there are none." She slipped the journal behind her, out of sight. "Just the story . . . in German." She hoped he wasn't fluent in the language. If he asked to see the book she'd be hard-set to comply.

"One would think, for a child's story, there would be an interest in illustrations," he said, apparently disappointed. "My brother, you know, is an exceptional artist. Now that he has a child, I wonder his thoughts on the subject."

"I would think illustrations would be a wonderful idea," she said. Strange to think of Bedford having a family and to hear a sort of yearning in his voice when he spoke of children. She hadn't thought to ask him his thoughts on family, so much of their conversations had been her lack of appropriate grace, her lack of appropriate etiquette, and recently her lack of appropriate fashion.

"You shall meet him soon enough. In his congratulatory telegraph he said he was anxious to make your acquaintance and reassure you that first impressions can be deceiving, though I'm not sure what he meant by that." He frowned. "I've asked him to join us at Deerfeld as I need to speak to him about some urgent matters that require his . . . unique knowledge."

She nodded, curious about his brother and envious of the way Bedford's tone changed when he spoke of him. The affection was apparent. What would it be like to have had a brother or sister with which to share stories and experiences, with which to share long, lonely hours?

"I know that newly married couples traditionally go on a honeymoon of sorts, but I'm afraid with Bertie's imminent arrival there just isn't time. There's much to be done and Nicholas can be of assistance."

She assumed this was his way of suggesting she would have to find her own way in this new household, that he would be unavailable. She was well experienced with the concept of alone. That did not concern her nearly as much as this grand reception for the Prince Regent. As hostess, she would again be placed on public display.

"I'm sure you'll enjoy meeting Nicholas's wife and child." He managed to smile in that particular way that set her rib cage aflutter, reminding her of her own need to advance her impregnation efforts. "What happened to the little girl when it was discovered the ball was lost?" He tilted his head, looking both earnest and concerned. One would think they were discussing the Indian wars or the women's suffrage movement, serious issues of the day, not the Frog King. His brows lowered. "Was she punished?"

His face held such a rapt expression of fear and curiosity that she wondered briefly if he had experienced harsh punishments as a child. Perhaps this too was another thing they had in common. But the sentiment was lost in the novel sensation of a man so engaged in her words. Especially as the subject matter was an innocent children's story.

She relaxed a bit, enjoying his interest. "She was afraid her father would do just that; fortunately a frog came to her rescue."

"A frog, you say?" He looked so puzzled, she was inclined to laugh. Then awareness lit his expression. "A most accommodating fellow."

"Yes, Your Grace." She couldn't hold by her laughter any longer as his face had betrayed the exact moment he made the connection between the story and his choice of costume for the ball. "Indeed," she said. "He was a most distinguished-looking frog, a king among frogs."

"Not a duke?" His eyes crinkled in laughter. "Tell me more."

Those three words triggered a flutter of appreciation in her rib cage. He wanted to hear more . . . from her! It was a simple concept and hardly the foundation upon which to build a marriage, but . . . perhaps a friendship?

She hadn't many friends, much less male friends—except maybe Randolph. That thought brought her up short. She urgently wanted to deny the comparison. Randolph was more than a friend, she told herself. Bedford was a mere acquaintance.

Bedford is more than a friend, a tiny voice whispered in her head. *He's your husband.* She mentally shook herself back to the conversation at hand.

"The frog makes several requests from the little girl before he agrees to retrieve her ball."

"I can't image what sort of requests a frog would make," Bedford said, fully engaged in the story. "New lily pads, perhaps? Another frog for companionship?"

"It's companionship he desires, but not for another frog." She caught the duke's gaze and felt suddenly demure, as if she'd just revealed her wishes and not that of a storybook character.

"I feel a certain affinity for this frog king." Bedford reached over and took her hand in his. That simple familiar act sparked a delicious warmth. "He made you laugh. That's the first time I've heard your laughter."

His thumb stroked the length of her fingers, raising her awareness to his touch and his close proximity. She lifted her gaze to his, finding a spark smoldering there as well. "I hope to hear more of it."

Her breath caught. How could the telling of a children's tale suddenly feel so incredibly carnal?

"This girl must have been very, very wealthy to have a ball of gold." The quirk of his brow and the low timber of his voice made her wonder if they were still conversing about a children's story. His fingers slipped in and out of the crevices between her own in a playful, teasing game. "I think she must be American."

"She was a princess," she answered, wishing she wasn't wearing the lightweight jacket so he could play this wonderful teasing game up the sensitive skin of her arm. "We haven't royalty in America."

"Ah, a princess . . ." he said, his lids half lowering over his eyes in a sleepy, seductive gaze. "What did the frog request of the princess for retrieving this immensely valuable ball?"

A delicious tingling played in her rib cage creating an urgency for more—more touch, more closeness, more sharing of secrets—as that's how the sharing of the story felt. She leaned a bit closer in his direction.

"He had three requests," she said, while something akin to warmed honey spread upward from her fingers. It pooled in the vicinity of her breasts, making the very tips of them ache. She recalled that last night his fingers—those very talented fingers that now stroked and teased her hand—had explored her breast in much the same fashion. Instantly, those tips remembered as well. She felt them rub the satin of her corset in their plea for attention. The temperature in the railcar seemed to raise a few degrees.

"The frog wanted to share her meals."

"Understandable." His lips turned in an enticing smile, causing her to wonder if he were speaking of himself or the green amphibian.

"The frog wanted to share her pillow at night."

"An assuredly intelligent beast, that frog." The quirk of his lips made her want to laugh, and yet his implication that the sharing of one's pillow was an intelligent request made her skittish deep inside. How would it feel to share her pillow with Bedford?

Had he moved closer? The distance between them felt reduced, and yet she wished it was reduced again.

"And he wanted to be kissed every night before bed," she said, gazing pointedly at his full lower lip. The very lips that had explored her own that very morning. Her own lips dried to the consistency of an abandoned honeycomb. She moistened them with her tongue as she waited for his response.

His eyebrows barely raised while his gaze locked on her lips. His throat must have been as dry as hers as his normal low smooth tones turned scratchy. His hand stopped its wonderful torment and lay heavy on hers. "And did she?"

Fran was suddenly embarrassed to tell him the true end to the story, that the girl's father forced her to comply with all the demands except the last. The little girl threw the frog against a wall rather than kiss him. It was just a children's story, but one with the wrong ending.

Instead Fran pitched her voice low, leaned close and held his gaze. "She should have."

HE WANTED TO KISS HER THEN. HE WANTED TO THROW her back against the pillows and kiss her senseless. Somehow she had taken a children's story and turned it into an invitation to bed her. And bed her, he longed to do. The attraction had been there from the first, but not yet. Not till he knew.

He should never have touched her hand. That began his undoing. But how could he resist when he heard the yearning in her voice when she said *companionship*. He wanted to reassure her. He wanted her to know she wasn't alone. He wanted to let her know he wished for the same. Simple companionship.

He should never have watched her lips. Yet it was difficult to resist when he had so recently tasted their sweetness. Impossible to resist when her tongue darted about leaving glistening honey in its wake. And when she spoke of pillows . . . did she not realize she was sitting on a bed? Every particle of masculinity in his body knew the temptation afforded by a mattress—and still demanded satisfaction.

He cleared his throat, averted his gaze, then reluctantly removed his hand from hers. "Right then." He stood and turned his back toward her to hide his lamentable condition. He wished he'd brought his top hat in the car with him, but how was he to know his Frosty Franny could melt an iceberg? "I suppose I should see about dinner."

"Will you be joining me, Your Grace?" Her voice held a hopeful lilt, much as he imagined the frog might have had in the sharing of pillows. For a moment he wasn't sure the manner of joining she implied.

Blast! She offered an invitation that was difficult to refuse, but if he stayed . . . well, he would never know if the babe was his or that of another. No. He had the right of it when he counseled himself to keep his distance. Counsel he should have obeyed when he thought to check on her earlier.

"No. I believe not. I've heard that several men with money meet in the smoking car for games of skill and chance. I believe I'll try my luck."

He headed for the vestibule door, but spoke over his shoulder. "Sleep tight, my duchess. I won't be disturbing your slumber tonight."

He had opened the car door and was about to step onto the platform between cars when he thought he heard spoken quietly behind him, "But you should have."

· Nine ·

RECALLING THE TEMPTATION AFFORDED BY LAST evening's brief interlude, William was hesitant to climb into the confined quarters of a carriage with his wife, even for the short journey to the White Star docks. At least this time she was dressed properly. The high-necked blue-and-white-striped bodice covered her chest completely. He should be pleased by that, he groused. Why wasn't he pleased by that?

It was her fault, of course. If she hadn't been so approachable last night, so inviting, he wouldn't have spent so much time in that card game with the American version of Twiddlebody. He hadn't especially enjoyed the game, but he wasn't confident he could resist her if he went back to the sleeping car. Instead, he returned late to the parlor car and tried unsuccessfully to sleep on an overstuffed divan. Now that his wife was properly dressed in a stylized version of a sailor suit, he shouldn't be tempted to stare indecently at her chest, and yet he fought the urge.

Her matching skirt was pulled tight on the sides, outlining her trim shape for all that looked twice. Once they reached the docks he imagined there would be plenty who would do just that. He rubbed the back of his neck, his ire starting to rise. Why should they have the pleasure of looking, while he had to avert his gaze to maintain his sanity?

Calm yourself, he counseled. As the new Duchess of Bedford, there would be many who would gawk after her. He was the Duke, after all, a pillar of society. Men would naturally be curious. Men would naturally pass judgment. He should acclimate himself toward such scrutiny. It just aggravated him that so many would assume he enjoyed the very husbandly privileges that he denied himself. The thought grated. He grimaced in her direction, but she never saw it. She was too busy watching the passing scenery.

The carriage slowed as they neared the wharf and rising cacophony of stevedores, immigrants, fine carriages, hackneys, wagons of luggage, wagons of produce, and all manner of man and beast swarming the docks. In the center of it all, massive and stationary like a slumbering beast surrounded by insignificant insects, waited the SS *Republic* bound for Southampton. With four masts and one funnel, she wasn't the biggest steamer, nor the fastest, but she did provide the most extravagant services to her first-class passengers—he smiled— services worthy of a duke.

Transferring Francesca's luggage from the Grand Central Depot to the rented carriage and wagon had taken more time than the entire trip to the White Star Line dock. Now the carriage rocked from side to side as the whole process began again. Already he could hear Mary and Hodgins, who accompanied the luggage wagon, shout directions as to the disposition of the trunks and boxes.

The driver opened the door and helped Francesca out a moment before William could escape the tight confines of the paneled interior. He eagerly stepped out into the bright light and invigorating atmosphere of adventure. He was going home.

He glanced at his bride, noting her stiff stance and wide, brown eyes. At first, he thought she looked overwhelmed by the activity surrounding them, then he reconsidered. She had tried to escape the engagement, she had tried to escape the marriage, and from the looks of her, she might still be scheming to disappear into the ubiquitous crowd.

Randolph. The name crept into his consciousness, bringing with it the taste of bile. Even though they were legally wed, she was perhaps thinking to slip away to rejoin her lover. In this crush, such a plan would be easy to implement given an opportunity. He set his teeth. No one was going to take from him what was legally his. No one.

He linked her arm with his, pulling her snug against him.

She glanced at him in surprise, which only confirmed his suspicions. Now let's just see her try to slip away. He congratulated himself on his swift analysis and precautionary measures.

With a thought to lead her toward the first-class boarding ramp, he stepped forward. She, however, remained anchored to the spot, pulling him back.

She appeared frozen, like the giant blocks of ice and sawdust currently loading into the ship's massive hold. He glanced at her stricken face, quickly analyzing the situation.

"Have you not crossed the Atlantic before?" he asked, feeling a bit smug in his superiority. "There's nothing to fear. The voyage here was my first crossing. I arrived fit as a fiddle." The last was a lie as he remembered his battle with seasickness, but there was no need to scare her with that possibility.

His question startled her. Her blank gaze shifted to find his, reminding him of how she looked when they had exchanged vows. "I've crossed on several occasions," she said. "My mother prefers to shop in Paris. We go every spring."

He hadn't expected that. He rather enjoyed the brief feeling of being the more experienced one, and now that fizzled. He frowned. "Then why are you so hesitant?"

"We always crossed on my father's private yacht with just the crew." He followed her gaze to the promenade deck where a small crowd had gathered by the rail.

"Yes, well, there are considerably more people on a transatlantic steamer"—he pulled her forward with a bit more authority—"but you needn't be concerned. I've reserved a parlor suite. We won't be in cramped quarters." Unlike his previous trip, he mentally added, when a hasty sale of an heirloom vase afforded him a shared berth in a first-class cabin, not the luxury of a full suite.

He tried to pull her forward, but their progress was slow. "This particular steamship has an open promenade deck and running water for a private bath. The food is most agreeable."

How lovely to have the money to pay for the finer comforts, like a suite that befit his status. Reassured he now had the means to enjoy the proper lifestyle of a duke, he took a deep

breath and promptly launched into a coughing fit. The scent of
sea air mingled with wharf refuse should never be taken in
large doses.

"It's not the quarters that concern me, Your Grace," she
said once he got his breath back.

"My dear, we will need to move a bit faster if we're going to
board this ship." At the speed of their approach, the bloody
thing could sail to England and back by the time they made it
to the ramp.

As if in possession of some alchemist's talent, a slight ad-
justment to her posture modified her natural quiet grace into
something regal and elegant. Amazed, he glanced around the
feminine gewgaws that decorated her hat to see her face, wondering if a change had occurred there as well.

Her eyes were closed, and her lips murmured something
that sounded remarkably like "just smile and nod." Her lips
lifted in a smug tilt, her eyes opened in something akin to a
blank stare. She planted the parasol that expressly matched
her dress by her feet with purpose and determination, and she
moved forward, breaking free of his clasp.

"My God," he said to himself. In the space of a heartbeat,
she replaced the warm, inviting companion who relayed stories
with childlike glee with the cold, distant, aloof society lady
that had exchanged vows with him before God and the congregation. She had the look of a perfect duchess, and yet something was missing. And already he felt its loss.

She hooked her parasol on her arm and lifted her skirts
slightly to manage the narrow steps that would take them up
to the first-class deck. He followed behind her, placing both
hands on the railings and thus eliminating her means of turning back, should she harbor such a plan. Her amply decorated
derriere swayed seductively in front of him, reminding him of
the price he was paying to establish paternity. Panels of white-
trimmed, blue-striped fabric with large white buttons dangled
enticingly over her rump for no practical purpose that he
could fathom, other than to call the viewer's attention to this
particular area.

And pay attention, he did. The short train of her outfit slid lightly over two risers immediately behind her. In order not to step on her skirts he stayed several risers back which placed the rhythmic swinging panels in direct line with his nose. It took all his control to keep his hands on the rail and not place them on her very tempting bottom. He offered a silent prayer that his brother would enlighten him on some telltale aspect of a woman's pregnancy that would eliminate the need to wait the necessary month or so before her belly would yield her secrets. If he had to wait long before he could slake this thirst, he'd go insane.

They reached the first-class deck where a man in the nautical cap of an officer greeted them and welcomed them aboard. Francesca, he noted, smiled and nodded. The officer handed William a key to their staterooms and assured him their luggage would be delivered directly. After noting the room's location, he passed the key on to Hodgins, who labored up the steps a distance behind them, then escorted Francesca to the promenade deck.

"Shouldn't we see to our rooms?" Francesca asked, with a backward glance at the retreating Hodgins.

"Mary and Hodgins will see to the luggage. That is their responsibility. Ours is to be seen." He guided her up the short flight of steps to the open air deck where fashionable men and well-turned ladies strolled arm in arm near the railings. "The other first-class passengers are here, thus we should be as well."

Her eyes widened a moment as she scanned the crowd on the deck. Her voice dropped to hushed tones. "Will it always be this way?"

"My dear, we have an obligation, an image to uphold." It would be impossible to explain to her the lessons of image and responsibility that had been burned into him at an early age. He had prepared for this his entire life. The promenade deck was a far cry from Mayfair, but only the best of society could travel to London first class. One never knew who would be sharing the trip with them.

So he shouldn't have been surprised to see Twiddlebody and his wife. And yet he was.

"Fancy seeing you again, Your Grace, and is this the new missus?"

William made the introductions. Francesca nodded and smiled.

"I read about the nuptials in the papers." He winked at William. "I'm glad this trip was a profitable one. A chip off the old man's block, don't you know. Guess I won't have to rush to your brother after all." He tipped his hat to Francesca. "Pleasure to make your acquaintance, Your Grace."

"That is an odious man," William said, watching the couple depart.

Francesca just continued to smile and nod. He didn't hear a word from her lips as they greeted several other well-connected couples. They joined the others at the rails as the massive ropes that secured the steamer to the docks were thrown clear: The engines rumbled, people shouted. Francesca smiled and nodded. She didn't show deference to anyone even though it was apparent through their appearance that some couples were of greater social prominence than others. She ignored all equally.

Perhaps this was how things were done in America, but then he remembered how her mother had catered to certain esteemed guests at the wedding luncheon. There was a definite social strata in attendance at that gathering, just as there would have been in London. Her mother knew how to play the strings. But the daughter . . . he glanced over at her glazed expression . . . would probably smile and nod at one from steerage as she did to the first-class passengers. Did she even recognize the difference?

He recalled her behavior on the night of their engagement, when she quickly disappeared after their engagement was announced. He recalled her behavior at the wedding luncheon when he caught her talking to walls. He recalled as well his threat to lock her in the attic. Perhaps not one of his finer moments, he reflected. He had thought it was an empty threat at the time, now he wasn't as sure.

A harbinger of doubt started to form. He had assumed based on his observation of the mother that the daughter would be able to assume her proper role in society, once she understood the proper delineations notated in the lineage volume. However, if she hadn't the appreciation of the respect those titles carried, would she be suitable? Would her lack of acumen make him a laughingstock?

He hooked a finger around his chin, letting his fist and arm support the weight of his heavy thoughts. What of Bertie's impending visit? The abbey wasn't ready, but his new financial status should ensure ready artisans and laborers to make the needed modifications. He'd already purchased sufficient items during his month in New York to mask his recent efforts to keep the estate afloat. What kind of modifications would Francesca require to be acceptable for the highest of society? Now that he had the means to pay his father's debts and salvage the family assets from embarrassing ruin, was his wife to become an albatross to hang heavy around his neck?

He stared out at the water gently slapping the sides of the *Republic* far below him. How would she react to the role she'd be expected to play? At least he still had his aunt to help her with the basics.

Fran glanced at her husband. She would have expected him to be pleased to be on his way home, instead he looked as if he were contemplating jumping over the rail. Indeed, with her own homeland receding in the distance, and a dismal, bleak future in a land of strangers as an immediate future, she should be the morose one, not him.

"Is something wrong, Your Grace?" she asked.

He glanced at her as if startled, then squinted as if he could still make out details on the distant land. "Your country has many interesting qualities, but I don't think I could ever be truly happy there." His brow creased. He shifted his gaze back to her. "It makes me wonder if you'll be happy living in England?" He lifted a brow in her direction.

Her heart expanded a little for his concern. He was the first to seem to care about her feelings, though it was a bit late to change the course of events as a result. However tempted she was to truthfully speak of her fears and anxieties, her mother's precautions to never disclose her true feelings held her back.

"I admit I am leery of living among strangers." She glanced

down at her parasol. "But my needs are few. I will do my best to be happy there."

He turned and leaned his back against the rail, crossing his arms in front of him. "I would like to think you consider me more than a stranger."

Her cheeks warmed under his regard. Ever since their quiet conversation yesterday on the train, she considered him less and less as a stranger. When they had first met, she thought he was an extremely attractive means to end a very unwanted engagement. Then he became a difficult though attractive means to create a passage back home. When he wasn't an ogre spouting decrees about social responsibilities, she had begun to think that a quiet life shared with him in front of a warm hearth might not be difficult.

"The more we learn about each other, the more I consider you a friend," she said, declining to admit she hoped to become more than a friend.

A smile teased his eyes and cheeks. Black hair flitted across his forehead, pushed by an ocean breeze. He looked like a repentant child. "I suppose we didn't have the best start, but we can rectify that on our trip to England. By the time we set foot in Southampton, we'll be the closest of friends."

She was about to respond that she would like that very much when he patted his jacket pockets with a sort of urgency.

"Blast. I'd almost forgotten." He produced a small box from one of the pockets and held it out to her. "I should have presented this to you earlier. Go ahead. It's a gift."

She reluctantly took the box from his outstretched hand. Although it was customary for the groom to present the bride with an intimate gift on the occurrence of their wedding, that precluded that the bride and groom actually knew each other. She hadn't anticipated anything from him and certainly hadn't had the foresight to purchase something for him in return. Her lips pulled in a tight smile. She should check with Mary; perhaps her mother had the foresight to purchase a groom's gift, although she suspected the lacy negligee qualified.

"Open it," he encouraged.

She slipped the lid from the box. "It's a locket," she said. Her words to Mary describing a gift from Bedford haunted her with its accuracy. "And a rather large locket at that."

"Yes. My aunt had it designed just for you." His voice echoed with pride. "That's an etching of the abbey on the casing. She wanted to welcome you into the family."

His aunt's enthusiasm apparently overshadowed her sense of taste. The size was more appropriate for a pocket watch than for something one wore around a fragile neck. Millstones might weigh less.

"Deerfeld Abbey has been the ducal seat of my family for centuries. I'm sure you will find it appropriate for a duchess." If Bedford was a peacock, he'd have his brilliant plumage on full display. She hid her smile at the image, but glanced back at the etching on the locket.

The house was impressive in size if the miniature did it justice. Much larger than her parents' New York and Newport residences. Surely, it would be possible to find a quiet spot to translate her stories. That thought warmed her. It wasn't a quiet barrister's estate in the country, but she could carve a quiet secluded life there. Perhaps life in England would not be as difficult as she imagined.

"The estate suffered neglect recently, but nothing that can't be remedied," he said. "Workmen are currently employed to set it to rights. We shall entertain Bertie in the manner that is expected."

Her pleasant thoughts evaporated, replaced with a low panic. "In the manner that is expected?"

"Of course." He still beamed, apparently blind to her sudden distress. "There are social obligations that go with the title. Bertie's reception is only the first. We will host dignitaries, sponsor balls, dinner parties . . ." He finally glanced at her face. "But don't worry. Trust me. I'll be there to tell you what to do every step of the way."

Her eyes widened. Just the thought of what he was proposing . . . she felt dizzy, light-headed. Appropriate words wouldn't come to her aid. She didn't want to glance up for fear he would read the panic in her face. Her mother's warning sounded in her ears. *Don't let them know how you feel.* She fidgeted with the locket clasp to hide her thoughts and the golden lid flipped open.

"That's my sister, Arianne, on the right and my aunt, Lady Rosalyn, on the left."

She stared at the pictures, as if the two faces would suddenly come to life and offer a solution to her looming dilemma.

"Lady Rosalyn, in particular, should prove of great assistance to you. She has been responsible for the running of Deerfeld Abbey for some time. She's familiar, of course, with the ton and their strict requirements. The first few dinner parties may prove awkward"—his lips turned up in a smile—"but she'll shape you into a proper English wife in no time."

"I'm not an English wife." Did she say that? Her words sounded so quiet and weak, as if she dreamed she'd spoken. Could this be a dream? A cruel sort of nightmare?

"I realize that, but now you'll have to become one." He smiled as if he were bestowing some honor upon her. "Of course, you may have to refrain from some of your colorful American attributes. English society is one of decorum and place."

Shape! Parties! Strict requirements! He might as well sentence her to a torture chamber. They had those in these old estates, didn't they? She clenched her teeth to keep her lips from trembling. That action did nothing, though, to still the shaking that moved to her hand. The heavy chain tapped against the housing.

"It's just a locket. You can put another's likeness in it if you like." He sounded unsure, uncomfortable, as well he should, for what he was asking of her. Awkward silence settled between them.

"You're looking pale," he said. "Perhaps we should return to the stateroom so you can rest. A woman in your condition—"

"My condition?" She glanced up to meet his concerned gaze. "What condition would that be?"

He glanced away a moment before offering her a tight

smile. "A woman newly married to a stranger she doesn't yet trust."

She certainly couldn't argue with that.

"I assure you, Miss Winthrop, you can trust me. I recognize that sacrifices have been made, but I am honor bound to provide for you"—he glanced down below her face—"and yours, with decorum worthy of your position." His eyes narrowed slightly. "Perhaps there is something you wish to confide? Especially as we're to be more than friends?"

His stern gaze burned into her, making speech difficult. She just shook her head, not sure what she was supposed to say.

He sighed, then removed the locket from her hand. "Let me put this around your neck." He lifted the chain rather unceremoniously over her hat and high coiffure, then dropped the links carefully on her shoulders. The heavy weight of the locket pulled taut and found a resting place at the top of her corset, protruding like an old woman's quizzing glass. "We can talk more about my expectations after you've had a chance to rest."

Rest! She was more inclined to pace the carpet till it was threadbare than rest. It was bad enough that she and Bedford had nothing in common beyond a family history of wealth. However, to put her on public display, presumably to be mocked for her American attributes seemed cruel and insulting.

What to do? She gnawed on her bottom lip, a habit her mother had tried to unsuccessfully break. What could she do now that the deed was done? Before she had agonized over living in a country of strangers. Now, it appeared that even her own husband regarded her as such an oddity that she needed to be molded into acceptability.

"We should probably find our stateroom." He turned from the rail. "Hodgins will think we have leapt overboard."

She glanced at the wide benevolent ocean. For a moment, even that alternative held appeal.

· Ten ·

"YOU AND YOUR MAID WILL HAVE THE LUXURY OF a full stateroom," Bedford said.

"My maid and I?" Fran paused in the process of removing her hat. That would make the practicing of her courtesan ways much more difficult. Given the future Bedford had outlined on the promenade deck, a quick pregnancy was now even more urgent.

"Yes. Hodgins and I will occupy the other." He shifted his gaze to her. "I thought you might appreciate the privacy."

The man was making this whole concept of procreation difficult. She never imagined she would have had to work this hard. From what she had read in Bridget's journal, men had prodded her cunny without waiting for an invitation. Sometimes they hadn't waited for her to undress. She smiled at the vernacular she was developing as a result of her study. Who knew so many colorful descriptions existed for such fundamental bodily functions?

She had learned from the journal as well that one did not necessarily have to like, or even know, the person doing the prodding. This was essential information given that last discussion with Bedford. He was not necessarily the man she would have chosen to do the prodding, but it was too late to correct that now. That he hadn't yet performed the deed suggested she had not yet shed her Frosty Franny image.

They would be on the high seas for seven days. Surely in that time she might convince him to change the sleeping arrangements.

Bedford had secured two parlor suites, which Fran gathered allowed them more spacious quarters, though spacious was a generous description. The sleeping quarters consisted of two single narrow berths on opposite walls. A table ran between them and below a large porthole. A plush chair and writing table filled one end of the room, along with a sink, a mirror, and a changing screen. The entire allotted space was smaller than the size of her private sleeping room on her father's yacht.

While she could appreciate that the addition of the public rooms—the library, the women's saloon, and the dining areas— would greatly expand their freedom of movement on the vessel, she had no intention of utilizing any room that had the word public before it. The concept gave her shivers.

A basket of fruit occupied a table, a gift from the White Star Line. A box tied with a bow sat to its side. Bedford picked it up.

"There's no card, but the box says Stewarts." He glanced up at her. "Would those be the Stewarts that were at your luncheon?"

"I believe that is mine." She retrieved the box from his hands. "I discovered I'd forgotten to pack something of importance and asked the store to ship it here."

"Forgotten to pack?" His eyes widened. "I seem to recall a great deal of transferring of boxes and trunks from your home to this vessel. What could you possibly have forgotten?"

"You suggested I rest before dinner, Your Grace. I believe I shall take your advice." She removed herself and the box to her stateroom. Mary had already laid her evening dress on the bed.

"I selected the green crepe de chine with roses for tonight. I hope that's acceptable, Your Grace. It was getting late and—"

"The box from Stewarts has arrived," Fran interrupted, tucking the box under her arm so she could remove her gloves.

"It did? I must have missed it in the unpacking."

Fran quickly disposed of the ribbon and lid. She riffled through the tissue paper. Her breath caught. The corset was like none she'd ever seen. Red sateen stripes alternated with buttery soft tan leather that covered the whalebone supports shaping the garment into sensuous curves. A wide border of delicate scalloped lace accentuated the top, emphasizing the femininity of the piece, while four metal fasteners ran down the front along the two-part busk, making the garment easy to remove without disturbing the back lacing. This was a far cry from her standard lacy white fare.

"Lord Almighty," Mary said. "Even Pauline's corset can't hold a candle to that."

"Do you think it's unforgettable?"

"I won't be forgetting it anytime soon," Mary said.

"Help me get this off," Fran said, working the buttons down the front of the blue-stripe sailing suit. Mary started detaching the basque panels. Fran glanced over her shoulder. "Excellent choice of attire, Mary."

"Did you remember to sway your hips when you went up the steps?"

"Like the pendulum of a grandfather clock," Fran replied. "Do you think he noticed?"

"I suspect he couldn't help it." Mary laughed. She unhooked the skirts and untied the half cage. Fran disposed of the bodice jacket and began to unhook her white corset.

"Can I wear the new one under the crepe de chine?"

Mary loosened the ties on the new purchase. "I don't think so, Your Grace. I selected the green because it dips so low in the front. This corset is as pretty as a picture but I think the top trim will show above the cut of bodice."

Fran fitted the new corset in place while Mary tightened the lacings behind her. Then stepped back. "Lord in heaven above, I don't think any man would forget the sight of you in that corset."

"Do you think so?" She turned from side to side, then frowned. "I'm not sure he'll see it. I think he may be disappointed with me. He rubbed his shoulder."

"That's not a good thing?"

"I've noticed he does that when something upsets him. I'm afraid that I'm the culprit this time."

"Once he sees you in that corset, I'm sure all will be forgiven."

She had her doubts. He'd had a conniption over the sight of her without her fichu. This was such a far cry from her innocent and pure white corsets, she imagined she looked quite the tart. Would he approve?

Fran began to unhook the fasteners so she could change into her evening attire. "I hope you're right." Though she had her doubts.

THE MOMENT HE SAW HER IN HER EVENING GOWN, William knew he was a lucky man to have found such a beautiful woman to make his wife. If appearances alone where all that mattered, he had no doubt that she would be invited to the finest dining salons in London. Unfortunately, appearances were only part of the criteria for acceptance. Time would tell if she could master the other skills.

As they approached the top of the grand staircase he felt her stiffen. This time he was prepared for the subtle transformation. Her gaze dulled while her posture improved. She felt distant even as her gloved arm rested on his forearm. Together, they descended the stairway into the large dining salon.

He led her past a small gathering of Americans, past the French who appeared to have already imbibed much of the ship's wine inventory, and past the English who hadn't the social credentials to warrant the Duke's preferred seating at the captain's table. They were in the midst of introductions when a familiar voice interrupted.

"Your Grace, this is truly a surprise."

The fine hairs on the back of his head stood up and took notice. The last time he had heard that voice, he'd been ducking from a rather fine French carriage clock aimed at his head. What was she doing here? He forced a smile on his face and turned.

"My dear, may I present Lady Mandrake, wife of the Viscount Mandrake."

"It is an honor, Your Grace," Lady Mandrake said, with a quick curtsy to Francesca. "I read about the nuptials in the papers, of course. How fortunate Bedford found you in the nick of time."

Francesca just smiled and nodded. If she understood Lady Mandrake's insinuation, it didn't register in her face. William fought to keep the recognition from his. Decorum was to be maintained, even when presented with a viper. Had Lady Mandrake always been this way? Or had she that mysterious changing element that he had witnessed in Francesca in a public situation?

"I was not aware you were in the States," William said, casting about the room for her husband. "Are you crossing alone?"

"The Viscount should be here shortly. I imagine the cards run hot in the smoking room."

William nodded, keeping his smile in place. While her husband's fondness for cards had proved detrimental to their finances, it had been most helpful in arranging for the occasional tryst.

A beautiful woman in the manner of a fragile English rose, Lily looked much the same as she had when he left her two months ago. Yet something had changed. She had a hard edge to her features that he couldn't recall having noticed before. Now that the two stood conversing, he couldn't help comparing his former mistress to his present wife. Francesca had a wholesomeness to her, a vitality, even in her withdrawn state, that was sadly lacking in Lady Mandrake. Strange that he hadn't noticed that before.

"I hope we shall become better acquainted, Your Grace," Lily said to Francesca, sliding her gaze toward William. "I believe we may find we have several common interests."

A chill slipped down William's back. While Lily had been most accommodating in bed, she was hardly known for her congeniality with other women. He doubted Francesca had ever encountered anyone of Lily's deviousness and would be best parted from her company.

"Perhaps we should take our seats," he said to Francesca. "We wouldn't want to keep the others waiting."

Lily placed a restraining hand on his arm. "Before you do that, sir, I wonder if I may have a private word?"

He scowled. A private word was the last thing he wanted to share, but he could hardly refuse her in such a public forum. "My wife—"

"I should be happy to entertain the Duchess until your return, sir," the captain said, offering his arm to Francesca. "I believe you've been placed to my right."

Without a word to either of them, Francesca allowed the captain to escort her to her seat, thus eliminating William's excuse to deny Lady Mandrake her request. The two walked to a deserted corner of the dining salon to continue their conversation.

"I had thought I had made my position clear at our last meeting," William hissed as soon as they were out of earshot of the other passengers.

"Now that I see the mouse, I thought you might feel differently," Lady Mandrake replied. "I admit I had hoped you'd wait until Mandrake passed away before you decided upon another wife. But I understand your need for financial backing." She looked up at him with simpering eyes. "Now that the coffers are full, I thought you and I might continue as before."

"I see no need to—"

"You know they call her Frosty Franny, don't you?" She glanced toward Francesca with narrowed eyes and a curled lip. Her hand drifted up the front of his shirt. "Now that I see her I understand. I doubt she can warm your bed the way I can."

"I repeat." He grabbed her wrist, stopping its progress. "I see no need to continue our liaisons as before. I have a wife. You have a husband. Our past is just that—past."

He turned to rejoin his wife at the captain's table, but Lady Mandrake grabbed his arm. "We have a week before us, Bedford. These crossings are known for their boredom. Should you have need for a little entertainment, I shall be available."

William shrugged off her arm, straightened his dinner jacket, and returned to the dinner table, a smile hiding his suspicion that Lady Mandrake was up to no good.

The White Star Line lived up to its reputation for fine dining with courses presented and removed with efficiency. As was the custom, William sat opposite his wife but farther down the table to facilitate conversation. A cheerful Irish chap near William proposed a toast to the newlyweds and all raised their glasses in response. Thankfully, Lady Mandrake was placed at the farthest end of the table. Francesca bent her head in conversation with the captain. William's ears pricked at the sound of her laughter. He cast a quick glance in her direction in what he hoped was an inconspicuous manner as he didn't want to draw the ire of Lady Coulton, who was describing their stay in America in minute boring detail.

Damnation. When he'd mentioned yesterday that he wanted to hear more of her laughter, he meant it to be between the two of them, not with . . . strangers. What were they discussing that held her rapt attention?

"Your Grace? Is something wrong?"

Lady Coulton's question brought him back to the conversation. "Excuse me, madam. You were saying?"

"I was observing that if you continue to stroke your chin in such a fashion, you risk removing it from your face."

Caught in the action, he lowered his hand but not without another quick glance across the table.

"I see." Lady Coulton followed his glance. "Your duchess is a lovely woman and you just newly wed." Memory lit her eyes as she sipped from her wineglass. "I remember that time with great fondness."

William smiled. He'd learned to divide women into two types, those that enjoyed sexual play and those that "did their duty." Lady Coulton appeared to be the former, and from her age, a very experienced former.

"Tell me," he said with sudden inspiration. "Is it possible, just by looking at a woman, to tell if she's with child?"

"Anxious for an heir, are you?" Lady Coulton laughed and gazed at Franny as if trying to recapture a lost memory. "I suggest you keep improving the odds. You haven't been married a month yet, have you?"

"No." He smiled. "We haven't yet been married a week." The stress of not knowing her the way a husband should had made the week feel like a year. The moment she had stepped out of her stateroom in that green dress with a neckline that angled like an arrow toward the cleft of her breasts, he'd felt his groin respond.

At first, he'd thought that his consistent immediate physical response to Franny resulted from not having been with a woman for several months. But even the laced mutton he'd noticed working in the public cars of the train last night were of little interest to him. Lily had elicited no response, whatsoever. Perhaps his fascination with Franny was sparked by her unavailability at the moment. His was the yearning that comes with denied goods. That must be it.

"It takes at least a month for the woman to suspect, and two months to be certain. Enjoy the matrimonial, Your Grace. Some women lose interest once they are on the nest."

He almost choked on his wine. He was fairly certain this did not apply to his wife. She had been begging for his services from the moment they had exchanged vows. Of course, she had an ulterior motive, that of hiding the true parentage of her whelp.

He felt a subtle shift in his gut and attributed it to too much wine. The captain stood and apologized for his early departure. He was needed in the pilothouse as the ship had turned from the coastline and had entered deeper water. Franny stood as well, which served as a signal to the other women to leave the men to their port and cigars.

"I believe I'll return to our suite," Franny advised him as she passed him. "The day has been a trying one and I wish to retire early."

"Allow me to escort you to the room," he offered with an eye on Lily. She seemed involved with the other women and did not glance at Franny.

"There's no need. I'm capable of finding my own bed," Franny replied. "Good night, Your Grace."

He watched her leave and stilled a desire to go with her. He felt the need to hold on to her company, though he wasn't sure why. It just felt comfortable, as if she balanced him in some way. Without her, he was a bit off center, the floor less firm as it were.

Lady Mandrake glanced his way and smiled in an undeniable inviting fashion. Granted in the months before he ascended to his title, he would have answered her siren's call. He'd have her skirts up with little resistance. Now, however, the attraction just wasn't there.

He wished to bury himself beneath someone else's skirts, someone who laughed at children's stories, someone temporarily forbidden. Soon though—he glanced up the staircase at her retreating back. Lady Coulton had said a woman needed two months to be certain. How far along was his Franny? Must he wait another two months? Hopefully, Nicholas would know of a faster determination. He smiled. Perhaps he should have booked their Atlantic passage with an eye toward speed and not comfort.

THE FOLLOWING MORNING, HE COULD ONLY PRAY HE was dying and would thus end his misery. The entire stateroom rose, then dropped like a rock, taking his stomach with it. The elaborate meal from the night before threatened to make a reappearance in the most undignified, disgusting manner. "Hodgins," he called, his voice hoarse and gruff. "I need the pail."

"It's right beside you, Your Grace."

Damnation! When had Franny come into the room? She should be in her stateroom, not at his bedside observing his humiliation. He pulled the sheet high over his shoulders. "Go away," he groused. "Let me die in peace."

She didn't listen. She was still there. He could sense her presence even though his eyes remained tightly shut. Perhaps it was her scent, that rarified fresh honey scent that seemed to cling to the air surrounding her. Lord, even the thought of scent made his stomach roil. He listened for the sound of her departure even while trying to hold back the foul impending spew.

"Go," he repeated. Bloody hell, where was Hodgins when he needed him? He called his name once more but the effort set his stomach in motion. He launched himself over the side of the bed, holding the sheet in place, and emptied his innards into the conveniently placed ceramic pot. Exhausted and mortified, he spit the last bit of stinking drool into the receptacle and hung limp over the rail of the berth.

A cool hand gently tugged his shoulder, helping him to turn onto his back on the mattress. He felt useless, spent, as feeble as a child and it rankled his gut.

"I suppose I should let you die here all alone. I would enjoy being a wealthy widow." Like some angel of mercy, she pressed a moist cloth about his face, removing the vestiges of sweat and sickness.

"Seasickness is common enough," she said, coaxing the hair that had fallen forward on his forehead off to the side. "More so on this northern route."

He cracked open his eyes, letting her face fill his vision. "Not for you." He should be grateful for her administrations, but he couldn't help but feel shamed by her witness to his debasement and resentment that their positions were not reversed.

"My father once told me I was born with the sea legs of a mariner." He heard a smile in her voice. "I'm not prone to seasickness, but I've nursed many so afflicted."

She removed the chamber pot to the water closet, while he tried to gain composure. He was after all a duke, although at the moment, a rather reeking, wretched, foul, disgusting duke. Now emptied, his stomach settled a bit, but the room's movement suggested the comfort wouldn't last. She returned with a freshened pot.

"Where's Hodgins?" he managed with some difficulty. Her dress had a pattern of wheels that seemed to turn with the tilt of the floor. The heavy gold locket around her neck swayed back and forth like a metronome on a piano. The combination made him dizzy and disoriented.

"Your man is similarly affected and can be of no assistance," she said. "I sent him where you should be, above deck on the steamer chairs. I'm sure you'll be more comfortable. The fresh air—"

"I can't manage to stand, much less walk. How can I go above decks?" he groused. With the bounce of the vessel, he was liable to be tossed into the ocean. He already worried about the seaworthiness of the steamer in such turbulent waters. A bit of bile touched the back of his throat. Of course, even if the hull were to crack in two, he'd never be able to navigate his way to the lifeboat.

"Save yourself," he grumbled. "I don't want you to see me like this."

"Why not?" She moved closer. A ripple of freshness radiated about her like a shield against the foul stench in the room. "You're no different than—"

"I'm a duke." His chest rose and fell in shallow breaths. "A member of the peerage, a man of dignity. I will not be seen as a sickly weakling."

He tried to sit up, but she pressed on his shoulders to lie back down.

"Rest. The strongest of men are afflicted by mal de mer, none have died as yet. I've sent Mary to check with the cook staff for some ginger wine. It'll calm your stomach."

Did she suggest wine would be a deliverance? He had thought the quantities consumed the night before were partially responsible for his current malfeasance. Was she suggesting the hair of the dog as a cure? His stomach turned again at the thought.

She pulled the sheet to his waist. He stilled, waiting for her reaction. She might need the wine to fortify herself to care for him, now that the puckered flesh of his scar was visible. Water splashed into a bowl, then squeezed through a cloth. "What are you doing?" he asked with suspicion.

She smiled. "Attempting to make you more comfortable."

Her fingers slipped around his jaw, soft, gentle, sweet; hesitating for a moment on the whorl of his chin where the hair grew the thickest. "I'd attempt to give you a shave," she said. "But I'm not sure you'd trust me with a razor."

His lips twitched at that.

"I don't think I can harm you with a washcloth."

He thought of her gentle touch and kindness in tending to him in this most vile state. He thought about how she'd just exposed his naked chest to her hungry eyes and she'd not so much as flinched at the violence marked there. He thought about her sometimes inappropriate attire, the sway of her hips, the low-cut gowns. He doubted arousal was possible on such a bilious stomach but wondered if she was so desperate for consummation that she understood that. He glanced at the inviting cloth in her hand, then narrowed his eyes. "I'm not as certain."

"Ssh . . . lie still and close your eyes," she said. "It will be easier on your stomach if you just lie perfectly still."

Fran watched as he reluctantly closed his eyes yet gripped the bed rail as if bracing himself for assault. Even in the shadows of the attached berth, she could see he was a well-formed man, with a wide powerful chest. Enticing black hair that begged to be touched obscured his masculine nipples before trailing to an area beneath the sheet. She'd noted all this before on their wedding night, but she hadn't had the luxury of a prolonged study then.

She started at the top of the nearest shoulder and dragged the damp cloth down his muscular arm, cleansing the underside. As the cloth approached the inside of his elbow, it brushed his side as well. He sucked in his breath.

"Do you need the pot?" she asked, but he carefully shook his head.

"Then I'll continue." She waited for a reaction but saw only a tightening of his jaw. She rinsed out the cloth and cleansed his hand, pausing to admire his strong fingers. She'd felt their strength when he grasped her arm, but she hadn't appreciated the flat of his palm, marked with hardened calluses—the mark of a man not afraid to work.

"I thought dukes contented themselves by flaunting their

title and looking pretty." The words fled her mouth before she thought to retract them.

His brows dived in a scowl. One eye opened a crack, honing in on her scrutiny of his hand. "You think I'm pretty?"

"Not at this moment." She smiled. No, "pretty" would not do justice for this half-naked man. "I meant that I did not expect a duke to have hands hardened by labor."

"One does what one must when there's no one else," he said. "The abbey needs repairs."

"I see."

She placed his hand palm down on the mattress so she could cleanse the back of his arm. The cloth traveled the length, flattening and straightening the dark hair with moisture. Such an intimate sensation, viewing a man thus. Always before his arm had been covered with cloth. Even when he came to her room that first night, his smoking jacket had covered this very male component. As tempting as it was to dwell on the very maleness of this appendage, she didn't linger.

"I'm going to wash your chest now." She congratulated herself on the evenness of her voice, that she didn't let the novelty and her curiosity show. He nodded hesitantly, yet she thought she saw him brace his hands.

She rinsed the cloth, then swirled it around the base of his neck, raising her knuckles just enough to feel the abrasiveness of his unshaven chin and jaw. The scrape on the back of her hand sent a tremor through her, causing her to wonder at the reaction if that scratchy chin were to meet other more sensitive parts of her body. Just the thought warmed her far more than the radiator heat on the ship.

She brought the cloth down the wide plane of his chest, over the enticing mat of black hair that flattened under the layer of moisture. Like that on his arms, the hairs lay flat and straight, revealing a pebbled nipple. It felt hard beneath her washcloth like a tiny shell of a button, but as she didn't wish him to know of her interest, she continued to the other side.

She gasped. His eye opened a crack and watched her.

"What is that burned into your chest? Who would do such

a thing?" She stared horrified at the circular scar containing a helmet and shield with much filigree.

"My father. He marked me as a remembrance to do my duty as the future duke."

"He branded you, as if you were cattle?" The thought rankled, but then she thought of how her mother had made her, as a child, endure an unnecessary and painful back brace for years just to ensure she had straight posture.

"I covered for Nicholas when he abandoned the more traditional roles for a younger son. My father flew into a rage when he learned Nicholas had left. In his anger, he knocked his crested walking stick in the fire. It wasn't in the flames long, but when he retrieved it, he did this. It reminds me that I have responsibilities to future generations beyond my own pleasure."

Horrified, she felt a sudden empathy for the young man burned in such a malicious assault. "What did your brother do when he learned what happened?"

"Nicholas doesn't know." His eyes captured hers. "And he is never to know. It wasn't his fault that my father had too much to drink that night, or that I mistakenly assumed I was safe near my own hearth."

She understood about love and betrayal when it applied to family, having experienced both. Her scars, however, were not as visible as this. Strangely drawn to the image, her finger traced the shield.

He watched her carefully, an uncertainty in his eyes reminding her of his concern about punishment in the Frog King.

"Do you think it's hideous?" he asked.

"Your scar?" Surprised at his question, she shook her head. "Unexpected . . . unique, but not hideous." She rinsed the cloth in the bowl so as to avert her eyes. The scar was not grotesque in the way he imagined, but that it still pained him, embarrassed him, reminded her of her own youth. She didn't want him to see her wince. "Parents can be such bloody idiots at times."

His eyes crinkled in a smile moments before the ship took another dip, then righted itself. Bedford gulped, before turning rapidly on his side and emptying his stomach.

"That's good," she said, helping him to his back. "You'll

feel better when there's nothing left inside." She offered him water to rinse his mouth, then went to freshen the bowl. He'd accepted her assistance easier this time, she noted.

"It wasn't this bad when I crossed to America," he said. "Just a discomfort, then."

"It won't last. We've hit a patch of weather, that's all," she reassured him. A knock on the door sounded just as she was returning with a clean bowl.

His eyes opened wide. "No one to see," he warned.

She put her bowl aside and reluctantly pulled the sheet over Bedford's chest.

Mary waited outside the door with a bottle of ginger wine, a currant wine that contained enough ginger that it was known to settle a nervous stomach.

"Excellent," Fran said. "Let me pour some for you to dose Hodgins. How is he?"

"Anxious to be standing on British soil."

"This part of the trip is always the worst. Reassure him it doesn't last."

"I did, but I'm not sure he believes me."

Fran pulled some of the deep amber wine into a glass and handed it to Mary. "This should be enough for now. I'll keep the bottle here."

Mary nodded, then left. Fran brought the bottle to Bedford's side.

"I want you to drink this," she said, deciding the best way to elevate him to drink. "It's ginger wine." Her voice took a lighter note. "British ginger wine. It should help settle your stomach."

"Can't." He grimaced.

"Trust me, in this," she said, moments before she realized she had voiced her mother's favorite expression. She bit her lip, resolved to worry about similarities another time. After pouring some wine in a glass, she set the bottle in the bracket carved in the table.

She slipped her arm beneath Bedford's head to the opposite shoulder, lifting him up. Cradling him much as one might a baby, a very large and heavy baby, she was reminded that her objective would again be postponed. There would be no courtesan practice today. She pressed the glass to his lips.

"Drink."

He sipped the sweet wine, frowned his displeasure, then sipped again.

"More," she insisted.

"Sweet," he protested, but he obeyed. He hadn't much choice.

She set the wineglass in the carved bracket, then lowered Bedford back to the pillows. She tucked the sheet around him. "Rest now. I'll return in a moment. There's a book in my room . . . it'll be something to do . . . I'll return in a moment."

He didn't think she would be gone long. It was difficult to estimate time or direction in this state. The mattress beneath him continued to rise and fall but without her hand grounding him, he felt lost. True to her word, his stomach was not reacting with the violence it had earlier, but his head couldn't distinguish up from down. He was alone, utterly alone with just his memories of his father on that fateful night. The ship creaked and moaned around him, as if the surrounding vessel itself mourned the needless suffering of a young lad trying desperately to be the man his father demanded.

Was the branding the impulsive action of a drunken duke? Or was it intentional? He would never forget the smell of burning flesh or the anger in his father's eyes that bordered on hatred for just a moment before his lips curled into a satisfied sneer.

You're the eldest. You belong to me, damn you! You will be responsible. You can never turn away. Hot metal bit deep into his shoulder. *Sacrifice. Respect.* The words echoed about him as if spoken by God himself. Once again, he writhed on the hearth rug, his shoulder in undeniable agony while his father loomed overhead. He remembered the words spoken, though now he wondered for whose benefit they were repeated. *A duke never sheds a tear.* Indeed his father hadn't. Not on that day or on any of the others that followed.

His father's scorn swirled about him, even from the grave.

What would he say about a man too sick to stir from his berth? He would laugh. He was laughing now.

William pushed himself upright. His stomach rebelled and he retched up remnants of the wine.

"Franny," he called into the dark.

"I'm here." Her voice was nearby, calming. When had she returned? When had the room gotten so dark?

Was it his imagination, or did her voice sound different—warmer perhaps, gentler than before? It was difficult to tell as so much seemed out of sorts. Her touch soothed him. He raised his hand in the dark, inches off the mattress before she took his hand in hers.

"I'm here."

He took her cool hand and pulled it to the middle of his chest, securing it with both hands.

"Don't leave me."

"I won't."

But you want to, his mind argued. *You've wanted to all along. I'm not good enough. A duke is not good enough. You love another. Randolph.* Just the thought of that name brought a surge of bile to his throat, but he swallowed rather than let go of her hand.

"Tell me a story. One of your children's stories."

"Like *The Frog King*?" she asked.

"Yes. Tell me one like that. Just talk to me. Let me hear your voice. Let me know that I'm not alone."

Fran proceeded to tell him the French fairy tale about a beautiful maiden who was given in wedlock to an ugly beast. She hadn't advanced far when she suspected Bedford had fallen asleep again. She sat quietly beside him to see if he would protest her silence, but he did not. So she sat in the dark and listened to him breathe.

The storm had eased. Here at midship, the shifting underfoot wouldn't be as troublesome as at the bow or stern. Chambers would be out of sorts for another a day, she guessed, before he was back to normal. She watched him sleeping, almost sorry that in a day's time he would no longer call out to her, or require her company for anything more than show.

For the first time, she'd felt needed—not by her father's crew hands, or the local farmers who appreciated her bee-keeping skills, or the local shopkeepers who cared for her business—but by an equal. He needed her on a personal level, as a friend. That warmed her inside. Perhaps staying in England wouldn't be so bad. It seemed she already had a friend there, which was more than she could say of Newport.

There was a soft knock at the door. Mary waited outside to advise that they were serving light meals to those that could stomach them in the dining saloon. She also asked that Fran look in on Hodgins as he was peppering Mary with questions about the Duke's situation.

Mary agreed to sit with Chambers while Fran went above deck.

THE CRISP AIR, THOUGH CHILL FROM THE PROXIMITY TO the Artic, felt refreshing and invigorating after the fetid closed air of the cabin. She'd have to get Chambers up here as soon as he was able so as to cleanse the vestiges of seasickness from his memories. She walked the length of the deck past the row deck chairs, searching the faces of the huddled bundles for one that resembled Hodgins. He spotted her first.

"Your Grace," he called. "I'm here."

She settled in a vacant chair next to his and reassured Hodgins that his duke was still alive and improving. Yes, he'd managed a bit of that magic elixir, ginger wine. No, nothing stronger than a weak tea or broth for dinner. Yes, she would advise His Grace of how desperately Hodgins wished he was up for the task of serving him at this time. She reminded Hodgins that most probably, he'd be able to tell the Duke these things himself as the pitch and roll of the decks had calmed noticeably. She also warned him that he would be covered in salt and ice if he tried to sleep above deck. Mary would return to help him go below. She was certain the Duke would be grateful for his company.

She'd left Hodgins to make her way to the dining salon for a light repast. She smiled and nodded at the travelers she'd passed without thought. Until one young man stopped before her.

"Miss Winthrop?" he asked, with a look of uncertainty. His smile broadened, though it did not reach his eyes. "Though I suppose it would be Duchess now."

She nodded, but couldn't place the man. His features struck a familiar chord, yet there was an odd maliciousness in his glance, as if she had somehow offered personal insult to the man. Suddenly she wished she was in Chambers's company. Strangers would not dare approach her with such a threat by her side.

"I'm Mr. Randolph Stockwell's cousin, Joshua Hairston. We met at a polo match in Newport about a year ago?"

Randolph's cousin! The memory returned in minute clarity. Was it only a year ago that they were together? It seemed much longer, so much had happened between that occasion and this.

"Yes, I remember," she said, relieved to discover he was not a stranger after all. "What a pleasure to see you again."

"I shall have to write Randolph and tell him how well you look," he said, disapproval still evident in his expression.

"Please extend my best wishes to him," she responded stiffly. "And to his wife."

"His wife?" Mr. Hairston's brow creased. "You must be mistaken, my cousin is not married."

A cold pall as frigid as the icy waters of the Atlantic settled over her. Not married? "I was informed by Mr. Whitby himself that Randolph had married while on assignment in Germany."

"Mr. Whitby must be misinformed. I received a letter from my cousin the day we boarded the *Republic*. He writes that he hates the weather, the people, and the countryside and he's most anxious to return home to"—he hesitated and looked at her askance—"his parents. It was not the letter of a newly married man."

She recognized that his initial impulse was to say that Randolph was most anxious to return to her. He had remained faithful while she ran off and married someone else. It was of little wonder that the cousin looked at her with such distain.

There could be only one explanation. Her mother. She knew her mother would use devious means to achieve her goals. She had accurately assumed that Fran would not have believed Alva if she were the messenger of Randolph's matrimonial vows. So she convinced her attorney, Randolph's employer, to lie on her behalf. Righteous anger built within and apparently showed on Fran's face as Mr. Hairston's disregard turned into incredulous concern.

"You believed Randolph had married?"

"I had not received letters from him for several weeks before I was so informed. I thought . . ." She shook her head, amazed at the depths her mother would go to gain a duke as a son-in-law. "I believe I have been the victim of a most serious deceit."

Was the Duke a party to her mother's game? Did he endorse the lies to ensure his place as her husband?

Hairston regarded her with something akin to pity in his eyes. "I assume it is too late, then."

"I have spoken my vows before God and the congregation," Fran said. "Had I realized that Randolph was still a bachelor, I would have . . . waited." She couldn't bring herself to say she wouldn't have married Chambers. She honestly wasn't sure what she would have done. But she was angered that she wasn't offered the opportunity of a choice.

Hairston bowed his head. "I'm sorry to be the messenger of such bad news." He started to continue on his way, but turned. "I wish you and the Duke happiness."

She hoped she'd managed to say thank you, but quite honestly, she wasn't sure she had. She stood in a shocked stupor for a few moments trying to absorb this unexpected conversation. Randolph was still available and, it seemed, still in love with her. Did it matter? The world assumed she was the proper Duchess of Bedford. Even though she and the Duke had not taken the necessary actions to produce an heir, they had exchanged intimacies that would be improper if they were not

husband and wife. Her name would be forever linked with
Bedford's, even if her heart belonged to someone else. This
certainly was a complication.

As soon as she returned to the stateroom, she retrieved her
jewel case and rummaged for Randolph's pin. It would be her
sign of defiance. Her mother may have taken away her opportunity for a quiet, uneventful future as the wife of a barrister,
Chambers may insist she become involved in the social functions he seemed to favor, but they would all know she was
participating in protest. She found the elegant honeybee and
pinned it to her bodice lapel. She would flaunt this bit of Randolph and silently remind them all of what they had stolen
from her.

· Eleven ·

HE WASN'T SURE WHAT WOKE HIM FROM A FITFUL dream. Perhaps an overabundance of sleep had finally jolted his mind awake. He'd done little else since this stomach disorder began. William cracked his eyes open, allowing his brain to register his surroundings. The porthole admitted the pale cool light of the moon, washing the too-familiar stateroom of color. The soft grays and relative stillness of the room brought welcomed relief. They must have survived the gale and moved on to calmer seas. Tomorrow, when sunlight shone through the porthole, he'd be able to test his sea legs and remove himself from this miserable cabin. The anticipation of breathing fresh air once again brought a thin smile to his lips. Perhaps he needn't wait till morning.

A soft rustle of fabric and accompanying movement pulled his gaze to the aisle between the berths.

His breath caught. An expanse of smooth bare skin, broken only by wispy tendrils of dark hair, expanded above the most provocative corset he had ever had privilege to witness, and he had witnessed a great many in his time. Medium and dark stripes cleverly curved and molded the wearer into a tantalizing hourglass shape, while black lacing down the back teased the eye as it crisscrossed through a medium stripe. She stood so close, his hand was tempted to reach and tug loose the cleverly tied knots. But he didn't, believing this to be a dream, or a figment of his earlier delirium.

Yet she seemed so real in this pale unearthly light. He clenched his jaw. This must be what happens when a man is so long without a woman. He can vividly recall an angel at will, one who encompasses the best of all mortal women he'd known. Either that, or someone had blessed him with a highly paid strumpet, one who understood the tantalizing play of color and form.

His eyes followed the captivating trail of the lacings to silk-encased buttocks. As if by his very thought, his dream mistress bent forward as if to retrieve something from the floor, the motion pushing her backside even closer for his observation. Lord, his mouth and throat dried to dust. His fingers twitched to feel the firm mounds presented so. But he didn't for fear that one touch would cause this vision to disappear and return to the dream world from which she came. His bedsheet slid down his chest, the result of his rising erection.

She stood, a printed cotton garment with a design of tiny circular wheels in her hand. She placed it on the opposite mattress where more of the fabric lay. His brain whirled much like the tiny wheels; where had he seen that pattern before?

Her shoulder blades drew back, her elbows lifted at angles to her side; he knew she was unfastening the front of that amazing corset, and he prayed she'd turn around. He ardently wished it so, hoping that as before, she would act upon his thought command. Instead, she spread the unfastened garment wide across her back, like an erotic fan employed in the finest pleasure houses. She released one side of the corset and pulled it to the front of her, leaving a thin creased chemise in its wake. Just as he was enjoying the artistry of her disrobing, the memory of the pattern clicked with shocking reality.

"Franny?"

She gasped and spun about. Shielding her chest with her discarded corset, she pulled her elbows tight about her. Her eyes grew huge in the pale moonlight.

"What are you doing?" he asked, though the answer was obvious enough.

"I thought you were sleeping," she said, looking shocked as if she'd just been caught pilfering sweets from the pantry.

"Did you, now?" he said, more as an accusation. Obviously, she was preparing to slip into his berth, and thus claim they'd enjoyed sexual congress to establish paternity for her bastard. Was there no level to which she would stoop? Did she think he would not remember such an event?

"I thought to change into something more comfortable. I've been sitting in that chair for hours." She nodded toward a chair pulled near the foot of the bed.

He followed the tilt of her chin. "You've been watching me sleep?"

He couldn't recall that chair placed just so earlier. Indeed, it would have made walking between the berths impossible, so narrow was the space. Perhaps he'd been too hasty in his supposition?

"I've been watching to see that you had no need of the bowl, and to assist you if you had."

She'd been watching him, caring for him? Guilt challenged his earlier suspicions. He knew she had cared for him earlier in the day, but he hadn't considered she'd continue the task into the night. He shook his head, in part to clear it of lingering lascivious thoughts of all he had planned to do with his dream angel. This was his wife, the last woman he wanted to think about in those terms. Damnation, whoever coined the phrase "Frosty Franny" had never seen her in that corset!

"Your ginger wine helped considerably," he managed with guilt and gratitude. "My stomach has settled for the moment."

He glanced up at her, clinging to that tantalizing contraption of lace and whalebone as if it were some bit of armor that would protect her from ravishment. Now that was a contradiction . . . if she planned to seduce him to cover the tracks of an earlier encounter, why would she cower much like a virginal miss? For that matter, why would a virginal miss wear a strumpet's corset? It was too confusing to sort through at the moment. Then a new thought entered his tangled thoughts.

"Where is Hodgins? He's not—".

"We moved him into my stateroom, Your Grace." She looked askance. "It didn't seem proper for me to spend the night confined with two men."

"I see." So in spite of evidence to the contrary, she did have a sense of decorum. It was a pleasing thought. "And Mary?"

"It is fortunate that you reserved a parlor suite. She insisted that she could make do with the divan. To his credit, Hodgins did protest displacing Mary from the stateroom, but this arrangement provided us with more freedom of movement."

"Well considered." He continued to watch her while she shifted uncomfortably. He supposed as a gentleman he should turn and face the wall. But then, as he glanced at her in abject appreciation, he *was* the Duke . . .

"Do not let me stop you from becoming more comfortable," he said after a few awkward moments.

Her eyes grew impossibly large. "You'd watch me undress?"

"I am your husband." Bloody hell, her portrayal of interrupted innocence could put Sarah Bernhardt to shame. Still, it provoked the devil in him. How far would she go before proving her lack of virtue? "Go ahead," he said. "I'm in no condition to touch you."

It was a lie, of course. Had he not just admitted that he was no longer under the effects of that earlier malady? One could question his mental acuity, though. Inviting the one woman he had sworn to resist to disrobe was beyond lunacy. His fingers tightened in their grip on the rail in some vague hope that he could honor his statement. For one touch could well be his undoing.

Perhaps a stronger man would have requested she cover herself, but such a paragon had not seen Franny in the moonlight.

She hesitated a moment, then placed the corset alongside her day dress. She presented her back to him, then lifted the creased chemise over her head. She had the most beautiful, sensuous back he'd had ever seen. Skin that glowed in the moonlight and begged for touch like a luscious velvet. His groin ached in defiance of his earlier statement that he would not touch her.

"Turn around," he said, finding it difficult to give voice to his words.

She crossed her arms over her chest and looked over her

shoulder. "You'll laugh at me. I'm not"—she glanced down, then looked back—"I'm not very big."

"Let me be the judge of that." Damnation! Why was he causing himself such misery? His cock thickened with need. He was putty in her hands. She would squeeze the seed from him with her tight little cunny and he'd forever question the paternity of her issue. But issues of forever faded with the temptation before him. He was a duke accustomed to giving orders, and she was the wife who had vowed to obey.

She turned to face him, her arms crossed over her chest, her silky pantaloons still tied to her waist.

FRAN THOUGHT ABOUT HER PURPOSE IN READING BRIDget's journal. This was the moment she'd been planning for. Bridget would have dropped her arms and shown her bosoms without thought. Yet she hesitated, suspecting it must be easier to expose one's body to a stranger than to someone you would see the rest of your life, someone whose opinion mattered, because curiously, now his opinion did. As his wife, the Duke had a right to see her as God created.

Moonlight sliced down through the porthole highlighting her midriff while keeping her face in shadow. She bit her lip, summoning her courage, then slowly, very slowly, lowered her arms.

Her breath held in anticipation, she waited for his laughter. Granted, he had seen her in that lacy bit of nothing on their wedding night, but somehow this was different. She hadn't even a scrap of lace to hide behind.

"Come closer," he rasped.

She glanced down at her paltry denizens bathed in the soft light of the moon. He hadn't laughed, but neither had he praised. Perhaps the lift of her corsets had suggested there would be more of her. Upon impulse, she placed her hands beneath her breasts, lifting them as her stays might. Her thumb strayed across a begging nipple causing a jolt of awareness to slice through her clear to her toes.

"Do it again."

His strained voice rewarded her effort, boosting her confidence. Bridget would be proud of this inadvertent stumble into seduction. She glanced down at the Duke beneath lowered lids, wishing his lips—not her thumb—brushed the sensitive flesh. "Will you not do this, sir?"

"I promised not to touch you," he fairly gritted between his teeth.

Why did he promise such a ridiculous thing? Didn't he know how she yearned to feel the rasp of his chin against her tender skin, experience the pull of his lips on her berries? That promise he'd made to her on their wedding night about knowing her taste, the alluring stories from the courtesan's journal that fascinated her with the possibilities, her father's sage advice that she quickly get with child—none of these would come to fruition if he didn't touch her!

A bit of moonlight glinted off the dark green bottle of ginger wine bracketed over his berth. The Duke had sampled a wine made of currants, yet refused her offering of berries. Her frustration sparked inspiration. What if she were to combine the two?

The brash idea slammed into her natural sensibilities causing gooseflesh to lift on her arms. She could never be so bold!

A soft inner voice chided. Frosty Franny would never attempt such artful seduction, but a courtesan trained to call attention to her best assets . . .

She hesitated, then reached for the bottle.

"What are you doing?" Bedford asked.

She bit her lip, reluctant to explain her purpose. He'd resisted her earlier attempts at seduction and might do so again. She pulled on the opening lever, releasing the ginger aroma into the cabin.

"I don't need more of that," he protested. "My stomach is fine."

She tilted the bottle, pouring a shallow puddle of the golden liquid in her cupped palm. "Is it?" she asked with a false bravado.

Quickly, before the liquid could leak through her trembling

fingers, she leaned forward, alternately pressing her breasts into her raised palm. The ginger richness coated the aching bud of each and proceeded to race down her bosom like a track of tears. She bent forward, letting the moistened nipple barely touch his lips. "Then, you may have no need of this."

With a groan, he parted his lips and suckled her, sending intoxicating waves of ravishing heat through her veins. His tongue flicked over the appreciative nipple, making her knees buckle. He let the pebbled nub go, then dragged his abrasive chin over the side of her breast until he could again nip at the extended tip. She must have gasped though she wasn't conscious of making a sound.

"Do you enjoy that, you seductive minx?"

Seductive! Pleasure flashed through her at his unknowing compliment, one far distant from Frosty Franny.

"Give me the other," he demanded.

Happy to acquiesce, she braced one hand near the side of his head for balance. Her left breast hovered inches from his talented lips, while the right, still damp and aching from his administrations, stirred the black curling hair on his chest. Her other hand found purchase by his hip, pushing the sheet farther down his form. It was an amazing sensation, having a man draw at her breasts. No wonder women of Bridget's ilk flaunted their virtues. She would be hard-pressed not to offer her berries up to Bedford's lips at every turn.

While he energetically removed every trace of ginger wine from her breast, she noticed his manhood had stretched to great proportions, enough to nudge her arm. Rising from a nest of black hair, it reached toward her, begging attention.

Fascinated, she watched. Dare she touch it? Madame Aglionby had described the male member in detail, and Bridget had applied rather bawdy descriptions to this particular appendage, but nothing she had read or heard described could compare to the fully erect flesh-and-blood member, teasing her with its demanding tip.

She shuddered, as much from the stimulation of Bedford's talented lips as from the realization that she would have to take that thick, living shaft inside of her in what could only be described as a brutal fashion. Perhaps even tonight. The member brushed her arm again but this time, she reached out her hand . . .

William's eyes nearly closed at the ecstasy. Not only was he drawing on the sweetest, most intoxicating tit in all of creation, but a cool, gentle finger said up the side of the eager cock. For a moment he imagined he was in one of the best brothels in London, then he remembered he was in a steamer berth with—his eyes widened—his wife!

"Sweet God in heaven," Bedford swore, pushing at her shoulder, to bring her upright. "We can't do this."

Perhaps it was the moonlight that gave her that soft, dewy glow. She glanced at him as if she had been similarly caught up in a dream, but then awareness intervened. She hastily stood. "Are you not well? Do you have need of—"

"My stomach is well," he said, flattered that her immediate thought was of his well-being, yet still humiliated by what she had witnessed as his nurse. "What I meant was that we cannot continue along this course." He glanced at his cockstand, still high and firm. "In a matter of moments, I'd have been grinding away at your"—he glanced up, thinking to modify his brothel language—"at Cupid's arbor."

"But isn't that what husbands do to their wives?"

If her eagerness to engage in that very activity hadn't already given away her experienced nature, then that very question would have clued her game. Damnation. He should have been the first! William took a breath, noting that his arousal was already fading. He glanced back at her, trying to learn to distrust those wide, innocent eyes.

"I shouldn't have interrupted you in your change of attire. I'm sure that after the hours spent watching over me, you're in need of rest. Be assured my needs won't interrupt you again. Good night, Franny."

He pulled the sheet and blanket to cover his shoulders, then turned on his side to face the wall, cursing himself. He should have at least kissed her good night, but in his current state that might have led to the very thing he was trying to avoid.

He'd been a fool to demand she bare herself to him. He'd been a fool to believe avoiding consummation with her would be a simple affair. He grimaced at the wall. Perhaps his father was right, he lacked the inner strength to be a duke.

She must have watched him for a few moments, as he could hear naught but her breathing. Then the soft rustle of fabric sliding over her luscious body whispered in the silent room. After a few minutes of quiet, he heard a brush pulling through her hair. He closed his eyes tight against the image. He would have performed that small chore for her. After all she had done for him, it would have been an easy task.

Even the thought of his fingers slipping through her rich strands of silk caused his cock to take notice. He cursed himself for his incontrollable lust. He was a duke, after all, and a duke needed to think with his brain and not his privates.

He waited a few more minutes until he heard her crawl into the opposite berth. The morning would be upon them soon. Let her rest for now. Tomorrow they would talk about what was proper and what was not, and perhaps he could broach the topic of her courtesan's corset. Heaven help them both if Bertie were to catch her in that attire. Since the conclusion of his affair with that Langtry woman, the Prince of Wales was undoubtedly fishing for another married woman to call a paramour. By God, that would not be Franny.

Tomorrow. Tomorrow he'd make things right.

FRAN TOSSED FITFULLY IN THE SMALL, UNCOMFORTABLE berth. It was no wonder her parents had shunned these more public modes of transportation. However, she suspected it wasn't the thinness of the mattress or the narrow width of the berth that kept her awake.

What had she done wrong? Why did he turn away?

In her journal, Bridget had detailed the acts she performed to bring her clients to a state of arousal. Fran had touched the proof that she had done the same, but somehow she'd failed to complete her mission. Once again, it came back to her. She hadn't mastered the skills other wives employed to encourage their husbands to finish the task.

That woman, the one from dinner, entered her thoughts. She'd seen the way Madame Floozy, Lady Mandrake, had regarded her husband. More important, she'd noticed the way he responded. She suspected Bedford would not hesitate to bed that woman given an opportunity. That thought made her heart twist. It shouldn't, she scolded herself. She and Bedford had been linked for financial and social considerations. It hadn't been a love match. Had it? She glanced over at his back, listening to his soft snore.

Sometimes when he spoke her name a certain way, when he asked her opinion and cared about her stories, some-times . . . she felt a yearning, a pleasure, a tingling that felt very much like what she imagined love would be. Theirs was not that easy, comfortable, and compatible relationship that she'd enjoyed with Randolph. But her relationship with Randolph never made her feel like she was soaring effortlessly above ground. Bedford had done that to her. Was that love?

She didn't know.

Silly, to think about such things. She was married to Bedford now. What was done was done. If she were back home right now, she'd go out to her hives and work out a plan. The hum of the bees was always so soothing and their industry so predictable. It was easy to influence their direction with the proper plantings and . . .

That inspired a thought.

She'd found she'd been able to influence the taste of her bee's honey by the incorporation of various plants near the hives. She and the gardener had spent many hours observing the bee's preferences. They used that knowledge in the plant-ings to modify the flavor of the honey. Her bees were selective in the pollen they carried. Some plants they visited regularly, others they shunned.

What if people were like that? What if Bedford was like that?

By careful observation of his interaction with the various women on board, she might be able to tell the qualities to which he was most attracted. She smiled. Her courtesan's journal had given her the techniques to entice the body, now she would learn how to entice his mind. Her observations would complete the puzzle. Between the two she should garner the qualities sufficient to seduce a duke.

THE NEXT MORNING, BEFORE WILLIAM TESTED HIS LEGS, he noticed the berth opposite was empty. Franny had obviously risen. He was surprised that she would brave the dining salon alone, but then—he glanced at the partial bottle of ginger wine in the bracket near his berth—his little Franny was full of surprises. The memory of her magic potion, served most ingeniously, brought a smile to his lips. Under different circumstances, a man might welcome feeling under the weather if dosed in such an imaginative fashion.

He stood, mentally bracing himself for the lurch of his stomach, but all seemed well on that front. He quickly dressed and shaved without Hodgins's assistance as he was anxious to see Franny in the light of day. From her description, Hodgins was still fairly ill. If he was still asleep, William was loathe to wake him. If he still suffered from mal de mer, sleep would keep his stomach at bay.

He went to the dining salon, expecting he'd find Franny, but to no avail. It was most disconcerting to inquire as to the possible whereabouts of one's own wife. Yet no one could assist him.

"Drink with me."

William turned to find the gentleman from Ireland, the very one who sat across from William at the captain's table, slumped in a chair nursing a partially filled bottle of whiskey.

"A toast to our surviving the voyage." The man spilled as much liquor on the table as he managed to pour into the two glasses.

"Doyle, was it?" William scowled. "It's a bit early."

"Never too early. Whiskey has saved me from the bloody sickness. It'll save you, too."

William glanced at the other passengers, who just shook their heads. "Perhaps later, right now I need to find my wife." He turned to leave.

"A toast to the Queen," Doyle roared. "No respectable duke can resist a toast to the good Queen Victoria."

He knew it wasn't wise, as he hadn't eaten in several days, but the others were watching and if he wasn't mistaken, some of his fellow countrymen had a smirk on their faces. Doyle was calling his bluff. William turned around and picked up a glass.

"God save the Queen." While his toast was echoed by Doyle and the tea drinkers across the salon, William poured the more than generous portion of fine Irish whiskey down his throat. It scorched his empty gullet before the fumes burned a path back up through his nostrils. In order to get about his business, he took several large gulps, emptying a glass that should have been consumed over a much longer period of time. He slammed the glass back on the table. "Now, let me find Franny."

He wasn't sure if it was the whiskey or returning mal de mer, but he could feel the disheartening shifting beneath him once again. He resisted the foreboding queasiness as a stern test of manhood. Instead he strode to the promenade deck; at least the fresh air would help him to escape the bilious smells belowdecks.

He saw her near the stern of the ship in deep conversation with someone he didn't recognize and his pace quickened. No other woman he'd noted on the ship had Franny's proud, straight carriage. He could pick her from a crowd, from a distance. A smile crept to his lips remembering that not so long ago he required someone else to identify her. When had that changed?

Did anyone else on the ship recognize the sensual vixen that hid beneath that dull gray dress with black trim and fringe? Playful curiosity buoyed his spirits. If he were to unfasten those black buttons on her bodice, would he find that strumpet's corset? As he neared the couple, the ship lurched causing him to grasp the rail. He noted the stranger took hold of Franny's elbow as if to steady her. She smiled at him in return.

Bile rose in William's throat while something akin to jealousy burned in his stomach. Franny was his private angel of mercy, his wife, his duchess—he surged forward—no stranger had the right to touch. Franny should reward the stranger with a slap, not a smile.

"Your Grace," she said as he neared. "Allow me to introduce Mr. Hairston. We've discovered we have some mutual acquaintances."

William extended his hand if only to ensure this Hairston fellow released his wife. "Hairston," he acknowledged.

"Your wife is well acquainted with my cousin, who works indirectly for your father-in-law," Hairston explained. "He's in Germany at the moment. I'm en route to meet with him."

Now that he could scrutinize Hairston's expression, he could see that the man posed no threat to his Franny. Yet there was something in his words that sounded a bit of a fuzzy warning in his head. No time to think about that now. The motion of the ship was taking a toll.

"Yes. Well, I hope he shall come to visit us once we're settled in Deerfeld." He glanced at his wife, at his beautiful, seductive, charming wife. "I imagine the Duchess would appreciate a familiar face from her homeland now and again."

Her face fairly lit up. "Thank you, Your Grace. I would enjoy that." She turned to Mr. Hairston. "And you must come as well. I think when one suffers a crossing such as this together, the fellow passengers become much like family."

They laughed, though William hoped Franny was not issuing invitations to the entire passenger list. There were some faces on the manifest that he would prefer not to see in the abbey.

"I wonder if I might speak to you privately, my dear," he managed, though his tongue was just not cooperating. "I believe it's time for another dose of that ginger remedy?"

Her cheeks turned the most fascinating shade of pink, even if her eyes glanced at him suspiciously.

"Remedy? You must mean for seasickness," Hairston said. "I'm told West Indian pickles mixed with potatoes settles the stomach. A Frenchman swears that oysters do the trick."

Both suggestions were having the opposite effect on William's innards. Fortunately, Hairston tipped his hat and took his leave, allowing Franny to escort him back to the stateroom.

"I should like to see how you would dose up pickles and potatoes," he said with a distinctly lecherous glance to her bosom. "I'm afraid the oysters would slide right off."

"Stop that, Your Grace." She gave him a playful push on his arm. "Someone will hear."

"I'm afraid what they will hear is the formality in your references to me," he said in sudden solemnity. "May we dispense with the formal salu . . . salu . . . forms of address? You know certain details about me of which even my brother isn't aware."

She thought of the family crest burned into his shoulder and tried to hide her grimace. Her mother was proud of the Winthrop name and exploited it at every opportunity. She even married her daughter off to a stranger to secure a title in the bloodlines, but she would never brand another as the old duke had done.

"What should I call you, Your . . . er . . ."

"William should be fine." He smiled. "Or Bedford. Or"—his smile took a more seductive turn—"my dear, my dearest, my most esteemed husband. My magnificent—"

"I'm sure I'll determine something appropriate when the time is upon us." From the scent of his breath, he'd already sampled a bit more than the ginger remedy. Although she didn't approve of drunkenness, she rather liked this less rigid, less formal side of him.

"And I'll continue to call you Franny."

"Perhaps Fran," she said. "I'd prefer Fran. The other reminds me of a name I'd prefer to forget."

"Frosty Franny?"

She stopped her forward progress. "You know about that?"

He looked up and down the corridor, then slipped his arms about her waist, pulling her close. He nuzzled her ear, then murmured, "If it were true, this voyage would be a lot easier."

He stepped back, grinning like one of her mother's Pomeranians, then took her elbow, much as Hairston had done, and started her moving again.

She looked at him askance. What on earth did he mean by that? Did he want her to be cold and distant? Perhaps he had heard of that seasickness remedy that called for ice in an India rubber bag applied to the spinal cord and somehow imagined a frosty wife would be the equivalent. She sighed. Was it even possible when a man was in his cups to determine wit from wisdom?

They arrived at the stateroom. Fran immediately retrieved the ginger bottle, then turned around to find Bedford had followed close behind and, in fact, was backing her into the table.

"That's a lovely bee pin you have there." He started to unbutton her bodice.

Dear heavens, what was she to do now? Being undressed by a man in front of a large porthole with streaming daylight felt extraordinarily decadent. Did he truly plan to lap the wine from her breasts at every interval? Heat rose to her chest along with a yearning that he do just that.

"It . . . it was a gift," she said, as his hands neared the final button. What a delicious feeling to have another remove one's clothes with unbridled urgency. She couldn't recall that cited in her journal. Bridget never described details of the disrobing that Fran could recall. Both parties seemed to magically divest of clothing.

"Yes. I know. But the jeweler forgot an important component of the pin." He yanked the bodice back exposing her corset to his view, setting the wine to slosh in the bottle. "He forgot the crescent."

She had to admit this method of divesting of one's attire might not be ladylike, but it definitely set her insides to tingling. Her breasts seemed to swell with his gaze and a primitive sort of yearning throbbed at the juncture of her thighs. Bedford stepped back to survey his handiwork. "Now this," he said, "is a gift."

A smile twisted his lips and an image from the journal slipped to her mind. His lips, her juncture . . . a delicious shiver jolted through her. She reached for a bed rail for support.

His brows knit together and he helped her regain her balance. "Are you well? Has the mal de mer affected you?"

She shook her head, too embarrassed by the train of her thoughts to give them voice. "I just lost my footing for a moment."

"Pity, I had thought I would have to dose you. If my stomach weren't staging a revolt, I think I know of a fairly imaginative method to serve you ginger wine." He glanced down his front to his trousers.

Dear Lord and all the saints in heaven! Between the acts described by the journal and her chance encounter last night with the anatomy hidden by those trousers, she had a fairly good idea of the basis of his suggestion. From the heat engulfing her, she was probably as red as the stripes on her "unforgettable"—the likes of which he seemed to be memorizing, based on his lascivious stare.

"Do you require this ginger, sir?" she asked, the edge of the table pressing in just under her bustle. "Or was that merely a prevarication for removing my bodice?"

"Don't turn round," he grinned in a most appreciative way. "My Frosty Franny could melt the icebergs with that corset."

Now he was just teasing her. Her face cooled, a steady heartbeat returned along with a bereft sense of loss. It was bad enough when the papers made fun of her, but this hurt so much more. "I think you should lie down, sir."

"William," he said, moving forward, not back. "Say it."

"If it will assist you into your berth, Will—"

She didn't finish as his mouth crushed down on hers, transferring some of the intoxicating whiskey vapors from his tongue to hers. His arms slid up the back of her bodice, pulling her close. She gave herself up to him, letting him know how much she wanted this, how much she wanted him. No man had made her burn in this fashion. She wanted to experience it all.

He broke the kiss, but pulled her head to his shoulder. "Franny, Franny . . . I should have been the first. If you hadn't a babe growing in your belly—"

She pushed her head back. "A what?"

"A baby . . . that's why your mother arranged for a quick wedding, was it not?"

Her face screwed up. "I'm not with child."

He scowled. "But what of your lover, Randolph?"

She almost laughed at his insinuation that Randolph was her lover. She was fond of him, but he certainly never did anything to elevate that fondness to love. In fact, enticing Randolph to become her lover was the whole purpose behind securing Bridget's journal.

She wanted to laugh, but based on the deep crease between his brows in his scowl, she rather expected he wouldn't appreciate the irony. "I'm virginal, sir."

He stepped back and pointed an accusatory finger at her midriff. "That is not the corset of a virgin."

She glanced down at her unforgettable. "It's not white . . ."

"And you know things . . . Bloody hell, Franny, you do things that a virgin should not know how to do."

She didn't have a great response to that. She did know things, but it wasn't from firsthand experience. If she showed him the journal, she'd have to explain why she had it, and the accusations against Randolph would continue. It was better to say nothing.

He launched himself into his berth and covered his eyes with his arm. "I knew you'd say you weren't pregnant. I knew it. It's in your best interest to deny your . . . your indiscretion."

"Indiscretion?" His accusations raised her temper. "You think I'd be so shameless as to give myself to a man not my husband?"

"You're a passionate woman." His eyebrow raised with his statement of fact.

She stood awestruck. He clasped her hand in his, massaging small circles with his thumb. "Franny . . . my dear, dear Franny . . . I'll raise the child as my own, but this is too important to ignore. I must know the paternity of my heirs. If you'll just admit to carrying another's child, we can be as husband and wife. I want to be as husband and wife."

There was nothing she could say in her defense. She wasn't even sure if in his present state he would recognize her innocence. She'd heard that avid horsewomen sometimes don't bleed their first time. She certainly qualified as a horsewoman. So if she didn't bleed, how could she vindicate herself?

"You think I'm a whore?"

"Not a whore . . . not exactly." He glanced pointedly at her corset. "But if one were to judge by looks . . ."

She placed the bottle of ginger wine next to him before hastily buttoning her bodice. "You—can—not—judge a book by its cover. Good day, Your Grace."

She turned on her heel and left him to fend for his drunken—no good—uppity—branded self.

· Twelve ·

WHAT SHE WOULDN'T DO FOR A NEARBY HIVE OF bees. She stomped her way to the empty ladies' saloon, the only place she felt safe should Chambers try to pursue her. She wished she could decry his logic, but it all made perfect sense. Naturally, it would take a foreigner to believe that the very woman whom the rest of America knew as cold and dispassionate was, in fact, a desperate demimondaine. With the help of her courtesan journal, she'd certainly acted the part well and oh so convincingly.

When she thought of how proud she was when she "forgot" her fichu and encouraged Bedford to notice her breasts . . . she sunk her head in her hands. What a fool! What a childish, silly fool. What little pride she had left after her mother sold her as a wife, she freely gave away to be a . . . harlot. It's a good thing that alcohol had loosened his tongue enough to tell her of his suspicions, for who knows to what depths she would have descended in her pursuit of his affection.

Tears burned in her eyes. She held a balled handkerchief to her lips to keep the sobs from emerging. Such a fool!

One of the housekeeping stewardesses entered the saloon to see if it needed cleaning. Fran gave instructions for clean sheets to be delivered to the two staterooms. There was no way she would sleep in the same room with that man. He'd accuse her of tempting him, the absurdity of it all.

If she was pregnant, wouldn't there be noticeable signs by now? That put her in a quandary. She'd never really been around a pregnant woman before. Although she knew that as a child grew, so did the woman's belly, but she had no idea when this actually occurred.

But it would occur. She grasped on to her righteous indignity. When Bedford realized that no child grew within her, he'd come to reason. He'd recognize the error of his ways and humbly beg for her forgiveness. Well . . . perhaps not humbly . . . she couldn't imagine Bedford ever being humble—not in public, at least.

She'd bide her time, keep her distance, and let him feel all the chill that Frosty Franny could muster. In the meantime, she'd entertain herself by contemplating just the right act of contrition she'd require of him to return to her good graces.

"Oh, I hadn't expected to find anyone here." The distinctively accented voice of Lady Mandrake broke the comforting silence of the room. "I most certainly didn't expect to find our new blushing bride."

Fran sniffed and pasted on a smile. "I was just leaving."

"Please stay. I had hoped we could get better acquainted—you've been crying!" Instantly Lady Mandrake was by her side, pushing her to sit on the upholstered circular bench in the center of the room. "Has he done something to you? Bedford can be such a beast." Using her own handkerchief, she dabbed at Fran's eyes. "You poor dear. You can tell me anything. I've been married so long I've seen it all."

"Bedford has done nothing wrong," Fran said. "He's been a perfect gentleman." Fran gulped air trying to pull her emotions under control. How embarrassing to be caught in such a vulnerable position by this stranger. Her mother would certainly disapprove.

"Has he now?" Lady Mandrake said with a decided gleam in her eye. "Is that what has you upset? Sometimes a woman prefers a little cad in her man. It can be fun when it's a little rough. Believe me, I know."

Although Fran wasn't sure what "a little rough" meant, it didn't sound particularly pleasant, nor did it sound particularly appropriate given that they barely knew one another. She looked at "Bedford's old friend" askance, sensing another purpose behind the woman's words.

"I haven't seen him since that dinner the first night. He's not"—Lady Mandrake smiled—"indisposed by the rocking of the boat, is he?"

Fran remembered how insistent Bedford was about not letting anyone see that he was ill. It seemed a ridiculous concern to her at the time, but if Bedford wanted to perpetuate the perception that he was never ill, who was she to ignore his wishes? She straightened her spine. "Bedford and I are recently married. Neither of us have been outside our stateroom for long periods." She dabbed at the sides of her nose. "I'm sorry you caught me in a foolish bout of homesickness. I trust you will be discreet. However, I must return now to my husband."

Fran shook out her skirts and walked to the door. Yes. A hive of angry bees would certainly have been handy.

MUCH TO WILLIAM'S CHAGRIN, HODGINS MOVED BACK to share his stateroom. No longer would Franny be at his beck and call, to soothe his chest with cooling sponge baths, or to entertain him with children's stories when he was bored. Who would have thought that one rather full glass of whiskey could do such damage?

At least the truth was out between them. She knew that he knew so there'd be no more need for her delightful tricks to seduce him. Even though that was a depressing thought, part of him accepted that it was all for the best. They would both just watch to see what develops.

But what if he were wrong? What if she truly was a virgin? Banish the thought, a part of his brain—the part that had gotten him through a rocky youth to respectable manhood—shouted. If he was wrong, he'd simply buy her a bauble—he could afford to do that now—and all would be forgiven. Granted, she was American, and heaven knew those people had some strange suppositions. Once she was in England and found the way of it, she would surely understand how important issues of paternity were to the landed gentry.

He debated going to dinner. While nourishment might have some beneficial effects relating to the whiskey, his stomach and food had not been cooperating partners of late. Reluctantly, he dressed for dinner with Hodgins's limited help just for the opportunity to see Franny again. He knocked on her stateroom door and Mary advised that they were eating in, thank you so very much.

In the end, he sent Hodgins to the kitchen to rustle some bread as that was all William figured their stomachs could handle.

ON THE FOURTH DAY AT SEA, BOTH HE AND HODGINS felt much improved. The ship had traversed into calmer waters, and they could stand and walk without a threatening roll in their stomachs.

Finally able to emerge from the prisons of their berths, many of the passengers rediscovered the optimism and joviality they'd shared that first day of the voyage. William headed to breakfast in hopes Franny would be there as well. She was not.

He tried the promenade deck, again full of walking, smiling, happy passengers. But no Franny.

On a hunch, he checked the library, and there she was, bent over one of her books, writing in a journal of some sort. She was the only one in the cavernous room. The rest of the passengers were too busy enjoying the novelty of fresh air.

He imagined the Paris designer responsible for her intensely violet dress never intended it to be worn in such a studious endeavor. Yet the designer could not have picked a more advantageous model. Even the trims suited her as she was a woman of many unusual contrasts herself. He tried to be quiet in his approach, but as the room was empty of all save Franny, his addition was bound to be noted. She glanced up, frowned, and went back to work.

"Franny, I'm sorry," he said. "I didn't mean to hurt you."

She never stopped writing. "That's considerate of you, sir. Most gentlemen wouldn't show that kind of compassion for a common trollop."

"I don't think you're a trollop, Franny, and I certainly don't think of you as common. This is just too important for uncertainty. You can see that, can't you?"

She put her pen down and glanced up. The hurt he saw in her large brown eyes wounded him deeply. "Yes." She sighed. "I understand how important this seems to you. It's part of the reason I moved out of the stateroom, even though I am your legal wife."

That small concession lifted his spirits. "As your legal husband, may I request that we continue to take our meals together?"

She raised a brow.

"I would say this is necessary to maintain proper appearances, but the truth of the matter is . . . I rather miss your company."

Compassion flooded her at the sincerity in those last words. He shifted his weight uncomfortably as if her answer really mattered. That in itself was a novelty—that her opinions mattered to anyone.

"I will join you for meals if you come to call at my stateroom."

"Agreed."

She nodded acceptance and returned to her translations, but he continued to stand by her side even though the topic had clearly been settled. She glanced up at him. "Was there something else?"

"As a matter of fact, there is." He pulled a chair over to her side. "Franny, we still need to review and practice the lineage information." He held up a hand to still her rising protest. "I know this is not something you want to do. I realize the lines of my ancestry are not as exciting as your children's stories, but believe me, this information will be of crucial importance once we reach England. You will appreciate having spent the time studying it."

At least, this time he phrased this boring assignment as a request rather than a demand. On that basis alone she was inclined to agree. But something else bothered her and as he seemed in a cooperative mood . . .

"Tell me," she said. "You mentioned something about my bee pin yesterday."

"Yes." He scowled slightly as if confused. "I said the jewelers forgot the crescent, why?"

"Crescent?"

"Yes, a bar that would signify the crescent moon." He slipped his fingers under the wings of the bee pinned to her gown. "To be quite honest, I was surprised to see it on your bodice. I had supposed that it failed to be delivered before our departure."

"Then you commissioned it?" she asked, just to be certain.

"Of course." He smiled. "It's to symbolize our honeymoon. Normally, such a pin has a flower and a moon, but given your interest in these pesky little insects, I commissioned a bee. I must say"—he tilted his head in a critical fashion—"it turned out quite well, didn't it?"

She wasn't even sure he'd known of her interest in bees, and yet he knew enough to commission a unique pin, just for her. Her fingers sought the pin. She had worn it as a protest and now discovered it signified acceptance of the very situation she was protesting. She had thought the elegant pin was the creation of a poet, someone with superior taste and grace, all attributes she had assigned to Randolph. Now she wondered if those same attributes truly belonged to Bedford. Her head swam with the irony of this entire phase of her life.

"I think you're correct that I require additional information," she said, wondering what other attributes had she seemingly missed about her husband. Earlier she had little interest in learning all his connections, and the forced memorizations seemed more tortuous than necessary. Perhaps the shortened time available before she was to actually meet some of the names in that tome affected her logic. Or perhaps she was developing a different sort of appreciation for a man who noticed the small things about her, but suddenly she was curious about how his family . . . now her family . . . fit into the puzzle of British society.

A smile lit his eyes and she found herself to be smiling in

response. Something passed between them, perhaps a recognition and an appreciation for the other. A warm current infused her, like a fine tea slowly staining heated water.

"Excellent," he said. "But there is one other problem. This library is not the best place to review this information. It may be empty now as everyone is enjoying the sunshine that they'd been denied to date. However, as I recall from the passage over, this novelty will pass, the ennui will set in, and this room will be occupied by any number of passengers."

"Why would that be a concern?"

The smile turned wry. He studied his hands as if reluctant to continue.

"Perhaps there are dark sheep in your family that you don't wish to publicly acknowledge?" she teased, partly to bring the erstwhile smile back to his face. "Murderers, smugglers, robbers, and thieves, we all have family members we'd prefer not recognize."

Her strategy didn't work, his lips tightened. He was obviously uncomfortable with the topic at hand. "I'm sure we have all those and more. That, however, isn't my concern."

His solemnity tempered her enthusiasm.

He reached over and took her hand in his. "Franny, you know that if circumstances had been different, we might never have met, much less married." One corner of his lips twitched up. "I must admit that even if we hadn't married, I'm glad that we met. I've never known anyone quite like you."

That cup of tea was staining darker and darker. A low tingle started in her rib cage.

"If I married under normal circumstances, then my prospective bride would be presumed to already know those things I'm asking you to study. Not to know these relationships invites hurtful criticism and misrepresentation for both you and me."

"I understand that but—"

He squeezed her hand. "There are those, even aboard this vessel, that would use the occasion of our studying against us. As proof positive that you are not suited to be the wife of a duke."

He didn't mention a name, but the image of Lady Mandrake popped into her mind. Yes. She could see that such preparations should be handled privately.

"Of course." She glanced up at him. "Where do you propose we study?"

"Either your stateroom or mine, it matters not. Now that we both understand the restrictions surrounding our behavior, I'm sure we'll be able to manage responsibly."

She nodded again, a bit more hesitantly. The "restrictions surrounding our behavior" part of his speech dredged up memories that he still considered she was lying regarding her intimate history. The tingling stilled and her imagined cup of tea turned cold. "When would you like to begin this review?"

"We could begin today after the midday meal."

She agreed, but still he didn't leave. He glanced at her written pages.

"Is this the story of the beautiful girl who is forced to marry the beast? The one you told me about when I was ill? You never told me how that ended."

"I haven't decided yet, it's still something of a work in progress," she said. "I've found several different adaptations of the same tale with different endings. I haven't decided which ending will work best."

He looked pensive, so she continued. "I'm working on something else. It's called 'Ash Girl' and was written by the Brothers Grimm. I'm afraid they tend to have a rather nasty ending to their stories, so I may need to change this ending as well."

"Can you tell me about it? Perhaps I can help?"

So she told him the story of the ash girl as per the German text and he listened intently. She returned the favor that afternoon when they met in her stateroom parlor.

The remaining days on the *Republic* continued in a similar fashion. They discussed fairy tales and lineage, art and architectural—subjects she noted William to be particularly knowledgeable about—and beekeeping as a vital component of agriculture. Without the stress afforded by trying to seduce Bedford at every turn, she found him to be intelligent, well mannered, and often humorous.

Her plan to observe the women to which he seemed attracted did not provide any additional information. He seemed to focus his energies entirely on her.

Sometimes she'd catch him observing her with a peculiar expression, as if he wondered if she still wore her brightly striped corset beneath her high-neck dresses. The thought made her smile. Perhaps her "unforgettable" had lived up to its purpose after all. He escorted her at mealtimes, and she found that with him by her side, she began to relax more in the presence of strangers.

They laughed often about minor considerations. Throughout the day they indulged in friendly discourse, but in the evening without so much as a kiss, they reluctantly parted in the hallway outside their staterooms.

FINALLY, ON THE SEVENTH DAY FROM LEAVING PORT IN New York, they arrived at Southampton port. Even though Fran had initially not wanted to move to England, the prospect of solid ground made her mouth water.

She stood at the rail with Bedford and the other passengers to watch with great anticipation the misty lump on the horizon grow first into a full vista, then into the colorful, busy docks.

He placed his hand above the horsehair bustle tied at her waist. The heat of his touch warmed her through her many layers in a different way than the fierce sun overhead. Did he step closer or did she? Either way, his close presence comforted her jittery nerves as she glanced out at the foreign country that would be home for a few years at a minimum.

She had to admit that prospect was not as distasteful as before—now that she had learned that Bedford was not the beast that she'd envisioned. Of course, he was only one in an entire country of strangers.

"Is there someone waiting to greet you?" she asked, knowing for a certainty no one waited for her.

Ropes as thick as her arm swung out from the vessel to secure the *Republic* to the dock. The wharf swarmed with activity, like bees on a comb.

"This isn't the end of our journey," he said. "Deerfeld Abbey is north of London in Bedfordshire. The luggage will be hauled by a freight company, but we'll take the train. It's the quickest way home."

Lord, she was weary of travel. She believed her soul groaned, she just hadn't anticipated that it would be audible. "Mercy," she said. "I had hoped to sleep in a bed that doesn't move and in a room that doesn't moan."

She tilted her head to see his face. Fine creases fanned out from the corners of his eyes.

"I thought you were born with sea legs?"

"One does not sleep standing up."

His smile deepened a moment before his expression shifted. He held her gaze. "Sometimes one doesn't sleep at all."

They connected in that moment in words not spoken but deeply felt, words about unquenched desires, reluctant separations at one's stateroom door, revisiting memories of ginger wine. His head bent closer as if to kiss her—there in such a public venue—without care or concern for the appropriateness of such an action. Her eyes slipped shut, a willing accomplice to need and desire.

"Bedford," a familiar woman's voice called from behind. The moment was lost. Fran's eyes shot open as they both turned to see Lady Mandrake and her aged viscount. Fran offered her noncommittal smile.

"Mandrake." Bedford nodded. "You're looking a bit indisposed. Did the crossing not agree with you?"

"Worst crossing ever," the old man grumbled. "Now I'm stiff in all the wrong places, if you catch my meaning." He shifted his rheumy gaze to Fran. "This must be the new Duchess I've heard so much about."

Bedford handled the introductions.

"Will you be staying locally for the night before continuing?" Lady Mandrake asked, her eyes trained on Bedford.

Fran looked up at him hopefully. If her will alone could persuade his speech, his lips would mold into the word, *yes*.

She studied his face, waiting for his answer. He hesitated and held Lady Mandrake's glance. The overlong moment hung in the air, making her realize another form of communication had transpired.

"No," he said with a conciliatory glance at Fran. "I'm afraid we shall need to return to Deerfeld Abbey rather urgently. We'll go directly from here to the train station."

As disappointing as the prospect of more transit was to Fran, if she wasn't mistaken Lady Mandrake appeared flummoxed as well. Fran's eyes narrowed. There was something irritating about that woman, something akin to a stinging insect that always avoids the slap.

"Deerfeld Abbey is rather large." Bedford's brows took an apologetic tilt, taking some of the sting away from his refusal. "I'm sure we shall be able to carve out some private time there amid a busy schedule. Beside the fact that once we arrive at Deerfeld, we won't need to board a train or streamer for an extended period."

Fran sighed. "There is that."

To all, they must seem the perfect couple, and in a sense they were. However, in a most important sense they still weren't. The marriage had not yet been consummated and she still hadn't been able to convince Bedford of her lack of experience.

"Bully for you, Bedford. Your new duchess is a beauty, she is. Getting heirs on her won't be a hardship." The viscount laughed at his own wit. Bedford's smile tightened.

Fran glanced over her shoulder. "I believe they've lowered the ramp. Perhaps—"

"By all means," the Viscount interrupted. "Never been so sick on a crossing. Can't leave this steamer too soon. Come along, dear." He pulled on his wife's arm.

But she firmly stood her ground. "I'm so pleased we had occasion to meet again," she cooed to Bedford. "I'm sure we shall see you and your lovely American wife soon."

Fran had the impression that she'd just been insulted. The

woman made her nationality sound distasteful, perhaps much the same way her father made British sound fastidious.

Fortunately, the Viscount won the tug of war and both Mandrakes departed. Bedford watched after them, or was he watching the pronounced sway of Lady Mandrakes's bustle? A trace of discomfort stirred Fran's brain.

"Are you similarly as anxious as the Mandrakes to leave this confounded ship?" he asked, a brow raised.

"Yes," Fran replied, frowning at the audacious bow draped across Lady Mandrake's derriere. She stifled an urge to use the point of her fashionable parasol in an inappropriate manner. "But let's wait a little bit."

EVEN THOUGH THEY TRAVELED RESERVED CLASS ON THE train, it was not the luxurious conditions they had experienced in the private car in America. William could see that the lengthy trip to Deerfeld was taking a toll on Franny. Guilt burrowed in his gut. They could have stayed over in Southampton. While there was an inherent urgency to return to Deerfeld Abbey, a day's delay would not have mattered. The lure of a stable bed sat heavy with him, but that was part of the problem.

To maintain appearances of a newly married couple he would have had to reserve one room for both Franny and himself to share. After a week of fantasizing over striped corsets and ginger-coated breasts, he was likely to make that bed rock with a need fueled by her sensitive smile and engaging laughter. His resistance was wearing thin and in need of the discipline of separate bedrooms.

So they endured a hurried transition from ocean steamer to train, leaving much of their luggage behind for Mary and Hodgins to oversee and arrange delivery. Upon their arrival at Deerfeld's train station, they found the village had turned out with flowers and speeches from local dignitaries. He was beginning to recognize the signs of Franny's transition into her aloof public visage. He smiled, feeling privileged in his knowledge that the private woman was nothing like this cold, distant public apparition that smiled vacantly and nodded at the villagers.

He recalled her hesitation when she first saw the family crest on the carriage that was to deliver them to the abbey. Did it spring from a hesitancy to continue on in the tiring journey, or did it spark a memory and revulsion of his scar? Bedford mentally cursed his father once again for his drunken cruelty, but this curse, like the many that had gone before, would not change the past. He'd long ago resigned himself to the existence of the brand. In time, he hoped Franny would as well.

Franny had fallen asleep in the coach, her head nodding against his shoulder with the rhythmic gait of the horses. He was hesitant to wake her, but they were drawing near to the abbey.

"Franny, we're almost there," he said, gently prodding her awake. "I'd have liked for you to make your first sighting of the abbey in daylight, but it can be a welcoming sight in the light of a full moon."

She blinked rapidly before pulling herself upright and away from his shoulder. His aching shoulder registered relief at the removed weight, but he would have gladly suffered additional hours of the strain. It was unlikely he'd have the pleasure of Franny's sleeping head on his shoulder anytime in the near future.

"Where are we?" she asked with a yawn.

"Do you remember how I told you that Deerfeld Abbey was built atop the foundation of a twelfth-century Cistercian monastery?"

She nodded. "King Henry VIII confiscated the monastery after the abbot was found guilty of treason."

"Very good." He smiled his approval before pointing at the window. "We're on the lane approaching the gate. Do you see that oak tree?"

She followed the path of his finger, past the dark silhouettes of trees and hedges to one tree that stood a bit taller than the rest. She nodded.

"It's said that's where the abbot, Robert Hughes, is rumored to have hanged."

It seemed a tree like all the others, but suddenly took on a sinister bent. "Is the abbey haunted?" she asked.

"I suppose that depends on who you ask."

The iron gate was drawn back, indicating their arrival was anticipated. The carriage followed the dirt path that wove past some farm buildings and what appeared to be a stable. The carriage rolled effortlessly across a wooden bridge. Bedford smiled, obviously pleased to be home.

The ground was flat and grassy, dotted with trees and—she squinted—deer, some of which lifted great racks of antlers, curious, no doubt, about the evening interlopers. The great Palladian mansion, bleached white in the moonlight, loomed before them. Though torches flared near the doorway, and a few rooms within emitted a muted light through the windows, the building seemed cold and unwelcoming. She shivered more from the ominous sight than from the temperature.

"Will we live here year-round?" she asked hoping that this abbey, like her Newport cottage, would be utilized only a few months of the year.

"We have a London house," he said, "that I use in the winter." The carriage slowed and began a slow turn in front of the entrance. A door opened and uniformed staff poured out.

She noted the transition from "we" to "I" without comment. Her father often lived away from her mother and herself, presumably for business purposes, but there had been whispered rumors as well. Did Bedford maintain his London house as a vehicle for pleasure or commerce, or both? An unease settled over her as she remembered Lady Mandrake's question on the *Republic* and the awareness she saw flash between them. Was he planning to stow Frosty Franny at this country estate, while he satisfied his urges in London?

She winced. Perhaps she put away her courtesan's journal too soon.

The household staff had formed a double line that extended from the carriage to the doorway. Good Lord, there must be forty men and women standing in those two lines. What could they all possibly do?

"They should be in bed," Fran said, firmly ensconced in the comforting confinement of the carriage. "Their day starts earlier than ours. What are they doing?"

An older man made his way toward the carriage door. "They wanted to show respect for their new mistress," Bedford said, apparently surprised at her question. He took her hand. "Franny, don't be afraid. Trust me."

Those two words again. She fought her immediate instinct to recoil.

"Just think of it as meeting one person, for one moment, then another. You can meet one new person, can't you? I'll be there by your side."

Their driver opened the carriage door then pulled down the steps. Bedford exited first, then turned to assist Fran from the carriage. Ducking so her ostrich plumes could clear the doorway, she stepped out to meet her new household staff.

There were so many of them! As one they began to clap. What an odd tableaux they must make for the deer, standing and clapping in the moonlight.

"Carruthers," Bedford turned to the older gentleman, "allow me to present the new Duchess of Bedford."

"Your Grace," the butler bowed. "It shall be my pleasure to serve you at Deerfeld Abbey."

"My brother?" Bedford asked.

"He arrived yesterday, sir, and awaits your pleasure in the library. Lady Rosalyn, however, has retired for the evening. She has asked me to convey her regrets and disappointment that you did not arrive during the daylight hours. She says she will meet your bride in the morning, sir."

She noted Bedford's quick frown. She wasn't sure why he'd be disappointed that at least one person had the good sense to retire.

Carruthers led them forward and one by one the servants bowed or curtsied and wished her welcome. Fran's discomfort dissipated by the second greeting. She glanced back at Bedford and he nodded her forward. He was correct. As long as she approached each person as an individual, she managed without having to convince herself she was elsewhere.

They entered into a spacious foyer. Moonlight from windows on the upper level illuminated a wide staircase. Many paintings in gilded frames covered the walls. These must be the faces that accompanied the names she'd studied on the *Republic*. She'd have liked to study them, but Bedford was quickly leading her down a hallway.

"William!" An almost exact duplicate of her husband rested a hip on a George IV library table while he poured an amber liquid into a glass, a duplicate of a similarly filled glass by his side. She guessed by the walls of books that this was the library. She'd have to be careful marking the way back so she could find her way here again.

Bedford stood, tall and straight, a smile pulled at his lips. "Francesca, I'd like to present my brother, Lord Nicholas Chambers."

"It is indeed a pleasure to meet you, Your Grace." He straightened and offered a curt bow. "Allow me to welcome you to the Chambers family."

Fran curtsied, amazingly comfortable in this man's presence. There was something about his easy charm that put her instantly at ease. "I'm most pleased to make your acquaintance, sir. Your reputation precedes you."

He looked startled. For a moment, she thought she had inadvertently insulted him.

"As an artist, Nick. She's familiar with your paintings," William explained.

"That's reassuring." Chambers's lips curled into a lazy smile that reminded her so much of William she felt a bit giddy. "I was afraid Emma would have my head, otherwise."

"Emma came?" William asked. "I thought she might still be avoiding me after that . . . er . . . misunderstanding."

"Yes, she's here. She wanted to welcome the new Duchess properly but when I caught her nodding off to sleep I suggested she find her bed. As to her forgiveness," he said, sipping from his glass, "I suspect she also wished to offer condolences to your dear wife."

She looked to William for an explanation, noticing his smile faltered every so slightly. There was a story there, but she would not ferret it out tonight. She was just too tired.

A groan issued from the vicinity of the fireplace. She thought at first she'd discovered the answer to her question about ghosts. William smiled. "And that would be Spotted Dick, my dog."

She peeked around a chair and noted a long brown/gray beast covered with spots like freckles lying before the cold hearth. Like a lion to a kitten, this dog was to her mother's Pomeranians. The beast lifted its head, thumped its long, thin tail on the ground, then lay back down. "That's a dog?"

"Dick is a mastiff, an old mastiff." William patted his leg and the dog reluctantly pulled its body from the hearth and slowly advanced toward Fran. He was so tall, she could scratch between his ears without bending, and did so. The dog's jowl dropped and he panted in contentment.

"I believe your wife, Lord Chambers, has the most sense of the lot of us," Fran said. "I would gladly leave you to your brandy if I knew the way to my room."

William tugged on a tasseled cord. The butler appeared at the door moments later.

"Could you show the Duchess to her room, Carruthers? My brother and I have some concerns to discuss."

"Certainly, sir. Perhaps Her Grace would enjoy a hot bath after a long day of travel?"

"It's not too late? I shouldn't want to trouble anyone," Fran said, thinking of how wonderful a hot soak would be.

Carruthers frowned. "Serving you is to be our pleasure, madam. Do not think another second about it."

She turned to Nicholas. "It was a pleasure meeting you, sir. Perhaps we can improve upon our acquaintance tomorrow."

"I shall look forward to it."

William brushed his lips across her brow. "Sleep well, my dear. Tomorrow I'll introduce you to your new home."

With that she followed the butler down the wide hallway, hopefully to a hot bath and a stationary bed. Spotted Dick ambled slowly behind her.

NICHOLAS HANDED THE WAITING GLASS OF BRANDY TO his brother. "Congratulations. You've done well. You've found a wife who is both beautiful and wealthy. I bow before your magnificence," he said with great flourish.

"It's true that I expected someone of a different nature." William sipped the brandy, letting it warm the back of his throat before burning a path down his throat.

"What were you expecting?" Nicholas asked.

"I was prepared for Francesca to be plain, but as you can see she is not."

"No, she certainly isn't plain," Nicholas agreed. "Her portrait will be a welcome addition to the family gallery."

William concentrated on the swirl of liquid in his glass. "You plan to paint her portrait?"

"You believe I'm not capable?" Nicholas challenged.

"It's not that. I just . . . I would just insist that Emma be present when you do the painting."

A wolfish grin spread across Nicholas's face. "Once Emma meets the new Duchess, she'll insist on being present. You have no need to worry, Brother. I'm a happily married man and I plan to remain so. Your duchess will be fully clothed for her portrait."

William had to admit, he felt a bit foolish for making Nicholas state his intentions. However, he'd noted Franny's reaction to Nicholas's smile. Blast his brother! When properly motivated, Nicholas could charm the habit off a nun. He'd not have Franny become another of his conquests. He took another sip of the brandy.

"There's something else," William said, avoiding his brother's glance. "I believe I have need of your advice on something of a delicate nature."

"Is this the 'matter of great urgency' that required my appearance at the abbey?" Nicholas raised his brow. "Emma would have insisted we come to meet the new bride even if you hadn't sent such an intriguing—and demanding—telegram."

"If I hadn't sent my request, you may have waited to allow us time to settle. I need your immediate counsel."

Nicholas flopped into a chair, his walking stick by his side. "I cannot recall a single incident in which you've sought my advice. This promises to be most interesting."

Most difficult, more likely, William thought, carefully choosing his words. "As you have noted, Francesca is a most engaging woman of considerable means. She is beautiful, intelligent, compassionate . . ." He lingered a moment over that last description, recalling how she stayed with him while he was ill and read her stories to keep him entertained. She could have easily gone elsewhere on the *Republic* rather than stay in that foul stateroom.

"William?" Nicholas tapped his boot with his stick. "I see no problem with the qualities you've listed. You must be the luckiest man in all of England to cross the ocean to return with such a jewel—sight unseen. Where is the difficulty in this?"

This was proving most difficult to ask, especially of a younger brother. But he could see no way around it. He thought to appear nonchalant, but given his interest, even that was impossible.

"How can you tell if a woman is with child?"

"Are we speaking of your charming wife?" Nick's brows shot to his hairline before he laughed. "Lord, you do take your heir-producing obligations seriously. You'll know when your wife tells you, of course."

Nicholas glanced at William's face and sobered. "Unless of course, we are speaking of another charming female, that of a previous nature?"

William shook his head. "No. My concern is with Francesca." He sipped from his glass. "I've wondered why her mother would arrange to marry this beautiful, charming heiress, who had no interest in marriage herself, in such a swift and timely manner?" He didn't give Nicholas an opportunity to respond. "I believe the answer is that she is ruined goods and the mother was anxious to have her married before her dishonor affected the family name."

Nicholas frowned. "You surprise me, William. I had never considered you so provincial as to require the sacrifice of your bride's maidenhead on the marriage altar."

"It's not that." William raked a hand through his hair. "It's no secret that I married her for her fortune. I married her to save this." He swung his arm out to encompass the room. "I would have married a toothless crone with five brats clinging to her skirts if she brought the fortune I needed."

"Dare I say again, you are the luckiest man in all of England. I fail to see your difficulty."

William took a swallow from his glass, letting it burn down to his stomach. "The difficulty is this: if Francesca is breeding, I want to know it. I don't want to question if the babe is that of another man, or my own. It'll make no difference in the raising, mind you. I intend to honor my obligations as a husband and father under all circumstances, but I want to know. Damn it."

"Have you asked the lady?"

"Of course, I have."

"And?"

"She denies it, of course. But what value can I place on her word? If she is breeding, it would be in her interest to lie and pass the babe off as mine."

"So you haven't . . . dipped in the well?"

William pulled his lips taut, mentally preparing for the taunting that was sure to ensue. "No."

His brother whistled an exclamation, then held his glass high. "You're a more disciplined man than I, William Chambers. We of the baser instincts salute you." He took a drink then grimaced. "How can you sleep with such a beauty and not take advantage?"

"I've been careful not to share a bed with her thus far," William explained. "But she hasn't made it easy."

Nicholas choked on his brandy then lapsed into a coughing spasm. "What . . . what do you mean?" he rasped.

"She knows things." William's eyes narrowed. "Things that a proper, respectable woman should not know." He pointed at his brother. "It's as if she attended that bloody Pettibone School."

"I repeat, Brother." Nicholas chortled. "You are the luckiest man—"

"Spare me the laughter. It's not a humorous affair." He paced the floor like an Indian tiger brought round in a cage for display. "My life has been hell for nigh on the past week.

On one hand, she's perfect. She's unlike any other woman I've ever known, and I want her. I want her so bad, my cock throbs when she enters the room. When she smiles, I want to cover her in kisses. I want to taste every inch of her honey skin, and know her like no other man. I can't sleep. I can't think." He stopped for emphasis. "But if I yield, if I engage in intimacy in the manner she has so very clearly bloody well offered—then I may never know the parentage of the ensuing babe." He sank into a chair opposite his brother then buried his head in his hands.

Nicholas slowly shook his head. "I thought you looked tired when you first entered the library. I had assumed more pleasant activities were costing you sleep." He walked back to the decanter, placing his glass on the tray. "While I commiserate with your predicament, I'm not sure how you thought I might assist you in its solution."

"You've fathered a child, Nicholas. You've seen a woman in the various stages of her pregnancy, and I know your proclivity with a piece of charcoal. I thought perhaps you had done some studies of Emma that I might peruse—strictly to determine if Francesca is following a similar path."

"You want me to show you naked pictures of my wife?"

"Only for the purpose of studying the anatomy of a woman's pregnancy," William insisted. Surely, Nicholas didn't think he would make such a request for any other purpose? "Mine is a scientific interest, really."

"I swear, if you weren't my brother—"

"You've already hung a naked portrait of your wife in the Royal Academy for all of London to see," William argued. "Surely you wouldn't object to—"

"No. *You* hung that purloined portrait, and don't think I've forgiven you for it." Nicholas stomped his way across the room, leaning heavily on his stick. "I should have called you out then and there." He spun around. "I would have too if it hadn't meant I would have been stuck with all this." He waved his stick about the room, much as William had done earlier. "You're a better man for this, William. I have no desire to be the duke of anything, but you've been bred to it."

"I need your help," William pleaded.

"I won't deny that I've captured my Emma in all manner of her blossoming," Nicholas said, with a tightening of his lips. He pointed his stick at William. "But those sketches are in my private collection at Black Oak. You will have to get Emma's permission to view them, and quite frankly, I doubt she'll agree."

"Then you'll offer me no assistance?" He had clung to the hope that Nicholas would be able to confirm Franny's condition one way or the other. To learn that he could not was like the snuffing of a candle. He felt destitute.

"Time is your friend," Nicholas advised. "You've been gone more than a month, and it takes a month for the woman to suspect she's with child. If your Francesca is pregnant, you'll know soon enough."

"If I live that long," he grumbled. "So you're condemning me to continue to remain isolated from my wife?"

Nicholas nodded. "In the meantime, I'll speak to Emma. Your Francesca might be more inclined to speak openly with another woman. I'll set her to the task."

"Thank you."

"William." The hard edge left Nicholas's voice. "Not all women lie. Not all wives are like Catherine."

Begrudgingly, William nodded. There were few similarities between Franny and his first wife. Catherine, whom he thought he loved at one time, was a liar and a cheat. Franny, who was a complete stranger, appeared to be neither of those things. He could almost hear his father's laughter. His inability to judge women would be just another example of his inadequacy to be a duke.

His brother patted him on the shoulder, then headed for the door presumably to join his wife, another woman William had misjudged.

"I must say, Brother," Nicholas added at the door. "After all these years of your cold heavy-handedness, it is most gratifying to see you in a stew over a woman."

William threw a pillow toward the door.

· *Thirteen* ·

MORNING CAME EARLY AND LOUD IN THIS PART OF the world. A chambermaid drew the heavy draperies aside, allowing the streaming morning light to slice across the bed. Fran awoke with a start, disoriented for a moment with the unfamiliar surroundings and a distant pounding in her head.

"Would Your Grace like a breakfast tray?" the housekeeper, a Mrs. Tuberville if she remembered correctly, asked.

It took a moment for her to unravel the accent with her groggy brain. "Yes. Thank you," she replied.

Both the maid and the housekeeper finished their quick chores and departed, leaving her alone to scrutinize her surroundings. She'd been so tired the night before, it had taken all her energy to climb from the tepid bath and make her way to bed. That had been a surprise. Back home, heated water poured from a tap. In this centuries old abbey, the water was heated elsewhere then carried down long, drafty hallways. She regretted her request of the night before, not only because it kept so many servants from their beds but it also took much, much longer than she'd anticipated, which only delayed the time she could rest her head on a pillow.

She slipped from the bed, tying the sash of her wrapper around her. She'd speak to William about the need for indoor plumbing as part of the improvements he had planned. Meanwhile, she'd explore this room as she'd been informed, that of the many vacant rooms, this one was to be hers.

Back home, her mother had taken complete control over the decorating of all the family's households. As she had intended that Francesca would marry royalty, her mother had thought it best to prepare Fran to live in a barren environment such as what she might encounter in a castle. Having lived in that surrounding for so long, the femininity of rose wallpaper, though severely faded, brought a smile to her lips. Paintings of pastoral scenes hung on the walls as well as small mirrors. She noted two oil lamps, and several candle holders, but no fixtures for a gas jet. How extraordinary. Her room had a fireplace, one of many throughout the abbey, she supposed, and several chintz-covered chairs, a writing desk, and a rosewood settee. Luxurious.

The maid returned with a tray of fruits, breads and jams, eggs and some sort of meat, and two pots—one of chocolate, one of tea. "We didn't know which you'd prefer," the maid explained.

"I shall drink them both," Fran announced, happy to see that the liquids remained stable in their cups, and reflected neither the turbulence of crashing waves nor the turning of iron wheels. Like the bathwater, both were barely tepid.

"Has the Duke risen yet this morning?" she asked.

"I wouldn't know, Your Grace. I can ask his chambermaid, if you like," the girl replied with eyes as wide as saucers.

"I'm sure I'll discover myself, soon enough." She glanced about the walls. "Is there a connecting door of which I should be aware?" Her parents maintained separate rooms connected by a large sitting room. Her tutor had explained that the in-between room existed for private dinners or for those special private conversations, which Fran quickly ascertained meant arguments.

The maid glanced to a barely visible door handle on a far wall. "Will that be all, madam?"

"Thank you, yes," Fran replied. She waited till the servant had left before she tiptoed to the connecting door. Most likely, he'd still be asleep as it appeared he and his brother were settling in for a long discussion last night. She just wanted to peek in as she was hesitant to go downstairs to meet the rest of the household without him. But the door was locked, which brought the enormity of her situation home.

She was alone in a strange house, in a strange country, speaking the same language, but spoken differently enough to be almost impossible to comprehend. She didn't know the house routines, she didn't know the house layout, for that matter, she didn't even know the house inhabitants.

The only person she knew well enough to recognize in a crowd thought she was a lying slut—so much so he locked the door so she couldn't gain admittance to his person. Even Mary, the one person she trusted to help her face the unknown, was facing a travail of her own. Tears burned in her eyes. What had she done?

She gazed out her window that oversaw some gardens. Flowers opened their petals to the morning sun. She could almost hear the faint buzzing of bees about their business. Oh, how she wished she were back in Newport in her veiled bonnet and gloves, isolated from the world and confidant in her own abilities.

Just as she was wishing she had not so willingly participated in this venture, a group of rough-looking men, one with a hammer in hand, wandered through the garden. She drew back so as not to be seen. Perhaps that distant hammering wasn't just in her head.

There came a knock at the door. "Entrez," Fran called, hoping Mary had arrived.

"Good morning, Your Grace." A rather stout woman, about twenty years her senior and dressed in mourning attire, stood at the door. "I'm Mrs. Beckett, Lady Rosalyn's personal maid. As your maid has not yet arrived, Lady Rosalyn instructed that I am to help you dress."

She smiled. How considerate her new aunt must be to oversee her needs in this fashion.

"Thank you, I believe a riding habit was included in the garments sent earlier. I wonder—"

"That is not the attire Lady Rosalyn has chosen for you to wear," Mrs. Beckett replied. "I've been instructed to prepare the velvet for you."

"Velvet? Is it not August on this side of the world? I shall melt in the heat," Fran protested, trying not to dwell on the thought that William's aunt thought fit to rummage through the wardrobe Fran had sent over in advance of the wedding. How fortunate her mother had insisted that Fran's jewels be hand transported across the Atlantic. Those certainly would have been inspected without her presence as well.

"It is what Lady Rosalyn selected."

Fran acquiesced, feeling much as she had back in Newport when her mother dressed her in uncomfortable, expensive finery for the purpose of showing off their wealth. She became little more than a fashion plate with no participation in the styles she was told to wear. Funny, just moments earlier she had wished to be back in Newport, although not in this manner. Still, it would be wise to yield to Bedford's aunt to keep the harmony of the house.

After she was dressed in the seasonally inappropriate gown chosen by Lady Rosalyn, she added her tiny bee pin to the heavy collar before following Mrs. Beckett down the stairs to the blue salon where the aunt waited.

She paused in the hallway outside the salon to tug on her jacket to make sure it sat properly, when she heard voices from inside the salon.

"He married an American! My brother is probably turning over in his grave. Surely, William could have managed without scraping the gutter for gold coins."

"Lady Rosalyn, may I remind you that you haven't met—"

"I don't need to meet her! Her money is from trade, did you know that? She probably can't make a decent curtsy. We shall be lucky if she doesn't wear her hair in long braids with turkey feathers attached."

"Aunt! She's not an Indian. Nicholas said she was quite refined when he met her last night. You should have more faith in your nephew."

"You mark my words. William will turn this family into a jest to be bandied about the ton. He has no concept of what it means to be a duke. Never has."

The overheard insults set Fran's chest to burning, or maybe it was a reaction to the sweltering garments she'd worn for the aunt's edification. She thought to turn away and hide in her room, though she suspected the aunt's venom would not dilute with time.

No. She could do this. Reading the courtesan's journal had led her to do things of an intimate nature that she never thought she could manage, and yet she survived. This would be no different. Her mother's counsel whispered in her mind, *Never show emotion, or risk the scorn that follows.* She took a breath, patted her hair to make sure her "turkey feathers" were in place, and slipped through the doorway to face the two unknown women.

Something akin to delight flashed over the face of the youngest, a woman close to her own age. Fran smiled inwardly. Her mother would have criticized the young woman for allowing her emotions to show so openly on her face, but in this case, Fran was glad she had. From the overheard conversation, she thought she was stepping into a nest of vipers. It was reassuring to find one friendly face in the room.

"I'm sorry I could not greet you properly last night, Your Grace," the woman said with a wide smile. "I am Lady Nicholas Chambers. I believe you've met my husband?"

Fran nodded, perhaps a bit awkwardly, unsure as she was as how one proceeded to turn an acquaintance into a friend. Her mother had disapproved of Fran being exposed to other girls her own age. Consequently, her only close friend had been Randolph.

"Please call me Emma," the woman continued, offering her hands. "I hope we shall be friends as well as sisters-in-law."

"Yes," Fran managed. She squeezed Emma's hands lightly. "I hope—"

The sound of someone loudly clearing their throat issued from a corner of the room. Both women turned in response.

"Duchess," Emma said. "Allow me to introduce our aunt, Lady Rosalyn."

"Come here, girl," the matronly woman said. "Let me have a look at you."

Dressed in mourning, Lady Rosalyn's girth overflowed

her high-backed armchair. She kept a man's walking stick by her side. Fran squinted, barely discerning the slightly raised image of the family crest in the blackened metal. A shudder slipped down her spine.

This was the one with the hurtful insults. Remembering her mother's advice to keep her thoughts her own, Fran turned to the woman and dipped into a curtsy worthy of a queen. "My lady," she said.

Fran thought she heard a poorly concealed snicker from Emma's direction.

The aunt just frowned. "I suppose you'll do as long as you don't speak to anyone. Your accent grates on my ears." She looked Fran up and down. "I see Mrs. Beckett has you looking acceptable enough."

"Aunt, do you not feel it is too warm for fur-trimmed velvet?" Emma asked.

"I personally selected that gown," the matronly woman intoned. "As she'll be introduced to our neighboring estates, it's important to show that the Duke's American wife brings at least wealth to the marriage."

"Where is my husband?" Fran asked, her expression showing no cognizance of the continued insults. She was starting to appreciate why her mother kept her yappy Pomeranians with her at all times. She wouldn't object to exposing this woman to a nip or two from their sharp teeth.

"The abbey is swarming with laborers working on the west wall. The steward needed the Duke's counsel regarding dry rot. Bundles and boxes are arriving daily from all the recent purchases. None of that, however, is your concern. My nephew is far too busy to deal with petty issues. As soon as he is finished, we'll begin those calls."

Fran turned and began to unbutton her jacket, with the thought of using the intervening time to explore the house, or at least stand in the breeze from an open window.

"I hope you are not one of those unrestrained women like that Yznaga creature," the aunt snapped. "All the money in the world cannot buy character and respectability. You should remember that."

Fran hid her snicker. A former American heiress, Consuelo Yznaga, now the Duchess of Manchester, had been rumored to be beautiful, talented, and engaging. Her mother had often instructed Fran to follow her example. However, the well-known society hostess was a distant cry from Frosty Franny.

Fran took a deep breath. It was painfully obvious that no one would stand up for her if she did not do so herself. Her heart pounded a rhythm in her throat. She swallowed her fear and turned, smiling sweetly, "I'm sorry you've found the receipt of my money so troublesome, madam. I'm sure a word to the bankers will ensure that you won't suffer so needlessly again." She left the salon with the woman sputtering.

Once outside the room and removed from the sight of the irritating aunt, Fran leaned against the ancient wall to catch her breath. What had she done! She could not recall ever having deliberately insulted anyone before in her life. Yet she wasn't sorry, the woman had been absolutely hateful. She continued down the hallway, seeking to put needed distance between herself and Lady Rosalyn.

Emma caught up with her. "I'm beginning to understand how you had the fortitude to take on William. You truly crossed the Atlantic with him and didn't feel compelled to push him overboard at least once?"

Fran tilted her head toward Emma. "You know Bedford well then?"

She smiled. "I know that he acts on good intentions, if not good sense. He believes he knows what is best for all concerned and acts on those beliefs, even if others are hurt in the process."

Fran stopped and narrowed her eyes. "He hurt you?"

Emma blushed. "He thought he was helping Nicholas. I was inconsequential."

A handsomely attired, clean-shaved William turned a corner, placing him directly in their path. Fran caught her breath. The sight of him had intrigued her from that very first day and he still managed to cause a fluttering beneath her stays. Heat, not associated with her furs, sprang from her core.

"Ladies." He bowed his head, but his gaze remain fixed on Fran. He lifted an eyebrow. "Were you expecting snow, my dear?"

Emma laughed. "Lady Rosalyn selected her attire."

"Then I suppose it's appropriate enough. My aunt would rather go to her grave than be associated with something inappropriate."

"In my case, it seems she has little choice," Fran said.

He raised a brow. "For what purpose is my aunt choosing your attire?"

Fran explained about the calls. William frowned. "There's much to do and I haven't the time to go riding about the countryside making calls. Stone for the renovations will be arriving today. All those neighbors shall be here in due time for the ball. They can meet the new Duchess then. I'll inform my aunt." He turned to Emma. "I wonder if you could be so kind as to find your husband. I have need of his artistic sensibilities."

She grimaced. "I don't believe Nicholas—"

"Now, Emma." He flicked his intense gaze her way.

She nodded. "I'll find him and advise him of your wishes." She quickly glanced at Fran. "Not tempted? Not even once?"

Fran snapped open her fan and pushed an air current toward her face.

Once Emma had disappeared down the hall, he stepped nearer, his eyelids lowered in a lazy, seductive fashion. His lower lip extended just the smallest bit. "Did I understand my sister-in-law to say that I don't tempt you?"

He slipped his hands under her opened jacket and spanned her waist. "That I've never tempted you?"

His thumbs followed the path of her stays till they rubbed the tips of her breasts, turning them to pebbled peaks.

She smiled. "You've misunderstood the context of her question."

"Did I?" His lips started to descend for a kiss.

She wanted that kiss, not for any prelude to seduction, but just to feel wanted, desired. The moment she felt the gentle pressure of his lips, she opened for him in anticipation of deepening the embrace. His hands tightened on her waist. She heard a low groan, filling her with an amazing sense of accomplishment.

"There you are!" Nicholas's voice sounded from the opposite direction.

William's back had blocked her from Nicholas's view, but she knew embarrassment stained her cheeks. She hesitated, hoping the heat might be blamed for her heightened color, before stepping around Bedford to greet the brother. Nicholas, followed by the lumbering Spotted Dick, approached, then stopped. He glanced at Fran, then William, his face twisted in disbelief. "You can hardly expect her to go out like that. If she stands in the sun, you'll be a widower again before sundown."

Something about his reference to William's first wife sent a dampening shiver down her spine. The possibility of a pleasant conclusion to their brief interlude faded.

"Excuse me, gentlemen," she said. "I believe I need to change my attire."

"The trunks won't arrive till later today," Bedford advised. "Do you have something suitable?"

Fran raised her brow. "I believe I packed my buckskins in the earlier deliveries." She strode back toward the stairs, hoping she could find her room and wardrobe on her own.

William watched the mink tails trimming her jacket sway rather alluringly with her movement down the hall. Spotted Dick trotted behind her. Lucky dog.

"If I were a gambling man"—Nicholas gazed at his brother—"I would bet you won't last two weeks before you install her in your bed."

Franny disappeared around a corner.

"I'm sorry." William dragged his attention back to his brother. "What did you say? A bet?"

"I know you believe you have the sangfroid to keep your distance from your lovely American, but I beg to differ." Nicholas looked pensive. "I challenge you. If you consummate this marriage within the next two weeks, then I shall win . . . the Canaletto in the dining room."

Maintaining his outward calm, William gnashed his teeth. The Canaletto was the most valuable painting in the abbey. The others had been sold off earlier to keep the estate afloat. That Venice scene remained a remembrance of the glory the Chambers family once held, and he would not be pleased to part with it.

Still, if he was already determined to wait the next few weeks so as to know if she truly carried a bastard, then the opportunity to best his little brother would just make the waiting more enticing. He would prove that he was right in this, but the idea of betting on his ability to refuse Franny . . .

"And if I accept this foolish gambit, what do you intend to forfeit when you lose, *Artemis's Revenge*?" he suggested. Nicholas would never agree to forfeit the painting that had gained him his reputation, the naked portrait of the woman who later became his wife. But it would establish a high basis for stakes.

Nicholas's face reddened. "I believe we settled this last night." He turned, as if to leave the conversation, then reconsidered. "If you should win the bet and manage to avoid knowing your wife in the intimate way she deserves, then I will paint that portrait of the old Duke, as you requested, to complete the family gallery. I shall curse your name with every stroke, but I will do it."

William smiled. It wasn't that he necessarily wanted a portrait of his father, but the man was entitled to having a portrait hang at the abbey. It was William's responsibility to see that legacy fulfilled.

"Agreed," he said. They shook hands. "However, I'd like your advice on the redesign of the western façade. Let's talk in the library . . ."

SHE WAS LOST. SHE HADN'T INTENDED TO TAKE A TOUR of Deerfeld Abbey, but she must have taken a wrong turn. The long, drafty hallways looked remarkably alike. She'd discovered the abbey was laid out in the form of a great rectangle with

a courtyard in the center. She'd opened a massive wooden door
and discovered a breezeway whose arched openings opened to
the courtyard. One could well imagine garbed monks hurrying
through the passage on their way to chapel. A large scaffolding
erected along the opposite wall supported a number of noisy
workers, while even more worked on the ground. This must be
the swarming mentioned by Lady Rosalyn. Fran shrank back,
hesitant to make her presence known among the strangers.

Another hallway held the silence of undisturbed dust. Narrow wooden doors stood on each side of the stone corridor.
Most of the doors were locked, but some were so narrow as to
support only a small pallet and chair if furnished. A tiny window high on the wall gave the room the appearance of a
prison cell. She shuddered. Fortunately, William hadn't mentioned that particular use in the abbey's history.

She'd gained access to several rooms along a third hallway, but the dust coverings spread over the furnishings suggested they were not used. By her estimation, Deerfeld Abbey
could house the entire village of Deerfeld if pressed. It was
unfortunate that none of that vast army of servants she'd
noted yesterday seemed to service these far wings of the
house. Her steps echoed in the silence of the unused corridors.

She recalled her hope that she'd be able to find some solitude at the abbey so as to work on her translations. Given the
vast number of empty rooms, solitude should be easy to produce. Sufficient lighting by which to read, however, might
prove challenging. The centuries-old abbey was constructed
long before the invention of gas lighting—the method used
to light the rooms of her homes in Newport and New York.
Rumors abounded of a new form of lighting—electrical
lighting—that was being employed in various businesses.
Her father thought that soon this modern invention would
eventually make its way to city residences. However, she
imagined years could pass before that technology would find
its way here.

She negotiated around a full suit of armor standing guard

over empty unused hallways. Apparently, that was the last technological development that had made it to the abbey.

She heard laughter, a child's laugh. The sound urged her forward looking for the source. She hurried down the hall turning the corner to what appeared to be the utilized wing of the house. The laughter slipped through the opening of a door that stood slightly ajar. She peeked in.

"Find me now, Mama. Find me."

A beautiful little girl with soft brown curls stood barely hidden between a dollhouse twice her size and a chest of drawers. The woman she'd called mama stood a few feet away, her back turned to the child. She said in a loud voice, "Where can she be? Where can my dear Sarah be? Could she be under the table?"

The little girl couldn't contain her laughter. "No, no. I'm not there."

Fran opened the door the least little bit more, but the wincing shriek of hinges in need of oil betrayed her presence. The mother turned and smiled. "You found us."

Emma! The woman who had seemed so at ease around Lady Rosalyn. Fran hesitantly advanced. "I didn't mean to interrupt. I'm afraid I'm lost. If—"

"Sarah, come out and meet your new aunt," Emma said.

Fran's eyes widened with delight. She was an aunt? The little girl dutifully left her hiding place and dipped in a hastily executed curtsy. She glanced up at Fran with impossibly huge blue eyes. A jolt of awareness startled her as she realized she was gazing into Bedford's eyes. Though his were rarely crinkled with laughter, more likely they were narrowed in accusation. She hadn't seen Bedford laugh since—

"Can I touch your tail?" the little girl asked.

"Sarah!" Emma reprimanded the child before she shifted a shy glance to Fran and nodded to the jacket trim. "She means your sable tails."

"Oh, of course." Fran slipped out of the jacket and held it, tails up, toward Sarah. The little girl soothed a tiny perfect hand over the gray fur. "Soft."

"We didn't mean to bother you," Emma said. "The governess will be back in just a moment and I'll help you find your way. I just wanted to enjoy my little Sarah for a few moments."

"Do you know any stories?" Sarah asked. Her nose scrunched up in an otherwise earnest-looking face.

Fran wasn't sure exactly what about the little girl touched her heart, but her request for a story placed her securely there.

"I do indeed." Fran stooped down so she would be on an even level with those wide eyes. "I even know a story about a fox with a tail as soft as this."

Sarah clapped her hands. "Tell me, tell me."

"Not now, Sarah." Emma winked at Fran. "I'm sure Her Grace has more important things to do than tell stories to small, impertinent children."

Fran would have loved to stay and tell this angel fairy tale after fairy tale. Did she have more important things to do? She honestly didn't know. If there was something more important, she doubted it could be more pleasant. She had no desire to leave the confines of this bright, laughter-filled room to return to the gloomy staterooms of the abbey, or their equally gloomy occupants.

"Tell me the fox, please?" Sarah pleaded. "Just once."

Emma glanced to Fran. "Nicholas says we spoil her by indulging her whims, but he does little better at refusing her. Would it be an imposition?"

"Not at all. I would love to share a story." Fran spied an adult chair and settled herself there. Sarah sat at her feet, while Emma stood with her back to the door, watching them both.

WILLIAM PAUSED OUTSIDE OF THE DOOR OF THE MAKE-shift nursery. Was that Franny's voice? He had supposed she was with his aunt going through the litany of commandments for properly taking her place at the head of the household. Instead, she was telling a story—he peeked in the slightly ajar door—to Nicholas's daughter. The scene he beheld brought a smile to his lips. She was so involved in the fairy tale, she didn't see him standing there. All her attention centered on the child that sat enraptured at her feet. William felt a familiar pang of jealousy, wishing again that he could enjoy Nicholas's success in family and accomplishment.

Or was it the attention Franny gave the child that fueled his jealousy? He remembered the intimacy they had shared discussing the story of *The Frog King*. He had purposively avoided being alone with her so as not to be tempted to advance that intimacy, but he missed hearing her simple stories. That thought set him back. He was a grown man, a grown duke. Surely a duke shouldn't be jealous of the attention granted a child. Still, he yearned to be at Franny's feet listening to her passionate re-telling of some child's tale, watching her face contort with delight at the stories of magical animals and wishes granted.

Had he ever been entertained in such a manner? Even as a child, he couldn't recall an indulgent moment when he was allowed to think of anything but the task before him and the need to excel at it. To do any less brought repercussions, painful repercussions.

His finger circled a spot on his shoulder. He shouldn't dally here. He had much to do before Bertie's visit. Franny had much to do as well, but for now . . . he left the nostalgic scene with an unexplained despondency.

EMMA HELPED FRAN FIND HER WAY BACK TO HER ROOM. She noted a portrait of a rather stern-looking woman, a former duchess she assumed, hung outside of her door. She entered to find Mary setting the few personal items she'd brought from Newport about the room.

Mary cocked a critical eye. "Couldn't the maids here press out a summer dress? You look as if you're about to melt into a puddle."

"Mary, I'm so glad to see you. Come. Sit on the bed and tell me about your trip."

Mary accepted the offer of a seat on the bed, but glanced nervously about. "There's not much to tell, miss. It was a long trip and I'm glad to have arrived, but that housekeeper, Mrs. Tuberville, gave me a long list of chores and duties. I don't think I can stay and talk to you right now."

"Yes. Of course." Fran drew back, her enthusiasm checked. "I wish to change out of this velvet into something appropriate for the season."

"I know just the dress. Give me a moment to find it." Mary disappeared through a door that blended seamlessly into the wall. Already Mary seemed to know the house better than she did.

Fourteen

SHE HAD TO ADMIT, SHE WAS A BIT BRAZEN AT DIN-ner that evening.

But what choice did she have? With the exception of that unsuspected kiss in the hallway, Bedford seemed to be keeping his distance. The rude behavior of the aunt just solidified her reasons for wanting to return home. To do that, she needed to become pregnant. To become pregnant, she had to seduce the Duke, so she really had no other choice.

Her neckline was low, but not so low that she couldn't wear her unforgettable corset. She instructed Mary to wind scarlet and tan ribbons in her hair, just so Bedford would know what waited beneath. Her green and beige satin gown pulled tight at her hips, clearly defining her silhouette, then piled about on her bustle to exaggerate the sway of her hips when she walked.

She wore Bedford's locket, but adjusted the chain so that the gold fob would sit above her neckline in a sufficient manner to call attention to her chest. Finally, she carried a feather plume fan so that she could direct attention to any part of her person. The journal had taught her the importance of directing a man's eye to a woman's assets. Tonight, she had all her weapons at her disposal for doing just that. All she needed was the man.

Lady Rosalyn, Emma, and Nicholas had gathered in the blue salon. Between Lady Rosalyn's black and Emma's attractive but demure brown, Fran wore the only spot of color in the room. Had she not already been conspicuous by her speech and background, it appeared her fashion set her apart as well. She would have preferred to blend in, but she doubted she'd attract Bedford's eye if she dressed as did Emma.

Nicholas admired a new handsome horse sculpture cast in bronze that sat on the mantel. "I see my brother has already put your dowry to work refurbishing the house."

"Nonsense," Lady Rosalyn said. "Boxes and crates arrived weeks before the nuptials. I'm sure William found the necessary finances in the estate's coffers. I can't imagine her dowry could accommodate all the new purchases."

Nicholas lifted a brow, but did not respond to his aunt's opinion.

"Emma tells me Sarah begged a marvelous story earlier. I hope you didn't find her too tiring."

"Your daughter is an adorable child. I did not find her tiring at all." She glanced about the room. "Finding my way about this house though . . ."

"It helps if you know about the secret passageways," Nicholas said.

"There's no such thing," Lady Rosalyn intervened. "If there were, I would have found them long ago."

Nicholas just smiled. Between the two of them, Fran would have bet her dowry that Nicholas was right. She could see it there on his face, in the pull of his lips. He so much resembled William that when she had first entered the room, she thought it was Bedford standing by the mantel. However, Nicholas was more relaxed, more open with his expression. William kept his thoughts and emotions locked tight, much like herself, she realized.

Nicholas depended on his walking stick. Although, she was curious as to his malady, proper etiquette required she ignore its existence. William's malady was hidden, burned into his shoulder. Again, one open and one not.

William entered the salon looking every inch the aristocrat in his finely tailored dinner jacket. All eyes turned his way. He caught her gaze for just a moment, then turned away to speak to his aunt and sister-in-law.

"You've captured my brother's fancy, you know." Nicholas dropped his voice so the comments would remain private as they watched William's progress about the room.

"How can you tell?" she asked, using the plumes of her fan to mask her words.

Nicholas stiffened slightly, then turned toward her. He took her hand in his and lifted it to his lips. His mischievous gaze caught hers over the arch of her hand.

"Watch."

William was by her side in an instant. He lifted her hand from Nicholas's light grasp, then lowered it to waist height. His thumb lightly stroked her hand, much as it had other parts of her person. Those parts immediately lifted in response. She waved her fan to stir a cooling current, but the silky plumes just settled on her chest. A slight lift of his eyelid confirmed he recognized the power of his touch.

"You look lovely this evening." He smiled, melting a bit of her heart in the process.

"Do you like my hair ribbons?" she asked.

His glance flicked to her hair, then quickly lowered to her bosom. "I believe your wife waits on the other side of the room, Nicholas."

"But I find your wife so delightful," Nicholas replied. "She has just accepted my offer of drawing lessons."

William winced slightly. They both shifted their gazes to Nicholas. Fran was about to deny his invitation, but William spoke first.

"I'm not sure that would be best. Lady Rosalyn insists that Francesca has much to learn before Bertie's arrival."

Fran sighed. "She is trying to teach me to speak with a British accent. She finds my American accent offensive."

Both brothers smiled, but as she watched the interplay between them, she decided to trust Nicholas's lead. William's objective, after all, was to confine her for longer periods with his aunt, thus making the choice easy.

"Lessons of the nature you've indicated would make a wonderful addition to my translations." She turned toward William and batted her fan on his shoulder. "Didn't you suggest the same on the passage over?"

The soft tendrils drifted down the side of his face, drawing her gaze to his lips. Dear heaven, the fan was to draw his attention to her, not the other way around. His free hand captured the shaft of the fan, holding it in place, and preventing her from using it to mask the flush she felt spreading across her chest.

"Excellent, then it's settled," Nicholas said. "I'm sure Lady Rosalyn can spare her for an hour or so. Sketching can be quite the release." He patted his brother on the back, before crossing the room toward his wife. "You should indulge yourself sometime."

They stood that way, two halves of a circle connected by their hands for a moment. His eyes smoldered beneath lazy lids. He squeezed the hand held so tenderly in his own. "Be careful," he said, then released her.

He crossed the room to escort his aunt into the dining room. Nicholas already had Emma on his left arm, but he looked back and signaled Fran to join them. By rights, William should have the honor of accompaniment, but that fact seemed to have eluded him. Fran accepted Nicholas's right arm, but he held them back a moment instead of following behind William.

"I was serious, you know, about the secret passageways. William and I explored them as boys. They run throughout this abbey." He wriggled a brow at her. "When used properly, you can appear in the most unexpected places."

If Fran didn't know better, she'd think Nicholas was intent on helping her in her seduction of his brother. Why would he do that?

Emma shuddered. "Isn't there a ghost that's supposed to haunt those passages? Don't mention them to Sarah or I'll never be able to find her."

"A ghost?" Nicholas asked.

"That's right," Fran said. "William mentioned something to me about some poor monk that was hung by the gate."

"A ghost." Nicholas smiled. "That could prove interesting."

AFTER DINNER, WILLIAM POURED BRANDY INTO SNIFTERS set out on the recently purchased silver tray that sat on a new Hepplewhite carved side table. Amazing the treasures that could be found in the New York trading establishments. He'd been quite successful in procuring items to fill the public rooms. One would never know the desperate straits they had faced before Franny's rescue.

"She soon will be mine, you know," Nicholas observed from the divan on the far side of the smoking room.

"She?" William groused, still irritated by the prospect of Nicholas teaching Franny the finer points of illustration. When he had mentioned illustrations on the passage over it had not been his intent to closet his wife with his brother, a former rake and bounder, in pursuit of art lessons. Nicholas may have settled down in his new marital state, but he suspected his Franny could tempt a man to forget his vows.

"The Canaletto. She'll soon be mine. I saw the way your wife looks at you." Nicholas sipped from his snifter. "I don't know how you've lasted this long."

It hadn't been easy, William thought. He wasn't immune to her open invitations. He had to admit a certain relief when the ladies retired to the blue salon to leave the men to cigars and brandy. Neither he nor his brother were fond of cigars, but the brandy was another matter. "You call a painting 'she'?"

"I consider all great works of art to be of a feminine nature, and all great females to be great works of art." Nicholas smiled. "Take your wife, for instance."

William groaned. "Please don't."

"If Francesca can manipulate a piece of charcoal the way she managed that fan, her sketches will be hanging in the Royal Academy before long."

William felt his groin tighten with the memory. He hadn't realized anyone else had noticed.

"Did you see how she managed to frame her face with the

plumes when she was speaking to Emma?" Nicholas asked. "The feathers curled about her high cheekbones, drawing attention to her lively brown eyes. I was half tempted to do a sketch on the tablecloth. I could well imagine how her face would look resting on a white feather pillow."

"Nicholas . . ." William instilled as much warning into the name as possible. If his brother made mention of how those wispy plumes frequently rested on the exposed portion of her chest, sometimes reaching their curly tips inside her gown, most likely inside that strumpet's corset . . . well, he'd have to call him out. Those ribbons in her hair were a clear signal to those that could read them, and his shaft apparently had that ability. He had to admit that was the most uncomfortable dinner in recent history.

"What exactly did she do when the other ladies were leaving the room?"

William felt his face pale. He busied himself fidgeting with the items on the tray, but in reality he just couldn't bring himself to meet his brother's face. "Whatever do you mean?"

"We stood when the ladies rose to leave. Emma and Aunt Rosalyn left the room, but Francesca stopped to speak to you. I couldn't hear what was said, but I saw your knuckles whiten. You watched her departure for several minutes after she had left."

He couldn't bloody well say that Franny dragged that banner of femininity right up the front of his trousers. Good Lord, the audacity! Right in the middle of the dining room. A blast of heat roared through his veins, just as it had at the table. He hoped his brother didn't notice, then or now as his body reenacted his initial response. He purposively dawdled at the brandy decanter waiting till he could regain control. Of course, in order to do that, he had to stop wondering what that plume would have felt like without the benefit of a cloth interference.

"Did it have something to do with her hair ribbons?"

William choked on his brandy and spun about. "What do you know about her ribbons?"

"Only that the red was an unusual color to wear with green.

I thought it might have had some significance. From your reaction, I would guess that I was correct." He laughed and shook his head. "You're a lucky man, big brother." Nicholas's voice held a smugness that William wished he could forget. "I only hope that one of these days, you'll come off that high horse and recognize your good fortune."

"The recognition of fortune is not the difficult," William said. "I wish I could say the same of the partaking."

"She'll be mine," Nicholas said. "I have no doubt."

· *Fifteen* ·

THE FOLLOWING DAYS FOLLOWED A SIMILAR DIS-comforting pattern. Sarah kept Emma so busy that Emma often napped the same as Sarah. While Fran enjoyed her sketching sessions with Nicholas, they were often filled with long periods of silence for the purpose of drawing a vase or a statuette. On the other hand, her time with Lady Rosalyn was quite the opposite. Fran endured endless lectures with a liberal sprinkling of insults resulting from Fran's "unfortunate background." The one person she wished to see claimed he was too busy with matters concerning renovations to give her the time she wished. Since her experiment with the plume fan, he hadn't even appeared at the dinner table for three days.

Accompanied by Spotted Dick, she'd begun taking buckets of fresh water for refreshment out to the workers in the courtyard in the hope of catching William's eye. She'd see him directing someone in a corner, or even wielding a hammer himself, but he didn't acknowledge her. The experience had made her less terrified of the strange men, but frustrated in her attempts to seduce her husband.

"I believe he's avoiding me," she explained to Mary. "Just when I have more desire than ever to leave this wretched place, I can't find Bedford to encourage him to do what he must."

Mary paused in raising and fastening Fran's overskirt so that it would add to the height achieved by her bustle and not drag on the floor as originally designed. "Why do you call this a wretched place?"

"To be an American here is a great disadvantage. I'm lectured daily on how I am unfit to be a duchess." She ticked off on her fingers. "I am uncivilized, uncultured, grating to the ear, not knowledgeable in the running of a household, not knowledgeable about the responsibilities of servants, and unappreciative of the opportunity to reside in England. The only thing I have to my credit is my wealth, which of course is no longer mine."

"Sounds like you and I have been receiving the same lectures," Mary said, her voice barely audible above the swishing of fabric.

Fran twisted her head to glance over her shoulder. "You too, Mary? Why?"

Mary swung her head from side to side as she enumerated the reasons. "I'm American. I don't know my place. My family's not in the trade, and I argue with them when they talk about you."

"The servants talk about me?"

"Did you ask the chamber steward to remove a trunk instead of a footman?"

"Oh, yes," Fran recalled. "That precipitated the lecture on which servant can satisfy which request—no matter how menial the task."

"Because it is a menial task," Mary noted.

Fran sighed. "I should have just done it myself; it was an empty trunk." She tapped her foot. "Did you know that at the end of the meals, all the table scraps are mashed together into one tin and taken to the tenants for their meals? Peas, meats, sauces, and sweets—all combined in one glutinous mess to be shared in the name of charity." She crooked her hand on her hip. "I offered that the tenants might enjoy the gift more if the portions were kept separate in several small containers. Lady Rosalyn railed that her brother distributed scraps this way and nothing would be changed."

"What does the Duke say?"

"I haven't been able to talk to him. Either there are other people present, or he's off somewhere in this monstrous abbey." She glanced out the window, yearning a bit for the life she had left behind in Newport. "I'm lonely, Mary. I never thought I would say it. I thought I'd enjoy the solitude of a grand residence, but it's too quiet and so old and incredibly inconvenient."

"Done," Mary said, sitting back on her heels.

Fran turned and offered her hands to help Mary stand. "I don't know what I'd do without you here, Mary. You will always have a place with me."

"Thank you, Your Grace," she said with a curtsy. The gesture reminded Fran of the time she and Mary had practiced the art of the curtsy in anticipation of the costume ball so they could change roles. She almost wished they could do that again. Anything to alter the situation as it currently stood.

"Begging your pardon, madam, but why don't you use the private door to talk to His Grace?" Mary nodded to the connecting door between her and Bedford's suites, then walked toward it to retrieve a book propped against bottom.

"Leave it, Mary," Fran said. "I've been using the book to see if the Duke ever opens the door." She didn't mention her sense that someone entered her room at night. It was nothing she could prove, especially as the book remained upright every morning, but it was a feeling, an intuition. She shivered. Perhaps a ghost truly occupied the abbey after all.

"He keeps it locked. I truly believe he's dodging my presence." Fran sighed. "I suppose it doesn't matter. He has said time and time again that Lady Rosalyn's mission is to mold me into a proper English duchess so that I might impress the other proper dukes and duchesses. He would not care that the process of molding is so uncomfortable and degrading."

"Did you know that His Grace rides every morning before breakfast?" Mary said in the manner of an observation. "One of the grooms told me."

"Does he now?" Fran replied. "I must admit I've missed riding myself." She thought of her father's stables in Hyde Park and her rides in the Hudson Valley. Those had been simpler times, enjoyable times, with the wind in her face and the powerful grace of a horse beneath her. She could well understand William's need for a morning ride. "Perhaps it's time I became better acquainted with the stables."

She twisted to see the effect of the altered skirt in the mirror. "That should do. I just didn't want it to drag on the floor."

"You're still not going to tell me what you're up to?" Mary handed her an apron, and a bonnet, the sort used by the housemaids.

"It's a secret. But I'll be back here to change before dinner."

FRAN JOINED NICHOLAS IN THE ROOM HE'D ESTABLISHED as a studio while at Deerfeld Abbey. He waited with two lit candles secured behind glass chimneys.

"Are you sure you want to explore the passageways?" he asked. "I doubt anyone has been through them in decades."

"It will be like climbing through a honeycomb," she replied, slipping her arms beneath the apron straps. Nicholas tied the garment behind her while she tried to tuck as much of her hair in the protective bonnet as possible. "Besides, one never knows when I'll find need of an escape from Lady Rosalyn."

Nicholas offered a sympathetic smile. "Not every room is connected to the passageway. Perhaps they once were, but renovations and changes through the years have most likely eliminated the hidden mechanisms. You might have noted the elaborate molding surrounding the doors." He pointed to the beautiful wooden fruit and leaf carvings on the studio door frame.

"Yes." Fran nodded. "The craftsmanship and artistry are one aspect of the abbey that I've truly admired."

"Craftsmanship indeed. If the room has a portal to the passageway, it'll also have a grape cluster right here." He indicated a wooden carving of grapes about shoulder high on the right of the door. He pressed the trailing grape in the cluster and a doorway slid open on the adjacent wall. "I chose this room to use as my studio because it has a working passageway." He smiled. "As you indicated, you never know when one will find need of escaping Lady Rosalyn."

He handed her a lamp and led the way into the narrow passageway.

"How did you discover this?" Fran asked in awe.

"Quite innocently. As children, we found our own entertainment on dismal rainy days when our studies were done and the governess worn out. William liked to play King of the Hill, with himself as King, naturally."

"Of course," Fran said, imagining the haughty Duke as a child.

Once they both were through, Nicholas pressed a button on the passageway side of the door. The secret door slid shut, plunging them into a darkness that was only broken by their lit candles.

After an initial burst of panic of being trapped between interior walls, Fran discovered her curiosity banished her fear. Moving through the centuries-old passageway made her feel as if she was moving through history. Nicholas's walking stick proved invaluable for clearing the cobwebs that had formed in the years since he and William had roamed the passageway. Her fan cleared the ones his stick missed.

"William had placed a chair by the door frame to be his throne and stood on it so his head would be the highest," Nicholas said as they walked.

Fran tried unsuccessfully to stifle a laugh, remembering that she once thought that William would have included a similar clause in the marriage contract.

"It just so happened that he picked a doorway with a grape cluster and his head was of sufficient height to activate the mechanism. After that . . . well, we were fairly thorough explorers."

They came to a doorway. Nicholas felt along the side of the wall, then smiled. "It's still here. William insisted on marking the doorways so we'd know which door led to which room. According to the code, this door opens to the ballroom, which means the steps to the second floor should be just ahead."

"What kind of code?" Fran asked.

"It was something William devised. He was always doing things like that—taking charge, setting the rules. We used a picture code based on the room's function and letters for the bedrooms." Nicholas glanced over his shoulder at her. "I thought we could just draw the pictures on the backside of the door, but William insisted we carve them in the wood with our penknives so they could be discovered without benefit of light." He turned back forward. "He was right. I doubt my chalk renderings would have lasted this long."

They found the steps and climbed while Nicholas rattled off the picture renderings, a ball for the ballroom, a drumstick for the dining room, a chair for one salon, a table for the other. The third salon had no passageway. He explained that many doors weren't marked because they weren't used. Even in the days of their youth, Deerfeld Abbey was too large for one family to fill.

"This was my sister's room, Arianne. Can you feel the marking?"

Fran ran her fingers along the wood, instantly recognizing the crude carving of the letter *A*. "Where is Arianne?"

"She's wandering somewhere around Europe. William would know. He keeps track of her. He's the responsible one—always has been." Nicholas turned a lever and the door opened. As in the studio, one exited the passageway by virtue of the carved wooden panel next to the fireplace. Dust cloths covered what appeared to be a bed by the large shape, a table, and two chairs. The rugs had been rolled up and dust motes danced in the light from the windows.

"Did William keep track of you, as well?"

Nicholas laughed. "If you mean, did he interfere when his involvement was not appreciated? I would have to say, yes." He glanced out the window at the gardens beyond. "William was the family man, more so than my father. He was the one trying to keep us all together, but when I knew it was my time to go, he didn't stop me. He's never stopped trying to bring me back, though."

And he paid the price, Fran thought, recalling his scar.

She could understand his desire to keep his siblings together, especially as she knew the loneliness that comes with having none. If only he had a similar desire to keep her close. Not having seen him for three days was taking a toll.

"Can we see his room?"

"His room as a boy, or his room as a duke?"

She recognized her faux pas as soon as she said it. As a wife, she should be familiar with his room as a duke, yet Nicholas did not seem surprised by her question.

"As a boy, please."

"This way."

They went past an unmarked doorway that Nicholas speculated was Lady Rosalyn's room by its location, turned a corner and found the doorway with a *W*. Nicholas pulled the lever and Fran pushed through the exposed opening.

She had expected to see dust cloths and rolled rugs; instead it was obvious that the room was currently occupied. Nicholas followed behind her.

"That's odd. From the looks of things, he never moved into the Duke's master bedroom," he said.

In spite of her curiosity, Fran had the uncomfortable feeling that she shouldn't be here— not now. As much as she wished to see William, she had the distinct feeling that he wouldn't approve of her spying in this manner. "We need to leave."

"Aren't you curious? Not much has changed since we were boys. William is still fastidious." Nicholas enjoyed this surprising discovery too much. He poked around some papers neatly stacked on a desk. "He's working on designs for the eastern façade." He looked back at Fran. "Between dry rot and porous stone, maintaining the ancestral home is a tedious and expensive project at best."

"Come, we should leave." Fran slipped back through the narrow opening into the passage. At least now she understood why the book never toppled from the ever locked door, but why hadn't he assumed the master's bedroom?

She was too rattled by their discovery to continue so Nicholas led her back to the workroom. She removed the apron and cap, and returned to her room. Once inside she checked the doorway. A set of grape clusters hung shoulder high. She had obviously set her trap on the wrong door. Tonight, she would rectify that mistake.

"WHERE HAVE YOU BEEN?" MARY ASKED THE MOMENT she came in to help Fran dress for dinner. "Lady Rosalyn had everyone searching for you and Lord Nicholas. Visitors arrived earlier and neither of you were available to welcome them."

Fran felt a moment of guilt at not meeting her proper duties as the hostess of Deerfeld Abbey, but as she had not personally invited anyone, she wasn't sure how she could be held accountable for being absent upon their arrival. "Who has come?" she asked, expecting the answer to be a neighbor who decided not to wait till the official ball to meet the new duchess.

"I believe it may be that woman from the SS *Republic* and her husband. The one you mentioned that knew the Duke."

Lily Mandrake. Yes, Fran knew exactly who Mary alluded to. But why would she be here? Fran hadn't invited her.

"At least their arrival should insure the Duke's presence at dinner this evening," Fran said. How unfortunate that it took another woman's arrival for her to get a chance to see her own husband. Jealously twisted in her stomach. "For dinner this evening, I wish to look the part of a perfect hostess. I wish to be alluring, elegant, and refined, but not overbearing."

Mary smiled. "I know just the dress."

Two hours later, Fran descended the steps confident that she resembled a perfectly attired Newport hostess in her reception gown. The deceptively simple dropped-sleeve gown made a perfect foil for her diamond collar necklace. Black accents against the white faille brought interest to all the desired places, particularly the high bustle on her backside. Black plumes set in her chignon and a black lace fan completed the ensemble.

She stepped into the salon and all heads turned her way. Lady Rosalyn appeared appalled, Lady Mandrake smirked, and Fran immediately realized that Newport appropriateness equated to overdressed by English country estate standards.

Her confidence depleted, she searched the room for William. He stood in the corner with Emma and appeared momentarily stunned. Then he crossed to her, an appreciative look in his eye. "Francesca, my dear, you quite take my breath away."

He took her hand in his. "You recall, of course, Viscount and Lady Mandrake from the SS *Republic*?"

"Of course." Fran smiled in what she hoped appeared a sincere expression. "How lovely to see you again."

"Your Grace." Lady Mandrake curtsied. The Viscount inclined his head. "I can't tell you how delighted we were to receive Lady Rosalyn's invitation to stay at Deerfeld Abbey. I'm sure the welcoming ball will be the most memorable event this season."

"I thought it wise to invite Lady Mandrake so our American heiress could observe how a true English gentlewoman behaves," Lady Rosalyn said.

"Oh, how thoughtful," Fran improvised. "I had thought I could learn all I needed to know by observing your behavior, Lady Rosalyn. Thank you for providing yet another example," she managed, all the while seething inside. As if the Winthrops had not been already received by most of the royalty on the continent. If the height of correct behavior meant to publicly embarrass another, then Lady Rosalyn could keep her gentlewoman lessons.

"We had hoped, of course, to convey our appreciation to the hostess as soon as we arrived this afternoon," Lady Mandrake said, sliding a sideways glance toward Emma before returning her gaze to Fran. "But I understand that you were not available."

What was this woman implying? Fran glanced toward Emma for an answer but found none. Drawing on her mother's advice, Fran softened her smile. "Had I been aware that you and your husband were arriving, I would certainly have not been otherwise indisposed."

Lady Mandrake's eyes widened slightly as if in acknowledgment that the invitation had not come from the Duchess, but another. Her lips tightened in one corner before she turned her gaze to William. She lightly slapped her hand fan in one palm. "I wonder, Bedford, if you could tell me the history behind that amusing painting over on the far wall?"

"I'm sure my brother could—"

"But your brother is not in attendance at the moment," Lady Mandrake interrupted, using the closed fan to push some of her dark hair away from her pale ivory face.

William squeezed Fran's hand briefly, she supposed by way of an apology. "If you'll excuse us . . ." He led Lady Mandrake to the painting in question. The Viscount involved Lady Rosalyn in conversation, leaving Fran and Emma alone.

"I can't believe Lady Rosalyn invited her here," Emma said, her voice barely above a whisper.

"I suppose she meant well," Fran said. "She didn't know what to expect when William left for America. She must have sent the invitation before our return."

"But why would she invite his former mistress?" Emma said, her gaze trained on the couple admiring the painting. "If she truly felt an example was needed, why that woman?"

Shocked, Fran's voice caught. "His mistress?"

"It was fairly general knowledge at the time. I suppose even the Viscount was aware of the arrangement." She glanced up toward Fran, and her expression withered. "Oh, dear. You didn't know? I thought that as you both had been on the same ship on the return . . ."

Fran bit her lip. "William and I had a brief discussion about such matters. He did mention something about appetites; I just hadn't recognized his personal taste."

"Nicholas assures me that the arrangement is all in the past. William's not the sort to maintain a mistress while he has a wife."

Fran didn't comment. At this moment, she wasn't sure what label she could place on the marriage she shared with William. He certainly had not come to her for the sort of favor one would expect from a wife. Perhaps Emma was incorrect in her assertions about his character. Fran's father had enjoyed a mistress while married, yet he was a prominent and respected figure in society, wasn't he?

She watched the two whispering in front of the painting. This woman had captured William's interest in the past in a way Fran had yet to experience. Perhaps Lady Rosalyn was right. Lady Mandrake was a woman to be carefully observed and perhaps emulated—though not for the purposes Lady Rosalyn thought.

"I cannot believe the audacity of that woman," Emma said beside her. "Look at her."

So Fran did, noting how she smiled prettily up to William while lightly tapping the right side of her face with the closed fan. She seemed deeply engaged in the conversation.

"She's asking when she can see him," Emma observed. "Look at that!" Though hushed, Emma's voice clearly expressed her outrage. "She wants to speak privately with him, though by that look on her face, it's not talking she has in mind."

Fran studied Emma. She had heard of individuals who could read another's words by the shape of their lips. Did Emma possess that talent? "How do you know?"

"By the way she uses her fan. One of the spinsters teaches a class on the language of the fan at the Pettibone School for Young Ladies. With all those girls practicing, I've become rather expert at interpretation." Emma smiled.

Fran had heard mention of such a secret language but never gave it much credence. It could hardly be secret if another across the room could interpret the motions. But then perhaps this was another strange courtship ritual unique to England. "Did you speak with Nicholas by means of a fan?" Fran asked, intrigued.

Emma blushed for no apparent reason. "I'm afraid I lost my fan fairly early in our courtship." She averted her gaze. "We spoke in the ordinary fashion."

Fran glanced back at William. She couldn't tell if he was

responding to these apparent signals from Lady Mandrake. He did stroke a finger up the side of his face that sent a slight jolt of alarm through her. "Is there a secret language for men as well? One by which to respond?"

Emma thought a moment. "No, I don't think so. At least, there is nothing that we've covered at the school. I suppose I'll have to ask Nicholas about that."

That wouldn't help her for the present, Fran thought. She'd like to interpret these so-called signals sent by Lady Mandrake herself. Even more, she'd like to know how to send out signals herself in the event that William could interpret them. She turned her back to the assembly in the room. "Can you show me some of these motions?"

Emma managed to show her some of the basic movements before Nicholas joined the group. His eyes narrowed on the couple on the far side of the room before he shifted his gaze to his wife, then Fran. His expression brightened. "It appears I am once again honored by the company of the two most beautiful women in all of England."

"Now that we are all assembled," Lady Rosalyn announced. "Let us proceed to the dining room."

· Sixteen ·

DAMNATION! IF HE DIDN'T ALREADY HAVE ENOUGH on his hands with the abbey crumbling overhead, a royal visit for which to prepare, and a tantalizing wife to resist, now, thanks to his high-handed aunt, his former mistress seemed anxious to reestablish relations. There he sat, next to the viper that seemed determined to find a way into his bed, and across from his comely wife who would do the same given an opportunity. By his own determination, he had closed himself off from the one he wanted, which only served to encourage the one he didn't. His brother enjoyed his predicament entirely too much. While his aunt remained seemingly unaware of the problems she had wrought.

"Bedford, your aunt tells me you've been working ceaselessly to bring this magnificent abbey back to its formal glory. Have your efforts extended to the gardens?" Lily stopped the slow fluttering of her open fan to shield her next words from the rest of the table. "Meet me there later."

A loud snap like the crack of a whip pulled his attention across the table to his wife. She fluttered her aggressively opened fan with a passion. "We have a large pile of discarded weeds that you may examine, Lady Mandrake, but as we've only been back for a short period of time, the gardens haven't yet shown the benefit of our efforts."

Franny's finely drawn brows raised in what appeared to be a dare. He almost choked on his wine. When had his gentle, generally reclusive wife taken such an aggressive turn? Of course, he'd known of her rather forward efforts in the area of intimacy, but not in a social setting. Perhaps if he hadn't been trying to avoid her these past several days, he'd have been forewarned of her "sea change."

Lily slowly closed her fan. Franny mirrored the action, then pressed the closed fan to her left cheek, her gaze intent on Lady Mandrake.

William felt Lily stiffen beside him. He seemed to be in the midst of a silent duel, the weapons—the innocuous hand fan accompanied by intense, narrowed stares. Like two peacocks, engaged in spreading their plumage for a peahen's attention, so did these two repeatedly spread and close their fans. Emma and his aunt watched the volley with great intent, lips parted as if ready to cheer the victor. He glanced toward Nicholas who simply shrugged. The Viscount was too engaged with his roast venison to observe the proceedings.

"I know the ball is to occur within two weeks," Lily said, drawing her closed fan through a tunnel created by her fingers. "But when is the Prince of Wales to arrive?"

While William could have easily answered her query, he thought it best to remain silent. He settled back in his chair to watch his wife in this feminine battle of wills.

Franny smiled, then raised her fan above her left ear as if to lightly tap at the nest of plumes fastened there. Lady Rosalyn gasped. Emma smiled.

"I believe Bertie likes to keep his own schedule," Franny replied. "We hope he arrives after the repairs are complete on his room. They should be completed in a week." Her gaze shifted to him. "Do I not have that correct, Bedford?"

He nodded, enjoying his wife's apparent success at whatever was transpiring. Lily placed her closed fan on the table beside her plate. He wondered if that was some admission of defeat.

Franny tapped a partially opened fan on her lower lip as if deep in thought. "I believe most of the staterooms are under some sort of repair . . . in which room were you placed?"

Lady Rosalyn responded, a note of urgency in her voice. "I had them installed in the red stateroom, next to the Duke."

"Pity," William said, his gaze locked with Franny's. She had the most amazing twinkle in her eyes; it could rival the diamonds around her neck. "I believe that room is scheduled to be draped for plastering tomorrow." He glanced quickly at Lily. "Had we known you were coming . . ."

Lily narrowed her eyes at Franny. "It is well we haven't completely unpacked. We should be able to move to another room if it will accommodate your preparations."

"I believe all the staterooms will be worked to some extent," Franny said. "Perhaps we should leave things as they are and forgo the improvements on your room until after your departure. I would think that would result in the least upheaval to your comfort."

"Excellent suggestion," the Viscount offered from his seat next to Lady Rosalyn. "Our room will be fine just the way it is. We're just grateful to be welcomed into your hospitable home."

William nodded. He imagined given the Viscount's run of finances that the words were heartfelt and sincere. He glanced toward Franny. Her wrist extended just above the table and held her fully opened fan. When she turned her head from the Viscount's direction toward him, the black lace hid the lower part of her face leaving just her eyes visible. But what eyes! Her glance toward him smoldered with a passion that he felt square in his groin. If this was the result of winning an argument, by God, she could win every argument for the rest of his natural life.

"Yes." Aunt Rosalyn signaled for the footman to pull back her chair. "With that, I believe it's time for the ladies to leave the men to their port."

Fran felt a heat infuse her that no fan could alleviate. Already a bit giddy from her triumphant volley with the former mistress, when she caught William's gaze, a jolt of sensual awareness sizzled through her that glued her to her chair. Inexplicably, it had nothing to do with Bridget's journal, her corset, or any attempts to draw attention to her more feminine features. She saw admiration, appreciation, and desire for her in his gaze. Just her.

She almost regretted Lady Rosalyn's signal to leave and thus hesitated, perhaps a bit too long, as now she was filing out of the room with Lady Mandrake by her side.

"He doesn't love you," the woman said in low tones. "He only married you for your money."

Her words stung because Fran knew them to be true. William certainly had not spoken of love, yet that look they had shared . . .

"He'll be back in my bed," Mandrake hissed. "You'll see."

Fran stopped short, drawing Lady Mandrake to a halt as well. She called on her mother's training to mask both the hurt inflicted by the vile woman's words and the hope that William did indeed care for her. Exposing such a desire to this woman could only result in further scorn, so she kept that hidden. She did, however, appreciate the opportunity to use a bit of that colorful language she had acquired as a result of Bridget's journal.

"Should the Duke choose your affections over my own, I shall still be his wife. I shall still be the Duchess of Bedford. And that would make you, Lady Mandrake, little more than a carrion hunter with horns to sell and a cunny with the wear of a hobbyhorse."

She left the woman sputtering behind her as she hurried to catch Emma on her way to look in on her precious daughter.

PROGRESS WAS A NOISY PROPOSITION.

The urgency surrounding the renovations meant workers attacked the western façade at the first break of light. Echoes of hammers and chisels disrupted morning dreams, directions shouted from one laborer to another challenged decorum, wagons jostling heavy loads rattled illusions of tranquility.

Even though William frequently found himself in the midst of the renovation chaos and took great pride in leaving this stamp on the Chambers legacy, he found that he needed to occasionally escape it as well. On those occasions he had his stallion, Chiron, brought round, then he headed for the quiet of the countryside.

Paths wove through the surrounding plain to a stretch of woods that dampened the construction cacophony. Beyond the

woods, tenant farmers worked the estate land, turning fields
into productive acreage.

This was the true legacy of his dukedom, the land. Riding
along the paths proved a balm to the spirit, allowing him to
set aside the multitude of details requiring address before
Bertie's arrival. For a brief time he could dismiss his aunt's
continued complaints about Franny's appropriateness as a
duchess. The more he observed Franny, the more he was convinced she was eminently qualified for the role if she would
just assert herself in that position. He chuckled softly to himself. She fairly well asserted herself in that battle of fans last
night at dinner. Though he wasn't sure the exact nature of the
grievance that led to that feminine test of wills, he could tell
Franny emerged the victor. Even though Lady Rosalyn would
vehemently disagree, it was a good sign that Franny was coming into her own.

Of course, if he hadn't been purposively avoiding his wife,
he would have been able to support her in testing her authority. However, to be near her and not touch her . . . it was just
too difficult.

Stop that! He scolded himself. Stop tormenting yourself
with thoughts of Franny. It shouldn't be long before the truth
of her condition would be obvious. Then he would be free to
enjoy the full benefit of those marriage vows. He would be
able to touch her dewy skin and taste her honeyed sweetness
in the most intimate of settings. He would brush her silky hair
and she would tell him stories of talking beasts and magic
wishes. He found his lips turning into a smile, imagining the
light in her eyes when he presented her with the fairy-tale
books he'd ordered to help stock the depleted library. Imagining she would thank him with a kiss, or maybe with the artful
employment of that ostrich plume, or . . .

Damnation! He was doing it again!

Trying to extricate himself from thoughts of his wife, he
spied a mysterious swath of blue at the edge of a field dotted
with the yellow flowers of squash plants. He turned Chiron to
investigate.

Although the thickly veiled hat would hide her identity to most, the fashionable riding habit combined with the bee-keeper's protective netting, proclaimed that the wearer could only be Franny. He smiled. Who else would consort with a gnarled old beekeeper with a full set of whiskers in the middle of a vegetable patch and have no thought as to the appropriateness of her being or attire?

"Franny!" he shouted.

The hat tilted his way before she quickly passed a frame of sorts to farmer Thackett, then dashed toward the edge of the field. Her mount, Thalia, if he wasn't mistaken, waited a distance away from the series of boxed hives.

"Franny, wait!" he shouted as he urged Chiron forward to follow.

He was closing in, when she expertly mounted Thalia, turning the mare toward a path that would take her back toward the woods.

William followed close behind. What in blazes did she think she was doing? He had to admit as Thalia sailed over a fallen tree, his wife knew how to sit a horse. He would have felt more secure about her abilities if she weren't wearing that heavy veiling. It had pulled loose from her hat and whipped about behind her. He saw her reach toward the veiling a moment before a low tree branch caught her raised arm unaware. Thrown off balance, she fell from the racing horse, her cry of distress ending abruptly with a dull thud.

He pulled Chiron up short and dismounted, running to where she lay still in the grass. His own heartbeat pounded in his ears.

"Franny, are you hurt? Talk to me, Franny!" He knelt beside her, then gently turned her over, pushing the white netting from her face. Her eyes were wide, panicked. She gulped at the air like a fish jerked from the lake. Thank God, she was alive! A spill like that—

"Breathe in, Franny, slow . . . slow . . ."

Time seemed to stop as he watched her attempt to drag deep draughts of air into her lungs. He found himself breathing with her. "Another . . ."

Once it was apparent that she'd gotten back her wind, he moved to her legs, feeling each beneath the voluminous skirts of the riding habit. Her arms and fingers appeared to be unharmed as she moved them to her chest to feel the rise and fall of her lungs. Then the realization hit him that if she truly were pregnant . . .

An overwhelming sense of loss smacked him in the gut. A child, a poor innocent babe, one that he would have accepted even with its cloudy parentage, in all probability could not survive such a fall. A child whose laughter he'd now never hear was lost all due to his stubborn pride. Surely if he hadn't kept Franny at arm's length, she wouldn't have fled from him when he called her name. It was all his fault. For what? For the certainty of being right? To win a bet with his younger brother? A child lost in exchange for bragging rights? Anger and grief roiled within. He had promised Franny to protect her and hers, yet his arrogance caused this tragedy. He glanced at her, watching for awareness of the probable consequence of her fall.

Unshed tears burned in his eyes. *A duke never sheds a tear. Don't be a child, be a duke.* He winced. The child had deserved something better than a fool playacting as a duke for a father. The child, even one not of his making, deserved support, protection, shelter.

"Franny." He scooped her into his arms, lifting her. Her leather gloved hand reached to his shoulder, her head tucked toward his chest. A nearby fallen tree trunk provided a bench of sorts. He sat, letting his legs support her bottom while he pulled her tight to his chest. "I'm so sorry." He kissed the top of her head. "I was a fool. I'm so sorry."

She tested her voice. "You were a fool?"

She looked up at him with enormous brown eyes beneath a delicately arched brow . . . fragile eyes . . . trusting eyes . . . His heart wrenched.

He ran his hand down the front of her, pausing at the spot beneath the lowest fasteners of her corset. A spot about which he had shamelessly fantasized without proper regard to the precious cargo it sheltered. "The babe . . . a fall such as that . . ."

"The babe?" Awareness crept into her eyes. "Good Lord, William, are you still nourishing that foolish notion that I'm pregnant?"

Nothing. No sketches of a woman's changing form, no calendars with days carefully counted, no treatises on husbandry could have convinced him more completely of her lack of pregnancy than those words breathlessly uttered after such a fall. His heart, still heavy with grief for the lost child, flew to his throat. A giddiness filled his head. So many changes in such a short period of time left him speechless.

So he kissed her. He hadn't intended a passionate kiss. His thoughts were more of a celebratory nature. However, once her lips parted to receive him, and he felt her press back, urging him to drown in her moist sweetness, all his pent-up longings rushed to the forefront. He couldn't stop.

He could have her right there, his mind argued. The woods were private; no one would see. One hand explored the back of her tightly tailored riding jacket, then slid to the front. Buttons, too many tiny buttons fastened her in that first line of defense. Beneath that, there would be blouse buttons—his mind reasoned—a camisole, corset fasteners . . . Best to attack from the other direction. His hand slid down to her boot, then followed her leg up, tossing the material so as to get to the stocking-encased thigh he had checked earlier.

Lord, he wanted her so desperately! She could straddle him, right here on this fallen tree. He could bounce her delectable bottom and sink in to her warmth, if he could just make headway with these skirts, and petticoats, and stockings, and . . .

The sound of leather reins slapping horse hide and rumbling wooden wheels interrupted his progress. His hand froze in position. He glanced up.

"Thackett," he acknowledged.

"I heard her scream and thought she might be hurt," Thackett stated from the bench seat of his wagon, barely suppressing a wide grin. "But I see you've got things well in hand."

William glanced down the length of his wife. All pertinent areas seemed to be adequately covered by cascading yards of linen and lace, but it should be fairly obvious to the casual observer the intent of his exploring hand. He glanced back to the grinning Thackett. "Yes. It seems I do."

The farmer stood on the buckboard as if to search the environs. "She sure took off like she had a bee in her bonnet."

William glanced at Franny, who had tuned her face toward his chest, to hide her embarrassment, he supposed. "I was just about to ask her why she did that."

"I can see that you were," old Thackett said. The man had more years on him than many of the trees in this glen. William grinned. Who else would dare interrupt what was obviously developing into a romantic tryst?

"Her horse must be still running," Thackett observed.

"My horse?" Franny straightened, causing William to remove his hand from its accommodating shelter. She sat up in his lap. "She's gone?"

"She probably ran back to the stables," William said. "Chiron is here. I can take you back to the abbey."

Franny stood and dusted her skirts. "Thank you for coming to check on me, Mr. Thackett. That was most considerate of you."

He doffed his hat. "I was honored that you visited my hives, Your Grace. I'll give that advice some consideration."

"Thank you," she nodded curtly. "The conditions here may be different than in New England." She smiled. "Then again, there's a little bit of England in both locations."

They both chuckled.

"I can give you a ride back to the abbey if you prefer," he offered. "Two in a wagon is less crowded than two on a horse."

She glanced at William, who slowly shook his head. "Thank you for the offer, Mr. Thackett, but I believe His Grace has already considered the matter."

Thackett shrugged then sat back down on the wagon seat. He clicked the reins and maneuvered the wagon in a circle to return to the field.

While William snagged the reins of his patient horse, Franny retrieved the veiling she'd used to protect her head from potential bee sting. The white netting floated out in a

breeze before her, reminding him of her wedding veil. She'd
tried to run away from him then as well. The realization that
she still might not wish to be married to him stung. He brought
Chiron over to where she stood.

"Why is it you're always running away from me?" He
spanned her waist, then lifted her onto the saddle.

"Aren't you riding with me?" she asked.

"I think I'd prefer to walk alongside for a while."

"Then I should walk as well." She twisted as if to slide off
the saddle.

"No." He placed his hand on her leg. "I'd prefer that you
stay where I can see you." Once she righted herself, he tugged
on the reins, then walked beside the horse. "You didn't answer my question."

"I'm not always running away—"

He ticked off on his fingers. "The engagement, the wedding . . ."

She didn't respond.

"You heard me call your name. I saw you look up. Why
didn't you just wait for me to join you?"

She bit her lower lip and turned her face away.

Ire rose in his voice. "Then perhaps you can explain what
you were doing with old Thackett, or why you're riding out in
the woods alone? Don't you know how dangerous that can
be?"

"I miss my home," she said. "I miss riding in Hyde Park.
I miss the ocean and cliffwalk. I miss my hives." She dropped
her gaze to her hands. "I didn't expect to miss those things
this much."

The pain in her voice made him remember his joy when
they docked at Southampton. He understood about homesickness. Of course, his was only for a month's duration. Hers, on
the other hand, promised to last a lifetime.

"Your aunt despises me. She'll be disappointed that I didn't
break my neck out riding."

"Fran . . ." he said, in as stern a voice as he could muster.

"It's true," she stated. "I'm totally unsuitable to be a duchess. She's told me often enough. She said last night was the

proof to end all proofs. Now that you have control over my money, she wishes I would just crawl away somewhere and die."

"That's nonsense." He frowned. "I'm disappointed that you would repeat such things."

"Mr. Thackett, however, is kind to me and respects what I have to say about bees. Looking in on his hives reminds me of home."

"Thackett has farmed that land alone for as long as I can remember." Given her comparison of his aunt and Thackett, he could appreciate her desire to escape periodically. "He probably enjoys having an attractive young woman call on his bees."

"If I were gone, the way would be clear for you to marry that Mandrake woman."

A stone weight fell to the bottom of his stomach. "Why would I want to do something like that? Lady Mandrake is already married, remember? You met her husband."

"Your aunt says Lord Mandrake is wasting away. He can't last much longer. Then Lady Mandrake will be available."

"That's preposterous." He scowled. "I have no desire to wed Lady Mandrake."

"You certainly had no desire to marry me either," she said softly. He wished he could deny it, but her words were true. But he'd changed, by God. Couldn't she tell that he'd changed?

"What would it take for you, William?" she asked. "What would it take to make you love someone like me?"

"Why were you running away from me?" he asked perplexed. "Why didn't you wait when I called?"

She sighed. "I never wanted to be a duchess, William. I never wanted your title. Don't you understand? I was enjoying my inappropriate visit with Mr. Thackett. When you called, I knew you'd take me back to the abbey, so I ran. It's no wonder your entire family believes I'm unsuitable to be this grand society lady. It's not what I want to be."

"And what would that be?" he asked. How odd that so many women had pursued him with the thought of being the eventual duchess as their ultimate goal and yet he married the one woman who insisted she wasn't interested.

Her voice softened; perhaps she'd forgotten how sounds could carry on a breeze. He heard her clearly—both her words and her yearning hidden in them.

"Loved," she said. "Just once in my life, I wish to be loved."

He should have told her then that he loved her. He hadn't recognized the emotion until he thought he'd lost her on that fall. If he were to admit it now, she wouldn't believe him. She'd think he was just saying what she wanted to hear.

He would just have to prove it to her. If he could show his adoration of her vitality, wit, and charm, she'd know he loved her. Then he'd be content that she wasn't conspiring at every turn to disappear from his life. His stomach turned at that thought. No. He wouldn't let her disappear, and he knew one extremely satisfying, wrongfully delayed way that he could show his love.

He smiled, already anticipating the night.

· *Seventeen* ·

ONCE THEY CLEARED THE WOODS, WILLIAM MOUNTED Chiron and pulled Fran tight in front of him. Together, they rode back to the abbey.

Such a delicious feeling nestled up against a man in that fashion, Fran thought. She could feel the strength in his thighs as he directed the horse, helping her maintain her balance with an arm loosely about her waist. They were silent for much of the journey, though periodically William's lips would push through her hair to press a light kiss on her head. She wished the abbey was a bit more distant. But the sound of hammering gained in volume and Spotted Dick soon lumbered across the plain to meet them. In much too short a time William reined in Chiron in front of the abbey.

Before William could dismount, Carruthers opened the front door.

"I've rung for a groom, Your Grace. He should be here presently."

"Excellent," William said as he swung his leg over the horse's hindquarters and settled on the ground. He reached for her, catching her waist as she slid to the ground. She waited, brushing away the remnants of the woods that had journeyed on her skirts, hoping William would take her by the hand and lead her somewhere to finish what they'd earlier begun. However, activity by the gates at the far, far end of the long drive to the entrance of the abbey drew their attention.

"I don't suppose the grooms have taken to using carriages to collect the horses," Fran observed, noting an older barouche making its way up the lane.

William squinted. "It looks like one from the village." He gave Chiron an affectionate pat on the hindquarters before a groom led him off for the stable.

The front door opened behind them. Fran turned an instant before Emma clasped her in a painful hug. "Thank heavens, you're safe. When Thalia returned without a rider, we were in a panic to find you."

Fran smiled over Emma's shoulder at Nicholas, who lingered by the entry. It was a lovely feeling to have people who held such concern about one's well-being. Having Emma and Nicholas as family had proved a surprising unanticipated benefit to her married state.

"Then William was gone." Emma scowled at William. "We weren't certain what to do."

"I told her my older brother would take care of everything. He always does whether warranted or not." Nicholas squinted at the oncoming carriage. "Were you expecting someone?"

The carriage rounded the turn in front of the door. Carruthers advanced to inquire about the traveler who could be seen peering out the window, but Fran broke into a wide smile before the carriage came to a full halt.

"Randolph!" she exclaimed, starting to move forward but a dull pain in her chest drew her up short. She pressed the offending spot, while looking for confirmation that the brief glimpse of the passenger was reality. "Can it be?"

"It would seem so," William said, letting his displeasure seep into his voice. "The question should be: why?"

Emma grasped Franny's elbow. "Are you hurt?"

William watched for her response. He'd be surprised if there weren't some repercussions from that fall beyond her disheveled appearance. Franny, however, shook her head. "Just a bit sore. I fell from Thalia."

"Who is this Randolph fellow?" Nicholas asked, advancing to join the others. "Why is he here?"

"William invited him," Franny replied with a glance to her husband.

He scowled. "I've never met the man." He could have continued that he had no wish to meet him, but Franny's eyes were lit with such enthusiasm and delight—he refused to say anything to lessen her glow.

Carruthers advanced to open the carriage door.

"On the *Republic*," Franny said. "Do you not remember that you invited Mr. Hairston and his cousin to call upon us?" She slowly advanced toward the carriage, hand on hip.

"Mr. Hairston is not Randolph Stockwell," William said softly at her back, still puzzled by the sudden appearance of the man from Franny's past, especially at this inopportune moment.

She didn't stop but replied over her shoulder. "Randolph is Mr. Hairston's cousin."

"Bloody hell!" He swore softly to himself. He could have just as well as fallen victim to a tumbled load of marble block for the heavy burden this unexpected visit caused.

The door to the carriage opened and a tall, fuzzy-jawed American emerged, his gaze intent on Franny.

For her part, Franny seemed as giddy as a girl just introduced to society, even though in her current state of disarray, she looked more the part of a street urchin. She curtsied to the young man, even though she held the higher ranking according to British standards. William's lips tightened. She apparently had forgotten that as a duchess she need only curtsy to the Queen and other heads of state.

The Randolph fellow kissed her hand and, in William's opinion, lingered a bit too long at it. He started to move forward, but his brother blocked his path with his walking stick. Though tempted to break the impediment, he glanced at its owner. Nicholas nodded with a lifted brow, signaling restraint. Frustrated, William took a deep breath and worked to control his rising ire.

Franny introduced the young man—the young barrister, he modified, to the welcoming party. Her hand pressed to her side, she seemed to be having some minor difficulty. Before he could step forward, Randolph offered his arm for assistance. She took it—gladly, William silently fumed. She should be leaning on his arm, no one else's. When Franny guided Mr. Randolph Stockwell toward him, William offered a curt handshake and forced a tight smile. She guided her visitor toward the house, issuing orders to a footman in her wake. Dick trotted behind at her heels.

William scowled at their backs; the visitor's timing could not be worse. Still, William walked over to have a word with the driver of the barouche, one of the rentals available in town to transport rail passengers to their country destinations. The driver nodded, then wheeled his carriage about to return to the village.

"I take it you know this fellow?" Nicholas asked, waiting for his brother after the two Americans and Emma had entered the abbey.

"I'd never met him before, but I know of him," William replied, pausing outside. "Francesca fancied herself in love with the man before she was forced to marry me."

Nicholas whistled low. "And you invited him here?"

William squinted into the sunlight. "It would appear so."

"Your balls must be of tougher stuff than those slabs of stone they're hoisting on the west side."

FRAN TOOK RANDOLPH TO THE BLUE SALON TO GIVE the housekeeping staff time to prepare a room and to discover all that had transpired since she had last seen him. She introduced Randolph to Lady Rosalyn, who paled at his first utterance. She quickly excused herself, Fran assumed to find a vial of smelling salts. Lady Mandrake, on the other hand, took immediate interest in the newcomer. Good. Perhaps that bit of flash would shift her focus away from William and onto Randolph.

"I must admit I wasn't confident of my reception here," he said. "And you"—he surveyed her from head to toe with appreciation—"look different than I remembered."

She patted her hair, then realized the extent to which sections of Mary's elaborate upsweep now dangled about her shoulders. Her straw hat, dusty and battered from the fall, dangled in her hand. She imagined her appearance certainly didn't conform to the Newport de rigueur, much less a duchess persona. Perhaps Randolph wasn't the cause of Lady Rosalyn's distress, after all.

"I had a bit of a spill earlier. I usually look . . . cleaner." Hastily shoving some of the fallen tendrils behind her ear, she sat on one of the blue-satin cushioned chairs and invited by gesture that Randolph do the same.

"I'm so pleased you decided to act on William's invitation," Fran rushed. "I've been so homesick, it does my soul good to have you here. Please say that you'll stay till the grand ball for the Prince of Wales."

"The Prince of Wales is coming here?" Randolph asked, his face incredulous. "I would think making his acquaintance would make old Whitby stand up and take notice. But, Fran, I have to tell you," he said, suddenly looking very serious. "I didn't come here as the result of the Duke's invitation."

"You didn't?" Confused, she nevertheless maintained her smile. "Then what brought you here?"

"Your letter." His face expressed the confusion she felt. He reached in his inner jacket pocket and began to tug at a paper. "You were obviously under a delusion that—"

"There you are," William said, joining them in the salon. "I'm sorry to be detained. Apparently, some difficulties in the renovations presented themselves while the Duchess and I were riding."

Randolph quickly pushed the paper back into his pocket, then tugged at the bottom of his jacket, straightening it.

"Tell me, Stockwell. Do you know anything about British contract negotiations?"

"I was doing something along those lines for Mr. Winthrop's interests in Germany. I'm not sure—"

"Excellent. Allow me to show you the extensive renovations we're making on the abbey. As you can see the venture involves a number of guilds. Come." He waved Randolph forward.

Poor Randolph appeared flustered, Fran thought with a grin. But then he'd never encountered Williams's relentless determination. "But I was just explaining to the Duchess—"

"After our long ride this morning, I suspect my wife is

most anxious to soak in a hot tub and freshen her attire. Aren't you, my dear?" Before she could answer, he continued on. "We'll see the women again at dinner. You know how long it takes them to prepare. Come. Let me show you what we've done thus far."

She supposed she should have protested William's heavy-handedness with their new visitor, but quite honestly, a hot bath sounded wonderful. That spill had affected her more than she'd realized, in fact she wouldn't mind borrowing one of Nicholas's walking sticks. Fortunately, Emma came by to check on her and with very little persuasion assisted Fran up the stairs to her room where, she discovered, William had already ordered a bath be drawn for her. Such a considerate man, her husband.

"MR. STOCKWELL IS HERE? HE'S STAYING IN THE ABBEY?" Mary obviously had no reluctance to let her shock resonant in her voice. It brought a smile to Fran's lips as she soaked in the tub. Mary had tossed a handful of rose petals and lavender into the water and the resulting fragrance was wonderfully relaxing.

"I've asked him to stay till the ball. It'll be lovely to have another American on the grounds."

Mary shook her head. "Didn't you say he married some German girl?"

"I thought I'd mentioned it to you on the *Republic*. It seems that was a lie perpetuated by—"

A knock on the door interrupted. Mary cracked the door and spoke briefly with the person on the other side.

"The doctor is here to tend to you, Your Grace."

"Doctor? I don't think I need a doctor," Fran said, not wishing to leave the soothing comfort of the warm water.

Mary retrieved a night rail and placed it on the bed. "Nevertheless your husband sent for one." She picked up a towel and held it wide. "Up with you and let's get you ready."

Mary wouldn't allow the doctor entrance to the room before Fran was properly dressed and tucked into bed. Once she had Fran situated, she opened the door. "You may come in now."

An older man, about her father's age, entered the room with William on his heels. William quickly introduced Dr. Shipley.

"Your Grace," the doctor bowed to Fran. "We were introduced on the day of your arrival at Deerfeld, but I imagine with so many new faces, you may not recall mine."

"You are mistaken," Fran replied, finding it easy to slip into a mistress of the manor role with William in observance. "I've found it's always wise to memorize the faces of medical professionals whenever I travel to a new city. One never knows when such knowledge will be needed." She shifted to sit a bit straighter, but grimaced with a quick pain in the chest. "However, this is not one of those occasions."

"I believe the doctor should be the judge of that." William moved to the far side of her bed. "That was a nasty spill off your horse."

Irritated, she glanced at William. Surely, she would know if she needed a doctor. There had been no blood, her limbs functioned sufficiently, her muscles ached from her fall—but none of that justified another man examining her in this state of undress. She had no need of a doctor . . . unless . . . unless Bedford was using her fall as an excuse to have the doctor examine her for a possible pregnancy. She grimaced. Her word should have been sufficient, but if this is what it took . . .

"Will you stay?" she asked, directing her question to William.

"If you like." He sat on the mattress by her side.

"I'm going to first check your limbs for breaks," the doctor said. He ran his hand down her arms and legs, just as William had done immediately after the fall. The doctor, of course, found nothing just as she had anticipated.

"Now I'm going to check your breathing. Could you possibly sit straight, madam?"

William immediately braced her shoulder with his arm, helping her to lift into a sitting position. His close proximity reminded her of the quiet intimacy they'd shared on his horse. She nuzzled her forehead against his chin while the doctor placed a metal cup attached to rubber tubes on her chest. She had kept hold of the sheet to cover her breasts for decency's sake, but now she wondered if even the sheet would conceal the effect William's nearness had on her body.

"There's certainly nothing wrong with your heartbeat, madam. It's healthy and strong, perhaps a mite fast." He smiled down at her, then placed the metal cup on her back. "Take a breath, please."

She compiled, then he repeated the procedure a few more times before he would allow her to lie down. William continued to hold her hand, even after she lay back upon the pillows. She glanced at him, surprised he would do this in plain view of the doctor.

"I need to check her rib cage. Will you allow me to turn back the sheets?" His question was directed to William, which seemed odd. William nodded and the doctor turned back the top sheet in wide folds to her waist. He lightly pressed her nightgown down her sides, then pressed her chest in the vicinity of her rib cage. Her breath caught from the sharp pain, but it quickly abated.

"I believe that is all I need," the doctor said, unfolding the sheet to its original position. "Rest is all you need. You'll be sore, but there's nothing serious about which to be concerned." He removed a bottle of liquid from his bag and poured a bit into a spoon. "I'd like you to swallow this."

She let the sweet medicine slide down her throat.

"It's laudanum for the pain." He explained to William. "I'll leave this bottle for her use. Just let her take some as needed."

William appeared relieved. Fran would have drawn a deep breath but she thought it might hurt too much. She straightened in the bed and brushed the top of the sheet.

"While the doctor is here, Bedford, is there another examination you wish performed?" she asked with a meaningful glance to the juncture of her legs.

He raised a brow in her direction. "I don't believe that will be necessary."

The doctor's brow lowered as he glanced from Fran to

William, then he eased into a wide grin. "I'm afraid it's too early to tell if the seed has taken root, if that is your question, madam. You've only been married a few weeks." He raised his eyebrows. "Unless, of course, you two . . ."

"No," they both replied in unison.

The doctor chuckled. "Normally, I would counsel you both to continue in that vein, but under the circumstances the Duchess would fare better with an uninterrupted night's sleep. She shouldn't have any pressure placed on her chest." He looked intently at William.

"For how long?" he asked. Fran thought she could deduce a bit of panic in his voice. She smiled lazily his way, pleased to see that the doctor's pronouncement did not sit well. He apparently was as eager as she to advance their intimate relations. Refusing the examination was satisfying as well. He believed her. That knowledge warmed her more than the perfumed bathwater.

"I believe the Duchess's circumstance should be much improved in three weeks' time," the doctor pronounced. "Father Time is the ultimate healer and we cannot hasten his pace."

William's earlier expression of relief had dissolved into something of a more stoic nature. He offered to escort the doctor out, then kissed her lightly on the forehead. Another surprising public display of affection, she thought, her eyelids feeling heavy. Before the fall, he seemed to avoid touching her at all costs, now he appeared hesitant to be separated from her at all. She liked that. She liked that very much. She yawned, ignoring the faint pull in her side.

The men left the room and she closed her eyes. It had been a long, tiring, wonderful day.

SHE AWOKE WITH A START. THE ROOM WAS BLACK. IF A moon hung in the sky, it must have been buried beneath clouds. Panic leapt to her throat. Someone was in the room. She could sense a presence. She sniffed at the air, then relaxed.

"William?"

There was no answer.

"William, I know you're there."

"How can you tell?"

Relief flooded through her, as she wasn't completely convinced until she heard his voice. How did she know?

"There's a scent." Yes. Now that she said it, she recognized it was true. "Something mixed in beeswax, I can sense it when you're near." She had smelled it in his room when Nicholas showed her the way and, of course, on his skin when they shared a ride on Chiron. She had smelled it as well, she now realized, lingering in her room on those nights she had sensed a visitor. "You've come to see me several times this way."

"You knew?"

He was closer now. Her body tingled in recognition. She longed to feel the press of him down her length. She heard a dull thud, then another.

"I felt your benevolence in my dreams," she answered, thinking he should light a candle so she could see him, though there was something titillating about sharing a conversation in the dark.

"That was not benevolence, Franny." She felt the mattress sag on the far side. "That was lust."

He was next to her then, pulling her to curl along his length. He wore those silk trousers that she remembered from their wedding night, but his chest was bare for her touch.

"How do you feel?" he asked. "Do your muscles still pain you?"

Her fingers drifted across the plane of his chest, a mischievous thought came to mind. "Have you come to dose me?"

"Oh, Franny." He trapped her hand on his chest before it could drift down. "I've dreamed of having you like this, teaching you the pleasures that can be shared between a husband and wife."

"Teach me," she said. "I've always been a excellent student."

"Not now. Not till you've recovered from that fall. We've years before us. We can wait for now."

"We can kiss," she said hopefully. "My chest won't be hurt by a meeting of lips." She drew her finger across the shape of his lips. He captured her finger between his teeth, then drew on it as she wished he would her breasts.

"That's true," he said. "But once started, I'm not sure I could stop with a kiss." He kissed her forehead. "The doctor said that rest was the best medicine."

Sharing a bed with William was the closest thing to heaven she'd ever experienced in her entire lonely life. Having another breathe beside her, being held in another's arms—it was truly remarkable. She remembered once a long, long time ago, she had dreamed of a solitary life, a quiet life as the wife of a barrister left alone to tend her hives and do her translations. Now, she knew that would never suit. She wished to always be surrounded by another such as William and be welcomed in a family of brothers and sisters. She never would have discovered this wonder with Randolph.

"Randolph!" she exclaimed. "Did I sleep through dinner? What happened to Randolph?"

"Ssh . . . don't fret," he comforted. "Lady Mandrake kept Randolph occupied throughout dinner. He understood your need to rest. You'll be able to talk to him tomorrow. Rest now, here in my arms."

"After sleeping all evening, I'm not sure I can go back to sleep now," she said. It did feel marvelous and sheltered in his arms. She had no desire to rise and do anything of a productive nature. Her body sizzled with a unique sort of longing and she wasn't sure she could cause it to lull.

"Would you like me to tell you a story?" His words warmed her ear, turning her insides to warm honey. "I may have a new ending for that beast story you began before." He kissed her neck, sending lovely shivers down her spine.

"Close your eyes," he said. She obeyed, listening to the calming lilt of his low, mesmerizing voice. His voice was one of the first things she loved about him when they'd met in the dark on her Newport lawn. He was dressed as a frog, and she . . . she was wrapped in bed linens.

"Once upon a time," he said, tucking her fully into the curve of his body. "A hideous beast longed for the love of a beautiful American princess . . ."

· Eighteen ·

THE NEXT MORNING SHE WAS RAVENOUS AND alone. William had either returned to his room, or was involved with the workmen, or even out riding Chiron. It didn't matter. She had fallen asleep in his arms, secure in the knowledge that he cared for her. If it hadn't been for that doctor making those entirely unneeded recommendations, they might have done more than sleep. But William was right, they had time for that as they had a full future ahead of them.

Funny. She remembered how she wanted William at first for his seed. She wished to be pregnant to escape him. Now, she still longed for the same intimate union, but for different purposes. She wanted to be close to him in a way that no one else could share. She wanted to give him the kind of pleasure that earned Bridget fame in her journal and experience the pleasure William had promised last night. That set her core to tingling. If she were to become pregnant in the process, that would be wonderful. In the meantime, she'd have William.

"I see you're awake. How are you feeling this morning?" Mary brought a breakfast tray laden with meats, fruits, and chocolate, as well as the bottle of laudanum.

"Much better," Fran said, piling the pillows up behind her. "Much rested."

Mary looked pointedly at the indentation on the other side of the mattress.

"Yes. The Duke spent the night here," she replied to Mary's raised brow. "We could only sleep, due to my chest, but I know that will change."

"Thank the Lord, the man finally gained some sense. These

English chaps sure do take their time about getting to the basics." Mary settled the tray over Fran's lap.

"Why, Mary, is there some English chap that is taking his time around your basics?" Fran teased.

"Never you mind my basics," Mary said with a wide smile. "Finish your breakfast and we'll see if you need any of that medicine in order to get dressed."

SHE REFUSED TO TAKE ANY MORE LAUDANUM, AS THERE was simply too much to do to lose daylight to sleep. Mary loosened the lacing on her corset and fitted her into a comfortable day dress. Fran first went off in search of William. She spotted him in the courtyard discussing the renovation work with the lead builder. She paused to admire his broad back covered by a linen shirt, the strong arms with sleeves rolled up, and his authoritative stance. She idly opened her fan to start a current. To think she'd spent the night wrapped in those very competent arms.

"Are you admiring the renovation work, or the renovator himself?" Nicholas asked from behind her.

"Oh!" Heat spread across her chest. "I was hoping to find you. Will we be sketching later today? I missed my lesson yesterday."

"If you feel up to it." Nicholas smiled, then glanced toward the courtyard. "Perhaps it's time we moved on to the study of the human form. I could speak to William. There's nothing like a live model to inspire the artist's imagination."

She ducked her head and picked up the tempo of her fan, then continued down the hall. She could hear Nicholas's soft chuckle behind her.

She found Randolph in the library.

"Francesca, I had no idea that you were hurt yesterday," he exclaimed, quickly abandoning the book he'd been perusing. "When I heard the doctor had come to see you, I was most concerned. I'm glad you're well enough to be up and about."

She smiled. He seemed so much younger than she remembered. His jaw looked somehow lacking, she could never imagine it nuzzling her forehead the way William did. His muttonchops, that ridiculous extremity of facial hair that was currently the rage in men's fashion—old men's fashion—failed to add maturity to his features.

"I was surprised to see the doctor myself," she admitted. "William must have sent word without my knowledge. He's very . . . competent," she said, realizing how that word suited him in so many ways.

"Competent enough to marry a wealthy heiress," Randolph replied. "Of course he sent for a doctor; he wouldn't want anything to happen to his golden goose."

"It's not like that," Fran protested. "He's not like that."

"No? Why else would he marry an American heiress sight unseen? Open your eyes, Francesca. You can hear him spending your money." Randolph paused a moment, letting the noise of the renovations fill the void.

"I know that ours was an arranged marriage," Fran said. "It's true that he needed the money, but it's not true that it is his only concern."

"Has he said he loves you?" Randolph asked.

Fran couldn't answer. While she felt that William cared for her, and might even eventually grow to love her, he had never actually said those words. She had given him the perfect opportunity in the woods yesterday, but he remained mute. Was it because he didn't love her?

But the intimacies they had shared, the way she felt whenever he glanced at her with that raised brow and slight lift to his lips, or the way his voice reverberated all the way to her toes and back—didn't those things signify love? And if they did, had she told him she loved him?

"It doesn't matter if he told you he loved you or not. He'd be lying if he said those things." Randolph paced back and forth, his fingers lightly tapping his lips.

"Lying?" she asked, perplexed.

"Of course. He would tell you what you wanted to hear, don't you see? If he wants to keep your money, then he has an interest in lying. You can't trust what he says."

It struck her that this was very similar to the argument

William had advanced regarding her supposed pregnancy. He couldn't believe her if she said she wasn't breeding because she had an interest in convincing him he was the father. Did all men think this way? Or was this thinking limited to stubborn, arrogant men who had to be right even when they were wrong?

"The thing is—the reason I came here to see you—is to tell you that I love you, Francesca." He pulled a chair next to her, then sank his long frame on it, allowing his knee to barely touch hers. "If you had received my letters, you would have known that I loved you. Even when you didn't write back, I knew you were waiting for me. I knew that you felt as I did. Then I received that letter advising me of your wedding."

Her chest ached. Not from her sore muscles, but from the heartache she heard in his voice. She knew how he felt. Hadn't she felt the same way when Mr. Whitby advised her of Randolph's wedding?

"I'm so sorry, Randolph." She placed her hand on his. "You know that I never received your letters. I wrote you every day, I thought you'd forgotten about me."

"Forgotten about you? How could I ever forget someone who wrote me a letter like this?" He pulled her first letter from his pocket; she recognized Madame Aglionby's stationery. The creases were worn to the point of separation. A faint wisp of a floral perfume lingered as he unfolded the paper. "You said you burn for me, that you longed for the taste of my kisses, that there could never be anyone else."

She blushed. She could feel the embarrassment spread across her cheeks. "I was much younger then, Randolph. Maybe not in years, but in experience. When I wrote that, I didn't know what love was."

"And now you do?"

"Yes," she insisted. "I believe I do."

"But you're not sure. I can hear it in your voice."

"This is ridiculous," she said, flustered. "I don't think we should talk about this anymore."

Randolph stood in front of her, then leaned down, placing his hands on the wooden arms of the chair on either side of her, effectively trapping her. He brought his stern gaze on an even level with her own. "Francesca Winthrop, I want to marry you."

"But I'm already married."

"It doesn't matter. It doesn't matter that you're soiled goods. I still want to marry you."

"Soiled goods?" Her jaw dropped.

"He forced himself on you, didn't he?" He moved his face so close she could smell the morning kippers on his breath. "Did he hurt you? I'll kill him if he hurt you, Fran. Did he?"

She tried to straighten in the chair to put distance between them but it did no good. His gaze bored into her. Her eyes widened in panic. "I refuse to answer these questions. This is totally inappropriate." She averted her gaze.

"Look at me, Francesca. Look at me." He reached out and physically turned her face toward his. "Tell me the truth. Did he hurt you when he took you the first time?"

She didn't say anything. What could she say? Then it occurred to her to simply tell the truth. "No," she said evenly. "William didn't hurt me."

Randolph stared at her with the eyes of a crazy man, terrifying her. Then he smiled. "You haven't had sexual congress with him yet, have you?" He chuckled, his eyes boring into her as if he could read her mind and bypass her lips. "This is perfect. It all makes sense. If not for her money, why else would he marry Frosty Franny? He couldn't have had a great passion. Once he had your money, he didn't need to prod a cold fish. He probably thought he was being respectful not claiming you as a true wife. Hah, the fool!"

He released his grip on the chair and straightened. "You can have the marriage annulled, Francesca. You can claim fraudulent intent. You can annul the marriage and avoid the taint of divorce. Annul the marriage and marry me."

Now that he had moved, she was released from his confinement. She stood and straightened. Her heartbeat pounded in her ears. This was not the reunion she'd anticipated. "I was pleased to see you arrive here, Randolph. I would like to revisit our friendship the way it used to be. But I will not tolerate your suggestion that I annul my marriage. I have no desire to do so. Nor will I contemplate divorcing William, nor tolerate insults toward his character. If you continue on that path, then I shall be forced to ask you to leave. Do you understand me?"

It was his turn to gulp air. He hung his head and jammed his hands in the pockets of his jacket. "I . . . I apologize. I thought that you might still have feelings for me, the way I still have feelings for you."

"Ours may have been an arranged marriage, but I've grown to rejoice in the consequence. My mother may have played a heavy hand in her desire to gain a title for the family, but in retrospect, I wonder . . ." She dropped her head, feeling suddenly weary after that unanticipated argument. She pressed her hand on her side. "I think I should go upstairs now and rest. I'm feeling the effect of too much activity." She started to leave and then said, "If you should see Lord Nicholas Chambers, could you tell him I've reconsidered our sketching session. I don't think I'm quite up to it at present."

She was proud that she held her head high, that she managed to climb the steps with the help of the banister and stubborn pride, that she found her room in spite of the blur of tears that built in her eyes. A chambermaid was tidying up the room but after one look toward Fran, she curtsied and left. Fran lay down, too sore to even curl into a ball.

Why else would he marry Frosty Franny? Once he had your money, he didn't need to prod a cold fish. She could still hear Randolph's words. They shouldn't hurt the way they did. William had told her often enough that he didn't believe that insulting nickname, but the fact still remained that she was a wife in name only. *A cold fish. A cold fish.* Randolph brought memories of home but not the memories she'd sought. Was there some truth in his words? Is that why they stabbed at her heart with the intensity of that relentless pounding? Tears saturated her pillow. She had difficulty catching her breath, and she hurt. Lord, she hurt inside and out. .

She spied the laudanum bottle left behind from the breakfast tray. Take some for pain, the doctor had said, and so

she did. She didn't see a spoon available so she tipped the
bottle to her lips, sipping an amount she judged to be the
equivalent of what she had swallowed last night. She replaced
the cap on the bottle and stretched out on her bed, waiting for
the darkness to come.

HE WANTED—NEEDED—TO HIT SOMETHING. WILLIAM
stomped his way out of the abbey and into the busy courtyard.
Preferably something tall with an American twang and a
bushy fungus growing on both sides of his face. Men stood
waiting by long, thick ropes that would be used to hoist a giant triangle of stone to sit on the two new pillars beside the
carriage entrance to the courtyard. William strode to the end
of one line and placed the rope on his shoulder and turned his
back to the stone. As if that action had been a long-awaited
signal, the other workers picked up the rope as well. They
didn't wait long for the shout that caused them all to strain
their backs to the task at hand.

Nicholas had told him that he'd caught his wife ogling her
husband through a window to the courtyard. He had liked the
sound of that, his lusty wife ogling him. He had been pleased
as well to hear that she was up and about and not consigning
herself to her bed like a delicate English rose. He decided to
find her himself on the pretense of inquiring after her injuries.

Find her, he did—in the library with her American friend.
One of the consequences of living in an abbey was the amazing transference of sound. It seemed a whisper could be heard
a hallway away, and raised voices probably further. As the
door to the library was open, he could remain a respectable
distance away and still hear every gasp and sigh and bleat of
laughter.

Randolph had said he loved Franny, and that she loved him
too, and he had proof! William bent his legs and back, straining against the heavy weight that threatened to pull him back.
He could have tolerated that if that was all there was. By Franny's own admission she was younger and didn't know what
love meant.

But then the cheeky bugger suggested she have the marriage annulled. Just pretend that it had never happened. And the grounds? Lack of consummation! Well, William could pretend too. He could pretend the other end of this rope was wrapped around that American bastard's neck. He grunted and pulled harder, buoyed as well by shouts of encouragement around him.

He felt betrayed that Franny would admit such intimate details to a stranger. He felt betrayed that he didn't hear a resounding slap in answer to Stockwell's questions, but instead heard laughter. Laughter at him, the foolish Duke. The Duke who couldn't handle the responsibility that came with the title and married a woman whom he couldn't even mount. Then to add further insult, he felt betrayed that Franny invited him to stay on so that they could talk further. That's when he left the hallway in disgust. He couldn't stand to hear more.

The words he'd hoped to hear, the words that would have silenced Randolph, did not float on the currents that carried the full conversation to his ears. He waited to hear "I love my husband," but those words, those critical words, never passed her lips.

The weight on the other end of the rope seemed insurmountable. It pulled him back, made him lose ground. He dug in his heels and pressed his full weight forward.

"Your Grace," someone yelled beside him. "You can stop now. They need the slack. Let the rope go."

He looked to his side and noted the other lines had dropped the ropes so he did the same. Turning to admire the result of his labor, he noticed Randolph standing off to the side, pointing to the set stone. Damnation! Must that man ruin everything?

"You've got a strong back, Your Grace." The foremen of the crew handed him a towel to wipe the sweat from his face. "A strong back indeed. You can pull with me boys, anytime." He smacked the Duke on the back in a universal sign of acceptance. "We're going to drink some of your fine ale and toast the setting of this last piece. Will you join us, man?"

William smiled tightly, noting that the deletion of his title was meant as a compliment, a sign of acceptance. *I never wanted your title*, Franny had said yesterday. Right now, he wasn't sure he wanted it either. "Perhaps later," he replied to the invitation. "I think I need to celebrate the moment with something stronger."

SHE'D SLEPT THE MORNING, AFTERNOON, AND PERHAPS part of the early evening if she judged the light from the window correctly. She stretched out on her side, surprised to note that a blanket now covered her.

"You're awake now, are you?" Mary sat nearby, some mending on her lap. "You were sleeping like the dead. Did you take some of the laudanum, then?"

Fran groaned, noting her dress had been removed, and boots. She never felt a thing. "Mary, put that bottle away. It's too strong and too easy to take. I don't want to spend hours in this bed. I have guests."

"Are you saying you plan to join the others for dinner, then? If so, we should get you dressed. No time for a full bath, but I have water in the jug for a quick wash."

"A damp cloth sounds heavenly," Fran said, pulling herself to a sitting position. "Maybe it'll chase the fog from my head."

Mary busied herself with pouring water into the basin and setting the soap and washcloths to the side of the basin. "They set the capstone on the courtyard entrance today. There was quite a cheer."

"Oh, dear, I should have been there," Fran lamented. "William must be so proud." She should have been by his side to see the culmination of his plans. "Pick something out especially pretty for dinner tonight, Mary. We should toast the Duke's accomplishments."

"They say your duke was the lead man in the rope line to hoist the stone in place. It must have been quite a sight."

"William was in the line?" That would have been a sight to see; a tremor teased her core. How she wished she could have seen it, but she was sleeping away in her room. "You must put that laudanum away. I don't want to lose another day like today."

She washed her face and extremities. There'd be time for a full bath later, for now she wished to see William, hear his voice, congratulate him on witnessing the fulfillment of his plans.

She took the pins out of hair and vigorously applied a brush. Mary returned with an ice blue gown decorated with lace trim. The overskirt was covered with golden honeybees embroidered with a shiny gold thread. It had been one of her favorite gowns and perfect for this evening.

"I'll need to wear my honeymoon pin," she said, excited to see William's expression when he saw her in the gown. Would he remember that it was her trip to the hives that had inspired their interrupted tryst in the woods yesterday?

Urging Mary to hurry, she was dressed in record time. The occasional stabbing pain in her chest kept her from rushing down the steps, but she maintained her progress.

She entered the parlor and all eyes turned toward her—but not the eyes she sought. William wasn't there.

The lips below those many pairs of eyes did not lift in greeting, or even smile at her arrival; they all turned away. Except Randolph. His smile was wide and his eyes very appreciative.

"What has happened?" she asked, an uneasy panic building in her rib cage.

Randolph's eyes grew wide. "Nothing, nothing has happened."

She advanced into the room and tugged on Nicholas's arm. "Where's William?"

He looked away. "Does it matter?" He sipped at a glass of spirits.

"Of course, it matters," Fran replied. "I thought we would be celebrating."

Emma stepped before her, her gaze narrowed and hard. "You wish to celebrate? I am so disappointed in you, Francesca. I thought William had finally found a woman worthy of him."

"I thought you weren't fond of William," Fran said, confused by the many contradictions. Family she had thought cared for her were now cold and distant. The cold and distant acquaintances now acted as friends. Was she still experiencing the effects of the laudanum? Was this some awful opium-induced nightmare?

"I love William as a brother," Emma said, her back straightened. "I love my husband. What William did to me was out of love for my husband as well. I can forgive him for that, but I don't think I shall ever forgive you." She started to walk away, but Fran grabbed her elbow and pulled her out into the hallway.

"Emma, please, I don't understand. What has happened while I slept?" Fran captured Emma's gaze and held firm, all the while offering a silent prayer that William was not hurt or otherwise incapacitated.

Emma sighed. "William told Nicholas that you planned to seek an annulment and cancel your marriage. I told him that I did not believe it of you, but Nicholas suggested you might have grounds."

A cold, ugly stillness slipped through her. There is only one person who could have suggested that to William. She started to return to the parlor, but Emma caught her arm.

"William's a good man, Francesca. I don't know why you feel you should do this thing, but I urge you to reconsider. You've hurt him deeply."

Fran glanced back at Emma, letting her feel the full force of Frosty Franny's famed demeanor. Emma drew back instantly.

"I have not now, nor have I ever, had any intention of dissolving my union with my husband," she said, low and emphatically.

She walked directly to Randolph and smiled in the hope that it would assist cooperation.

"You look every inch a duchess in that dress, Your Grace," Randolph said.

"Thank you," she replied. "What exactly did you say to the Duke?"

He laughed as if she were speaking out of two heads. "I haven't said anything to your husband."

The crack of her slap reverberated like a gunshot. His

hand reached for the reddening spot on his cheek. "Honest, Francesca," he pleaded. "I haven't seen him except when he stood on line for the capstone. I haven't spoken to him at all. I thought he would arrive at any moment."

She turned and saw admiration dawn in Nicholas's eyes. Lady Mandrake quickly moved to offer condolences to Randolph.

"I have to find William," she said to Nicholas. "Do you know where I should look?"

He shook his head. "We spoke in the studio. I don't know where he went from there, but he was not necessarily thinking clearly, which was understandable at the time."

She nodded. "I will find him."

"Do we have to wait on him to eat?" the Viscount whined to Lady Rosalyn. "The food will get cold."

Fran stopped in the doorway, then turned. "You are guests in my husband's home and you will wait on the Duke's pleasure." She sent a cold glare about the room. "If that does not suit, I shall be happy to arrange a carriage to the rail in Deerfeld."

She checked the library and his study, which were in the same wing as the parlor. She was about to take the steps to check the upstairs bedrooms when she thought she heard singing—faint singing. Following her instincts, she stayed on the first floor and followed around to the far hallway. The doorway was open to the arched breezeway, the one she had imagined was trafficked by monks. She approached. The garbled bawdy tune grew louder.

It certainly wasn't a hooded monk that sat slouched with a bottle on the bench across from one of the arched openings. Spotted Dick lifted his head from his position at William's feet and looked at her with huge, sad eyes as if he too recognized the magnitude of William's pain. Her heart twisted to see her competent Duke in such a sad, vulnerable posture. She advanced slowly.

"There she is," he called. "My lovely, lusty Franny, come see what your money has wrought." He patted the seat beside him.

She wasn't sure if he was happy or sad, but she was certain he'd had too much to drink. The stench of stale beer and stronger spirits surrounded him.

"Look at that!" he exclaimed as she moved in front of him. "Your bees have swarmed to carry your train. It's just like one of your fairy tales."

That image made her smile. He waved his hand as if to chase them away, then smiled much like an innocent babe. "Those bees are loyal to you, Franny. They won't leave. Maybe they think you're the queen." He lifted his bottle in salute. "To Francesca Chambers, queen of the bees."

She sat on the bench next to him, while he took a swig from a whiskey bottle.

He placed his arm around her and tugged her close to his shoulder. "Look there, right through the arch. Can you see?"

This particular archway framed a magnificent view of the recently placed capstone and completed courtyard wall. The scaffolding that had been constructed to assist in the renovations had been torn down. She could smell smoke on the wind, a bonfire.

William's chin nuzzled against her forehead, his lips pressed her forehead in a kiss. She closed her eyes soaking in his attention. Even deep in his cups, he cared for her. His finger reached and traced the bee pin he'd given her.

"I think you must be the queen of bees, Franny. Your barb is greater than the rest, deadly, painful." He shook his head then took another drink from his bottle. He rubbed his mouth on his sleeve. "When you leave me, I'll have to come here and sit and remember that we did this, you and I."

"I'm not leaving you," Fran said, tilting her head toward him. "I don't think I could ever leave you."

"See, there you go. Stinging at me with that barb again." His lips pulled into that half smile she loved, but his eyes didn't share the mirth. "I heard you in the library. You and that Randy fellow. You said you were going to have the magistrate annul our marriage because I wasn't man enough."

Even the knowledge that she said no such thing couldn't compensate for the undeserved pain caused her husband because he thought she had considered such a vile proposal. Her heart twisted in agony.

"William, listen to me," she pleaded. "I love you. I have no wish to annul our marriage. You heard Randolph talking. You didn't hear my agreement."

"Yesterday you said you didn't want to be a duchess." He caught her gaze and her heart melted. "If you don't want to be my duchess, I don't think I want to be a duke."

"But you are." She took the bottle from his fingers and set it on the far side of her. "I may not want to be a duchess, but if it's required to stay here with you, then I'll be your duchess."

"We could run away together." He looked at her hopefully. "I helped set that capstone. The foreman said I could work on his crew anytime. I was with them at the bonfire. They're a good sort, Franny. You know that and they all like you. We could run away, and I'll be a laborer and you'll be a laborer's wife." He patted her hand.

"As pleasant as that sounds," she said with a smile, "who would be left to watch over Nicholas and Emma, and keep in touch with Arianne? Who would keep the abbey intact for our children?"

"Children?" His eyebrows rose to impossible heights, which caused an immediate lift to her lips. He placed a hand on her belly. "You'd have my children?"

"I'd have you plant your seed tonight," she said.

"But the doctor said—"

"I think I know of a way. I have a book that talks about positions and—"

He frowned. "You have a book of positions for the four-legged frolic?" He shook his head. "You Americans. Where are the morals in providing young women with books—"

"It's French," Fran said.

"Oh, that explains it." A sly smile twisted his lips. "Does it have pictures?"

"Let's get you cleaned up," Fran said, her spirits lifted. She rose from the bench and held out her arms for assistance. "You have guests."

He accepted her hands and gazed up at her.

"I didn't invite any of those people. You know that, Franny?" He glanced away. "Well, I did invite Nicholas and Emma, but I'd hoped Nicholas could tell me how to determine if you were pregnant or not so I would know if I could—you know—"

"The four-legged frolic?"

"Precisely." He stood grinning. "He wouldn't let me look at his nude sketches of Emma."

"You asked if you could look at nude pictures of his wife?" She placed his arm around her shoulders so she could assist him, then shook her head. "And you complain about the morals of Americans?"

"It was only for sci . . . scientific purposes," William said solemnly. "I wouldn't want to see nude pictures of her otherwise."

Trying to manipulate William through the door to the staterooms apparently raised enough of a ruckus that Carruthers came to investigate. He quickly advanced to offer assistance.

"His Grace is in need of a bath," Fran said with her most upper-class smile, in spite of the fact that her muscles were complaining. "Where is the nearest hip bath?"

"I shall have one delivered immediately to the study, Your Grace."

That would require them walking past the dining room and the salon. She didn't want anyone to see William in this state. She looked about. The nursery was on this wing. "Is Miss Sarah sleeping in the nursery?"

"No, madam. Miss Sarah is staying with her governess for the moment."

"Then let's have the hip bath delivered to the nursery. I'll need towels, a maid's apron"—she glanced at William—"some black coffee, and if you could send Hodgins and Mary, that would be helpful."

"Yes, madam." He left to issue his long string of orders.

Fran opened the door to the nursery and guided William inside. She lowered him to a chair she'd remembered from her earlier visits before locating candles and matches.

Hodgins and Mary arrived together shortly after she had the room ablaze with candles. Their timing was such that she wondered if Hodgins was Mary's Englishman. She glanced between the two of them but hadn't time for inquiries.

She sent Hodgins to retrieve the necessary toiletries and clothing to look the part of a duke. She sent Mary to hurry along the coffee in necessary quantities.

She gazed at William, who was examining a piece of paper.

"What is that?" she asked.

"I believe it's an example of my niece's artwork. She seems to have inherited her father's talents."

She stepped to look over his shoulder at the drawing. She almost laughed. There on the paper in childlike scrawl was a line drawing of a fat frog with a tiny lopsided crown.

William tilted his head up to her. "I love you, Franny. I truly do."

She would prefer to hear the words from him when sober, but she had no doubt of his sincerity. She smiled back. "I love you too, Your Grace."

· Nineteen ·

IT TOOK THE CONCERTED EFFORTS OF THE THREE OF them to flush the alcohol out of him. Not an easy task. His hair was still wet from several jugs of cold water poured overhead, and his stomach soured at the sight of dark liquid in a cup, but he could stand and walk on his own power. Franny hovered nearby, her determined gaze buoying him when he wasn't sure he could remain upright. He wished he could remember all that had happened. He remembered the overheard conversation in the library, but Franny was here, her eyes wide and compassionate. His heart leapt into his throat. Did she have any idea of the devastating effect it would have on him if she should leave? Probably not. He should tell her, he thought, but not now.

She looked magnificent in her blue frock. She wore his pin, he noted. The significance gave him hope that he had misunderstood that earlier overheard conversation. He would rectify that tonight after this infernal dinner. He seemed to recall Franny mentioning that she had some sort of a bawdy book that would at least eliminate the possibility of an annulment. Of course, that sounded too much like something from her fairy tale books. Hmmm . . . did such things exist? Bawdy fairy tales?

The entire company was subdued, especially the Viscount, who he suspected was asleep. He couldn't bring himself to engage Franny's American friend in conversation, but as she likewise avoided the man, he didn't feel extremely guilty.

Nicholas raised a wineglass. "To the man of the hour that set the capstone in place through design and by deed."

"Hear, hear," the others repeated and toasted his accomplishment.

He raised a glass. "To my wonderful wife. I could not have done it without the assistance of the Duchess of Bedford. She, indeed, is my capstone."

After a moment's silence, Emma's cheer of "hear, hear" led to an echoing from the others.

This time Franny rose from her chair first, leading the ladies out of the dining room. He watched her retreating back to the point that she stopped in the door frame, letting the others pass her by as she glanced back at him. Lord, he loved that woman.

The footman advanced to pour wine, but William placed his hand on his glass and requested more coffee instead. He'd need his wits about him a bit longer.

"You disappeared for a while, Brother; could you tell us where you went?" Nicholas asked.

William smiled. "I enjoyed the rewards found at a bonfire with my fellow laborers. Perhaps I enjoyed the rewards a little too much."

The men laughed.

"I must say I was surprised to see a duke at the end of that rope line when it came to raise the stone," Randolph said. "I always thought the English gentry were more concerned with keeping their hands callous-free than putting them to work."

"I think you'll find that dukes, lords, and viscounts"— William nodded to the softly snoring Lord Mandrake—"are basically just men at heart. Some may be more inclined to heavy labor than others, but all are men." He narrowed his gaze toward Randolph. "Very possessive men."

Thankfully, they did not stay at their wine long. When they went to rejoin the ladies, he discovered that Franny had claimed her injury was paining her and had thus retired. William took the steps two risers at a time to check on her condition. He knocked on her door to no avail. She wasn't within.

Worried and frustrated, he walked down the hall to his own removed room. As he approached, a distinct scent of lavender and rose teased his nose. He opened the door and heard the swish of water a moment before he found his luscious naked wife in a bath illuminated by the flickering light of numerous candles.

He stepped inside, taking care to lock the door behind him. Then he tugged free the bow of his white silk cravat before pulling the material free of his collar. "This is a pleasant surprise. I was told your injuries were paining you."

"They were mental injuries, Your Grace."

"Such formality." The imp was grinning like a she-cat. He raised a brow while he set the neck cloth aside. "What is the nature of these mental injuries?"

She changed positions in the tub, the sound of splashing water amplified by the copper sheeting that saved the heat and covered her lower torso. Bloody design hid what he'd most like to see. Red rose petals and blue lavender seed heads floated on top of the water, obscuring what lay beneath. His manhood recognized what his eyes couldn't quite see and thickened in response. Rose petals jostled her skin about the same spot as her neckline, but knowing that eventually she'd need to rise from the water . . . his mouth dried to ash.

"I was mentally wounded that you wanted to look at nude sketches of my sister-in-law and not of me," she pouted.

He grimaced. When had he mentioned that particular request? He couldn't recall. He unfastened the three buttons of his waistcoat. "It was not Emma that I wished to see, just the progression of her belly as her breeding advanced." He stooped and stirred the water with his fingers, but captured her eyes with his gaze. "I hope never to see nude sketches of you, dear Franny, unless they are drawn by my own hand."

She moved her breast toward his fingers, allowing the tips of his fingers to follow the contour to the pebbled peak. "Do you have your brother's talent?" she asked.

He almost choked. "My brother has many talents, but if you refer to his particular one with a paintbrush, I'd have to say no. However, if you will model for me, I will endeavor to practice very, very hard."

She leaned back in the water till petals kissed her chin, then she arched her back allowing the rosy tips of her breasts to break the surface, but those bloody flowers clung to the most interesting parts. He reached to pluck a soft velvet petal from her tip, and briefly fondled the pebbled perfection underneath. Then she submerged them again.

"Are all American virgins as forward as you, or am I extraordinarily lucky?" He slipped out of his waistcoat, then quickly tossed it behind him, God knows where. Hodgins would be undoubtedly tightlipped tomorrow.

She smiled. "You're extraordinarily fortunate. I'm only this way because you forced me to take such extreme measures to encourage you to notice me."

"Nonsense," he protested. "I noticed you that first night when you presented yourself in bed linens."

"Then you hid your interest well." She sighed. "Even though I was forced to adopt such extreme measures, I did enjoy the results of my more forward attempts at seduction." She cupped her breasts with her hands much as she had on the ship. This time, however he wasn't hindered by sea sickness, or hamstringed by a mistaken belief that he couldn't have her. A bulge formed in the front of his trousers.

"So if you find me too forward," she said with a sly grin, "then it's of your own doing."

He unfastened his cuff links and set them aside. Another issue for Hodgins. Then, he rolled up the sleeve on one of his arms. Lifting the copper lid on the bottom part of the tub, he sunk his hand in the water capturing her foot.

She laughed and splashed at him, but he slid his hand all the way up her leg to its juncture. Urging her legs apart, he cupped her mound. She stilled and gazed up at him with impossibly large brown eyes. He traced her slit with one finger and entered slowly wiggling back and forth.

Her eyes closed and her head tilted back. She gripped both sides of the tub and gave him full access.

"There, you little minx." He added more fingers to the intimate water play. "Two can play this teasing game."

"William, if you continue, I fear I may drown. But please don't stop."

He withdrew his hand. "I can't fit in that bath with you,

Franny. If you want more, you'll have to come out." He shook his hand and started unfastening the buttons on his shirt. She opened her eyes and watched him.

"I like watching you undress," she said. "I think I should like to watch you undress every night."

"You'll tire of it soon enough," he said. " 'Sweets grown common lose their dear delight.' "

"Shakespeare?"

He nodded. "What I lack in fairy tales, I make up in poetry. It was one of Nicholas's obsessions." He pulled his arms out of his shirt and sent it the way of the waistcoat. Her lips formed a moue of appreciation. She might eventually become disinterested with his undressing, but he would never lose interest when she looked at him like that. Ogling. Is that what Nicholas called it?

" 'Familiar acts are beautiful through love,' " she quoted.

He paused in the act of removing his boots. "You can quote Shelley? I'm impressed," he said, pulling off the first boot.

She glanced about the room. "Why are we here, William?" she asked.

He suspected the water was losing much of its heat so he tried to hurry his disrobing. "Long ago, my great ancestor led a revolt on the king's behalf—"

"No. I don't mean the abbey. I meant why are we in this room and not the one that connects to mine?"

He pulled the second boot free, and then picked up the towel and stretched it wide. "Come out, your lower lip is trembling."

She bit her lower lip. A scared expression flitted across her face. "Perhaps you could close your eyes while I stand?"

He sighed audibly, then tilted his head to look down at her. "Franny, my dear. In the next twenty-four hours, I plan to explore your luscious body so thoroughly that there will not be an inch that I have not tasted, stroked, or kissed. I intend to pump you so full of seed that the suggestion that we have not been as man and wife will be laughable at best. And I intend to pleasure you in such meticulous detail that you will never entertain a thought of leaving me. Now stand."

She did, quickly and without complaint. His breath caught. She resembled a garden nymph, rose petals clung to her moist skin in the most intriguing of places, fragrant lavender heads pressed her belly and rode her fleece. "My God, you are beautiful. We should have done this long ago."

She nodded, too nervous to speak, he imagined. He swathed her in a towel, allowing her to hold the fabric closed in front of her. He used another to briskly rub her dry and dislodge the floral elements. He thought he saw her shiver.

"Are you cold?"

"Not cold . . . nervous," she replied.

And probably a bit scared, he thought. How could he have thought she was an experienced woman when her innocence radiated all around her? In one swooping motion, he lifted her in his arms, kissing her in reassurance. Her arms tangled about his neck, encouraging the kiss to mount in passion. He had intended to carry her to the bed but the doctor's warning sounded in his head. He glanced about the room, and carried her to the table he used as a desk, and set her on the edge.

Placing himself between her legs, he quickly dispensed with the buttons on his waistband letting both his drawers and trousers slide down his legs while he responded to her urgent kisses. Probably afraid to look down, he thought. Just as well. His thick cock felt double in size, which of course was a problem, given her untried cunny.

He slipped a hand down to the spot he'd fingered earlier and lightly ran a finger about the circumference. He felt her stiffen.

"Relax, dear Franny. They call this the honey pot, you know. Which means this"—he rimmed his finger around the button he sought—"would be the queen."

While she continued to cling to his shoulders, her head fell back, her breathing shallow. "The queen doesn't have a stinger," she said.

"No. No. Of course, she doesn't." Strange pillow talk, but

Franny was proving to be a unique woman. He continued to tease the bud with his thumb, while he slipped one finger into her tight sheath, then two. Franny gasped, then sighed. He could hear the sound of his movements in her juices. It was time.

"Wrap your legs around my waist, Franny." She complied.

He fitted himself to her opening. "This may hurt a bit but not for long. Are you ready?"

He felt her nod against his shoulder. "Hold on."

He fitted his hands beneath her lovely buttocks and lifted her off the table. Determining it was best to be quick, he let the weight of her settle on his straining cock, while he thrust upward. Her back stiffened. His scarred shoulder muffled the sound of her shout. He held her suspended on his grateful and eager cock, allowing her sheath to adjust to his thickness. When he could wait no longer, he shifted to his left, pressing her spine against the paneled wall while he thrust repeatedly into her tunnel.

Lord, she was so tight. She pressed him on all sides, drawing him in, urging him on, higher, deeper. He twisted his hips, adding more power to his thrust, but when he could no longer control it, his seed exploded into her womb again and again. His knees threatened to buckle, he sagged against her, feeling the combined product of their intimate act sliding down to coat his genitals.

He shifted her back to his desk, letting the wood take her weight while he withdrew. They both held each other, waiting for their heartbeats to slow, their breath to deepen.

"Dear heaven," she gasped. "I never imagined . . ."

"A woman's first time is often marked with pain." His fingers traced patterns on her back, learning every nuance. "The next time will be more enjoyable, I promise."

She pushed back slightly, her eyes widened. "Dear heaven!"

He smiled and pushed her head back to his shoulder where it belonged.

"That's it, then?" she asked. "There will be no question?"

He kissed her neck. "There can be no question. You are mine and no one will take you away."

SHE WAS HIS A FEW MORE TIMES THAT NIGHT AS WELL. They certainly didn't rise for breakfast, and would have missed lunch as well if William hadn't wanted to see the completed renovation in the light of day. She felt quite sated, used, and absolutely wonderful.

She hadn't realized from her courtesan's journal how truly intimate the act of mating, the taking of another into one's body, was. How could Bridget do it with strange men? She couldn't imagine sharing that closeness with anyone but William.

He looked different, younger, and most certainly happier. He kept glancing her way, then shaking his head as if to some silent jest.

"Why do you look at me that way?" she asked, watching him dress, which was not nearly as exciting as watching him undress, but pleasurable nonetheless.

"I just can't believe my good fortune," he said. "I had no idea when I journeyed to America that I was to meet my perfect match."

"Yes, it truly is an amazing twist of fate." She thought for a moment, wondering if it was pure fate or had someone else played a hand. "William, had you ever met my parents before that the engagement ball?"

"No. I'd heard of the Winthrops, of course, but prior to the correspondence from my solicitors I'd not known of your existence."

"Then I suppose it is a matter of good fortune." She stretched back on his pillows, flaunting her naked body for his pleasure. "My good fortune."

They'd tried several positions last night, many she recognized from Bridget's journal, but her favorite was still the first. She had dug her fingers into the hard muscles of his upper arms, feeling their power and protection, and then he rammed into her, claiming her for his own. Her core clenched just remembering the moment.

He picked her discarded towel off the floor, then tossed it over her, a smile on his lips. "If you keep that up, our guests will be storming the doors as neither of us will have left this room for days. Hodgins might be out in the hallway as we speak." He glanced to the door.

"I'll slip back through the passage as soon as you've gone," she said. "Tell me though, you never answered my question last night about this room. The connecting door to the master's bedroom would be more convenient than the secret passageway."

"That was my father's room, the old Duke of Bedford. The one that gave me this." He touched his shoulder. "He lived his life to tell me that I was never good enough to assume responsibility for the dukedom, no matter how hard I tried to prove otherwise." He paused, a wistful expression crossed his face. "It was the strangest thing. Sometimes I thought he was proud of us, that he cared. Then the next moment, you could see pure hatred in his eyes."

He leaned down and stroked her face. "Then he died, and I discovered he hadn't been a very good steward of all that had been entrusted to him. That's what led me to you." He smiled, but only for a moment. He straightened.

"I just couldn't move into his room. Too many unpleasant memories remain. After the ball, after the London season, when we return here next summer, perhaps then my feelings will have changed." He kissed her. "Go along now. I don't know how long I can last if I know you're up here waiting for me."

HE LEFT AND SHE SLIPPED INTO THE NIGHT RAIL AND wrapper that she had worn to go through the passageway last night. Mary waited for her on the other end and assisted her in dressing for the remainder of the day.

"There's talk that the ghost of the abbey has awakened. Several people heard him last night moaning and groaning," Mary advised with a grin on her face.

"Oh?" Fran felt her cheeks warm, thinking perhaps she hadn't fully closed the mantel door last night.

"I'd say it's about time," Mary said. Fran smiled, thinking how blessed she was with her maid.

Fran stopped by the nursery first to ensure everything had been cleared from last night's sobering activities with William. The room could still use a nice airing out, but nothing of consequence remained to suggest William was less than the Duke he strove hard to be.

It was time now for her to be the Duchess he wished her to be.

As if wakened from a long sleep, Fran suddenly recognized all that needed to be accomplished for the abbey to be brought to a standard worthy of a duke in the few days before Bertie's arrival. She needed to speak to the cook about the possibility of adding herbs, spices, and more honey to her repertoire. She wanted to check the guest rooms to see they'd been properly refurbished. And, she wanted to visit the old Duke's bedroom to see what changes she could make that might cleanse the room of memories.

She was on her way to find Lady Rosalyn, to settle the past disputes between them and request her opinion on some changes she wished to make, but Randolph found her first. He pulled her into the library to talk.

"I've been waiting all morning to speak to you, Francesca," he said. "I wanted to apologize. I had thought you were forced into this marriage, but I could tell from the dinner last night that you have strong feelings toward Bedford. I hope he is good to you, Fran. I should never have interfered."

"No," she agreed. "You should not have."

"I didn't want to lose your friendship over this." He issued a sly smile. "We were good friends at one time. Do you remember?"

"Those days seem so long ago, but yes, I remember." This was more like the Randolph whose friendship she'd enjoyed in Newport.

He traced the title of one of the books lying on the table,

something about classical architecture. She smiled. Undoubtedly one of William's books.

"I've left the law firm. When I learned how Whitby had intercepted our letters and told you that untruth about my supposed marriage, I knew I couldn't stay there."

"Oh, Randolph, I'm so sorry," she said.

"That's when I decided to come here and plead my case." He smiled. "I'm a lawyer, after all. A good one, I thought."

"My father was always complimentary toward your work."

His eyes reflected his appreciation. "Thank you. I'm hoping I might be able to get a position directly with his company. A letter from you might help. Or perhaps . . . the Duke?" He glanced at her hopefully.

"I shall speak with him about it," Fran promised. He sighed his gratitude. "But I won't tolerate any more talk of annulments," she said, waving a finger.

"I'm guessing as you haven't taken a seat that you no longer have grounds." He chuckled. "I heard the famed abbey ghost moan repeatedly last night."

"Oh, dear!" She opened her fan and whipped up a current.

"Now, your only option is a divorce. In that case, the Duke will keep all your money and you will get your freedom amid scandalous innuendo, of course."

"I have no desire to pursue such an option," she insisted.

"I thought you might say as much," Randolph said. "But circumstances have been known to change and if you ever reconsider . . . don't forget my offer of marriage still stands." He smiled sheepishly.

She patted his hand. "I hope one day you'll find the same happiness that I enjoy with Bedford." She held his gaze for a moment. "Now I'm off. I have a long list of things to do and little time to see them accomplished."

He accompanied her to the door. Before she left, she turned and placed her hand on his shoulder. "I know somewhere in the world there's an adoring woman who will be both honored and delighted to be your wife. You deserve nothing less."

She hadn't gone far down the hallway when she heard

Randolph say, "I thought I had found such a woman. I thought I had found you."

THE TRULY LOVELY THING ABOUT BEING A GUEST AT Deerfeld Abbey was that private conversations could be so easily overheard, Lady Mandrake reflected as she stood in the recess of a doorway down the hall. So a divorce would leave Bedford with all the money of Midas, and that disrespectful bit of baggage, not a farthing. She rather liked the sound of that. She could appreciate that the Duchess would not seek a divorce; after all, Lily had heard the ghost moaning last night as well, and darn irritating it was when she knew precisely what Bedford was doing to his willing wife. He'd done the same to her until Miss American Heiress came along.

What was it about Frosty Franny that had men falling at her feet with marriage proposals, anyway? Could it be that they found her remote disinterest alluring in some way? She doubted it. Lily had found her success in giving men what they wanted, then blackmailing them into marriage or money. No need to alter a proven formula.

Funny that the barrister said he had left his employer. Was that the American way of saying, "discharged"? At least that's what he had admitted to her after a few glasses of Bedford's excellent brandy. He was obviously still moon-faced over the American tart. Marriage to her would go far with the employer-to-be father, wouldn't it? She was sure she could use that knowledge in her planning.

So how could she convince Bedford that he should divorce his wife? One thing she knew about Bedford was his constant insistence on maintaining at least the appearance of respectability. So if she could prove his new wife was an embarrassment, that she was causing him dishonor, that might do the trick. She'd stick around to console him, of course, and resume their previous affair. The Viscount should expire any day now; a little more antimony in his food might do the trick. Then she would be the new Duchess of Bedford, and a far better job she would do of it than some American transplant.

She just needed the right set of circumstances to paint the sort of picture even Bedford couldn't deny. Bertie's arrival later in the week and his well-known predilection for married women might prove just the thing. Just the thing indeed.

· Twenty ·

MRS. TUBERVILLE OPENED THE OLD DUKE'S BED-room. Unlike the other unused rooms, this one had been maintained just as if the old man had stepped out for a moment. Fran looked to the housekeeper for an explanation.

"Lady Rosalyn insisted it be kept like this. Perhaps she thought her brother would return someday."

"But he died, didn't he?" she asked.

Mrs. Tuberville nodded. "They carried him out and put him in the ground."

"Then I see no need to keep this shrine to the old Duke," Fran said. A mammoth wooden carving of the family crest mounted on the wall opposite the bed gave the entire room a sinister and unholy feel. Had it been small enough to hang over a fireplace, she might have granted it a place in another bedroom, but it was truly out of place, even in this, the grandest of bedrooms.

Of course, her opinion may have been different if she hadn't seen the same image used as a form of torture. "That thing needs to come down," Fran indicated. "It's too large for this room."

The housekeeper's lips thinned. "Lady Rosalyn will not approve."

"Lady Rosalyn is not the Duchess of Bedford," Fran reminded her. "I shall deal with my aunt."

How strange the words "my aunt" sounded. Yet if she were to make the changes she desired and still maintain family harmony, she'd have to convince Lady Rosalyn to think of her as "her niece." It might take some doing.

"It's an impressive piece," she admitted. "The workmanship should be on public display . . ."

That's it. That's the argument to set before Lady Rosalyn. Surely she wouldn't object to displaying something that would speak to the magnificence of her family's history. Pleased she had constructed a winning argument to present to her aunt, she confidently advised Mrs. Tuberville. "Please arrange for its removal from this wall. I'll give instruction later where to place it. I'd like that dark portrait removed as well."

"That's the old Duke's father, Your Grace. The current Duke's grandfather."

She peered a little closer. Fortunately William and his brother must have taken after their mother. She could see little family resemblance in this portrait. Obviously maintaining an arrogant, stubborn expression was a family trait. William had come by that honestly enough. "Is there a portrait of the current Duke's mother in the abbey?" she asked, suddenly curious.

The housekeeper's brows lowered in thought. "I believe there was at one time, but I can't recall having seen it for years now."

"Nevertheless, this one goes down to be placed with others in the portrait gallery," Fran said. "I think I know just the painting I'd like to hang in its stead." She would have to enlist the assistance of her parents to purchase the painting of horses she'd seen by an American artist, but the painting so suited William, it would be of a par with his consideration in commissioning her pin.

She rubbed her arms. "It's so cold in this room, dark and cold. After the ball is past, we'll have this room painted a lighter color. This dark green must swallow the light at night." There should be ample room for William's desk, and a bookcase or two, but without good lighting they would be little use. She'd have to talk to William about modernization of the abbey.

"It's a start," she said. "Let's see the progress of the rest of the rooms."

LADY ROSALYN INSISTED LADY MANDRAKE ACCOMPANY her to the old Duke's bedroom. "She has no right. No right! I've been the mistress of the abbey for almost as long as she's been born."

"She *is* the new Duchess of Bedford," Lady Mandrake said, hoping to stir the waters. "I know I wouldn't have taken such drastic measures had I been the Duchess."

"You've always been the perfect English lady," Lady Rosalyn said, her distress evident. "If you hadn't already been married, I would have recommended to William that he consider you for that position."

Lily had to bite back her laughter. William would never have given serious consideration to any of Rosalyn's recommendations. If he had, he surely wouldn't have married an American.

Lady Rosalyn unlocked the bedroom door. "Look. Just look at what she's done!"

A hideous dark green paint covered most of the room, except for one gigantic pale blue splotch predominately placed on the wall facing the bed. Below the spot, a wooden coat of arms, as large as the abbey's front door leaned against the wall.

"My brother specifically had that family crest placed in this very room so he could see it every morning as soon as he woke. He never wanted to forget his family responsibilities." She dabbed at the corner of her eye with a handkerchief. "It was the last thing he saw before he died." She took a moment to compose herself, then added, "One would think William would have wanted that same inspiration."

Lily surveyed the room, noting its pristine, yet undisturbed appearance. "Is Bedford not sleeping here?"

Lady Rosalyn glanced about. "No. I believe he decided to stay in his old room. He just isn't ready to take on the mantle of dukedom. I've kept my brother's room just as he left it for that time when William chose to rightly ascend to the title. That American, though, she certainly has no such restraints."

"What is that in the wall?" Lady Mandrake squinted. "There's something cut into the wall." The two ladies moved closer to investigate.

"What an extraordinary place to keep a safe," Lady Rosalyn observed. "The coat of arms would take several strong men to move. You'd think my brother didn't want to get into his own safe." She laughed. "Imagine that."

"It has a key lock," Lily said. "Do you have the key?"

"Heavens no. It must be long gone by now. Whatever is in that safe will be there for eternity, I'm afraid." Lady Rosalyn hesitated for just a moment. "But look what she did. It's bad enough she removed the crest but there's that awful spot left behind. I can't put anyone in this room now. It's of little wonder that my brother's spirit is restless."

Lily shifted her gaze to the older woman. "Your brother's spirit?"

"Have you not heard the moaning late at night?" Rosalyn eyes widened. "I'm convinced it's my brother's spirit that is angry at the things that woman is doing to his legacy."

"Lady Rosalyn," Lily said. "As no one is using this room, may I have your permission to sleep here? The Viscount has an abominable snore and I haven't had a good night's rest since we came to the abbey at your invitation." She reached over and took Lady Rosalyn's hand in hers. "I promise I won't disturb any of your brother's effects. I just wish for a quiet place to rest my head."

She seemed hesitant, so Lily added, "Your sainted brother's spirit may even like the company."

"As long as you are sensitive to his things, and don't mind the mark on the wall, I don't see why not," Rosalyn said.

Excellent. Lily would bet that key was still in the room somewhere and if so, she'd find it. A safe, and a rather large safe at that, purposefully hidden behind a mammoth sculpture, especially one as significant as a coat of arms, would likely hold the kind of secrets only a woman of her ambitions would know how to use.

OVER THE ENSUING DAYS WILLIAM WATCHED AS THE abbey magically transformed from a cold, drafty stone cairn to something resembling a warm family home. Franny had distributed his many purchases in such a way as to add a fresh touch of sparkle to each stateroom, drawing the eye away from the old and faded. She scolded him for not purchasing fabrics with which to fashion draperies and comforters. But he pleaded ignorance and promised that he'd take her wherever she wished to purchase such items after the ball.

"We'd have to cross the water to find the best cloth," she teased.

He grimaced. "As long as you dose me with ginger wine in that unique American fashion, I'll take you anywhere."

Even the food tasted better as a result of Franny's involvement. By God, he was a lucky man. The only point of contention remained that blasted coat of arms. So much so that they discussed it that night when she came to his room.

"Franny, I told you I harbor some bad memories about that family crest. Before, I could lock the door to the old Duke's room and never look at the thing. But if you hang it in the ballroom, I won't be able to avoid it."

"You can still avoid the ballroom when it's not in use. It just didn't fit in any other bedroom. It was much too large an accessory. That crest was obviously meant to hang in the ballroom where it would be in proportion to the room." She stroked the side of his face, trying to coax his smile.

"Besides," she added. "If we're to cleanse the room of bad memories so as to make better ones, then the crest had to be removed."

"My aunt is fit to be tied. She's spoken of nothing else but your lack of respect and decorum all day."

"Your aunt is angry because I'm here," Fran said. "She's not willing to let go of the reins."

"Are you ready to take them?" he asked.

"I believe I am," she responded, with conviction. Running a household was similar on both sides of the Atlantic. She knew her mother's methods and standards by virtue of close observation. Consequently, she discovered she knew more than she had thought she would about managing staff and menus. Now that she felt a part of this household and not a visitor, she found it easy to take control.

"And my aunt?" he asked.

"She can stay here as long as she wishes, we certainly have enough room. During the months that we are not in residence, she can be mistress."

"So you enjoy taking command?" he asked, a mischievous twinkle in his eye.

"It's strange," she admitted, "but I think I do."

"Then," he said, lifting her to settle on top of him, "show me."

MOANING FROM THE GHOST FLOWED THROUGH THE walls every night on a consistent basis. The coat of arms was hung in the ballroom where it fit naturally as if it was meant to be there all along. The guest rooms had all been freshly painted and refurbished as much as time allowed. The cabriolet had been uncovered and cleaned to transport the party to Deerfeld to bring back the prince. The frantic pace of the prior week eased. William was still involved in designing projects for other areas including modernization of lighting, water closets, and heating issues, and thus closed off in his study or in consultation with others who knew the mechanics of such things.

Fran, though, was able to spend more time sketching with Nicholas, who seemed exceptionally pleased with her for some reason, telling stories to Sarah, and going for an occasional ride with Randolph. She introduced Randolph to Thackett and showed him the hives. They traveled as well into Deerfeld to purchase items for the abbey and to meet the villagers. She and Randolph fell back into the easy friendship that they'd enjoyed in Newport.

They laughed and talked, but now that she understood how it felt to love someone, truly love someone, she knew that what she had shared with Randolph was not love. In a way, her mother's interference had saved her from what might have been a very unfortunate marriage.

Randolph could not make her weak in the knees the way William could with just a lift of an eyebrow. If Randolph should pout, he just looked silly. If William's lower lip should protrude a mere fraction of an inch, she knew he was really posturing for a kiss, which she eagerly granted. She had, on one occasion, clasped Randolph's forearm and chanced to note how it lacked the hard strength of William's arms. If anything, her time with Randolph just made her all the more eager to return home to her husband.

She was happy, marvelously happy. The problems that did exist, like Lady Rosalyn's tsk-tsking whenever she made the smallest change in the household, or Lady Mandrake's snide comments, or the mysterious ailment that seemed to plague the Viscount's health, well, they diminished in importance in face of the delight she'd discovered in her life with William and his family.

AT FIRST, LILY WAS EXTREMELY CAUTIOUS WITH HER search for the key to the safe. After all, the pathetic little heiress was installed in the room next door. Should Francesca hear any unusual noises through the walls, well, she might just have Rosalyn investigate. Rosalyn would change the room assignments if she suspected her sainted brother's belongings were being rifled.

It didn't help that the old Duke seemed to have an interest in collecting keys of all natures. She found room keys, keys for snuff boxes, keys for drawers, and keys that didn't fit anything in the room—certainly not the safe.

The key to the door that connected to the Duchess's room

proved a fortuitous find. In hindsight, she should have realized that the Duchess was spending her nights with Bedford. Heaven knew that's where Lily would be if the situations were reversed. She gritted her teeth, reminding herself the situation would be reversed if she could just find the bleeding safe key.

Knowing that Francesca was not actually in her room at night allowed Lily to be a bit more aggressive in her search. And, of course, she couldn't resist exploring the Duchess's room with no one the wiser. The chit was smart enough to lock up her jewels; that was a disappointment. Rumor had it that the heiress had diamonds the size of pigeon's eggs, though she certainly didn't wear them to the evening meals. She found a bottle of laudanum on the mantel, which she brought back to the old Duke's room. It could prove handy. The duchess most likely wouldn't even miss the painkiller; she didn't seem to be in a great deal of pain. And if she did—Lily smiled—if would serve her right to not have the means to relieve it. She should have stayed on her side of the Atlantic. Her presence had certainly caused Lily enough suffering.

On the third night of searching, she found a locked box in the back of a drawer of gentlemen's unmentionables. One of her earlier discoveries unlocked the box. Inside lay a key, a single key. She carried it to the safe and turned.

Click.

ALBERT EDWARD, THE PRINCE OF WALES, ARRIVED ON Thursday. With prayers and hopes that the rain would hold off until they returned home, the Duke and Duchess and their various guests took both the cabriolet and the brougham to Deerfeld for the welcoming ceremonies. Much to her surprise, Fran didn't feel the need to disassociate herself from the crowd. Instead, she was able to greet many of the now-familiar faces.

When the Prince stepped onto the platform, and the spontaneous cheering and clapping subsided, William stepped forward to make introductions.

"Your Highness, allow me to introduce my wife, the Duchess of Bedford."

Fran dropped into a curtsy.

"Francesca, it has been a very long time," he said as she rose.

"That it has," she replied with a quick glance to her husband. His eyes widened, his lips separated, and she thought that if she weren't careful, she'd knock him off the platform with the plume of her hat. Her smile deepened. She was afraid to check Lady Rosalyn's reaction. "I'm surprised you remember," she said to the Prince.

"You have met my wife before?" William finally managed.

"I believe we were rather young," Fran said.

"You were a skinny, reclusive thing, as I recall." The handsome barrel-chested Prince took her other hand and held her at arm's length. "I see you have grown into a beautiful woman."

She blushed. "Thank you, Your Highness."

He leaned over and murmured in her ear. "It's Bertie to my friends." He stepped back. "I'm sorry we were unable to attend the nuptials." He glanced at Bedford. "You have married one of our finest, Francesca."

She smiled. "I believe I may have done just that."

Bertie tucked her arm in his and advanced to receive the official welcome from the village dignitaries.

Fran was glad she had insisted that they take the open-air cabriolet so the Prince could wave and be seen by the village folk who had come en masse for his visit. Both he and William sat face forward while she and Nicholas's family took the other seat. The Mandrakes, Lady Rosalyn, and Randolph were resigned to the brougham.

"How are your parents, Francesca?" Bertie turned to William. "Your mother-in-law enjoys a certain celebrity, as I recall."

"I am greatly indebted to my mother-in-law," William said, smiling at Fran. She had to admit she was feeling rather grateful to her mother these days as well. She'd have to ask Randolph to convey her great happiness to her mother when he returned to Newport next week. Letters simply couldn't convey the wonder of the last month.

"I'm sorry your wife was not able to accompany you," Fran said. "I would have enjoyed seeing her again as well."

He gazed at her in appraisal. "She just didn't feel well enough for a trip. My wife is something of a homebody these days."

"Perhaps another time," she said.

He glanced at William. "What kind of entertainments are in store this weekend, Bedford?"

"I'm afraid it's likely to be somewhat quiet. But the stables are full so there's riding and hunting, if you like. We've planned a ball in your honor on Saturday. We certainly have enough hands for a round of cards or two. Otherwise, it should be a restful time."

"We have a ghost," Nicholas inserted. "He's been carrying on quite a bit lately. I'm not sure restful is the right word to describe a night at the abbey."

Fran was tempted to stab his good foot with her parasol. Fortunately, Emma must have felt similarly as Nicholas jumped a bit in his seat. A well-applied pinch, she suspected.

"A ghost, you say?" Bertie smiled. "That might prove amusing."

KNOWING HOW IMPORTANT THIS WEEKEND WAS TO William, Fran dressed to the nines in one of her Parisian acquisitions for dinner that evening. The blue satin cuirasse showed her form in very flattering lines. The neckline was low enough to tease William throughout dinner, but the modesty piece of shirred crepe and gauze fichu made a more demure statement. The skirts abounded with fringe and a garland of wild roses and leaves. This latest fashion called for back interest that fell from the hips so she could forgo the bustle this evening, but she would still be trailing yards of blue satin and trimmed gauze behind her. She wore a rose at the top of one of her puffed sleeves and in her hair, and accessorized with a strand of perfectly matched pearls.

William came to her room so they could make an entrance together, however, the moment she saw him, she regretted the need to accompany him anywhere. If Mary had not been straightening the room after the dressing ritual, she'd have been tempted to simply close the door behind him and let the others enjoy their dinners without the hosts. Heavens, he was handsome, and even more attractive as she knew what lay beneath the waistcoat and cravat, the linen shirt, and the perfectly pressed trousers. Perhaps, he was thinking of her in the same way, as his eyes skimmed over her in a most appreciative way. He bit his lip.

"Franny, how well do you know Bertie?" he asked.

She laughed. "My father's fortune opened many doors for us when we traveled. I believe I was about thirteen, and the Prince was already a married man. Otherwise my mother would have set her sights on him for me." She slipped her hands beneath his jacket. "I'm glad that she did not."

He kissed her quickly. "As am I, but . . . I just wanted to warn you that the Prince has a reputation for dallying with married women. I saw his gaze settle on you in the carriage."

"You don't think I'd consent to something like that?" she protested.

"No. Of course not. I just wanted to warn you that he might make overtures."

She thought a minute. "In that case . . ." She exchanged her tussie-mussie of fragrant blossoms for her hand fan with the bone handles. "Now I'm prepared."

FRANNY PUT THE REST OF THE WOMEN TO SHAME, William thought, entering the salon with his wife on his arm. As proud as he was to be her husband, he almost wished she didn't look as delectable as she did this evening with both the eyes of Prince of Wales and that American fellow ogling her. He glanced toward his brother and noted that even his wife was surprisingly subdued in fashion this evening. Emma was a beautiful woman. Otherwise, he would never have so foolishly propositioned her so many years ago. His brother had achieved enough success with his artwork to keep her in the best of fashion, but tonight there was not an inch of exposed skin from her chin to the floor. Smart man, his brother.

Lily looked to make a play for the Prince based on her attire, and he wished her luck. Anything to draw Bertie's attention from his wife.

His aunt seemed determined to remind Bertie of everything the old duke had said in his lifetime. Nicholas repeatedly called the group's attention to the Canaletto and William's generosity in letting him take the painting back with him. William smiled. It was the first bet he'd been pleased to lose.

The food was superb, the service superior. William could have burst his buttons with pride; everything was perfection. Then Lily began a conversation alluding to recent society scandals and the effect they'd had on the individuals involved. William would have been a bit more vocal in defending the need for honor and respectability in all facets of society, but Bertie seemed disconcerted by the topic. Probably because he'd been in the center of some of those scandals. Not necessarily named, of course, but most definitely involved.

He wasn't sure how much Franny knew about the English aristocracy; she certainly didn't participate in the conversation, but rather just listened intently. Perhaps she sensed the shift in temperament from the Prince who sat to her left as she promptly stood, leading the women out of the dining room.

"You've done well, Bedford. I knew you'd admirably fill the hole left by your father's passing," Bertie observed.

"My brother has been preparing for this role since birth," Nicholas said. "With Francesca by his side, he will be an able steward for God and country." He lifted his glass of port. "To William, the most able Duke of Bedford."

All sipped from their glasses. They had barely returned them to the table when Randolph proposed another toast. "And to the amazing and lovely Francesca Winthrop, may she grace our lives and intellects for years to come."

William narrowed his gaze. "You mean Francesca Chambers. I assure you she is well and truly married."

Nicholas laughed. "It appears Americans have difficulty

holding on to both memories and port simultaneously." He extended his glass. "To Francesca Chambers, the Duchess of Bedford."

They drank. "You are returning to American shortly, Mr. Stockwell, are you not?" William asked.

"I've booked passage for next week," Randolph replied.

"Please let me know if you need assistance to make that departure," William said. "I know my wife has enjoyed your company these past two weeks, and will be sorry to see you leave, but all good things must come to an end."

"Sage advice, Your Grace," Randolph replied, with a steady stare. "You may call it to mind in the days ahead."

It was spoken as a challenge, a glove slapped across the face, but William hadn't a clue what the lad was suggesting, or why. The sooner Stockwell returned to New England, the better.

The Prince, watching the confrontational play, squinted down the table. "Mandrake, are you feeling all right? Are you still with us?" He glanced at William, dropping his voice. "The man looks like death."

The dinner party was perfect, as was the private celebration in the bedroom after. Though if someone had told him it was the last time he would see Franny, he would have made it last a lot longer.

· Twenty-One ·

THE NEXT MORNING, FRAN HAD BARELY TAKEN TWO steps from her bedroom when she noted the door next to hers was open. She went to the old Duke's room to investigate and was quickly pulled inside by Lady Mandrake. Randolph shut the door behind her.

"What is the meaning of this?" Fran asked, her gaze alternating between them. "What are you two doing in here?"

"We needed to talk somewhere private," Lily said. "Somewhere where we won't be overheard."

Fran glanced past Lily and noted the giant blue spot and an open safe inside it. That ominous feeling inspired by the room hit her triple-fold. Her gaze narrowed on Lily. "What is this about?"

"I found something." She picked up what looked to be a diary from the desk. "Something that will ruin Bedford."

Her blood turned to ice. Gooseflesh rose on her arms. "Ruin? His reputation is impeccable. What could possibly ruin the Duke?"

"Perhaps the information that he's not really a duke." Lily's lips spread in a wicked smile, savoring Fran's shocked expression. "He's not, you know, not really."

"Of course, he's a duke. Did you not hear Bertie say as much?" Fran scowled. As much as she disliked Lily Mandrake, the woman was not an idiot. What was she up to?

"That's because Bertie doesn't know what I know." Lily settled down on a chair. Randolph paced behind her. "If you don't do exactly what I say, I will inform Bertie and the rest of your guests of the information that has recently come into my possession."

"What information?" Was she purposively speaking in circles? Or was it Fran's head that spun with the implied threats to William's reputation?

Lily tapped the book. "It says here that the old Duke couldn't get children on his wife, something about a childhood illness. He wanted an heir so he told his wife to find someone else. Someone who knew how to keep his mouth shut. Someone who would be willing to pump up a lather in the Duchess till she bore his bastard."

"That is absurd," Fran protested with a laugh. "One has to only look at the Duke and Lord Chambers and know they are brothers. They are years apart, yet look so much alike that they must have the same parentage." She thought of the locket she'd fastened to a chain and wore today near her hip. "And there's a sister as well."

"They all have the same parentage, but none of it comes from ducal bloodlines. Once the Duchess had sampled his sausage, she went back for more. They're all bastards. Sprung from the Duchess and the seed of . . ." She opened the diary to a place marked by a ribbon, then glanced at Fran. "Could be anyone . . . a laborer, a servant, a farmer."

Lily laughed, a diabolical sound. Randolph smirked behind her.

"It's no wonder the Duke can plow straight and true and . . . deep." She glared at Fran. "As I'm sure you've noticed."

Heat spread across Fran's cheeks, but refused to be embarrassed by Lily's crude sexual innuendos.

"It's all here," Lily assured her, waving the book. "Here in the Duchess's diary."

"I don't believe you," Fran said. "Is that a book of fairy tales? Where else would you find such a fantastical story?"

"Read it for yourself." Lily handed the book to Fran. "Start here, but don't leave the room. We're watching you."

Randolph offered Fran a seat on a hard wooden chair, all

the while averting his gaze. As he should. She would have a
word with him later, after she dispelled this ridiculous story.
She sat with the diary on her lap. Beginning at the place indicated by the ribbon, she read of the Duke's demand and the
Duchess's reluctant obedience. She went to someone she'd
known from her childhood. Someone who could use the
money the Duke had offered and provide her the emotional
refuge the Duke couldn't.

As she turned the pages that bled frustration, fear, pain,
and . . . eventual acceptance, it became clear that Grace Chambers, the Duchess of Bedford, was falling in love with another
man at the behest of her own husband. Fran didn't need to read
it all to see the damage the diary would cause her husband.
Lily's snickers and crude comments would be whispered behind screening fans and palms across the ton. William would
become the source of jibes and laughter.

"Where did you get this?" Fran demanded.

"In a sense, you gave it to me," Lily said, enjoying her
moment of importance. "When you had that hideous crest
pulled off the wall, I discovered a safe. Inside, I found this
diary, the portrait of the Duchess, and a box of records
showing payment of 'stud fees.' " Lily snickered, then looked
at the portrait of a beautiful woman with sad, compassionate
eyes. "It must have made the Duke furious that his pretty
little wife was being used like a bit of tail. That must be why
he locked her portrait in the safe, then buried it behind that
crest."

"What do you want for the lot?" Fran asked, looking inside the diary for verification of its owner. Unfortunately, it
was on the first page. She marshaled her skills as Frosty
Franny to keep the panic screaming inside her head from revealing itself on her face. "William cannot know about any of
this. I'll pay whatever you want."

Dear heaven, the revelation would kill him. His entire life
revolved around being the proper Duke and meeting the obligations tied to the title. And to think she had inadvertently led
to this discovery. Guilt joined the churning vile mixture in
her stomach.

"Oh, you will pay. I want money and more." Lily smiled. "It's a shame, though, that you don't have any money, not anymore. Everything that was yours, now belongs to Bedford."

"It doesn't matter." Fran was adamant. "I'll find a way to get what you want. I'll sell my jewels. I'll speak to my parents. Just tell me what you want."

"I want you to leave your husband," Lily said.

Fran gasped. "What do you mean?"

"How much clearer can I be?" She raised her brows, feigning a look of innocence. "I want you to leave today with Stockwell and go home to wherever you came from. Once you're gone, I'll tell Bedford that you've run off with your lover and eventually convince him to divorce you."

"Lily, it will kill him." Her whole body shook with her fury at what Lily required. "It'll break his heart. If you care at all for him, don't do this. Let the dead keep its secrets."

"Nonsense," she scoffed. "You know his first wife cheated on him, yet he survived. When you desert him, he'll survive again. That you ran off will upset him but not as much as this." She raised the diary as if Fran had somehow forgotten its existence. She would never forget that diary as long as she lived.

"This will ruin him, his brother, and his sister for the rest of their lives," Lily said. "But if you disappear, you . . . you'll be like that storm last night, loud and painful for a little while, then you'll fade to a few low grumbles and then nothing. Bedford will still have your money, even if he doesn't have you. That should give you some small comfort."

She glared at Randolph. "How could you take part in this?"

"I'm really helping you." He smiled in a feeble way. "By leaving with me, you'll be protecting Bedford. He'll never know about the diary. We'll go back to New England and things will be as they were."

Fran shook her head. "Things will never be as they were." How could she have ever thought—in her wildest dreams— that she could love this . . . this weasel?

"And you"—she shifted her glare to Lily—"how will you profit? Bedford will have my money, not you."

"I should be a widow in a week's time," Lily said, patting her hair. "I'll be here when you are not. We'll console each other regarding our losses. I'll encourage him to divorce you, then I'll marry him and become the Duchess of Bedford. I had him once. I'll have him again."

The thought of the two of them together made bile come up the back of her throat. "And if I don't agree to this insidious plan?"

"Then I shall make the information public at the ball tomorrow night." Lily smoothed out her skirt. "I must thank you for gathering so many of your neighbors and family to celebrate. It will make a most gratifying audience for the utter destruction of your husband. You'll be able to measure the spread of the news by the looks of astonishment and the bursts of laughter."

Tears blurred her vision; she couldn't let that happen to him. "Why would you do this? Why can't you just let him be?"

Lily scowled. "If you hadn't come along, Bedford would have married me once I rid myself of the Viscount. You ruined that. Even if I can't have the Duke, I'll take comfort in your ruin. You have a choice. You can be perceived as a cheating and conniving homesick heiress, or a servant's wife who won't be received in the finest homes of London. The choice is yours."

She had no difficulty being a servant's wife, as long as the servant was William. She'd never wanted the title of duchess. But William could not be anything but a duke. It was bred into him, no matter who sired him. His greatest fear was not measuring up to his responsibilities. To take away his bloodlines would be akin to taking his very essence. She couldn't be the cause of that.

If she left with Randolph, her heart would break. She could never love another man the way she loved William. But Lily was right. In time, he would forget about her. As Lily had so ungraciously explained, he'd been through this before. He had his family here to comfort him. Who would comfort her, she wondered? She could guarantee it would not be Randolph. But if she went home to Newport, maybe her father could help. He had influence. But could he fix this? Could anyone?

"How do I know that if I go along with your plan, you won't still expose him?" she asked.

Lily laughed. "Why would I do that? I want to be the Duchess, not the wife to a man broken by scandal."

Fran knew she would rather sacrifice herself than William. She supposed Lily knew that as well, judging from her she-wolf expression. William was important to too many people, while she was . . . important to only one, the man whose heart she was about to break. She consoled herself by thinking that if she went along, she might find a way out of this mess. But, Lord, she didn't know how.

She stood. "I'll have to pack."

"No. No packing." Lily grinned, gloating over Fran's imminent destruction. "You will not say a word about this to anyone. You will go out on a ride with Stockwell, just as you've been doing all week. Only this time you won't come back. By the time Bedford discovers you've gone, it'll be too late."

"It's already too late," Fran murmured, feeling life drain from her heart.

"One more thing," Lily said. She handed her a piece of stationery Fran recognized as coming from her own desk. "You're going to write a letter and I'm going to tell you what to say."

ABOUT NOON, CARRUTHERS RAPPED HIS KNUCKLES ON the door frame to William's study. "Beg your pardon, Your Grace, but your guests are beginning to arrive."

William glanced up. "Already? Have you informed the Duchess?"

"That's just it, sir. We can not find Her Grace," Carruthers said in a level monotone.

"Can't find her?" William grimaced. Franny had been preparing for this weekend for some time. He didn't think she'd

miss meeting the guests. She'd been memorizing the relationships as per that lineage tome just for this occasion.

"Check with the stables, perhaps she went out for a ride,"
he said. "Meanwhile, I'll play the role of affable host."

Carruthers nodded. "Thank you, sir."

AS SOON AS ONE CARRIAGE UNLOADED AND THE PAS-
sengers welcomed to the abbey, another carriage replaced the
previous. He had absolutely no time to inquire further about
Franny's disappearance and was getting damned tired of
making excuses for her absence. Carruthers informed him
that the Duchess had indeed gone out riding with her bushy-
cheeked American friend earlier that morning. So where
could she be? Totally irresponsible of her and downright in-
considerate. So very unlike the woman with whom he'd fallen
in love. A growing concern jabbed at his gut. What if something had happened to her? The rain had made the grounds
slick in spots. What if she'd taken another fall?

By late afternoon, Mary sought him out. She was worried
something may have happened to the Duchess. She hadn't
been to the room to change or prepare for the evening meal. It
was totally unlike her, Mary had said. The stables reported
that the two mounts had not returned. His stomach churned
with suppositions. Something was very, very wrong.

He was pacing in the library when the housekeeper asked
him about serving dinner to the house full of guests. He replied in a yell that he didn't give a bloody farthing about dinner. He was worried about his wife. Bertie stuck his head in to
inquire what in blue blazes was happening. That's when Lady
Mandrake presented the letter.

RANDOLPH LED HER TO A DILAPIDATED TENANT DWELL-
ing that appeared not to have entertained human occupants
for decades. Occupants of a four-footed nature were undoubtedly still in residence. Cold, wet, heartbroken, and miserable,

Fran had lost the ability to care about such trivial things, unless some wild animal currently in residence would favor her by eating Randolph. But that was unlikely.

"I found this building when we were out riding the other day. It looks abandoned. No one will find us here." He dismounted from his horse and attempted to help Fran from hers. She slapped his hands away.

"Randolph, why are you doing this? You know that I love my husband." She had pleaded with him to reconsider his role in Lily's plan during the entire ride. The cool wind pushed droplets of rain off the trees, showering them yet again. The whole world cried with her plight.

"I know you don't believe me, Francesca, but I do love you." He led her to the rickety front porch, then pushed the door open. "You only think you love Bedford, but he's not worthy of you. In time, you'd realize that he's the wrong man for you, but then it would be too late."

He pulled a candle and safety matches from his pocket. He finally lit the candle after several strikes. "You'll see, divorce doesn't carry the same stigma in America as it does here. You may hate me for a while, but eventually you'll come around. You'll see that I'm willing to sacrifice on your behalf."

"Sacrifice?" She glanced around the dismal interior of the single-room dwelling. Some straw had been piled in one corner. A wobbly table and rough-hewn chairs sat to one side by several cupboards and boxes. "What are you possibly sacrificing?"

"Well, I doubt your father is going to hire me now." He issued a weak laugh. "That's all right. I'll find another means of employment to keep you in fairy tales."

Fairy tales! What was he talking about? She'd been living a fairy tale. Her beast had transformed into a handsome prince. Just as she was settling in for her happily ever after, Randolph and Lily took it all away. William would be so worried. Tears welled in her eyes again. She thought she had cried all her tears out when she wrote that letter, yet more tracked down her cheeks on the way to this place. Was there any limit to the amount of tears one woman could shed?

"Not again." Randolph pulled a used handkerchief from his pocket. "I've never seen one woman cry so much in my life."

"I can't help it," Fran sobbed. "When William reads that letter, it'll break his heart. I wish . . . I wish I had never met you, Randolph Stockwell. I thought you were kind, and good, and concerned with justice and honor. How could I have misjudged a person so badly?" She sat on one of the chairs and buried her head in the nest of her arms. Her shoulders shook with her cries.

"I've stocked this place with minimal provisions so we should have enough to eat and drink while we're here." She heard him rustling about at one of the cupboards. She could run for the door, but where could she go? If she went back to the abbey, Lily would spew her venom. The only way to protect William was to stay away at least until after the ball when Bertie and some of the guests would leave.

"Drink this," Randolph said. "A drink of water will make you feel better." He handed her a metal cup. "Then I'll start a fire in the fireplace to take the chill out of the air."

She was thirsty after all the crying. She drank the full glass and too late recognized the sweet aftertaste—laudanum.

Her eyes narrowed on him. "You tricked me!"

He smiled, then became a bit fuzzy around the edges. "I couldn't very well sit here and listen to your caterwauling all day."

My Dearest Bedford,

I'm so sorry to have to leave you in this manner. I only married you because I wanted to be a duchess. I thought I could learn to love you, but I miss my home too much. Don't look for me. I've left with Mr. Stockwell and will be returning to America. I'm sorry if this hurts you, but there really is nothing else I can do.

Yours truly,
Francesca

The handwriting was hers, he'd seen enough of her translations to know that. The stationery was hers as well, but he knew Franny did not write this letter—not as a consequence of her own free will. The sentences did not sound like her and the sentiments were all wrong. She loved him. She'd told him numerous times and in numerous ways. "This letter is a fraud," he said.

"She handed it directly to me," Lily said, all wide-eyed innocence.

"I don't care if the Queen handed it to you," William bellowed. "Francesca did not write this."

"Caution, Bedford," Bertie murmured.

He turned to Bertie. "I apologize. It's just—"

"I agree," Nicholas said. "I've spent some time with Francesca these past weeks and I know she loved my brother. If she wrote this, it was because someone forced her."

William glanced to Nicholas in gratitude.

"I admit she certainly seemed like a woman in love yesterday, but women can be great actresses. Believe me, I know," Bertie said.

"I'm sorry, Bedford," Lily said, placing a hand on Bedford's upper arm. "I know how this must pain you, especially as you've lost one wife before, but I don't think she ever really felt comfortable here. It would be difficult for a foreigner to assume the role of a duchess. Perhaps she felt it was too much for her to handle."

"Excuse me, sir." Mary stood at the door. "I know it's not my place, but I thought you should know that she didn't take her clothes or jewels. The bee pin is still in her case. If she was running away, I think she would have taken her clothes."

"Franny never wanted to be a duchess," he stabbed at the letter. "It says here that she married me for my title but she never wanted it. She also addressed me as Bedford. That's not what she calls me. My Franny did not write this letter." He didn't say that just days earlier she could have had the marriage annulled and not gone through all this, but some things should remain between the two of them.

"Okay, William," Nicholas said. "What do you want us to do?"

"Find her!" he shouted. "She could be hurt. She's most likely in jeopardy to be forced to write this gibberish. Find her." Unshed tears burned his eyes, his throat was so tight so as to make swallowing painful. *A duke never sheds a tear.* But if Franny couldn't be his Duchess, he'd just as soon not be a duke.

"We're losing light if we want to search outside," Nicholas said. "I say we do this. Let's gather up some of the men and send them out with torches to search the adjacent properties. Her horse never returned so she could be somewhere in the neighboring vicinities."

"Her missing horse could be a decoy," Bertie cautioned. "We don't want to leave a stone unturned."

"Then the rest of the guests can organize in teams and search the abbey," Nicholas said. "We'll find her, William. If she's to be found, we'll do it."

"I'll go with the outside group," William said heading for the door. "I know the surrounding land."

"You'll stay here," Nicholas said, blocking his path. "You can't look for her thoroughly in your current state. We'll need someone to keep track of the teams, know what areas have been searched—that's your strength, William. Right now we need a list of the neighbors so we can collect them on our way."

"When we find her, you'll be the one she needs to see," Emma said, her voice shaking. "We'll need to know where to find you . . . for her."

He turned to his sister-in-law. She, more than the others, seemed to understand what was happening from Franny's position. A bond had formed between them that he hadn't recognized before. He wrapped his arms around Emma in a hug.

"We'll find her, William," she said softly. "We have to."

William pulled a sheet of paper from his desk and started writing down names.

The men filed out of the study, calling for volunteers. As soon as William finished his task, he joined the gathering groups in the foyer.

Lily and Rosalyn stayed behind.

"I don't know why they're trying to find her," Rosalyn said. "They should just let her go back home. She isn't needed here."

"Bedford will come to his senses," Lily said. "When he can't find her no matter how hard he looks, he'll have to accept that she left on her own accord. It'll just take some time."

Rosalyn straightened. "Well, now that she's gone, I believe we should see that the buffet is set up so the ladies remaining can eat, as well as the hunting parties before they venture out. They may be searching a long time if the girl doesn't want to be found. We certainly wouldn't want to appear inhospitable."

· Twenty-Two ·

WHEN SHE WOKE, ALL WAS DARK, HER STOMACH felt queasy, and her throat was thick and dry. She stirred, hearing a rustling beneath her. A faint scent of horses, smoke, and mold assaulted her senses. Dull panic rattled her brain. "William?" she called.

"He can't hear you. By now, he won't want to hear you."

Randolph! Her situation came rushing back. She sat up, experiencing an abrasive sliding on her wrist.

"How do you think your husband will feel when he learns you spent the entire day and night with me? I wonder who's sneering down their aristocratic nose now?"

His words were a bit slurred. As her eyes adjusted to the dark room, she heard the slosh of liquid in a glass bottle. Randolph was drinking.

"Even if you somehow find a way back to him now, he won't want you anymore." He laughed low. "Especially that one, so proud and arrogant, bet he's not so proud anymore. Now he knows"—Randolph struck a match, filling the room with a hazy yellow light, before he lit a candle—"how all good things come to an end. Quicker than he thought, I imagine."

He grinned at her. "Would you like a drink?"

She wasn't going to fall for that trick again. She shook her head, then glanced about the room. She lay on a sheet tossed over the pile of straw. A rope had been knotted at her wrist, not tight, but secure. Panic hit her hard and she patted herself down, checking that all layers remained intact.

"I haven't touched you, if that's what you're thinking." Randolph leered. "I wanted to, but I prefer a participating partner, not someone lost in opium dreams. We'll have time for that later when we cross the Atlantic."

"Randolph," she said, trying to keep her voice calm and even kind, but it required all her training to suppress her loathing. "I need to . . . you know . . ." She nodded toward the window. ". . . Relieve myself."

"Are you thinking you can escape? Where can you go? If you go to the abbey, Lily will make sure the world knows the truth about your husband. Besides, he'll toss you out for your betrayal."

"You don't need to remind me of the consequences of what I've done." Her eyes burned, but she had no more tears left. William would be sorely hurt, but still protected by her action. "I won't run."

"I know that, not with that rope around your wrist." He held up his arm and she saw that he'd attached the other end of the rope to himself. "If you try, you'll have to take me with you." He crossed the room to help her stand, but she refused to take his hand.

"Francesca," he said softly. "I'm not going to hurt you. I've never wanted to hurt you. This was the only way to get you free."

Reluctantly, she let him assist her. She needed him off his guard. For what purpose, she wasn't sure. As he'd so elegantly stated, her betrayal made returning impossible.

He led her to the door. "There's sufficient length for you to have some privacy, but I still need to come with you. Let me check to make sure it's safe."

She grimaced. She doubted Randolph could protect her from anything more aggressive than a stack of papers. Not like William. She could face her worst nightmares if he were by her side.

Randolph stepped outside, looking right and left. He turned to tell her she could come out when something metallic flashed, then smacked him on the head. Randolph crumbled beneath the blow.

Fran screamed, a short burst of sound. She backed into the house, unsure what kind of danger faced her. She couldn't close the door, not with the rope attaching her to Randolph's unconscious body. She raked her fingers over the rope bracelet, trying to pull it from her wrist.

The tall shrubs rustled by the side of the porch, then Thackett stepped into the doorway, a shovel in his hand. His gaze narrowed, focusing on the rope tied to her wrist. "Are you hurt? Did he hurt you?"

She nearly collapsed with relief. Perhaps she did as Thackett was suddenly there, supporting her. "You best sit, Missy," he said.

Her father had always called her by that name. That Thackett should do the same gave her a needed comfort. "Thackett . . ."

"Just sit here while I get that rope off ye." He pulled a folding knife from his pocket and sawed at a spot that would still leave almost a foot dangling from her wrist. "This should work until the Duke can remove the bracelet."

"Don't take me back!" Her eyes widened. "Something terrible will happen to the Duke if you take me to the abbey."

He paused in his cutting and glanced at her. "What do you mean?" He nodded toward the door. "You don't want to stay with that fellow, do you?"

"No. No. I don't want to stay with him," Fran quickly asserted. "I just can't go back. I . . . I don't know where to go."

Thackett continued his work on the rope. "Let's get this off ye and we'll figure it out."

"Is Randolph dead?" she asked, a tremor in her voice. It was bad enough she was responsible for causing injury to William, to add the death of another to her burden . . .

Thackett glanced toward the door. "No. I didn't hit him hard enough to do that kind of damage. He'll wake up with a powerful headache. We'll have you gone by then."

"How did you know where to find me?" she asked, thankful nonetheless for his interference.

"I smelled your fire and saw horses where they had no business being, so I've been watching. I thought maybe you were poachers." He smiled. "When that fellow lit the candle, I saw you in the corner with a rope and knew something was up."

"Thank you for your rescue." She felt a wash of compassion for the old man. But then tears threatened again. Randolph was right. She had no place to go.

He glanced at her face, then shifted uncomfortably. "Come on then. I'll take you back to my cottage."

He'd hidden his rig in the surrounding woods. After helping her up to the buckboard, he disappeared for a few moments. Just as Fran was beginning to wonder what he was about, he returned with the Duke's horses and tied them to the rig as well. "He won't be needing these."

She assumed he meant Randolph.

SHE KNEW THAT THACKETT'S CONCEPT OF A COTTAGE would not rival her mother's Newport concept. Still, his residence pleasantly surprised her, the sort of cottage one might encounter in a fairy tale. He helped her off the rig, then led her inside. An oil flame cast a low flame inside the small abode. Within moments, he had more lamps lit and water boiling on a stove. She glanced about at his cozy surroundings. She felt safe here, comfortable. He hadn't a great deal of furnishings in the manner of the typical cluttered parlor, but he had a few baubles, a plant set here and there, and a series of sketches on the wall. Flowers and herbs—the beekeeper's pantry—some had swabs of watercolor, one had a bee about to land on an outstretched petal. She noted a few books scattered about, so it was obvious he read. Yes, a cozy habitation indeed.

He called her to the kitchen table, then laid out butter, jam, and, of course, honey. He set a plate of coarse bread on the table and some sort of cold meat. "I'm guessing you haven't eaten. It's not worthy of a duchess, but—"

"This is wonderful, thank you." She hadn't realized how hungry she was until the scent of the meager repast reached her nose. She lathered honey onto a thick piece of bread and indulged. Once the water was ready, he made tea in heavy earthenware mugs. She spooned some honey into her tea and sipped the hot brew. Heavenly.

"Are those your sketches on the wall?" She wasn't ready to explain what had brought her here. "They're lovely."

He nodded.

"The Duke's brother is an artist. Did you know that? He's been teaching me to sketch so I can illustrate fairy tales." She was babbling, but it was easier than talking about the things that would have to be said.

He seemed to understand. He sat patiently waiting for her to finish, then he refilled her cup.

"Now suppose you tell me why I can't take you back to your husband." He settled down across from her. "I think he'll be madder than a swarm of angry bees if he found that I kept you away without good reason."

How to tell this story. Speaking of her discoveries to one of the estate's tenants seemed another possible form of betrayal. But if she didn't say anything, he could take her back, triggering an even greater treachery.

"Some malicious people have uncovered scandalous information that will ruin the Duke. In order to keep the information secret, I had to agree to go away with that man, and . . ." This was difficult. Much more difficult than she had imagined. Her throat constricted, and tears formed in her eyes. "I had to make it appear that I had run away. That I didn't truly love my husband and planned to shame him." The tears overflowed her eyes; apparently she hadn't cried them out after all. "They said if I go back, the information will be made public."

She glanced up into the kindly face of the beekeeper. "So you see I can't go back. I can't do that to him."

"So these malicious people, they're still back there, surrounding him, and he doesn't know it?"

She nodded. "One is. The other you left in the mud at that shelter."

He dropped his head and mumbled something that sounded like "should have bashed in his brains," but with his heavy accent she wasn't sure.

"So you decided for him? You didn't give him a chance to decide for himself whether this scandalous information was worth the loss of his wife?"

She read the accusation in his glance. "I was protecting him. You don't understand. Honor is everything to him. If he were to discover his bloodlines were not . . ." She caught herself before she completely spilled the secret.

Thackett looked at her intently. "Are his bloodlines so important that you can't love him knowing the truth?"

"No. I love William. How he came into being is of little concern. I never wanted to be a duchess. He could be anything and I'd still love him."

His lips tightened a moment, then he idly stirred his tea. "I'm just an old farmer, Missy, not the sort to be giving advice to high-and-mighty dukes and duchesses. But I know what it's like to lose someone you love, someone who loves you, and it's a pain like no other. I would think my . . . Duke would be able to deal with whatever this malicious person wants to do, as long as you were by his side." He glanced up at her with a sympathetic expression. "When you lose the one you love, you're lost. Utterly, totally lost."

"I know," she said quietly. Wasn't she experiencing that same emotion? She was lost and alone and miserable. She knew William felt the same almost as if they had a special connection to each other's thoughts.

Thackett raised his brows in the same way William did, and it wrenched her heart. She'd noted Nicholas had that ability as well. Could all men do this? Or was it something unique . . .

Puzzle pieces slipped into place in her mind. William had said Thackett had farmed the estate alone for as long as he could remember, the sketches on the wall, the way he lifted his brows . . . *he could be a farmer.* Fran's eyes widened.

"It's you, isn't it?" she said. "You're the father."

He looked away and squinted. "I'm not sure what you're talking about."

But she knew. She was as certain that this man was related to the one she loved as she was certain she could never love another.

"The diary said the old Duke couldn't produce children so his wife found someone who could provide the Duke with an heir. That was you."

"A diary? Grace kept a diary?" His eyes narrowed. "Did she mention my name? Where is the diary now?"

She was right! She knew it. Excitement bubbled within her. "I don't believe your name was mentioned, at least Lady Mandrake didn't know your identity. I imagine she's read every word written in that book in her eagerness to blackmail William."

His lips tightened. "Grace and I were of a similar age, but worlds apart. She being a lady and everything, and me the son of a farmer working the Duke's soil. Her parents negotiated the marriage. It was never a love match. The day she approached me with her request, I thought I was the cock of the walk. Neither of us had been with another so we learned the ways of the night together. It takes more than once for the seed to take and even then, it takes time to know it's growing."

Fran smiled, remembering how William was so obsessed to know the signs of the growing.

"I was living in that croft you were in earlier. She'd show up on my porch at night and leave in the morning. In the process of begetting, I fell in love." He smiled with the memories of a happier time. "She was so good and kind. It didn't matter that I had calloused hands or dirt under my nails. She taught me to read. I taught her about the flowers."

Fran reached out and took his hand in hers. She remembered how she had been impressed with William's calloused hands and strong, muscular frame. Yes, she could understand a woman of quality falling in love with this gentle man.

"The day she knew she was carrying, she brought a letter from the Duke. It promised that her child would be considered legitimate and noble born. He would be the heir to the dukedom and the secret of his true parentage would die with the old Duke. He promised me a lifetime tenancy for my silence and money besides, but I could never tell the boy that I was his father." He glanced at Fran. "Do you know what that's like? Watching your own flesh and blood grow up in another's house? Seeing them but never able to touch or talk without waiting for them to talk to you first? But as long as I kept my silence, they got the benefits that I could never provide—fine food, fancy clothes, an easier life. They got a good education." His face radiated that of a proud father. "William was a fine boy, and he turned into a fine man . . . and duke."

He didn't need to convince her of that. She squeezed his hand. "And Nicholas?"

"After William was born and growing like a weed, Grace appeared at my door again. There was sickness in the city that could spread out. The Duke felt they should have another child, just in case something happened to William. It was important, of course, for the two boys to look alike, so it was necessary that she come back to me."

He hung his head. "I should have said no. I had suffered so much with not seeing William, you know? I knew that Grace was my love, and would always be my love. There wouldn't be another."

He paused to wipe the dampness from the corners of his eyes. "After William was born, she couldn't come to the croft. Now that he wanted another son, I had a chance to be with my Grace again. I'd be able to leave something behind for when I leave this world, and they'd have such a better life than me. Such opportunities. I couldn't deny her, and so we had Nicholas." He smiled. "Nicholas was my father's name. Grace insisted she name this one."

He sipped his tea, most likely cold by now, but it didn't seem to matter. She imagined this was the first time Thackett could tell his story. Once he started, he seemed determined to finish.

"The Duke was like a man with two heads. He remained true to our agreement, but he treated Grace badly. I think he blamed her for obliging his requests. When times were bad, Grace would come to my door, not always for sporting times but just to be held, for speaking kind words, for listening. But sometimes we naturally fell into the old ways. It's hard to forget the comfort that comes when two are like one."

Fran knew exactly what he meant. Being with William in that way was more than finding pleasure. It was more than the acts mentioned in her courtesan's journal. It was more about the unconditional giving and acceptance, of bearing one's soul and knowing it would not be rejected. It was comfort and more.

"We tried to be careful. Grace had some 'mother's helper' solution that she said would keep the seed from taking root, and it worked for a number of years. Then it was obvious she was carrying again and it wasn't by the Duke's direction. I think he might have been afraid that I'd spill his secret about the others, so he made the same sort of agreements for this babe, which was a girl." He smiled. "A little girl who looked just like Grace."

Then his face grew more serious. "The Duke never forgave her after that. She never returned to the croft. I saw her once or twice in the distance, never touching close. She looked withered, sad. I don't know that he did anything to her, but she was dead in a living shell. Eventually, she passed, and a part of me went with her."

Tears streamed down Fran's cheeks, though she hadn't been aware she was crying till Thackett handed her a clean flannel handkerchief.

"I've been happy to see my boys back at the abbey, and I've been honored to meet you as well. A beekeeper! I was smiling for days after learning that." He squeezed her hand that time. She grinned as she swabbed her cheeks.

"I made a trip to the Royal Academy when they hung my boy's painting. I was so proud of him. I only wish my daughter would come back to the abbey in a way that I could see her. I haven't seen her since she was a young one."

Fran remembered her locket and detached it from the chain and handed it to Thackett. "I've not met her, but here's a likeness."

He pushed the clasp and opened the locket the size of a pocket watch. Gratitude that the larger size allowed a larger picture seized her. It was an amazing gift.

Thackett balked at first when he glanced at Rosalyn's picture, but his eyes softened the moment they met the likeness of Arianne. "That's my Grace," he said. "As I live and breathe." A tear slipped from his eye.

"You have a grandchild, did you know that?" Fran asked,

excited on his behalf. "Nicholas and Emma—you'll like her—have a baby girl named Sarah. They have an adopted daughter as well, I believe her name is Alice, who is grown up. You have a whole family who, I'm sure, can't wait to meet you."

She gazed at him enthusiastically. He just stared back.

"I don't have a family. You're running away to keep the Duke from knowing the truth, remember? You're taking from him all the love and joy he will ever find in life, to save him from possibly knowing his sire. You're taking his opportunity to choose for himself the road of his life."

She hadn't thought in those terms, that she was robbing William of a choice concerning his own future. William was always annoyed if someone turned to another for advice instead of him. What would he think to learn of the choices she made about his future without his consent or advice?

If Thackett was correct, by returning to America, she would spare William the pain of knowing that his bloodlines were not those from a line of dukes, but she would also doom him and herself to a lifetime of misery and loneliness. Thackett would be denied the chance to meet his legacy, but he accepted that as part of the bargain struck long ago.

If she returned to the abbey, she'd have to face the effect of her disappearance on William. Would he ever trust her again? She'd be the one who would have to explain the truth of his past and witness the private pain that revelation would cause. And if she were to do all that, given the lofty standards he'd set for himself as a duke, should she tell him that his true father was a tenant farmer—one who'd been given table scraps from William's dinners, one who had been ignored by William for decades? Should she tell him that, or let Thackett's role remain a mystery?

"You believe I should go back, then." Both afraid and anxious to return, she wasn't sure how she could face William after what had occurred.

"It doesn't matter what I believe, Your Grace. You need to do what your heart directs you to do."

· Twenty-Three ·

THE SEARCH PARTIES RETURNED WITH NOTHING TO report. Nicholas rode hard to Deerfeld to interview the train station manager. He reported back that no one had seen Franny and Randolph boarding a train.

That was good news of a sort, but it didn't provide a definitive answer as to her whereabouts. Most of the guests had long since gone to their beds. Nicholas offered to wait with him, but William sent him off to find Emma. One of them should endeavor to get enough sleep to be clearheaded tomorrow when the search continued. William knew he would not sleep until he found her. So help him God, even it meant he had to cross that bloody ocean again, he would do it and bring her home—here with him, where she belonged.

He'd not been a great believer in religion. The abbey chapel had been maintained primarily for the use of his aunt, the servants, and tenants. Tonight, though, it was the Duke who sank to his knees on the cold, hard floor with his head bent in prayer. "Please, God, bring her back. Keep her safe. Bring her home." It was not the most eloquent of prayers, but those were the only words streaming through his brain. "Bring her back. Keep her safe. Bring her home."

He wasn't above bargaining with God. He offered a number of promises if he could just see her again. He suspected God realized William would have bargained with the devil as well if it would bring his wife home safely. Franny, though, was more likely one of God's earthbound angels and so he sent his prayers skyward.

He returned to his study so as to be near the front door if

there was news. Spotted Dick waited with him. The dog had followed William all night as he roamed the empty hallways, giving into the restlessness that came with knowing something was wrong and being unable to fix it. For the most part, Dick had been a silent companion, but now he'd issued a low growl.

"Dick. Be still!" William warned, debating whether to indulge in another glass of brandy. It wasn't dulling the pain the way he'd hoped. He doubted anything could.

"Still no word?" Lily lounged in the study's doorway, wearing a nightgown that had no business being in an abbey.

"No. No word."

"I hate to see you suffer this way, Bedford." She entered the room uninvited. "Wouldn't it make sense to accept that she's run off and just forget about her? You know she'd been riding alone with that Randolph fellow for some time. Keep her money and divorce her, that should punish her for what she's done."

"This is not about money, Lily," he snarled.

She laughed. "Bedford, dear, it's always about money."

He narrowed his gaze. "Don't you have a sick husband to attend to?"

She shrugged. "He's sleeping. I'd much rather attend to you," she said in low, suggestive voice.

He sighed. "Go to your bed, Lily. I'm not interested in what you're peddling. I'm not sure I was all that interested before. You were . . . convenient. Nothing more."

"You'll pay for that, Bedford," she said, straightening. "You'll regret tossing me aside like dirty linen."

Her threat sounded strangely familiar. Like those words uttered by Randolph about good things coming to an end. He was about to explore the possibility of a connection between those two, when Dick perked his ears and started to wag his tail.

The dog heard something. It was probably deer wandering too close to the abbey, but what if it was something else . . . like horse hooves? William left his study with Spotted Dick in tow and strode to the front door. Even Carruthers, who had the uncanny ability to know when a carriage had arrived, had not appeared as yet. William opened the massive oak door, then peered down the long drive. A delivery wagon approached, but one trailing two horses. Why would a delivery come at this hour, it was barely breaking dawn, and why to the front entrance?

Dick became more animated. He trotted toward the wagon.

William stood rooted to the spot, his heart pounding in his eardrums, his throat so full of hope that he wasn't sure he could swallow.

The wagon pulled closer. Two people sat on the front bench. Judging from the whiskers, Thackett held the reins. The other was wrapped in a horse blanket to fend off the morning chill. It was a she, definitely a she, could it be . . . ? He ran toward the wagon. "Franny!" he yelled.

Thackett hadn't reached the circle before William pulled Franny into his arms. He couldn't hold her tight enough, kiss her face, her neck her forehead enough. "Franny, you're alive. I was so afraid . . ."

And then he'd have to kiss her again just to make sure she wasn't an illusion. Spotted Dick pranced around them, barking in celebration. William pressed his chin to the side of Franny's head and offered a silent prayer of gratitude. Then he glanced to Thackett. "I'm greatly indebted to you, sir. I'm not sure I can find a sufficient reward but I'll try. Come back near noon, and I'll be able to express my gratitude more coherently."

Franny pushed back from his embrace. "William, wait."

That's when he noticed the rope around her wrist; he grabbed her arm, holding it at length. Frustration that had simmered so near the surface burst into fury. "Who did this? Who did this? I will kill them."

It may have been the dog barking, or his yelling, but soon others became witness to his reunion with his wife. Carruthers arrived without his jacket, a sight William had never seen before. Nicholas appeared as if he'd pulled on a pair of trousers for decency's sake but was otherwise bare. Lily Mandrake hovered near the abbey door.

"William, please wait." Fran separated herself from him, then walked to the far side of the rig.

"Thackett!" William yelled.

"In the back," the farmer replied with a jerk of his head. "He's trussed up with his own rope."

Franny reached Thackett's side then and spoke with him in tones William couldn't hear. He couldn't take his eyes off her, afraid she'd disappear if he blinked. He saw her point in his direction. Thackett straightened and followed the direction of her finger. What was going on?

"If I recall correctly," Nicholas said, drawing to his side. "There's a hanging tree out front. That poor abbey ghost could use some company, I would think. Do you want the honors, or shall I?"

Franny started to return to him, and Thackett heaved himself down off the buckboard.

"What the devil is going on here?" Bertie, dressed in a long nightshirt and cap, stomped toward William. "I just went to sleep a few hours ago and now—oh, Francesca, you're back . . . with a rope." He looked at William with a raised brow.

"The criminal that was at the other end of that rope is in the back of the wagon," William said. He turned to Nicholas after pulling Franny tight to his side, "Get him out and lock him in one of the monk's cells. The magistrate can deal with him later."

Carruthers had arranged for a groomsman to take the two trailing horses back to their stalls. But it appeared the wagon would be staying in the curve of the driveway for a while. Thackett stood off from the crowd.

William hugged Franny again. "I'm never letting you out of my sight, ever. I knew you wouldn't leave me, especially for the likes of him," he said as Nicholas marched Randolph past the bystanders. "I knew that letter was a fraud. I knew you wouldn't run away."

"William," she said. "We need to talk."

Her voice was even, reminiscent of her Frosty Franny days. He'd have expected her to be overjoyed to be reunited, but then he realized she hadn't said all that much—at least to him. He glanced up at Thackett still standing off to the side, waiting. For what? An ominous feeling gripped his throat. He pulled back and captured her gaze.

"Did he hurt you, Franny? Did he . . ." He didn't want to say the word "rape." It was too vile and ugly to consider.

Franny shook her head. "He didn't touch me. I was drugged and unconscious most of the time, but I know . . . he didn't do that."

"Thank God." He hugged her again, but she pushed back.

"William, we need to speak privately, but first . . ." She turned to Bertie. "I wonder if I might have a moment of your time. I have a question and I'd like your answer before I speak with the Duke."

"This sounds intriguing." He glanced up at William. "May I borrow your wife for a moment?" William scowled but nodded. Franny led Bertie away from the crowd at the door, but remained in sight of William. He couldn't hear the question asked or the answer given.

"Why is Franny consulting Bertie?" Nicholas asked, returning to William's side. "I put Stockwell in that first cell, the one with the rat." He smiled maliciously.

William didn't feel like smiling. "Why is Thackett still here?"

Something was definitely wrong. William stood with his arms crossed, his legs braced, ready for the next threat to surface. Whatever it was she asked, Bertie stroked his chin in a sobering fashion, before answering. Not a crinkle of humor appeared on his face as he and Franny returned.

"Before I tell you about the circumstances that lead to our separation," Franny said, "I have to tell you that Mr. Stockwell did not operate alone. There is someone in the abbey who intends to do harm to you, William. That would be Lady Mandrake."

"Lily?" He almost laughed. Could this just be more of that feminine rivalry he'd witnessed at the dinner table? He glanced toward the front door, but she was no longer in sight. "I know she's upset because I won't participate in the tryst she envisions, but I don't think she'd do serious harm."

Franny did not smile. Bertie did not smile. William felt his own faltering. He turned to Nicholas. "Find her."

"No," Franny said. "Send someone else. This concerns Nicholas as well."

He and Nicholas exchanged confused glances, but Bertie intervened. "I'll take care of it. I suspect the three of you need some privacy."

The sky was well lit with the pinkish light of dawn. The three walked toward the front door. William clasped Franny's hand. He wasn't about to let go. He had some questions of his own that he wouldn't ask in his brother's company, and he didn't want her to disappear before he had answers. As they neared the top of the curve, Franny signaled for Thackett to follow them inside.

"We can talk in William's study," she said. "I'll join you in a moment."

Nicholas started down the hall, but William would not let go of her hand. When Thackett entered the foyer, he gave William a curt nod. "Your Grace."

The old man's face softened considerably when his glance settled on Franny. Something seemed different about the man, yet oddly familiar. Franny asked Thackett if he'd mind waiting in the library until they were through. Thackett smiled as if she had invited him to dance with her at tonight's ball. She accompanied him, with William and Spotted Dick in tow, to the library, then returned to the study where Nicholas waited.

Thankfully, Nicholas had lit a fire in the fireplace. The sun hadn't had sufficient time to burn away the chill of dawn, so the softly crackling fire was welcomed.

She closed the door, then set the horse blanket aside. William recognized her cold exterior, which meant she was struggling to hide her fear. Fear of what? Certainly not of him!

"I have some news that you are likely to disbelieve, but I assure you I've seen evidence that it is true. I was threatened that if I did not willingly go away with Randolph Stockwell and write that horrid letter, the news would be made public and embroil William in a public scandal."

William stiffened, struggling to digest her words. "Wait . . .

let me understand this. You went with Randolph *willingly*? You wrote that letter *willingly*? You destroyed my sanity, my desire to go forward *willingly*? All to avoid some silly scandal?"

"It was not an easy decision, Your Grace," she replied calmly. "It would not have seemed silly to you of all people. I was trying to protect you."

"Protect me?" His voice rose. "You sought to destroy me in the name of protection?"

She sucked in her lower lip. Her eyes betrayed that his words had stung. Which was just as well. He wanted her to feel a bit of the pain she'd caused by her willing escapade. Nicholas placed a restraining hand on his shoulder. "Let her continue, William."

He crossed his arms in front of him and waited. How could she? How could she do this to him? Her gaze flicked his way a moment before she glanced away, focusing instead on the view outside the window.

"A diary has surfaced that belonged to your mother, Grace Chambers, the Duchess of Bedford." Her lower lip trembled. "In the diary, she reveals that the old Duke is not your father."

William barked a laugh. "Preposterous! You're saying that my mother had a tryst and I was the result?" He shook his head. "Have you not looked at my brother? Is it not evident that we are the sons of the same father?"

Even Nicholas managed a nervous smile.

Franny gazed at him, her face a mask of solemnity. "You are."

The silence lasted the space of two rapid heartbeats, then she added, "The old Duke was impotent."

Damnation!

"I think you've taken the fairy tale a bit far this time," William said with censure. "This is not America. Bloodlines are taken seriously here especially when titles and inheritance issues are at stake."

She caught his gaze and held it, but didn't say a word. She just waited. A cold dread settled in his stomach. She was deadly serious.

"You say there is evidence of this?" Nicholas asked.

"There's a diary, and it's in the possession of Lady Mandrake. She found it hidden in a secret safe in the old Duke's bedroom."

"A secret safe? I've been in that room a number of times. There's no safe there," William protested.

"It was behind the coat of arms that I had removed to the ballroom." Her eyes pleaded with him. "I'm so sorry, William. My interference caused this mess."

"The old Duke was not our father?" he said, letting the concept sink in. It would explain, perhaps, the anger and almost hatred, sometimes unleashed on his sons. Perhaps it explained as well the old Duke's constant chiding that William wasn't good enough to carry the title.

"What about Arianne?" Nicholas asked. "Is she our sister? Or perhaps our half sister?"

"She is your sister. Your mother came to love the man she'd chosen to sire her sons. Your sister was the consequence of her continued affair with him."

"It explains why the old Duke never kept any portrait or record of our mother," William observed to Nicholas.

"It explains many things," Nicholas replied.

William's shoulder ached. He rubbed the familiar spot. *You're the eldest. You belong to me. I will have one. You're responsible. You can never turn away.*

Franny looked pointedly at his shoulder, then caught his gaze. Yes. It explained many things.

"I asked Bertie," she said, watching him intently. "Hypothetically, of course, that if a child sired by another man was born to a duke, wouldn't that child still be considered the legal heir to that duke? He said that this would be correct."

"You asked Bertie if Nicholas and I were considered legitimate because of this sudden revelation?" He could feel his anger mounting again.

"I believe he thought I was asking under the assumption that Randolph forced himself upon me," she said. "If a child were to result, would that child be your heir?"

"And, of course, the answer would be yes." He glanced at

Franny. "I had considered such a consequence when I thought you were pregnant by another." He thought he'd be able to treat that child as he would one of his own. He supposed the old Duke felt similarly. Inasmuch as he and his brother never suspected another sired them, the old Duke was successful on some level—but unsuccessful on others.

"So you see, you are still the Duke," she said, her lips turned in a weak smile. "Nothing has changed."

But everything had changed. Perhaps not in a legal fashion, but in a more fundamental way. He hadn't the bloodlines of the ancestors hanging in portraits on the wall. The abbey was filled with people he thought were his relatives, but no longer. In his darkest moments, he couldn't trust that his instincts had been honed by generations of past peers.

"Do you know," Nicholas asked, "who our real father is?"

"It was not disclosed in the diary," she said, "but yes, I know who your father is."

"Is he an earl, or perhaps another duke?" William asked. "I would assume our mother would have turned to another titled peer."

Franny just shook her head. William had an awful feeling that he knew why Thackett was ensconced in the library. He turned to Franny, scrutinizing her face, asking without words if the man down the hall was his father.

A knock on the door caused everyone to jump a little in their skins. Franny opened the door, thanked the person on the other side, then closed it again. She held a journal in her hand. "This is your mother's diary. I'm going to leave it here so you two can read it to verify that what I've said is true."

She caught his gaze, and he knew there would be no need to scrutinize the pages. She wouldn't have left him if she hadn't believed the legitimacy of the diary. It pained her that she was inadvertently hurting him.

"I have some other matters to attend to," she said.

William started forward, his heart in his throat. "I'll go with you."

"No." She placed a restraining hand on his chest. "Stay here." She gazed up at him, her eyes so full of hope and hurt.

"I promise. I won't leave the abbey." Her lips twisted in a small nervous smile. "And if I'm forced, I shall scream bloody murder."

Then she rose up on her tiptoes to kiss him, a quick kiss, a promise. He raised a brow, imploring her to return, and she said the most damnable thing. She said, "That's how I knew he was your father."

· Twenty-Four ·

SHE PAUSED OUTSIDE THE STUDY TO TAKE A BREATH. The worst was over. William and Nicholas knew that their family was not as they had believed them to be. She went to the library where Thackett had assembled a large stack of books beside him. He obviously expected to wait there for some time. He glanced up from a copy of *Great Expectations*.

"I will always value this gift she left me," he said with a sad smile.

It was a gift, Fran realized. The gift of an education, the gift of life experiences. That's what her parents had given her. She hadn't really appreciated that until she met this man who gave up his own children so they could have those benefits.

"I've told William and Nicholas that the old Duke was not their true father. They are reading their mother's diary now so they can see for themselves."

Thackett nodded. "Have they asked about me?"

"They asked if I knew who their father was. I said I did but I haven't told them about you." She caught his gaze so he'd understand. "I need for them to specifically ask. They may choose never to know."

Thackett's lips tightened. He'd come so close to acknowledging himself to his sons. It would be a shame if they decided to remain in ignorance. At least, he'd be able to share his heavy burden with her.

"William suspects," Fran said. She could almost read his thoughts. "But he may take some convincing."

Thackett smiled, so obviously proud of his sons. "Grace always said William was the practical one. He weighed all aspects of a problem and then chose the solution for himself and his siblings. He always watched over his brother and sister. He was the responsible one."

Yes. That would be her William. She felt a moment's yearning to have been able to talk to his mother, to learn a mother's knowledge about the man she loved so dearly.

"May I get you something to make you more comfortable while you wait?" she asked. "Something to drink or eat?" From the sunlight in the windows behind him, the kitchens would be fully functioning, preparing a breakfast buffet for the guests. Guests she'd yet to meet.

"You've already given me so much," Thackett said. "You've relieved this heavy burden I've carried alone all these years. You've told me of my children and their children. I shall be indebted to you always, Your Grace."

She smiled. "I preferred it when you called me Missy. It is my father's pet name for me."

"It's what I called Grace before she became the Duchess." They both smiled at that. Sometimes life spins in a circle.

"I see you're still wearing that rope bracelet," he said. "I can take it off of you now, if you like."

She raised her arm, looking at the dangling length. "It's loose enough that I forget it's there." She glanced up. "I think I should let William remove it. He needs a reminder that I was forced to do the things I did."

She left Thackett and headed upstairs. She wanted to check that safe before any more incriminating evidence slipped into some other unsavory hands.

WILLIAM HAD READ ENOUGH TO KNOW THE TRUTH OF Franny's words. There could be no denial. He hadn't the pedigree bloodline that he had believed he possessed. He left Nicholas in the study reading the diary and walked down to the library. The older man he'd known all his life as just "that old farmer" sat in a chair, his nose buried in a book.

"It's you, isn't it?" William asked from the doorway. "You're my father."

Thackett lowered the book and smiled. "Your wife asked me in precisely those words." William did not return his levity. Thackett nodded, closed the book, then placed it on the table. William closed the door and joined him.

"Yes, it's true," he said. "The Duchess of Bedford sought me out for the purpose of producing a child—for producing you."

"Did you love her? My mother?" William challenged.

"Very much. My eyes once had that same light that I see in yours when you look upon your wife." His face softened as if from a fond memory.

"Damnation!" William replied. "Why didn't you say something before? Why did you allow me to believe you were just a tenant farmer?"

"Would you have believed me if I did?" Thackett asked. William had to concede he had a point.

"I am who I am, son. I haven't your education, your knowledge, your polish. I'm a farmer, and the proud father of two strong men and a daughter."

So many thoughts raced through William's fatigued head about bloodlines and history. He couldn't keep them straight. But he had one overriding question. "Tell me exactly what happened tonight."

And so Thackett did. William's blood boiled anew when Thackett mentioned the rope, and Franny's tears at being forced to leave him in the name of protection.

"But how did she know it was you?" William asked as the story ended.

"I'm not sure," Thackett admitted. "She said it had to do with my sketches on the wall, and that I've lived here all my life, and something about the way I looked." He raised his brows in confusion.

"Yes, she said something similar to me," William said, still trying to make the connection. How did she, a relative newcomer, discover this decades-old secret, while he still couldn't see the similarities?

"Your wife is an amazing woman," Thackett said. "You're fortunate to have her."

"I know," William answered absently.

"I don't think you do," Thackett replied.

That brought his head up. He wasn't used to having anyone contradict him, much less a tenant farmer.

"That girl went through hell for you, lad," Thackett said. "You could see her heart dying in her eyes for what she was forced to do to protect your name. Coming back to you was no easy task either. She's a strong woman and she loves you in a way that only comes once in a lifetime."

William hung his head. He'd been so focused on Franny's revelations he hadn't given much thought to what she had gone through.

"If you understood how truly fortunate you were," Thackett said, "you would not be sitting here talking to an old farmer who lives a very short distance away."

William glanced up, surprised to be receiving such good advice from this source.

"Don't waste these moments, son. You don't know what's around the bend."

The old Duke never referred to him as son. That Thackett did was a strange and unfamiliar comfort. But one he'd be willing to get used to. He stood, having made up his mind.

"Come with me. I would like to introduce you to your other son."

HE FOUND HER, OR AT LEAST HER BACKSIDE, IN THE OLD Duke's room.

After she found the key to the safe, she emptied it of the box of receipts and the portrait of Grace Chambers, Duchess of Bedford. She'd bent into the empty safe, just to make sure she hadn't missed anything when his voice startled her.

"Now that I know I'm not the product of the old Duke's seed, this room has lost the menace it once held." She backed out of the safe in time to see him run his fingers up the molding surrounding the door, pressing the grape cluster that released the mantel door.

He had that mischievous glint in his eye, the one that

instantly signaled butterflies to take wing in her rib cage. She pushed some stray tendrils off her face. "No more bad memories?"

He glanced about the room, then sighed. "I understand now why he was always so angry with me, and why he was convinced I couldn't live up to the responsibilities of being the Duke." He advanced slowly toward her.

"But you do live up to the responsibilities," she insisted. "Your title doesn't automatically grant you honor. You bring honor to the title. And you always have." He was so close. Her heartbeat increased its tempo.

He bent close to her lips. "I've missed you."

She was in the process of rising up to meet his kiss when he snagged the rope dangling from her wrist. He tugged it, pulling her toward the passageway.

"William, what are you doing?" She grabbed the box of receipts, not wanting to leave them out in the open.

He struck a match and lit a candle that sat on the mantel. "Do you remember the story about the little girl who lied to the frog about the liberties she'd allow if only he'd retrieve her ball?"

"Yes, of course."

William led the way into the passageway; they walked past her room and headed toward his. "Do you remember that the father punished the little girl for not honoring her word?"

"I don't recall any aspects of punishment in the story."

William stopped and glanced back over his shoulder at her. "Well, she should have been punished."

She had some difficulty negotiating the passageway while carrying the box and being led by her wrist, but she managed. Anticipation of spending time alone with William in his bed made the trip less cumbersome.

"I seem to recall that you promised you'd never leave me." He pulled the lever that opened the door to his room.

Her heart dropped into her stomach. "It wasn't something I wanted to do—"

He gave a sharp tug on the rope, causing her to stumble through the secret door and smack into his hard chest. He took the box from her and set it aside. "Nevertheless"—he leaned low to her ear, letting his warm breath send titillating currents down to her toes and back—"you need to be punished."

Holding the end of the rope in his hand, he undressed her. What an amazing feeling, being undressed by a man. His lips would come close to her skin, but he wouldn't kiss her. She supposed that was her punishment, and a cruel one it was. She wanted those kisses, ached for them. He removed her bodice and lifted a brow at her "unforgettable."

"You thought to run away from me in this?" he scowled. "Didn't you know I would have braved the Atlantic just to see you in this corset?"

"They wouldn't allow me to change."

He unhooked and unfastened the tapes and hooks at her waist, letting the bulk of fabric slide to the floor. He tugged her forward to step out of the fabric puddle. Then, he took the rope and tied it to the side of the headboard of his bed.

"William, what are you doing?" she asked.

He tugged at his neck cloth, pulling it loose, and with one swift jerk, removed it from his collar. He gazed at her through those half-shuttered eyes.

"Lie down."

She did, ripples of anticipation slipping through her veins.

He clasped her other arm, then using his silk neck cloth tied it to the other side of the bed. She couldn't escape whatever he had planned, but honestly, she didn't want to.

He walked away from the bed and started to undress.

"It seems to me, Miss Winthrop, you're always running away from me." He quickly unbuttoned his shirt and pulled it off.

Lord, he was a sight to behold. Her breasts tingled. "William, I—"

"Is it because you think you'll find more pleasure with someone else?" He unfastened his pants, letting them fall to the floor.

"No. William, I—"

"Because you won't." He removed his drawers and stood before her totally naked, his cock thick and hard.

She felt a pooling between her legs and a delicious thrill of anticipation.

He knelt at her feet and slipped off her shoe. Taking her foot in his hand, he massaged it, then applied pressure to a spot beneath her instep that sent a jolt of dizzying sensation straight to her core. Her toes curled. Sweet heaven! He did the same with the other.

"I think you need to be reminded why you shouldn't run," he said.

He slid his hand up her stocking, following the silk beneath her pantalettes. She pulled a bit at the restraints when his hands reached that sensitive patch of skin above her stocking and beneath her garter. Her eyes closed at the intensity of his strong fingers on that tender spot. The sound of ripping cloth had her opening her eyes wide. He'd ripped her pantalettes right off her!

Clad only in her corset and stockings, she lay totally exposed to him. He pushed her legs wide, a mischievous glint in his eye as he peered at her at a level with her legs.

"William . . . we have a house full of family and guests."

"Let them wait. They're not my family. Not anymore." His hand slipped to the juncture of her legs, rimming her, testing her.

"You're still the son of a duchess and—Sweet Lord in heaven!" His tongue replaced the exploration of his fingers. She twisted at the restraints, but his exquisite assault continued. She was at his mercy, and he was relentless. Waves of delicious sensation urged her higher and higher, until . . .

EMMA GLANCED UP FROM WATCHING SARAH CHARM HER new grandfather. "Did you hear something?"

Nicholas raised his brow. "The ghost?"

"At this time of day?" Emma shook her head, a knowing smile in place.

HE WAITED TILL FRANNY WAS ASLEEP. AFTER THE NIGHT she'd had, she would need a few hours to manage the ball tonight. His eyes burned with fatigue, reminding him that a few hours rest for him wouldn't hurt. But open matters pressed heavily on his mind. He needed to settle the matter of Lady Mandrake and Randolph Stockwell, of course, but also there was something else. A matter of honor and respectability relating to impressions and otherwise.

He sent word requesting Bertie and Nicholas join him in the study. With the box of receipts for the money paid to Thackett and his mother's portrait in hand, he joined them there.

"I just wanted to offer my sympathies for all that has transpired here since my arrival," Bertie said. "I'm sure that Stockwell will receive swift and proper justice for what he's done." William handed the Prince a snifter of brandy and sipped from his own.

"Now that I have my wife back, I'm inclined to believe that no crime has been committed." William raised his gaze. Swallowing his pride came easier, now that he knew his true origins. Perhaps he had been a bit pompous in the past about such things. His lips turned in a slight smile. "I shall be happy to see Mr. Stockwell leave England and I will do everything in my power to make that occur as soon as possible. But my wife is adamant that she went with him willingly in the mistaken belief that she was protecting me."

That last was a bit rough. He couldn't recall anyone making the kind of sacrifice she had made for his benefit. It twisted his heart. At least, now she understood they would face such problems and threats together, and not separately.

Bertie gazed at him suspiciously. "You do know what went on at that place he took her to. You can't just walk away from that."

"I think you may be under a misimpression, Your Highness," William said. "I know the question she asked of you, but it was not because of a possible consequence of her abduction. Mr. Stockwell did not touch her in that manner. Quite honestly, if he had, he would disappear only to be discovered in the crypts beneath this abbey years hence."

Bertie chuckled but it was clear he believed William to be the one misinformed.

William glanced quickly to Nicholas, who nodded.

"You see, her question was concerning me," William captured Bertie's gaze and held it. "I'm the bastard born to a duke."

The Prince's jaw dropped. "What?"

He glanced to Nicholas who added, "As am I."

"This . . . this is extraordinary," Bertie gushed.

"Lady Mandrake stumbled upon evidence that the old Duke was impotent. Nicholas and I were sired by another man for purposes of providing the Duke of Bedford with an heir. This information was used to blackmail my wife into leaving with her American friend."

Bertie looked down at his glass of brandy. "You realize, of course, that if a baby is born to a legal wife within a marriage and claimed by the husband, there can be no question as to the child's legitimacy?" He lifted his gaze to William. "It's been that way for centuries. I know that it's even been suggested that I . . . well . . . I believe it's fair to say that your claim to the title of Duke of Bedford stands." He smiled broadly. "If the old Duke did not disclaim you, neither will I."

"Thank you, Your Highness." He bowed his head slightly. "I felt that as a matter of honor, you should know the truth. Which brings me to Lady Mandrake."

"Oh, that's a sorry lot." Bertie shook his head. "She knew her plot had failed when your wife returned. I found her hastily dressed with that mysterious diary and this." He pulled a bag of white powder from his pocket. "I'm not sure what it is, but I believe it might have something to do with her husband's fading health."

"How is he? Does anyone know?" Nicholas asked.

"Not well, I understand, but improving steadily since your aunt . . . er . . . Lady Rosalyn has seen to his care."

"Lady Rosalyn might just save Lily from the gallows," William said.

"What do you want to do about her?" Bertie asked.

"The evidence to her claim is confined to the diary and

this box of receipts." William placed his hand on the box, then looked to his brother. "The diary is . . . ?"

"In the hands of someone who will pose no threat to our family," Nicholas replied. "He wanted it for sentimental purposes. It's the only link he has to someone he once loved."

Bertie's brows rose. "Then you know who your sire was?"

He glanced at the both of them, but neither responded by word or expression.

"Right then," Bertie said. "I truly do not need to know. You say that box also contains evidence of Lady Mandrake's claim?"

William nodded.

Bertie picked up the box and threw it on the embers from the earlier fire. The box blackened and the receipts curled inward before disappearing in quick bursts of flame and crumbling ash. He dusted his hands. "I believe that takes care of that."

"I trust we can count on your support that should malicious rumors resulting from these revelations surface, they will be discarded as nonsensical?"

"I see no reason to support any claims to the contrary," Bertie reassured them.

"Excellent." William lifted his glass in salute. "Normally, I wouldn't concern myself with rumors true or otherwise, but our sister, Arianne, might be adversely affected should the truth be revealed."

"I'd forgotten about Arianne," Bertie conceded. "How is she?"

"She sent her love and congratulations on my recent nuptials from . . . Switzerland, I believe?"

He glanced at Nicholas, who shrugged. "Our sister does enjoy her travels."

"Is that it, gentlemen?" Bertie asked.

"I believe so," Nicholas said. "We will keep Mr. Stockwell here tonight and I will personally put him on the train tomorrow."

"Along with Lily Mandrake," William added. "Her husband

can stay until he's well enough to travel, then heaven help him."

"Or her," Nicholas added.

The men clicked glasses and then dispersed to prepare for the evening's entertainment.

· Twenty-Five ·

THE BALL WAS TRULY THE SOCIAL HIGHLIGHT OF the summer in Bedfordshire and surrounding counties. The repairs to the ballroom floor had been completed on time, the many new gilded mirrors added a touch of richness, while the recently installed wood carving of the Bedford crest of arms reminded all of the long ancestry of the Bedford line. William had to admit Franny had been right about its proper placement. She'd been right about so many things.

Albert Edward, Prince of Wales, stood handsome and regal in his evening attire. The young debutants fairly swooned when he looked their way. Several young women in questionable marriages flirted outrageously with him as well. Normally, William would expect to see Lady Mandrake in that group, but she wisely chose not to attend this evening's festivities.

The Chambers relatives had turned out in full force to gawk at William's American bride. He was so proud to have her on his arm during the introductions, he thought he might burst his buttons. She was magnificent, elegant, and engaging. The perfect duchess.

Funny how life had changed in such a short period of time. He recalled how he feared his American bride would make him a laughingstock. He, William Chambers—raised to be the perfect duke—discovered he was not so perfect after all. While his wife, who had no interest in being a duchess, could be held as a standard for all others to emulate. He chuckled softly to himself, remembering how he had thought that once married, he could hide his American bride in the country, while he spent her fortune ensuring the continuation of the estate. Now he could not imagine being without her. When he returned to his London town house, Franny would be there as well. Now that would be fun to watch. Franny taking on the ton in London.

There she was out on the dance floor—again—this time on the Prince's arm. Bertie's acceptance this afternoon enabled William to begrudge the Prince a longing look or two at Franny's low neckline. Some things even a Prince was denied, and a dalliance with his wife was one of them. Nicholas and Emma spun by in a waltz. There was a time when Nicholas refused to dance, claiming his leg injury made the movements too awkward. Emma had obviously cured him of that. They made a striking couple and if he wasn't mistaken, Emma was thickening about the middle. Could there have been a breeding female under his roof all this time and he was too foolish to know it? He watched them all with a silly smile on his lips, sipping champagne.

"What are you doing, lad?"

Startled, William glanced at the footman dressed in livery that looked to be a tad tight. Thackett!

"You should be out there dancing with her."

"What are you doing here?" William asked.

"I wanted to see my boys like this," he waved his arm about the ballroom. "All dressed up, dancing with their beautiful wives. So I asked Nicholas to find a way."

"Nicholas?" William scowled. "You asked Nicholas?"

Thackett raised his brows and William suddenly noticed the resemblance Franny had noted immediately. "You were busy at the time," Thackett said. "Something about a ghost moaning."

William smiled. There was that. Franny enjoyed her punishment so much, she vowed to be wicked, just so he could do it again.

"Now go dance with your wife and make this old farmer's dream come true," he said. "Before Carruthers discovers this footman doesn't know squat about fancy doings."

William handed Thackett his champagne glass and set out

to claim his wife. Fortunately, the set ended before he was forced to cut the Prince. Bertie kissed Franny's glove in parting and turned her over to William.

The music began and he guided her effortlessly about the ballroom.

"I had no idea you were such a wonderful dancer," she exclaimed.

"Had you not been hiding on the lawn looking to pounce on innocent strangers, we would have danced at our engagement ball," he said.

"With that large frog head?" She laughed, an infectiously happy sound he hoped to hear the rest of his life.

He smiled, then sobered. As they approached the doors that led to the courtyard he asked that they go outside for fresh air.

Franny had refurbished the gardens, he noted, by hanging baskets of potted flowers from the village. They stood outside, surrounded by their abbey.

"You look magnificent," he said for the umpteenth time.

She smoothed her hands down his lapels. "And you look every inch the perfect duke."

"Perhaps not so perfect," he said, thinking of Thackett.

She sighed. "William, you need to accept that bloodlines do not make a duke. Honor, respect, education, compassion, fairness—those are the qualities of a duke, and those are your qualities as well." She rubbed his shoulder, knowing the mark that existed below the cloth. "I must admit I'm pleased that the blood of someone who could do this to a child is not in your veins. I'd be concerned for our children."

He gazed down at her moonlit cheeks. "I hadn't thought about that, though I do like the sound of 'our children.'"

"The old Duke of Bedford decided you would be his heir. He could have denounced your birthright a long time ago, but he knew you were the one. He took steps to ensure that you would never know you were anything less that the perfect duke."

She tilted her face up to his. "And you're not less. You're perfect."

He slipped his hands around her trim waist and kissed her. Right there, in full view of the dancers inside, in full view of his family, in full view of anyone who might have assumed he was only interested in her money.

And to anyone watching, it was just as obvious that she was interested in only one thing, the seduction of the Duke.

· Epilogue ·

"ARE YOU SURE YOU HAVE ENOUGH ROSES?" ALVA Winthrop asked. "Everyone expects roses at a wedding. Some say orange blossoms as they denote innocence, but I say roses—big red ones—they stand for passion. That's what makes a marriage, passion."

"There are plenty of roses," Fran said. And plenty of passion, she mentally added.

"Your duke looks very handsome," Alva said. She looked at Fran askance. "I haven't heard you thank me yet."

"Thank you?" Fran exclaimed. "You married me off to a stranger; granted he turned out to be a handsome stranger . . . an incredibly handsome stranger . . . but you had no way of knowing that."

"What makes you say that?" Alva responded a little too smugly for comfort. "Do you really think I'd arrange the marriage of my only daughter, my much loved only daughter, to a complete stranger?"

Fran was about to respond, to ask exactly what her *maman* meant, but there was a knock on the door. William walked in.

He took her breath away. Even after three months. In his cutaway tuxedo, he was so incredibly attractive that she sent a skyward prayer of undying gratitude for her good fortune. But then, to listen to her mother, perhaps it wasn't merely good fortune, after all?

"Are you ladies ready? It's about time to go to the chapel."

"William," she scolded. "You shouldn't be here. You're supposed to be waiting at the chapel. It's bad luck to see the bride before the ceremony."

"I just wanted to check that you weren't going to try and escape again." He grinned. "Besides, I'd say our luck has been pretty good so far."

"Escape? What does he mean escape?" Alva asked Fran.

"Didn't she tell you?" William said. "She tried to sneak out on the wedding in Newport." He walked over and kissed her on the cheek. "But I nabbed her in the act and forced her to become a duchess . . . my duchess."

"I think it's lovely that you two are having a second wedding, but I still don't see the need," Alva said. "I would think the extravagant one in Newport would be sufficient."

"Several of William's family members couldn't attend that one, Maman."

"To say nothing of the tenants and villagers." He winked at Fran. "The real reason, though, is I didn't want anyone to think we weren't legally married because we married in America instead of England. I want there to be no question."

"There's also the matter of vows," Fran said. "It's more meaningful to vow to love, honor, and obey someone you actually know."

"And plan to obey," he whispered in her ear.

"Or risk punishment?" she whispered back. His eyelids lowered seductively causing an anticipatory shiver to tingle through her.

"So your family will be there?" Alva asked.

William didn't break eye contact with her. "My brother, Nicholas, will stand up as my best man."

"His wife, Emma, is to be my maid of honor and their daughter, Sarah, will be my flower girl," Emma said, still lost in his gaze.

"How about Arianne?" Alva asked. "Will she be here?"

"You've met Arianne?" Fran quickly shifted her gaze to her mother.

"Oh, yes. Lovely girl. I'm not sure exactly where we met . . . somewhere in Europe. You know how it is, so many countries in a short time. She told me quite a bit about William." Her mother winked at her. "And I'm pleased to say it all appears true."

"I suppose I owe Arianne a debt of gratitude," Fran said suspiciously. Did her mother truly plan a betrothal based on a chance meeting with William's sister?

"As do I." William scowled. "Arianne?"

"Let me make sure everything is ready for the ceremony. It is lovely that you have a newly refurbished chapel right on the grounds. So convenient." Alva left the abbey's master bedroom where Fran had been preparing.

William took advantage of the privacy by pulling Fran up from her chair for a kiss.

"The person you should really thank is my father for incorporating that clause in the marriage contract about our children being educated in the United States," Fran said, enjoying the comfort of William's arms around her. "If it hadn't been for that, I probably would never have consulted that courtesan's diary."

William frowned. "I don't recall a clause to that effect."

"My father said it was there. He didn't want his grandchildren educated in hoity-toity English schools. They were to be educated in America and I would be allowed to stay there with them." She looked at him aghast. "That's why I tried to seduce you so aggressively. I wanted to have your child."

"You wanted to become pregnant so as to escape me?" He scowled. "Marriage contracts aside, a wife stays with her husband, especially this wife and this husband."

"There was no clause?" This day seemed to be full of revelations.

"Not that I recall, but I would have agreed to any terms under the circumstances." He kissed the top of her head. "However, as we haven't any children, there's plenty of time to discuss the best educational choices for our offspring."

"There's not as much time as you may think," Fran said to his shoulder.

He pushed her back, his forehead creased. "What do you mean?"

She smiled and slid her hand down to her belly. "I think it's time to start renovations on the nursery."

Bedford Square, 1922

ESTELLE LEANED OUT FROM THE TINY BALCONY OFF
her bedroom, her face tilted to the sky over Bedford Square.
Rain fell from a blanket of leaden clouds, the droplets cool
and fresh as they struck her skin. She was fifteen. Gawky.
Bookish. Almost too shy to know how to make a friend. Fortunately, none of that mattered on this stormy May evening.

Her life had changed forever today.

She'd met the most marvelous man this morning. To him
she hadn't been invisible. To him she'd been a person worthy
not just of notice but of trust as well.

She'd noticed *him* at once. The schoolyard had been full,
cliques of girls whispering to each other, boys running between them, screaming like lunatics. Estelle was neither
popular nor bold enough to interest either group. Her banker
father's desire to seem more successful than he was did not
extend to kitting out his daughter in the latest styles. She
wore last year's dress and last year's shoes. She wasn't growing anymore, he'd blustered when she'd dared to ask if she
could have new. Why shouldn't she wear what still fit? This
he'd had the bottle to say after buying a real gold cigarette
case for himself, the same as his biggest rival at the bank
carried.

Other events had blotted out those annoyances this morning. She'd been leaning against her usual wall with her latest
book, her I-don't-bloody-well-care demeanor protecting her
from the chaos. A motion had caught her eye: a man, leading
a small golden-haired girl into the schoolyard.

His presence had straightened her from her slouch, had brought her head out of her mystery. It was rare to see a father escort his daughter, and rarer still for him to be so youthful and good-looking. This one certainly didn't resemble any father she knew. He was tall and lean, with a dark brimmed trilby pulled rakishly over one brow. As he parted the crowd his strides were different from other men's, tension and grace in them, like a big predator stalking antelope across the veld. The way his dark brown suit flowed with his movements was as much a testament to his fitness as his tailor's skill. Estelle's own muscles tightened as if she were secretly longing to run from him—though not, perhaps, to escape.

He must be a widower, she thought. *That's why his wife isn't here instead.*

Given Estelle's fascination, it took a moment for her to notice his daughter had been crying. Tears streaked her little cheeks as she clung desperately to his hand. Estelle could have told her she needn't fear her strange surroundings. The child was pretty, her clothes stylish and expensive, her flaxen curls shiny. Nary a wrinkle marred the perfection of her navy frock. She was like a doll from the very best department store. Odds were good she'd have a dozen tiny sycophants before the day was through, all vying to be her new best friend. Appearances mattered in a place like this, as did who one's parents were. No amount of Great Wars could level the youngest child's understanding of who belonged on what rung of the class ladder.

Estelle pegged this girl's father as a resident of considerably loftier reaches than her own.

A cynicism beyond her years had her burying her nose back in *The Mysterious Affair at Styles*. Books didn't care which year's footwear one was shod in. Books let one step into their characters' shoes instead. She was trying to focus on doing that when the sound of someone politely clearing his throat brought her head up again. Her breath whooshed from her as if a giant's hand had given her ribs a squeeze. The throat-clearer was the tall man in the trilby. His little girl was beside him, still clinging tearfully, but Estelle scarcely had a scrap of awareness for her.

Up close, the man was shockingly beautiful. Beneath the slanting shadow of his hat, his hair was a darker gold than his daughter's and surprisingly poet-long. Pansies were not bluer than his eyes, which seemed to glow with their rich, dark hue. His mouth was cut to perfection, like stone buffed to the finest of smooth edges. Estelle couldn't help but lick her own nervously.

"Forgive me," said the man as if he hadn't just laid all her Rudolph Valentino fantasies to rest. His voice was deep and cool. "I'm sorry to intrude, but you have a wonderfully kind face. Do you think you might look out for my daughter, Sally? Just until she gets settled in her class. She's a little nervous about her first day in school."

He thought *she* had a kind face? Was something wrong with his eyes? Resentful was more like it. Or sulky. As if her mind wished to prove this, all the not-so-kind things Estelle had been thinking about his daughter flew through her head and out again.

"Only if you wouldn't mind," the beautiful man added. "I know it's a lot to ask."

"*You* stay," pleaded his daughter, tugging his jacket sleeve. "You stay with me, Daddy."

He looked down at her, such love and patience in his expression that Estelle's throat went tight. She didn't think either of her parents had ever looked at her that way. They didn't look at her *any* way very much.

"You know I would, Lovey, if I could."

"I like it better at home," Sally insisted. "Ben can teach me to read when he gets back from boarding school."

The man knelt before her and squeezed her hands.

"I'll look out for her," Estelle said, before he could utter whatever parental platitude he was searching for.

Clearly surprised to be interrupted, man and girl turned their faces to her in unison. Estelle had the odd sensation that she was being put to the test by both sets of eyes. She felt dishonest, but couldn't she decide to be kind if she wanted to? Was what this man saw in her necessarily a lie?

"I'll look out for you, Sally," she repeated, meaning it—a bit to her own surprise. "I'm one of the big girls. You'll be perfectly safe with me."

Sally bit her lip and looked at her father.

"You see?" he said, bracing her little shoulders between his palms. "What could be better than having a lovely young lady like this to show you around?"

"I *have* to stay?" Sally asked.

"You do," her father confirmed, that gentle smile lifting his mouth as he rose.

"This is awfully decent of you," he said to Estelle. "You've no idea what a load you've taken off my mind."

"'S nothing," Estelle mumbled, still off balance from being called lovely.

Her shyness seemed to amuse him.

"I'm Edmund Fitz Clare," he said and held out his hand. "I'm a professor of history at the university."

He must mean London University. That was the closest one to here. But who would have guessed he was a *professor*? His clothes seemed too Savile Row for that. Conscious that her thoughts were rude, Estelle shook his hand awkwardly, nearly dropping her Agatha Christie as she tried to tuck the book out of the way beneath her other arm. "I'm Estelle Berenger."

He put his second hand over hers, easily swallowing it between his gloves. Within the supple leather, his fingers seemed very hard. "A star among women, to be sure."

She knew he was making a joke about the meaning of her name—Estelle, star, all that rot—but a flush washed through her exactly as if he were serious. What would it be like to be a star among women, and to be one to a man like this? She wasn't worldly enough to know what that might entail, but trying to imagine caused her to grow hot so swiftly that all her clothes went prickly.

She could almost feel his smooth, cool lips on her neck.

So softly she almost didn't hear it, Professor Fitz Clare

drew a sharpened breath. Perhaps the timing of the inhalation was only chance. Perhaps she was listening too hard to him. But if he'd guessed what she was thinking . . . what his inadvertently exciting touch had done to her . . .

She couldn't finish the thought. His eyes looked darker than before, the faintest quiver widening his nostrils.

She yanked back her hand at the same time he released it.

"Well," he said. He turned up the collar of his coat, despite the mild morning temperature. His neck was pink, she noticed, as if he had a slight sunburn. "I should be getting back to my books."

"Bye, Daddy," Sally said forlornly.

"Bye, Sunshine," he returned.

As a pair, Estelle and Sally watched him hurriedly cross the street, loping toward the shelter of a waiting Model T. Considering how graceful he'd been before, his gait was oddly unsteady.

"The professor drinks," Sally announced sadly with the wise-innocent air of a child repeating something she's heard adults say. "That's why he sleeps all day."

The words rang false for Estelle. The professor hadn't smelled of liquor, nor had his speech been slurred. "Perhaps he's a night owl," she said, giving Sally's soft curls a tentative stroke. "Even if he isn't, you probably shouldn't tell everyone you meet that he drinks."

"I shouldn't?" Sally asked.

"You shouldn't," Estelle said firmly.

Luckily, Sally believed her, and her first day of school unfolded exactly as Estelle foretold. Estelle gave Sally what help she needed to fit in: predictably, not much. The girl was bubbling with enjoyment by the time her father picked her up again. She remembered to thank Estelle without prompting, which Estelle couldn't help but be impressed by. That Sally's father's thanks were what really warmed her Estelle kept to herself.

Never mind that Sally—her chattiness irrepressible—had revealed that her father wasn't married, that he'd adopted Sally and two older boys after they were orphaned in the last war. Estelle knew Edmund Fitz Clare wasn't thinking of her romantically. No matter how kind he seemed, Estelle was just a girl to him.

A lovely young lady, she repeated soundlessly to the sky. It was darker now, almost night. Lightning flickered yellow within the clouds, the sight exhilarating to her wound-up nerves. A dog bayed with longing down in the square, invisible beneath the trees. Estelle could have hugged the sound to her in delight. Wolves howled like that when they missed their companions— though of course no real wolf would be racketing around London!

She wondered if Sally's father would speak to her tomorrow.

"Estelle!" her mother called from behind her closed bedroom door. "Your father's home from the bank. It's time to come down for tea."

"In a tick," she responded, loath to lose the magic of her own daydreams.

Tea with her parents was a tiresome business, a pro forma family gathering not a one of them was interested in. Her father would grumble over Britain's monetary policy, how it kept men like him from advancing as they deserved, her mother would say "yes, dear," and Estelle would entertain herself by stabbing her fork into her toast points until her mother ordered her to stop. Watching a storm approach was much more thrilling, hearing the thunder rumble, seeing the power of nature snake inexorably closer. Estelle would have to change her clothes for tea, in any case. She was wet through, the rain spitting hard against her cotton dress. The clinging cloth made her more aware of her body, of its strength and femininity. Maybe she was becoming a woman. Maybe this day had been a part of it.

What came next unfolded without warning.

The mournful dog howled again, and then a flash filled the air above her balcony. Estelle couldn't believe what she was seeing: lightning blooming into being right in front of her. Fine hairs stood on end all across her skin. The electric burst was streaking toward her blinding as the sun. She was going to die, but she didn't have a chance to feel more than surprised.

Really? she thought in the millisecond left to her. *I'm supposed to go now?*

She could have sworn she heard someone growl, "*No!*"

Thunder buffeted her ears just as a shadow leapt between her and the blazing light. She would have blinked if she'd had time. The shadow looked like a wolf at full gallop—a hallucination, she was sure. The lightning bolt pierced straight through the phantasm, breaking into rainbow shards. One stabbed her right eye, ran down her arm and out her middle fingertip. She flew backward like she'd been thrown, sailing clear across the room. Her back crashed into the wall behind her bed, the plaster cracking beneath the flowered wallpaper. None of her limbs would move. Helpless to brace for the fall, she slid until she half sat, half slumped on the mattress. Smoke issued in gray tendrils from the soles of her shoes.

Her right ear felt like a burning coal had lodged in it.

"Estelle!" her mother screamed, but Estelle had lost her power to answer.

She was seeing pictures through her lightning blasted eye. Knights on horseback. A diminutive dark-haired woman with skin like snow.

Goodness, she thought. *Maybe I did die, after all.*

Paddington Station, 1933

GRAHAM FITZ CLARE WAS A SECRET AGENT.

He had to repeat that to himself sometimes, because the situation seemed too ludicrous otherwise. He was ordinary, he thought, no one more so, but he fit the profile apparently. Eton. Oxford. No nascent Bolshevik tendencies. MI5 had recruited him two years ago, soon after he'd accepted a job as personal assistant to an American manufacturer. Arnold Anderson traveled the world on business, and Graham—who had a knack for languages—served as his translator and dogsbody.

He supposed it was the built-in cover that shined him up for spywork, though he couldn't see as he'd done anything important yet. He hadn't pilfered any secret papers, hadn't seduced an enemy agent—which wasn't to suggest he thought he could! For the most part, he'd simply reported back on factories he and his employer had visited, along with writing up impressions of their associated owners and officials.

Tonight, in fact, was the most spylike experience he'd had to date.

His instructions had been tucked into the copy of *The Times* he'd bought at the newsagent down the street from his home.

"Paddington Station," the note had said in curt, telegraphic style. "11:45 tonight. Come by Underground and carry this paper under your left arm."

Graham stood at the station now, carrying the paper and feeling vaguely foolish. The platform was empty and far darker than during the day. The cast iron arches of the roof curved gloomily above his head, the musty smell of soot stinging in his nose. A single train, unlit and silent except for the occasional sigh of escaping steam, sat on the track to the right of him. One bored porter had eyed him when he arrived, shaken his head, and then retired to presumably cozier environs.

Possibly the porter had been bribed to disappear. All Graham knew for sure was that he'd been waiting here fifteen minutes while his feet froze to the concrete floor, without the slightest sign of whomever he was supposed to meet. Doubly vexed to hear a church clock striking midnight, he tried not to shiver in the icy November damp. His overcoat was new, at least, a present from the professor on Graham's twenty-fifth birthday.

That memory made him smile despite his discomfort. His guardian was notoriously shy about giving gifts. They were always generous, always exactly what the person wanted—as if Edmund had plucked the wish from their minds. He always acted as if he'd presumed by wanting to give whatever it was to them. The habit, and so many others, endeared him to his adopted brood more than any parent by blood could have. The professor seemed to think it a privilege to have been allowed to care for them.

All of them, even flighty little Sally, knew the privilege was theirs.

Though Graham was old enough to occasionally be embarrassed by the fact, there really was no mystery to why Edmund's charges remained at home. Graham's lips pressed together at the thought of causing Edmund concern. If tonight's business kept him waiting long enough to have to lie to the professor about where he'd been, he was not going to be amused.

Metal creaked, drawing his eyes to the darkened train. Evidently, it wasn't empty. One of the doors had opened, and a dainty Oriental woman was stepping down the stairs of the central car. Her skintight emerald dress looked straight out of wardrobe for a Charlie Chan picture. Actually, she looked straight out of one, too, so exotically gorgeous that Graham's tongue was practically sticking to the roof of his mouth.

He forced himself to swallow as her eyes raked him up and down.

"Hm," she said, flicking a length of night-black hair behind one slender shoulder. "You're tall at least, and you look healthy."

Graham flushed at her dismissive tone, and again—even harder—when she turned her back on him to reascend the stairs. Holy hell, her rear view was smashing, her waist nipped in, her bum round and firm. Graham knew he wasn't the sort of man women swooned over, not like his younger brother, Ben, or even the professor, whose much-younger female students occasionally followed him home. No, Graham had a plain English face, not ugly but forgettable. Normally, this didn't bother him—or not much. It just seemed a bit humiliating to find the woman who'd insulted him so very attractive herself.

That green dress was tight enough to show the cleft between the halves of her arse. His groin grew heavy, his shaft beginning to swell. The sight of her lack of underclothes was so inspiring he forgot he was supposed to move.

"Don't just stand there," she said impatiently over her shoulder. "Follow me."

Shoving *The Times* into his pocket, he followed her, dumbstruck, into a private compartment. She yanked down the shades before flicking on two dim sconces.

"Sit," she said, pointing to the black leather seat opposite her own. Her hand was slim and pale, her nails lacquered red as blood.

Graham sat with difficulty. He was erect and aching and too polite to shift the cause of the trouble to a different position. Hoping his condition wasn't obvious to her, he wrapped his hands around his knees and waited.

The woman stared at him unblinking—taking his stock, he guessed. She resembled a painted statue, or maybe a mannequin in a store window. In spite of his attraction to her, Graham's irritation rose. This woman had kept him hanging long enough.

"What's this about?" he asked.

She leaned back and crossed a pair of incredibly shapely

lcgs, a move that seemed too practiced to be casual. Her dress was shorter than the current fashion, ending just below her knee. Graham wasn't certain, but from the hissing sound her calves made, she might be wearing real silk stockings.

"We're giving you a new assignment," she said.

"A new assignment."

"If we decide you're up for it."

"Look," Graham said, "you people came to me. It's hardly cricket to suggest that *you're* doing *me* favors."

The woman smiled, her teeth a gleaming flash of white behind ruby lips. Graham noticed her incisors were unusually sharp. "I think you'll find this assignment more intriguing than your previous one. It does, however, require a higher level of vetting." She leaned forward, her slender forearm resting gracefully on one thigh. The way her small breasts shifted behind her dress told him her top half wore no more undergarments than her bottom. Graham's collar began to feel as tight as his crotch. The space between their seats wasn't nearly great enough.

"Tell me, Graham," she said, her index finger almost brushing his, "what do you know about X Section?"

"Never heard of it," he said, because as far as he knew, MI5 sections only went up to F.

"What if I told you it hunts things?"

"*Things?*"

"Unnatural things. Dangerous things. Beasts who shouldn't exist in the human realm."

Her face was suddenly very close to his. Her eyes were as dark as coffee, mysterious golden lights seeming to flicker behind the irises. Graham felt dizzy staring into them, his heart thumping far too fast. He didn't recall seeing her move, but she was kneeling on the floor of the compartment in the space that gaped between his knees. Her pale strong hands were sliding up his thighs. His cock lurched like it could hasten their possible meeting.

"We need information," she whispered, her breath as cool and sweet as mint pastilles. "So we can destroy these monsters. And we need you to get it for us."

"You're crazy." He had to gasp it; his breath was coming so fast.

"No, I'm not, Graham. I'm the sanest person you've ever met."

Her fingers had reached the bend between his legs and torso, her thumbs sliding inward over the giant arch of his erection. She scratched him gently with the edge of her blood-red nails.

"Christ," Graham choked out. The feathery touch blazed through him like a welder's torch. His nerves were on fire, his penis slit weeping with desire. He shifted on the seat in help-less reaction. Her mouth was following her thumbs, her exha-lations whispering over his grossly stretched trouser front.

"I'm going to give you clearance," she said. "I'm going to make sure we can trust you."

He cried out when she undid his zip fastener, and again when her small, cool fingers dug into his smalls to lift out his engorged cock. Blimey, he was big, his skin stretched like it would split. She stroked the whole shuddering length of him, causing his spine to arch uncontrollably.

"Watch me," she ordered as his head lolled back. "Watch me suck you into my mouth."

Graham was no monk. He watched her, and felt her, and thought his soul was going to spill out his body where her lips drew strong and tight on him.

He didn't want to admit this was the first time a woman had performed this particular act on him. He could see why men liked it. The sensations were incredible, streaking in hot, sharp tingles from the tip of his throbbing penis to the arch-ing soles of his feet. She was smearing her ruby lipstick up and down his shaft, humming at the swell of him, taking him into her throat, it felt like. Her tongue was rubbing him every place he craved.

The fact that she was barking mad completely slipped his mind.

"Oh, God," he breathed, lightly touching her hair where she'd tucked it neatly behind her ears. The strands were silk under his fingertips, so smooth they seemed unreal. "Oh, Christ. Don't stop."

She didn't stop. She sucked and sucked until his seed exploded from his balls in a fiery rush. He cried out hoarsely, sorry and elated at the same time. And then she did something he couldn't quite believe.

She bit him.

Her teeth sank into him halfway down his shaft, those sharp incisors even sharper than he'd thought. The pain was as piercing as the pleasure had been a second earlier. He grabbed her ears, wondering if he dared to pull her off. Her clever tongue fluttered against him, wet, strong . . . and then she drew his blood from him.

He moaned, his world abruptly turned inside out. Ecstasy washed through him in drowning waves. She was drinking from him in a whole new way, swallowing, licking, moaning herself like a starving puppy suckling at a teat. All his senses went golden and soft. *So good. So sweet.* Like floating on a current of pure well-being.

He didn't know how long it lasted, but he was sorry when her head came up.

"You're mine now," she said.

He blinked sleepily into her glowing eyes. Was it queer that they were lit up? Right at that moment, he couldn't decide.

"I'm yours," he said, though he wasn't certain he meant it.

"You're not going to remember me biting you."

"No," he agreed. "That would be awkward."

"When I give you instructions, you'll follow them."

"I expect I will," he said.

She narrowed her eyes at him, her winglike little brows furrowing.

"I will," he repeated, because she seemed to require it.

She rose, licking one last smear of blood from her upper lip. As soon as it disappeared, he forgot that it had been there.

"Zip yourself," she said.

He obeyed and got to his feet as well. It seemed wrong to

be towering over his handler, though he couldn't really claim to mind. She handed him a slip of paper with a meeting place in Hampstead Heath. As had been the case with the note tucked into his paper, the directions were neatly typed—no bobbles or mistakes. He had the idle thought that Estelle would have approved.

"Tomorrow night," the woman said. "Eleven sharp. You'll know when you've seen what we need you to."

"Will you be there?"

He thought this was a natural question. Any male with blood in his veins would want to repeat the pleasures of this night, if only to return the favor she'd shown him. But perhaps he wasn't supposed to ask. She wrinkled her brow again.

"*I* won't be," she said, "but chances are our enemy will."